"So you didn't get to see this witch's face, or where they were?"

"I saw an alley—and I had the name."

Sully mulled over his words. "But I don't understand. *My* name?"

"Yep. Sullivan Timmerman." Dave frowned, then glanced down at the tea. "What's in this?"

"Oh, it's just a little lavender, lemon balm, a tidge of nutmeg..."

His eyes narrowed. "Antianxiety?"

She shrugged. "A calmative. I thought you could use it."

He had to admit, it worked. He'd come here with his gut roiling, concerned about how she'd receive him. But...how did she know? Realization dawned.

"You're an empath."

She stepped back. "What—what makes you say that?"

"Oh, just putting the pieces together. I don't know how many witches would patch me up, hear me out and make me tea after I've tried to kill them."

"Maybe I'm just a sucker for a bad boy."

His lips quirked. "Ah, now that's where you're wrong, Sully," he said in a low voice, leaning forward. "I can be very, very good."

WITCH HUNTER

&

KINDLING
THE DARKNESS

SHANNON CURTIS
AND
JANE KINDRED

HARLEQUIN® NOCTURNE™

Recycling programs
for this product may
not exist in your area.

ISBN-13: 978-1-335-45150-7

Witch Hunter & Kindling the Darkness

Copyright © 2019 by Harlequin Books S.A.

The publisher acknowledges the copyright holders
of the individual works as follows:

Witch Hunter
Copyright © 2018 by Shannon Curtis

Kindling the Darkness
Copyright © 2018 by Jane Kindred

HARLEQUIN®
™ www.Harlequin.com

Printed in U.S.A.

CONTENTS

Shannon Curtis grew up picnicking in graveyards (long story) and reading by flashlight, and has worked in various roles, such as office admin manager, logistics supervisor and betting agent, to mention a few. Her first love—after reading, and her husband—is writing, and she writes romantic suspense, paranormal and contemporary romance. From faeries to cowboys, military men to business tycoons, she loves crafting stories of thrills, chills, kills and kisses. She divides her time between being an office administrator for the Romance Writers of Australia and creating spellbinding tales of mischief, mayhem and the occasional murder. She lives in Sydney, Australia, with her best-friend husband, three children, a woolly dog and a very disdainful cat. Shannon can be found lurking on Twitter, @2bshannoncurtis, and Facebook, or you can email her at contactme@shannoncurtis.com— she loves hearing from readers. Like...LOVES it. Disturbingly so.

Books by Shannon Curtis

Harlequin Nocturne

Lycan Unleashed
Warrior Untamed
Vampire Undone
Wolf Undaunted

WITCH HUNTER

Shannon Curtis

This book is dedicated to all the readers
who have supported me by reading this series.
You have no idea how meaningful and humbling
your consideration and time have meant to me.

And thank you to Coleen,
for the inspiration that has become Dave Carter,
tattoo artist and witch hunter.

Chapter 1

"Why do you have so many tattoos?"

Dave lifted the tip of his needle from his client's inner wrist and gently dabbed at the skin. The woman was looking up at the ceiling, and she was exhaling slowly through her lips, as though trying not to flinch. Scream. Pee. Puke. Whatever.

"I'm a tattoo artist. Perks of the job." He eyed the intricate linework he'd inked onto her wrist. He just needed to close the top of the loop of one twist of the knot, and he was finished.

He dabbed at the skin again. He was only doing a simple line tattoo for this woman. It was her first tattoo, and she didn't think she could stand a lot of shading. He had to agree. The whole time she'd breathed as though she was in a Lamaze class. He was surprised she hadn't hyperventilated.

"I can't quite make it out…?" Her tone was raised in query.

He leaned forward, gently pressing his foot on the pedal, and the woman snapped her gaze from the mark on his arm to the ceiling again. The skin on his left breast itched.

Damn.

"I can, and that's what matters," he said, smiling at the woman as he carefully pressed the needle against her skin. He focused intently, despite the itch that was getting more annoying—and bound to become more so.

He worked as quickly as he could, his lips tightening as the itch became warm. He didn't have long.

"Are you sure you can see with those glasses on?" The woman bit her lip as he wiped petroleum jelly across her wrist to hydrate the skin, and then pressed the needle against her, concentrating on drawing out the ink.

"I'm nearly finished and you're asking me that now?" Dave raised an eyebrow, but didn't stop his work. The itch began to heat. Sweat broke out on his forehead and upper lip, and he worked faster, gritting his teeth at the burn.

He finished the line perfectly, closing the loop and preventing any breach to the protection spell he'd drawn into her tattoo.

"Right, that's done," he rasped, reaching for the anti-septic liquid soap on his table. He washed her skin and gently held her arm so that she could see the intricate linework. It looked like a delicate lace band around her wrist.

"And this will stop him…?" she asked tentatively.

He nodded. "He won't be able to raise his hand against you." He worked quickly, placing low adherent bandages over her new tattoo and taping them carefully into place.

"Leave those on for about twenty-four hours—or until tomorrow morning at the earliest. It will probably look shiny and gross—don't worry, that's normal." Damn, what had started as an itch now felt like someone was directing a heat lamp on his chest. "Shower and soap it up—antiseptic soap only, nothing scented, and for God's sake, no scrubs, and don't scratch it."

Ow. Crap. The burn! He'd run out of time.

He reached over with his left hand to pick up a flyer he'd had printed. "Here are the instructions for aftercare, call me if you need anything and leave your money on the counter on the way out."

He rose from his wheeled stool, and she gaped at him, her gaze dropping to his torso. "Hey, are you all rig—?"

"Fine," he said brusquely, leaving his room and jogging down the hall. He flung open a door marked Private and ran down the metal stairs to the apartment below his tattoo parlor, below street level. He raised his hand, pushing the door at the bottom of the stairs open with his magic, and then flicking it closed behind him. He jogged down the rock-hewn corridor to the door to his private quarters, and thrust it open, kicking it closed behind him, swearing in a soft hiss as he pulled the fabric of his gray T-shirt away from the blooming stain over his left pectoral muscle. He lifted the garment over his head, moving his left arm gingerly as he removed the T-shirt.

He always left the lamp next to his armchair on in his subterranean quarters, and it gave out a low, warm light. At the moment, it was just enough light to show him the damage.

The skin on his breast was blistered, bleeding. He sucked in and held his breath, trying not to yell or scream as it happened again.

The marking glowed as it seared into his skin, and he gritted his teeth, closing his eyes and tilting his head back as his skin was branded. The name was scorched into the very fiber of his being, and he let out a soft, pained growl as the searing seemed to continue forever. He started breathing like his recent client, short hitched gasps that stopped him from crying like a baby. The heat, the pain—it was excruciating, and left him temporarily powerless until the etching was complete.

He opened his eyes and stared at the bare-chested figure in the mirror on the wall by the door. The glow was beginning to darken, and he tried to slow his breathing down as the mark was completed, the wound glistening with his blood. He swallowed, his shoulders sagging.

Christ. That was a long name.

He stumbled closer to the mirror, and tilted his head to the side as he translated the script. *S. U.* double letters… more double letters. He turned back to the natural-edged hardwood table that was his dining table, kitchen prep, spellcasting, office desk and anything else he thought to use it for. He grabbed the pencil and notepad, then turned back to the mirror.

S.U.L.L… He jotted down the letters, gaze flicking between the notepad and the mirror, until he was sure he'd gotten it right—because he sure as hell couldn't get this wrong. Of course, it would be much easier if the Ancestors would try scripting their messages in English, and not in a language that hadn't been spoken in seven hundred years.

He held the paper in front of him and closely compared the lettering. Yep, he was right.

It was damn long name.

Sullivan Timmerman.

Dave's lips tightened. So what was Timmerman's crime?

He removed the sunglasses he always wore and took a deep breath.

"Sullivan Timmerman."

Bright light lanced his vision, and then all of a sudden he could see not his rock-walled apartment beneath his tattoo parlor, but a dark alley instead, as he gazed through Timmerman's eyes. He gazed down at the body he knelt over, and removed the blade from the man's heart. Dave watched as gloved hands picked up the limp right wrist and used the intricately carved blade to incise a rough *X* into the skin, and held a—Dave squinted—a horn?

Timmerman drained some blood into the horn and—Dave's stomach heaved as the killer drank the blood. He couldn't hear the words that were uttered, but the *X* on the wrist turned an inky black—and then Dave's vision went dark, and he blinked, his vision clearing to reveal his dim apartment.

What the—how had Timmerman kicked him out? He was usually able to piggyback on the vision of the killer until he could identify his location. This time, though, Timmerman had consumed the blood, said a few words and then blocked him.

Dave pressed his lips together. It was easy to see the witch was using dark magic, and he'd taken a life. No wonder the Ancestors had assigned him a new target.

Well, tracking the damned was part of his job, and he was good at it. He'd start looking—right after he'd patched himself up. He winced as he looked down at the brand that was already beginning to heal. Damn. It was over his heart, too. He shook his head as he stalked over to his bathroom door. The Ancestors didn't seem to care where he got the message, as long as he got it. Well, he'd received it, loud and clear.

He had a witch to kill.

Sully Timmerman glanced cautiously about the school-room.

"Relax, Sully. The kids are having their lunch out-side," Jenny Forsyth said with a smile as she set out test papers on the students' desks.

"The day I relax is the day I get caught," Sully said, then smiled as she leaned her hip against the teacher's desk. "How are the munchkins?"

Jenny smiled. "They're good, right now. They don't know they have a math test this afternoon."

Sully grinned. "You are such a cruel woman."

"And you love it." Jenny put the paper on the last desk, then strolled toward the front of the classroom. "How is work going?"

Sully nodded. "It's slowly picking up. I have a deliv-ery in the car for the diner, and it looks like the mayor's wife wants a new set of cutlery for their anniversary."

"Cutlery? For an anniversary?"

"Twenty-five years, silver." Sully shrugged. "Hey, it's an order, so I'm happy." Being a cutler was a dying art. There were so many cheaper options for pretty cutlery in a home, but Sully's reputation as a master cutler was finally beginning to bring in some new business, and now that she had a website, she was getting orders com-ing in from all over the place. She glanced at her watch and winced. "I'd better get going. I want to get Lucy in between the lunch and dinner rush."

She picked up her satchel, and the not-so-subtle clink

reminded her of the unofficial delivery in her bag. "Oops, nearly forgot."

She pulled the heavy cloth bag out of her satchel, and set it down on Jenny's desk with a dull chink. "Better find a good place for this lot."

Jenny's eyebrows rose as she undid the drawstring and peered inside. She whistled. "Wow. That is a lot of silver dollars. That will help quite a few families," she said quietly. She lifted her gaze to Sully's. "You take a big risk, you know."

Sully shrugged. "Hey, every little bit counts, right? It's not much, but if it helps, than that's the main thing." She was satisfied with this particular delivery. She'd counterfeited over two thousand dollars, this time, and that bag contained only about half that. Jenny would make sure it got to those who most needed it. This null community was struggling, more so than most, and if the off-cuts from the pieces she made could help put food on the table for some of these people, then the risk was worth it. She pulled her strap up over her shoulder as the school bell chimed outside, signaling the end of the lunch play period. "Now, hide it, or we'll both be in trouble."

Jenny opened her desk drawer and dropped the bag inside as the door to the classroom burst open, and her students swarmed inside. Their eyes brightened when they saw Sully, and she was nearly bowled over when the twenty or so seven-year-olds rushed to her. She hugged as many as she could as she made her way through the throng to the door.

"Hey, Sully, you want to join us next month for the school fete?" Jenny called.

The school fete was scheduled to coincide with the Harvest Moon Festival. Sully turned as the kids cheered, and she folded her arms and frowned. "I don't know. Is it worth it, Noah?" she looked at the young red-haired boy, who nodded, his blue eyes bright. Noah's mother, Susanne, was another of Sully's friends.

"It is, Sully. We've got rides and *donkeys*."

Sully's eyebrows rose. "Donkeys?" She glanced over at Jenny.

"Petting zoo," Jenny explained. She leaned closer. "Jacob will be there, too."

Sully shot her friend an exasperated look. Jenny had been trying to fix her up with her brother since she'd moved to Serenity Cove, and to date Sully had successfully avoided the hookup. Jacob was nice—good-looking, too, but she just wasn't interested. In anyone. She turned back to Noah.

"Donkeys, huh? Oh, well, I'll have to come for that." She winked at him. "Tell your mom hi from me." She waved to the kids as she closed the door behind her, grinning. A day surrounded by nulls? Yes, please.

She strode out of the two-story building that was elementary, middle and high school to the resident null community, and over to her beat-up sky blue station wagon. She sat in the driver's seat for a moment, enjoying the peace, the quiet. All the kids were back in class, but she was still close enough she was affected by their presence.

She closed her eyes. She was surrounded by…nothing. It was so beautiful. Dark. Silent. Peaceful. It was the absence, the void, that embraced her, and she loved it. She knew most witches avoided nulls like a hex, but she found there was a tranquility in their presence that she couldn't find anywhere else.

She opened her eyes, and shored up her shields, making sure that there were no cracks, no fractures in her defenses. When she was satisfied her mental walls were strong, and no light could cut through, she started her engine and drove the ten minutes into Serenity Cove.

She pulled the box out from the back of her car, lifting the tailgate with her hip. She didn't bother winding up the window or locking it. Anybody with half a mind to steal her car must be desperate, and welcome to it. Besides, everyone in town knew this was her car, and you didn't steal from a witch. The resulting curse wasn't worth it.

She walked up the steps to the Brewhaus Diner, and her flip-flops made a smacking sound on the veranda. She pushed through the door and the tinkling sound of the bell above the door brought an almost instinctive response as she stepped inside. She put a smile on her face as she ignored muffled emotions knocking at her protective walls.

Cheryl Conners, the waitress, was hiding her hurt that Sheriff Clinton was absorbed in his phone and not her. Sheriff Clinton was worried—but that seemed to be his default setting. Harold's gout was troubling him, Graham, the cook, was tired and his feet hurt, Mrs. Peterson was fighting off a strong cold, and Lucy—

Sully halted at the diner counter. Lucy wasn't happy. No, she was…heartbroken. She couldn't see the woman, but she could feel her pain—and that was with her shields up.

She placed the box on the counter and looked over at Cheryl as the waitress walked over to her.

"I'm here to see Lucy," Sully said softly. She glanced toward the swing door that led to the kitchen and the office beyond. "Is she okay?"

Cheryl shook her head. "She got some bad news." She

lifted her chin in the direction of the sheriff. "They found Gary's body last night."

Sully gasped, then lifted her hand to cover her mouth. "Oh, no."

Gary Adler was the coach over at the null comprehensive school, and Lucy's longtime boyfriend. No wonder the woman emitted the feel of devastation.

Sully patted the box on the counter. "Look, I'll leave these here, we can talk about sorting stuff out later. She's got enough on her plate, tell her not to worry about this. We can talk when she's ready, but don't stress over it." She adjusted the strap of her bag on her shoulder. "When is the funeral?"

"Won't be for a few days, yet," Sheriff Clinton said, glancing up from his phone. "We've got to wait for the autopsy."

Sully nodded. Gary had watched what he ate, exercised regularly, and apart from that one Christmas festival, didn't drink much. She wasn't aware of him suffering from any illness. They'd have to do an autopsy to find out what had made a relatively healthy man drop dead.

"Any ideas what the cause was?" she asked the sheriff.

He grimaced. "We're guessing it was the stab wound to the heart that did it."

Cheryl's jaw dropped. "What?"

Sully's eyes widened. "Are you saying he was murdered?"

"Well, it didn't look like he fell on the knife, or stabbed himself," the sheriff commented dryly.

"Oh, no, poor Lucy," Sully murmured. "I'll go home and put together a tea for her." She nodded to herself. "I should go visit with Gary's mother, too." Gary's mother lived in a tiny cottage on the northern tip of the seaside town, along with the bulk of the null community. "She'll be devastated."

Sheriff Clinton nodded. "Yeah. I'm sure Mary Anne would appreciate a visit, but I don't think a tea will help her."

Sully smiled sadly. "Not in the usual way, but herbs can still affect a Null, just like any other person, and there's always a little comfort to be found in a shared brew."

She waved briefly to the sheriff and Cheryl, and was nearly at the door when she snapped her fingers. She walked back over to Mrs. Peterson, and gently placed her hand over the older woman's.

"How are you, Mrs. Peterson?" she asked loudly so the woman could hear.

"What's that, dear?" Mrs. Peterson leaned forward.

"I said, how are you?" Sully said as loud as she could without shouting at the woman.

She opened her shield a crack and pulled in some of the pain she could sense in the swollen knuckles, and fed some warmth through in return, laced with a little calm.

The older woman's face creased like a scrunched-up piece of paper when she smiled up at Sully.

"I'm doing well, Sully," she said in her wavery voice.

"You're looking nice today. I like your dress," Sully said, gently patting the back of the woman's hand. She could already sense the easing of tension in the old woman as her arthritic pain subsided.

"What mess?" Mrs. Peterson glanced down in confusion at the table.

"Your *dress*," Sully repeated. "I like your dress." Pity she couldn't do anything about the woman's hearing— but she was an empath witch, not a god.

"Oh, thank you, dear," Mrs. Peterson said, and her face scrunched up even further as her smile broadened.

Sully nodded and winked, then turned in the direction of the door, cradling her hand on the top of her satchel. She closed her mental walls, ensuring nothing else leaked in she wasn't ready for. She walked on toward the door and waved at Harold when he signaled her. "Don't worry, I'll bring you something back later, too, Harold." She wagged a finger at him. "But you really do need to lay off the shellfish."

She pushed through the door, her smile tightening as the pain in her hand throbbed. Poor Mrs. Peterson. That really was a painful condition.

She skipped down the steps and dusted her hands as she walked to her car. To anyone else it looked like she was shaking black pepper off her hands as she discarded the pain she'd drawn in from Mrs. Peterson.

She considered the teas she'd make for Lucy and Mary Anne Adler as she climbed into her car. Lemon balm, linden and motherwort, she decided. They each had a calming effect, and the motherwort would be especially helpful with the heartache and grief. She waited for a motorcycle to turn across the intersection in front of her, and then pulled out. She sighed. Poor Gary. Murdered. Who would do such a thing?

Chapter 2

Dave pulled his motorbike into a spot on Main Street, and slid his helmet off his head. He looked around. So this was Serenity Cove, huh? The town was picture-postcard quaint. Victorian cottages, cute little boutiques and stores, and lots of white picket fences and ornate trim. Lots and lots. This place looked so damned sweet, he could feel a toothache coming on.

There were a few people wandering around. Admittedly, he thought there'd be more. It was summer and Serenity Cove had a fishing marina, nice little beaches—if his online searches could be trusted—but for some reason there wasn't the usual vacationers drifting around with beet-red sunburns and sarongs. A local bar also seemed to be missing from the scene. He eyed the diner across the street. In lieu of a bar to visit and source information, this place would have to do. Maybe someone in there could tell him where the bar was—after he got some intel on Sullivan Timmerman.

He swung his leg over the bike and placed his helmet over the dash and ignition, uttering a simple security spell. It never paid to mess with a witch's stuff.

It had been surprisingly easy to track down the witch. The guy had a website, for crying out loud. It was obviously a front, though. A cutler? He'd never heard of the trade. Most people just went to the store and bought their cutlery. Who would have a set made?

He crossed the street and entered the diner, the tinkling of the bell over the door causing the patrons to look up. He didn't remove his sunglasses, but then he didn't have a problem seeing inside. An older man, an even older lady and—oh, good. A sheriff. Dave sighed. He wasn't sure if it was the bike leathers, or the tattoos, but the law always seemed to want to chat with him.

He strolled down to the opposite end of the diner counter and slid onto a stool. The solitary waitress bustled over to him, a smile on her face. Dave smiled back. He read her name tag. Cheryl.

"Hey, stranger, can I get you something?" She leaned a hand on the counter and gave him a wink.

He grinned as he removed his gloves. "That depends, Cheryl." Her smile broadened at his use of her name. "What can you recommend?" He kept his tone light and flirtatious, and out of the corner of his eye he saw the sheriff lift his gaze from his phone.

She folded her arms on the counter and leaned forward. "Well," she said, drawing the word out slowly. "I've just put a fresh pot of coffee on, so I haven't had a chance to burn it, yet, and the peach pie is pretty good."

He nodded. "I'll take that. For starters," He winked

back at her. She was pretty, she was nice and liked to flirt. Serenity Cove might be all right, after all.

"What brings you to Serenity Cove?" The sheriff put his phone away and directed his full attention to him. His tone was casual, conversational, but the look in the man's eyes was anything but.

"I'm looking for someone," Dave replied as Cheryl placed a plate in front of him. She reached for the coffee carafe and poured him a cup, and he took care not to touch anything until she was finished. He waved away the cream and sugar she offered.

"Who?" the sheriff asked. This time his tone wasn't so casual or conversational.

"Tyler," Cheryl chided. "Be nice to our visitor."

"No, it's okay," Dave said. If there had been a murder, this officer would know about it—had to, in a place as small as Serenity Cove. He needed information from the man, and he didn't want to seem threatening or dangerous, because that would lead to an entirely different conversation.

"I'm looking for a friend," Dave said, flashing a smile at the sheriff in an effort to appear friendly. "I was in the area, so I thought I'd catch up."

"You have a friend?" the older man sitting at a booth near the door piped up. "Here?"

Dave kept his face impassive. Was the guy surprised at the idea of him having a friend in Serenity Cove or having a friend at all? "Yeah."

"Who?" Cheryl asked as she leaned against the counter. She didn't bother to hide her curiosity.

"Sullivan Timmerman."

Cheryl's eyes widened. "You know Sully?" her expression was incredulous as she looked him up and down.

"How do you know Sully?" the sheriff asked, his brow dipping.

Sully, huh? Dave took a moment to slip a bit of the peach pie into his mouth as he thought about his response. He always had an explanation ready for barflies, but talking with law enforcement required finesse and strategy. He swallowed the mouthful of pie—and Cheryl was right, it was pretty good.

"Are you an old boyfriend?" the older guy in the booth asked.

Dave coughed into the coffee mug he held to his lips. Boyfriend? Sullivan Timmerman had boyfriends?

"We went to school together," he responded cautiously once he'd cleared his throat. He hoped to hell Timmerman hadn't gone to school around here, although the information he'd found online suggested probably not. Timmerman had set up his business four years ago, but he hadn't been able to find any mention of the guy in the local schools' hall of fame lists for athletics or other clubs.

"Did you date?" Cheryl asked, waggling her eyebrows.

"Uh…" He ate some more pie as he thought of an appropriate response.

"What's that about Sully?" the old lady called out, cupping her hand to her ear.

"This guy used to date Sully," the guy in the booth yelled back.

"Why do you hate Sully?" the woman asked, horrified.

Dave blinked as Cheryl leaned over the counter. "Date, Mrs. Peterson. *Date.*"

"Oh." The old woman looked him up and down, then raised her eyebrows. "You don't say."

"You just missed her," Cheryl told him, then waved toward the door. "She left about five minutes ago."

Her. *Her.* He dipped his head for a moment. Phew. Then he frowned. He'd somehow felt a masculine energy in his vision and had assumed he was looking for a man. In his line of work, he couldn't rest on assumptions. The radio on the sheriff's hip squawked, and the man sighed as he levered himself off the chair.

"Gotta go." He grabbed his hat off the seat next to him and put it on his head. "How long are you intending to stay in Serenity Cove?" he asked Dave.

Dave waved a hand. "Oh, I'm only passing through." This kind of job never took long.

The sheriff nodded, satisfied, then turned to walk out the door.

"Bye, Tyler," Cheryl called. The sheriff didn't turn back, but lifted his hand in a casual wave of farewell. Dave caught the fleeting look of disappointment on her face before she masked it with a smile. "So, you used to date Sully, huh?"

Wow. These people were good. He bet that by the time he got back to his bike, he and this Sully would be in a serious, angst-ridden relationship. Which could work for him, really.

"Yeah," he said, folding his arms on the table and leaning forward conspiratorially. "I want to surprise her, though. Uh, do you know where I can find her?" He sent a compulsion spell in Cheryl's direction.

"She lives out at Crescent Head, north end, overlooking Driftwood Beach," Cheryl responded automatically, then blinked.

"Thanks." Dave scooped up the last of his pie, and nodded farewell as he rose from his seat. He donned his gloves and waved politely to the older patrons as he passed them.

He halted outside the diner. Two youths were checking out his bike. One of them even had the audacity to reach for the handlebars and pretend to steer. He frowned. His security spell should have knocked the kid off his feet. He flicked his fingers at him, but encountered…nothing. He frowned and tried to again.

Nothing.

He grimaced. Great. Nulls. He glanced about. Where there was one—or in this case, two—there were always more. Hopefully, though, it wouldn't interfere with what he had to do.

He sauntered across the street, and the teens took off as soon as they noticed him. He might not be able to cast a spell on them, but at least he could still look fierce.

Good. Because he had a witch to hunt.

Sully ignored the sparks as she ground the steel against the wheel. She turned the arrowhead slowly, shifting now and then to avoid smoothing the sharp angles she'd hammered into the steel. She pulled back, lifting the arrowhead to the light. Just a little more off there…

She held it back to the wheel and evened out the side, sliding the steel across the spinning wheel. When she was satisfied, she took her foot off the pedal and switched off the grinder.

She crossed over to the forge she'd made out of a soup can, sand and plaster. She'd turned the torch on a little while ago, so it was now ready for her. Using pliers, she carefully placed the arrowhead inside the forge, and then waited for it to glow. She stepped back and lifted her mask to take a sip of water from the glass on the shed sill. It was hot in the shed, and she was sweating profusely.

It didn't take too long before the arrowhead was glowing. She reached in with the pliers, and carefully dunked it into her bucket of oil, pausing for a long moment before withdrawing it.

Sully smiled. The arrowhead was in the square-headed bodkin style. Sure, the broadhead arrows were sharper and caused more damage, but every now and then it was a nice change to go for a classic shape. Besides, it had worked for the Vikings, so it wasn't completely useless. And it was exactly what Trey Mackie wanted—he wanted to try hunting just like his computer game avatar did. When the set of arrows were completed, she'd have to have a word with him about aiming at folks. She didn't make weapons for "fun". Weapons weren't toys. She'd bespell them, but she also wanted to make sure the youth used them responsibly.

She placed the arrowhead on the bench next to the other four she'd made that day. Damn, she must reek. She'd go for a quick dip before heading out to see Mary Anne. She shut down the torch on the forge and cleaned up, then quickly strode across her back garden to her cottage. Within minutes she'd donned a bikini, then threw on a peasant-style top and her long, flowing skirt. She didn't bother to fasten the belt that already twined through the loops on her skirt. The loose clothes were her stock standard wardrobe, especially for summer. She grabbed a ratty old towel, slipped her feet into her flip-flops and trotted to the end of her street. A path led from there to the stairs at the top of the cliff, and then down to the beach below. She paused at the grassy verge at the top of the stairs and took a moment to tilt her head back and let the sun shine down on her. This was one of her favorite spots, offering a one-hundred-and-eighty-degree view of the ocean. She could feel the kiss of a breeze against her skin, the heat of the sun as it beat down on her. The smell of salt and grass and the summer blossoms in her garden... The waves crashing on the beach below. This was one of her recharge places, where she could give herself up to elements of nature and restore her own energy. She gazed out at the vista. Dark clouds were gathering on the horizon. Whether a storm was coming, or about to pass, she couldn't tell. She sighed and then headed for the stairs.

Driftwood Beach was pretty much deserted. She saw a man walking his dog down the other end, but it looked like he was at the end of his walk, rather than the start. She was the only other person to walk across the sands. Most folks preferred the more sheltered Crescent Beach for a swim, just on the other side of the headland. Occasionally surfers would venture this far north out of town, but the surf at Caves' Beach was much better. She hadn't necessarily been looking for a private beach when she settled here at Crescent Head, it had just worked out that way. And she loved it. The less people she had to deal with, the better.

The surf was crisp and cool, exactly what she needed. The water embraced her, shielded her. She couldn't feel when she was fully immersed in the water. It was just her and the deep void, the occasional sea creature and strands of seaweed that always startled her into thinking it was a shark. For some reason, though, she was never bothered by the predators of the sea. No matter how far she swam out, it was like the sea provided a shelter for her. Buoyant, enveloping...peaceful. She let herself go, relaxed her mental shields and surrendered to utter unguarded enjoyment. This was as good as being surrounded by nulls, and the void their presence created.

After diving beneath a couple of waves she strode out of the water, lifting her knees so she could walk faster. Within minutes she'd patted herself dry, pulled her clothes on over the top of her swimsuit and fastened her belt. She stood on the beach, looking out over the water. By now it was late afternoon. She'd like to stay a little longer, maybe watch the sunset, but she'd promised teas for Lucy and Mrs. Peterson, and Harold something for his gout. She decided she'd take a double-prong attack with Harold. Something to rub on his toe for instant comfort and a tea to start working from the inside.

She remained where she was and closed her eyes. She mentally pictured her shutters rolling down to shield her mind. As she was going to be visiting grief-stricken women, she added a couple of extra layers to ensure she was protected from the waves of heartbreak she'd encounter. Once Sully was sure she could stand calmly in a room with them both and not crumble to the floor, curl into the fetal position and sob at the overwhelming pain, she opened her eyes.

A movement in the corner of her vision made her turn her head. A guy was walking along the beach. No, walking was too gentle a word. He was striding purposefully, his gait even and rhythmic. His broad shoulders moved with each step he took, like the slinky stalk of a predatory big cat. Graceful. That's what it was. Little puffs of sand rose at each step, catching in the breeze to dance a little before falling back to the beach. The man moved with a physical grace that suggested he was used to moving, with an added strength that made him look dangerous.

And way sexy. Sully took a moment to enjoy the view. He was built. Like, stripper-at-a-bachelorette-party built, with broad shoulders and lean hips, and thighs that looked… Her lips curled inward. Strong. Despite the heat, the man wore leather pants, boots and a black leather jacket over what she hoped was a T-shirt, for his sake. His hair was cropped short, and the sunglasses hid his eyes. She briefly wondered if he looked just as good out of them as in them. She'd once dated a guy, Marty, who looked hot in his shades, but when he'd removed them he'd revealed his sunken eyes, the dark shadows beneath and the enlarged pupils of a drug addict—which was never a good combination when mixed with his witch talents—such as they were.

Sully shook her head as she turned her back on the leather-clad man. Cute, but she wasn't interested. She sure knew how to pick 'em, as her grandmother would say. Marty was the reason she'd moved clear across the country and settled herself in a Null-saturated area. Never trust a guy who hides his eyes.

She scooped up her flip-flops and started to trudge along the waterline in the opposite direction, toward the timber stairs that hugged the cliff and led to the cliff-top walk.

She normally cut her herbs at either sunrise or sunset, when they were most potent. She'd have to hurry so she could collect all the ingredients for the teas she planned to make for her patients. Clients. Whatever you wanted to call them.

A soft breeze, warm and whispery, teased at the hem of her skirt. She grasped some of the fabric in her hand, lifting the skirt as she waded through the shallows, her lips curving at the rhythmic, refreshing chill of the waves washing over her feet.

"Sullivan Timmerman!"

Sully frowned at the sound of her name and glanced

over her shoulder. The man in black was closer to her, his expression—well, it didn't look flirty or friendly. No, he looked determined.

"What?"

"Are you Sullivan Timmerman?" the man asked again, and Sully nodded, although the movement was more a cautious dip of her head. She halted, but still looked over her shoulder at him, ready to bolt if need be. At this distance, though, she could see more of his face. He was unshaven, but not unkempt. The dusting of a beard along his jawline was closely trimmed, but it didn't hide the strong line of his jaw, or the sculpted shape of his lips. His cheekbones were balanced, his sunglasses revealing tiny lines at the corners of his eyes that could be from laughter, or scowling, she had no idea. Although she couldn't see his eyes, she could feel his stare boring into her.

There was an intensity about this man, a focus, that sparked a flare of attraction, yet the overwhelming impression she got was one of danger. She instinctively bolstered her shields with more protection. Whatever this guy was going through, she didn't want to feel it.

And yet…she knew she'd never seen this man, but there was something familiar about him, something she couldn't quite put her finger on, but it was intuitive, a bone-deep recognition she couldn't quite fathom.

"Uh, yes," she answered. She turned to face him warily. "Who wants to know?"

The man raised both of his arms out from his sides, palms up, fingers curled slightly. He started to murmur in a low voice, and it took Sully a moment to realize he was talking in the Old Language. She frowned as she struggled to decipher his words.

"…for your dark crimes, and the Ancestors call upon

your return to the Other Realm, to a place of execution—"

Sully's eyes widened in shock. Holy crap. A memory, lessons long since learned and nearly forgotten, fluttered in her mind, but it was dread that hit her, followed by comprehension.

"—until you are dead. May the Ancestors have mercy upon your soul."

His wrists rolled as he brought his arms around in front, toward her, and still clutching her flip-flops, she brought her own arms up, crossing them in front of her chest to brace against the magical blast that rolled over her.

Her feet created long burrows in the sand as she was pushed back under the force—a force that should have crushed her, but was mostly deflected by her shields.

The man blinked when he realized she remained standing.

"What the—?" Sully gaped at him, stunned dismay warring with anger. The Witch Hunter. He was here. Now. For *her*.

The man tilted his head. "Hmm." He raised his arms again, and Sully narrowed her eyes.

"Oh, no you don't." She refused to be at another man's mercy. She summoned her own magic, drawing from deep within and hurling her own cloud of badassery in his direction. Their powers met with a thunderous clap. Sully's shields coalesced into swirling colors as his magic rolled over her safeguards, and she twisted, guiding the force around and beyond her. Away from her.

Holy capital H.C. Crap. The Witch Hunter. One of the most powerful witches in existence, and he wanted to return her to the Other Realm.

She sidestepped another supernatural blast, deflecting it right back at him. He grunted as it hit him, sending him stumbling for a few steps. It gave her enough of a respite to bolster up her shields. She didn't have the juice to kill him—and she couldn't begin to fathom the karma that would come from killing the Witch Hunter—but she might be able hold him off long enough to—*oh, crap.*

It seemed he'd figured he couldn't pierce her shields, and had decided a more direct approach was in order. He roared something that could have been a battle cry in the Old Language—or perhaps a curse word—then lowered his head and charged straight at her.

Sully dipped to the side and started to run, but he flung out his arm and caught her around the knees. She hit the sand hard. She tried to wriggle away as he pulled her toward him.

Chapter 3

Dave swore as the witch flung a handful of sand in his face. What the—how the hell was Timmerman so damn strong? She'd shaken off his initial blast like a dog shaking off water.

She muttered something, and then her bare foot connected with his chest, sending him flying. A percussion incantation. Damn it. He flung another blast in her direction, but saw the sparks as it rolled over the armor she'd shielded herself with. Any other time he'd admit to being impressed, but right now he was annoyed. He had a duty to perform, and her impressive damn barriers were preventing him from doing it.

He murmured a spell, raising his hands, fingers splayed, satisfied when he felt the erosion spell spread over her shield like a wave of acid, eroding her safeguards.

She flinched, her face paling, and she murmured something. A wall of sand rose around him, enclosing him. He uttered a quick spell, and the sand erupted away from him.

A flip-flop slapped him in the face. His head whipped back at the sting. He blinked, shaking his head, then focused on his—where the hell did she go?

The beach was empty. He narrowed his eyes, scanning the sand. There. His lips curved. The damn witch had covered herself with an unseen spell, but that didn't mean she didn't leave tracks.

He saw the footprints and the little puffs of sand as she ran up the beach. He took off after her. He gritted his teeth. He hated running in sand. It always felt like it was clawing at you, pulling you back, slowing you down. He angled across the wet sand, where it was firmer under foot, then growled. *Screw it.*

He raised his hand toward her, murmuring a restraining spell, and a lariat of power lashed from his hand, encircling his target. He heard her surprised cry when he yanked her back. The sand was forming thrashing mounds, until finally she couldn't hold her invisibility *and* fight off his magical restraint, and her concealment gave way to show the struggling woman as he dragged her toward him.

A wave of water edged around his boots. Damn it. His favorite boots were getting a bath in salt water.

He grasped her thighs, and she roared—*roared* at him, her fist connecting with his jaw. His teeth snapped, and he blinked, then jerked to avoid the feet that kicked uncomfortably close to his groin. He tugged her farther along the sand.

"Sullivan Timmerman," he panted, straddling her

thighs to keep her from turning him into a eunuch. "You have been found guilty of—"

He closed his eyes instinctively as her hand flashed toward him, catching him on the cheek in an openhanded, stinging slap. By the time he focused again, she held a short but wickedly sharp blade in each hand, one pointed at his groin, the other against his throat.

He froze, and his eyebrows rose. "Well, aren't you full of surprises?" That was an understatement. The woman had deflected his power with a skill he hadn't seen before, and now had him at a slight disadvantage. Only slight, though. He outweighed, outmuscled and outpowered her. If outpowered was a thing.

"This is a little extreme for some coins, don't you think?" she panted up at him.

He frowned. "What?" Coins? What? The memory of her victim, the man in the alley with the X carved in his flesh…the draining of his blood. The blade in his chest… he didn't recall seeing any money. What the hell did all that have to do with coins?

"What the hell do the Ancestors have against the nulls?" she demanded.

His frown deepened. What the—? He was having trouble keeping up with the conversation. And why were they even having this conversation? Was she completely mad? Did she seriously not comprehend the damage she'd done—to an innocent, to the balance of nature itself? He'd never really had a witch withstand justice before, at least, not long enough to challenge the Ancestors. The blade at his neck pressed against his skin just a little harder.

"Get off me. Now." Her blue eyes glared at him, and her slightly lopsided mouth formed a tight pout. Her hair

hung in a tangled curtain behind her, dark and wet and...
okay, maybe a little bit more than mildly sexy. She was
attractive, slim yet curvy beneath him. Her cotton top
clung to the wet triangles of her red bikini, and despite
the toned strength of her arms and the thighs he straddled, she still had a softness about her that would have
had him buying her a drink in a bar under different circumstances. Very different. Like, without the execution
directive.

Maybe that was one of the reasons this woman was
so damn dangerous. She looked like some sexy beach
goddess, but he'd seen the blade in the man's heart, the
carving on his wrist, and...ugh. His eyes flicked to those
pouty little lips. She'd drunk his blood. She'd killed a
human. And it hadn't been in self-defense. It hadn't been
to protect others. It had been calculated and cruel. It was
intentional harm to an innocent, to the personal benefit
of the witch. He had no idea *why* she'd killed the man,
or why she'd murdered in the manner she had, but he
was the enforcer, his authority was recognized by Reform society and by the witch population. No matter how
damn smoking hot sexy the witch was, she'd committed
a crime against nature, against all of witchery, and she
had to be punished.

He held up his hands, palms out, in a nonthreatening
manner as he rose. She shuffled out from beneath him,
her daggers still held in a guarded, defensive position.
He eyed her outfit. Loose sleeves, loose skirt—where the
hell had she hidden those blades?

He let her back up a little. She thought she now had
the upper hand. She was so wrong, but for now he'd let
her go with it.

"This is not fair," she hissed at him as she took another step backward.

His eyebrows rose. "Not fair? Do you think I haven't heard that before?"

She shook her head, frowning at him. "What I did—sure, some might consider it a crime, but I was doing it for the greater good."

He shook his head. "Yeah, I've heard that before, too."

"Damn it, I mean it. There was no harm done!"

"No harm?" he repeated, incredulous. His brows dipped. "Are you kidding me? You think that what you did was *harmless*?"

"I was doing a service for the community," she snapped back at him.

"A service." His lips tightened, and he had to look away for a brief moment. Her words sparked a flare of anger in him that he didn't normally let himself feel. "You want to talk service? I live my life in service, and what you did—" he wagged a finger at her. "You should be ashamed. You've brought darkness to all of witchery for your actions."

Her eyebrows rose. "Darkness? To all of witchery? Wow. They've really set the bar low, then, haven't they? What I did, and how it affects others, should have no bearing whatsoever on all of witchery. For the Ancestors to call upon the Witch Hunter over such a trifling matter—that's extreme."

He gaped at her. She talked about murder so callously, as though it was of such little consequence. He couldn't begin to imagine the damage this woman could do if she wasn't stopped.

He took a step forward, and she shifted, angling the

blades toward him. "I can defend every damn thing I've done," she said in a low voice.

Disappointment, hot and sickening, roiled through him. "You defend the indefensible," he said. "And for that, the Ancestors call you to—"

He dived for her, thigh muscles bunching as he launched himself at her. He caught her hands and raised them above her head as he tackled her to the ground. Her breath left her in a grunt as she hit the sand. He spread his body over hers, using his weight to anchor her beneath him.

That's when it hit him. It was as though their powers met and coalesced in a sensory explosion. Her scent, salty and sweet, clouded his mind, as though blanketing him in an awareness of the woman beneath him. Her hair, wet and dark, still showed the odd strand of burnished gold. Her skin, smooth and warm, her eyes so blue and stormy, and her mouth—a delicate, lopsided pout that drew his attention.

For a moment, they both halted, staring at each other. Her mouth opened, and her expression showed her confusion, her surprise. His gaze dropped down to her lips, and he could hear his heartbeat throbbing in his ears—or was it her heartbeat? He couldn't tell. He lifted his stare to hers, dazed. He blinked—and time snapped its fingers, speeding up through the last few moments, folding itself over so that he felt a little unbalanced, a little bereft and a whole lot shaken.

She was supposed to be a hit, damn it. As though she was also catching up to speed—or perhaps she hadn't felt whatever the hell that was—the woman beneath him frowned up at him and started to struggle again.

She was surprisingly strong, and tried to free her arms,

those blades glinting in the light from the setting sun. His grasp tightened on her wrists until she whimpered slightly and released her hold on the short daggers.

He stared down at her. Her cheeks were flushed, her blue eyes bright with outrage and perhaps a tiny bit of fear. Her chest was heaving beneath his, her breasts brushing against his pecs. His legs were tangled with hers, and as his gaze drifted down her body, he saw the fabric of her skirt had hiked up in the struggle, revealing a shapely calf and toned thigh. He'd have to be a dead man not to find the woman attractive, and it was with a heavy heart that he returned his gaze to hers.

She was young. Passionate. Highly skilled. What a waste of a witch. She could have done so much good, and yet she'd acted against nature, against humanity— the vulnerable people they were charged to protect from the shadow breeds.

"Please, don't," she whispered, shaking her head.

"I have to," he told her quietly. "This brings me no joy."

Her pouty lips trembled, and she nodded. "I know."

He blinked at the unexpected concession from the witch he was about to kill. He eyed her face, the resignation in her expression, despite the resistance in her eyes. He wished… He shut that thought down. That way led to madness. Wishes were for fools. His lips firmed, and he sucked in a breath.

"The Ancestors call upon your return to—"

"The Other Realm, yeah, I know the drill," she said. "I remember the First Degree classes. Why don't we skip the speech and get to it?"

He frowned. She had just fought him off with skill and power of an elder, she'd almost gotten away from him, had pulled a knife—two, actually—on him, and now she wanted him to hurry up and kill her. This woman was doing his head in.

"Why are you suddenly so eager to die?" He dipped his head to gaze directly into her eyes, despite his sunglasses. Admittedly, this was possibly the most conversation he'd ever had with one of his hits, but he couldn't help it. She was an intriguing package of contradictions.

"I just realized that death isn't all bad," she said softly, lifting her chin.

He tilted his head, surprised. "You do realize that being summoned to the Other Realm is kind of...*bad*." It was hell—at least, a witch's version of it. Being summoned by the Ancestors who watched from beyond the veil was most definitely not good. The Ancestors had been there long enough to know how to tailor punishment to an excruciating degree for the individual witch who dared to act contrary to the beliefs and morality of the universal covens.

Her expression softened into one of sadness, a weariness that was a stark contrast to the young, vibrant woman she'd seemed just a short while ago as she'd tried to kick his ass.

"I'm ready."

He hesitated. He didn't often come across a target resigned and accepting of their fate. This particular hit was proving a first on many fronts. He nodded. "Okay, then." His frown deepened. After holding a blade to his balls, this witch was proving to be quite civil.

He moved back, just a little bit, one hand still grasping both of her wrists as he pulled his other hand back, almost as though to strike. "May the Ancestors have mercy upon your soul."

He summoned his inherited powers and sparks flickered at his fingertips.

Heat blazed across his chest. He cried out in pain and grasped his left pec as he rolled off her. He blinked furiously, trying to catch his breath.

What was happening? What the *hell* was—?

"Argh," he growled as the name branded on his chest flared to life. He shook his head. No. No, this can't be happening. She's here, he was about—

He winced as the wound blistered anew, and pulled at his T-shirt, tearing the fabric from neck to hem. He grunted when the cloth pulled away from the burn.

The witch on the ground next to him rolled, grabbing one of the blades in the sand before she scrambled to his side. She clasped the dagger in both hands and raised it above her head, poised to bring it down on him.

The pain was blinding, all-consuming, and he couldn't do anything to defend himself. When the ancestral fire was branded into his skin, he was powerless. He stared up at the woman above him, confused. She was here, and yet her name was being rebranded into his flesh.

Another innocent had been killed.

But not by this witch.

The woman started to bring the blade down, but she gasped when she looked down at his body.

Sully dropped the knife, her gaze locked on the Witch Hunter's chest. His T-shirt hung in tatters at his side. His chest was broadly muscled, his skin a light golden tan, his toned torso lined with dark tattoos that looked both beautiful and dangerous, but it was the glowing mark that drew her gaze, and made the sweat break out on her brow as she tried resurrect her shields.

Sullivan Timmerman.

It was written in the Old Language, but she couldn't mistake it.

Her name radiated on his chest, searing through his skin as though borne from a fire within, and the cords of his neck stuck out in stark relief as he tilted his head, growling in pain.

Holy capital H.C. Crap. She was too late.

She sucked in a breath at the hot wave that flashed through her, over her. It was *everywhere*. Pain. Tormented heat. Searing agony. Guilt. Self-loathing. Confusion. Loyalty. So many more emotions, too fast, too ferocious to name, bombarded her. The sensations were excruciating.

The Witch Hunter writhed on the ground, his teeth gritted, until she felt the pain drop from excruciating agony to aggravating throb. He gasped as he rolled over and onto his knees, wheezing slightly.

Sully looked away, mustering all the strength she could from within to shakily layer up some protections, although they were weak and tattered. Holy f—

"Sullivan Timmerman," the man at her side gasped, turning away from her as he removed his sunglasses to stare at the sea.

She eyed him warily. She tried to swallow, but couldn't quite get past the lump in her throat. Her arms hung limply by her side and she trembled all over. It didn't seem to matter, though. The Witch Hunter didn't look like he was talking to her, though. He was on his knees, hands fisted in the sand, and she stared at the back of his head as his chest rose and fell with deep, shuddering breaths. How the hell could the man still be conscious after that experience? Her gut twisted, and she felt shaky and nauseous, and quite frankly wanted to curl up on the sand and pass out.

After a moment he dipped his head, then he slid his sunglasses on. Sully rose to her feet, stumbled on her shaky knees and almost face-planted in the sand when she bent over to scoop up her blades. If he was coming for her again, she was going to fight. He'd obliterated her shields, and it would take her some time to rebuild them, but she could still hit.

Right now, though, all she could feel was him. His pain, his shock, his confusion.

He glanced over his shoulder to her, his brows drawn. "Sullivan Timmerman…?"

This time, his tone was uncertain, and she raised her arms in front of her in a defensive block, blades ready. She didn't bother to answer him. She'd almost gotten herself killed the last time she'd responded.

He shook his head as he rose to his feet. "You're not the right one." Even if she couldn't hear it in his tone, or see it in his face, she could feel the shock reverberating through him, the dismay. The guilt.

Her eyes widened, and she gaped at him. "Are you—? What the—? Holy—." She blinked at him. He'd just attacked her. Nearly killed her. And she wasn't the *right one*? She'd almost *died*. For the briefest of moments, she'd *wanted* to die. She squished that thought down deep, buried it under a fragile barrier.

He drew himself up to his full height, and she could see his wound was already beginning to heal, the lettering darkening to a semblance of what she'd assume would become a tattoo that matched the rest of the markings on his body.

He touched his abdomen and dipped his head. "I have

made a grave mistake. My duty is not with you. Please forgive me, Sullivan Timmerman."

His apology was sincere, his gestures faintly noble. Courtly. His earnestness was almost tangible, along with a profound sense of guilt, of sadness and of dismayed shock. And pain.

"For—forgive you?" she responded, her mouth slack.

She'd practically begged him to kill her.

Her lips tightened, her eyes narrowed. "Screw you, Witch Hunter."

She backed away from him, then turned and headed toward the cliff stairs. He'd tried to kill her, and normally she wouldn't be turning her back on a man who'd just tried to kill her, but she'd felt his remorse, his guilt. His exhaustion. He wouldn't come after her again.

"I'm so sorry," he called after her. She didn't look back as she flipped him the bird, then realized she still carried her blades. She slid them into the slim-line sheath that formed part of her belt, and it wasn't until she put her foot on the bottom step that she realized she'd left her flip-flops behind.

She glanced back at the beach in frustration, just in time to see the Witch Hunter drop to his knees, then collapse on the sand, his unconscious body an inert dark form on the sand.

Chapter 4

Dave's eyes fluttered open. He frowned. Stars? He blinked. Yep. Stars. A cool breeze—not unpleasant—brushed across him, and he could hear the rhythmic roar of waves. He shifted and groaned. His neck was supported by a mound of sand, but it felt like he'd been lying there for hours. He moved his arms and realized a light cloth covered him. He glanced down. Despite it being some-time in the night, the stars and a glimmer of the moon gave enough light to see a little. He picked at the cloth. A towel?

He sat up, hissing at the pull of skin on his chest. He flicked off the towel. A white patch was taped to his chest. What the—? He peeled back a corner of the ban-dage and caught a whiff of something disgusting. He scrunched his nose up. Ew. He could smell marigold, aloe vera, maybe jasmine and something else he couldn't quite put his finger on, but whatever it was, it smelled gross. He patted the tape back down. Someone had made him an herbal poultice to help heal his wound and limit infection and inflammation. He could think of only one person in the area that would have the plant knowledge for it, yet he couldn't quite believe she'd do that for him, not after what he'd attempted to do to her. Where was she? He glanced around. He was alone on the beach, with just the waves to keep him company.

He rolled to his knees, then his feet, groaning as the kinks in his neck and back straightened themselves out. He shook out his shoulders. Sleeping on the beach worked only if you were drunk and in the company of a woman. Here, he was neither.

His tattered T-shirt fluttered in the breeze, and he shrugged out of his jacket so he could discard the ruined garment. His mouth tightened. Damn. He'd almost killed her.

He dragged his thumb across his forehead. What the hell happened? He'd struggled to comprehend when his chest had started to burn again. He'd had Sullivan Timmerman right where he wanted her, and had been about to send her across the veil, but then…

It was still so hard to accept, to make sense of. Another innocent had died at the hands of Sullivan Timmerman, yet the woman had been right in front of him at the time, ready to accept her fate. When he'd uttered the name and channeled the killer's vision, he'd seen the latest victim. An older woman, tears running down her face as she'd stared up at him with confusion, horror and pain, and then with shock as the blade had pierced her heart. Once again, the killer had carved that mark on her wrist and used that same horn to capture the woman's blood. And once again, Dave had been booted out of the vision when the killer had consumed the blood and uttered his spell—whatever that damn spell was.

He placed his hand over the dressing. He'd had the wrong person. His stomach clenched, and he had to suck in some deep breaths to stop from throwing up. He'd almost killed an innocent—a crime that would send *him* across the veil to the Ancestors. How could that be?

Sullivan Timmerman wasn't a common name. How could he have gotten it so damn wrong? Guilt, hot and sickening, wrung his gut. The woman had answered his call, and had confirmed her identity—she'd even mentioned something about coins, as though she knew she was guilty of some wrongdoing… He looked down as the towel fluttered in the breeze, then rolled a little along the sand. He reached down and picked it up.

Death isn't all bad.

What the hell did she mean? She was so young, so full of life, so full of power when she'd fought him—the first witch to be able to maintain a defense against him…ever. She was also the first witch to halt him in his tracks, mid-hit. What the hell was that all about? And yet, when he'd had her down on the sand, it was as if all her fight had left her, and she was ready to cross the veil. He'd nearly killed an innocent witch. How…? What…?

He started to walk across the beach toward the trail at the edge of the dunes that would lead him to where he'd parked his bike. He ducked his head as he trudged through the sand. He'd fought with a woman, for God's sake. He—the guy who inked up women with protective spells against their abusers, who was committed to never hurting an innocent, who believed the women in his life, however fiery and frustrating they could be—and his mother and sister could be plenty of both—should be safeguarded, whatever the cost.

He stumbled. Hell. He'd tackled the woman. He'd threatened her, dominated her. He was no better than the monsters he hunted.

His toe hit something, and he glanced down. A white flip-flop lay half-buried in the sand.

Hers.

He scooped it up, turning it over to look at it. It was well worn, with dents in the rubber from her heel and the ball of her foot. He sighed as he continued along the beach. He'd have to make it up to her. Somehow. He didn't apologize very often, but words couldn't make up for his transgressions against her. Part of his job as the Witch Hunter was to redress the balance, wherever possible—especially by counteracting the misdeeds of the malefactors. What he'd done today with this Sullivan Timmerman—well, he had some counteracting to do.

After he caught the real Sullivan Timmerman and put an end to these murders.

He crested the last rise and walked over to his bike. He slipped the flip-flop and towel into one of his panniers. He wasn't quite sure where to start. All he'd managed to see was the female victim, an older woman, and what looked like a wooden floor beneath her, and the claw foot of a threadbare sofa.

He straddled his bike, started it and flicked up the kickstand with his heel.

Kill one Sullivan Timmerman, then make it up to the other Sullivan Timmerman. He'd better get busy.

Sully boxed up the teas she'd cut for Lucy and Mary Anne Adler. She realized her hands were trembling, and she curled her fingers over. Tears formed in her eyes. She'd been ready to die.

She blinked, sniffing, as she gathered the boxes and grabbed her satchel. She wasn't going to think about it. Nope. She was going to be a good little witch and completely ignore the ramifications of this afternoon's incident. She wasn't going to think about that moment when his body lay across hers. She should have felt threatened, frightened, but she felt—nope. Not going there.

She hesitated at the front door, gazing out at the sea that reflected the light of the moon and stars. From this point she couldn't see directly down to the beach. She'd have to walk to the edge of the headland to be able to do that.

She wasn't going to walk anywhere near the headland at the moment. What if he was still there?

Well, it would serve him right. She slammed the door closed behind her and stalked over to her car. The guy had tried to kill her.

He was just doing his duty.

Screw duty. The man was the Witch Hunter. She climbed into her car and started the engine, reversing out of the drive. All coven children were taught about the Witch Hunter. Much like the bogeyman, the Witch Hunter was someone to fear, someone who would come after you if you did something wrong. You never knew what the Witch Hunter looked like—only that he was out there, and ready to hunt you down if you so much as hinted at violating the universal laws of the covens. Witchery lore claimed there were Witch Hunters in every generation, chosen by the Ancestors, and assigned with the duty of preserving nature's balance. Only a hunted

witch could recognize the Witch Hunter for who he—
or she—was.

No wonder he'd seemed "familiar".

She drove down the dark road. Her cottage was the
last one in a street of four, with a considerable distance
between neighbors. They had no streetlights, and the real
estate agent who'd handled the sale had told her to be
thankful she had indoor plumbing, a landline and electricity. Cell phone reception kind of sucked, though. With
the expanse of the ocean on three sides, the nearest cell
tower was quite a distance away. She had to go into town
to her shop to get access to the internet, and even there
connectivity was a little spotty.

She still couldn't believe it. The Witch Hunter had
come after *her*. She shook her head as she turned left
onto the coast road. The only crime she committed was
a pesky little Reform one, and not one against an individual, a coven, or nature. Why the hell were the Ancestors
upset by a little coin-making? Sure, counterfeiting was
slightly illegal, but it was all to help others, so really they
should be proud of her, right? Witches blurred the legal
lines often, with the making of potions and toxins, and
spells designed to reveal or conceal…but she'd never used
nature's power to provoke another to an unlawful act, nor
had she sought power through the suffering of others, or
personal or financial gain at the risk of another. Those
were pretty much the deal breakers with the Ancestors,
and as far as she was concerned, she'd done neither.

You're not the right one.

She frowned. The Ancestors had gotten it wrong…she
grimaced at the memory of the lettering blazing across
the man's chest. That had looked painful. Oh, not the
chest. No, the chest had looked damn fine, actually. All

those glorious muscles… She shook her head. She was lusting after a guy who'd tried to kill her. She thought she was better than that, now. That she'd grown some insight, maybe even some self-respect and dignity. She needed her head examined. Or to get laid. She preferred…neither. She hadn't had a companion since she'd left the West Coast and arrived in Serenity Cove four years ago. If she thought the Witch Hunter was a long drink of sex on the beach, it was either too long between lovers, or she really hadn't experienced the personal growth she'd fooled herself into thinking she had.

No, damn it. She'd learned her lesson, and wasn't prepared to make those same disastrous mistakes again. Ever.

She wound down the driver's window, trying to get some fresh air, some snap to reality. Her car was so old it didn't have air-conditioning. She lifted her chin as the wind ruffled her hair. The warm breeze carried the scent of salt and brine, and almost as though he had a homing device in her brain, her thoughts returned to the man on the beach.

She'd been shocked to see him collapse, and had reluctantly, cautiously approached him. She'd lightly kicked him, but he hadn't stirred. She'd tentatively relaxed her shields and discovered he truly was unconscious. She couldn't blame him. That branding—damn, that had stung like the bejeebus.

She should have left him there for the crabs, or for the tide. Her mouth tightened. When he'd been poised above her, ready to deliver the death strike, she'd sensed him.

He'd been fighting his own reluctance to kill her. She'd felt the burden of his duty, his responsibility to the Ancestors, to the covens. She'd sensed—of all things—his honor that gave him a core of steel. She'd felt his pain, too, over the killing, and his absolute commitment to delivering her to the Ancestors for her crimes, and his determination to save the vulnerable from her actions. Having all these emotions, the true metal of his character, she'd glimpsed something she wasn't expecting. She'd seen beyond his actions, beyond his awareness, and she'd seen through the veil. She'd sensed the nothingness. No dark, no light, no pain…no emotion. She'd seen a glimpse of…peace. No emotions to dodge or defend herself from. No effort required to constantly shore up her defenses, to protect her own heart and mind from the pain of others. And for the briefest of moments, that oblivion seemed heaven-sent.

She'd spent so much energy shielding herself, the constant effort to mute the emotions of others on a daily basis was tiring. At that moment, when the veil parted, and time stood still for her, offering her a glimpse of what could be, she'd realized how alone she was, and how tired she was of playing at being someone else for those who thought they were closest to her, yet knew her not.

For that briefest of moments, she was ready to step through the veil into the Other Realm, and accept the solace it offered.

And then he'd received that bodyline text from the Ancestors, and she'd snapped out of it, thank goodness.

She was such a *sucker*. The guy had passed out on her after expending all that cosmic energy fighting her, and then enduring some epic pain, and what had she done? Checked on him. What a sap. She'd gone and made him a darn poultice for his wound. She'd even packed the sand into a pillow for him. She told herself it was to get back on the good side of the Ancestors, by looking after their Witch Hunter.

But she was an empath witch, and she didn't have the luxury of being able to walk away from a person in pain without making some effort to help. That, and he was the *Witch Hunter*, for crying out loud. She couldn't begin to imagine how pissed off the Ancestors would be if she turned her back on their warrior.

She sighed as she rounded a bend in the road. He certainly looked the part. Hard muscles, skin that was warm and smooth, and strong, handsome facial features. She was surprised the Ancestors had chosen such a hunk for their most difficult job. She'd always expected the Witch Hunter to be some twisted, not-so-attractive guy who looked on the outside as mean and harsh as she thought he'd have to be on the inside.

Only he hadn't been mean and harsh on the inside. He'd been determined, yes, and ruthless to boot, but she'd sensed a surprising hint of fairness in him, and a heavy dose of honor. Surprising as she hadn't expected to find either in the Ancestors' assassin.

She turned off the highway, and after a short drive turned onto the street where Mary Anne Adler lived. She frowned at the flashing red-and-blue lights, and slowed to a stop when a county deputy held up his hand.

A man emerged from Mary Anne's house, his hat in his hands, and the sheriff nodded when he saw Sully's car. He trotted down the stairs and over to her car, and she propped her elbow on the window frame. She leaned her head out slightly to look up at him.

"Evening, Tyler."

"Sully. I'm afraid I'm going to have to ask you to move on," he said, resting his hand on the roof of her car.

She frowned, and picked up the boxes that sat on the passenger seat. "I'm here with some tea for Lucy and Mary Anne." She knew Lucy and Gary had moved in with Mary Anne for a little while, to help her get her house ready for sale so that the older woman could downsize and move to a place closer to town.

The sheriff grimaced. "Well, Lucy's in the back of an ambulance on her way to St. Michael's Hospital," he told her.

"Is she all right?" Sully asked, concerned, then realized what a stupid question that was. Of course the woman wasn't all right. She was on her way to the hospital.

Tyler nodded. "She will be."

"Uh, well, do you want me to stay with Mary Anne until she gets back home?" Sully offered. The poor woman had to be devastated by her son's murder, and probably just a little anxious with her daughter-in-law being rushed to hospital.

Tyler's face grew grim. "Mary Anne isn't going to be needing your tea anymore, Sully. She died earlier tonight."

Sully gaped, and sorrow pierced her from within. Mary Anne was a sweet lady. "Oh, no. That's so sad. Gary's death was too much for her, huh?"

Tyler shrugged. "We'll never know. She was murdered."

Sully blanched, stunned. "No."

"Well, we're still investigating, obviously, but from what I saw, I'm pretty sure it wasn't a suicide or an accident."

Sully tilted her head against the backrest. "How—how

did it…?" she couldn't quite finish the sentence. How did Mary Anne die?

Tyler glanced back at the house. "I can't say. Not yet." He looked down at Sully. "But I will say this—go home and lock your doors. Stay safe."

He tapped the roof of her car, then turned back to the Adler house. A deputy was unravelling yellow tape along the front veranda railing, and Sully's blood cooled in her veins at the sight, and what it meant.

The Adler house was a crime scene. Sweet little Mary Anne had been murdered in her home. That woman was so lovely, Sully couldn't imagine anyone having enough animosity, enough rage, to want to kill the older woman. And so soon after her son's murder. Were they connected? She couldn't quite believe that one murder had been committed in their sleepy little cove, let alone two. What were the odds that they were two separate, random acts? What were the odds they were connected? Poor Mary Anne. Sully shifted gears and reversed down the street until she could do a U-turn. It wasn't until she was pulling into her darkened yard, with only the moonlight and the stars to illuminate her garden, that Tyler's words really sank in.

Lock the doors. Stay safe.

What the hell kind of danger was out there? And why did he think it could visit her?

Chapter 5

Dave frowned at the Closed sign on the shop door. There was a lot of that going around Serenity Cove, today. He'd just tried to get some breakfast at the diner in town, only to find it was temporarily closed for business. He'd managed to find a burger joint down near Crescent Beach. He'd also found a bar, but it was too early to open.

He had not found a certain witch, though. He'd checked the beach he'd first seen her on, and then had taken the walk up the stairs to the top of the cliff. He'd found a cleared area at the top, and then a little road that led back to the highway. He'd found her home—her garden was very impressive, along with a little shed out the back. He hadn't been able to find her, though.

And he needed to find her. He needed to…seek forgiveness. Redemption, maybe. His gut tightened inside him, like a corkscrew twisting into a cork. What he did, killing witches, it was a crap job that someone had to do. He was there to stop witches from abusing power, abusing the vulnerable. It was an ordained vocation, and he was *supposed* to be doing *good*. He had a witch to hunt, but he'd found he couldn't concentrate until he made it right with the witch he'd wronged. His shoulders tensed. He didn't want to think about what he'd nearly done, but he didn't usually shy away from the difficult—that's why the Ancestors had picked him in the first place. Still, he felt like a heel for what he'd done, how close he'd come to really hurting her.

He glanced down at the flip-flop he gripped. He'd used it to perform a locator spell, and even now it was tugging away from him, toward the door that was closed to customers. He glanced about. Sullivan Timmerman's shop was on the edge of town. It was set back a little from the road, with a parking area in front. Just like the rest of the stores in the area, it had a sweet facade of Victorian wood trim, painted white, and a soft pastel blue on the clapboards. It gave an impression of welcome and charm, the kind of thing he'd associate with a sweet little grandmother—only the witch inside was no grandma, and after seeing her defense against him, he'd say sweet wasn't his first descriptor for her. Fiery, maybe. Sweet, not so much.

He was trying to ignore the towel, the sand pillow and the dressing that had soothed the pain in his chest.

He knocked on the door, then peered through the glass pane. For a moment all he could see was his reflection, his sunglasses glinting in the sunshine. He had to cup his hands around his eyes and press up against the window to see inside. The shop interior was dark. A little on the small side, and devoid of anyone, including the witch he sought. She was in here, somewhere, damn it. The flip-flop told him. He glanced carefully about in the gloom and finally noticed the flickering light through a transom window above a door that led from the shop room into an area behind.

He knew it. She was here. He shrugged out of his leather jacket and draped carefully, silently, over the glass-topped counter display. The garment was great on a bike, lousy in the summer, and creaky when he wanted to be quiet.

He muttered a quick yield spell, and the door un-locked, swinging inward. He shook his head. She hadn't bespelled her property at all, from the looks of it. He stepped inside and closed the door behind him. He hesi-tated, then flicked the lock. He had to apologize, and he'd prefer no interruptions, and no witnesses.

He stepped up to the door that led out back, and tested the doorknob. He shook his head when it twisted at his touch. Security was not a priority for this witch. He opened the door a little and peered through it. It opened into some sort of workshop. There was large machinery, grinding wheels, anvils and sharpening blocks. There was an artist's desk, with a number of sketches pinned to the corkboard above it. His eyes widened when he saw the wicked-looking blades lined up on a magnetic knife rack on one wall. Different lengths—hell, was that a *sword*?

He could hear a regular thump, thump, thump, accom-panied with a faint grinding sound. It took a moment, but he finally narrowed down the source of the sounds. She sat at a machine, and every time she pressed her foot on the pedal, a weight would descend, making the thump, thump noise he could hear. He realized it was a press of some sort. She'd place a metal prong into the press, and the weight would descend, and then she'd remove and slide into another chute, and thump again. When she removed the prong, he could see tines had been cut into the metal end.

Forks. She was making…forks? He watched her for a moment. Her blond hair was tied back into a thick braid, and she wore a loose-fitting blouse over a long patterned skirt. She was so intent on her work, her head and shoulders dipped each time she set the prongs in the chutes. At one point she arched her back, and his gaze was drawn to the long line of her body as she tilted her head back and rubbed her neck. The flowing clothes made her look willowy and lithe, but he could see the strength in her arms as she placed the newly formed forks onto a tray next to her. Then she returned to her task, inserting the metal prongs into the chutes and cutting tines in the ends.

He stepped inside the room, and the floorboard creaked beneath his feet. She whirled, and he ducked, hearing the thud as the fork hit the timber door behind him. He glanced over his shoulder. The fork had impaled in the wood, quivering, at roughly the same position his head had been mere seconds before. Yeah, he guessed he deserved that reaction—and a whole lot more.

He turned, and she'd already picked up another fork and held it poised to throw again.

"Whoa, whoa," he said, hands up as he straightened. "I come in peace."

"Then go in peace—or pieces. Your choice."

Okay, so he could understand her…resistance to meeting with him. Fair enough. "Please," he said. He tried to send her some calming waves, only he could sense the block between them. Damn, she was good.

"Why are you here?" she asked, slowly rising from her stool to face him properly, her movement fluid and graceful. She'd lowered her hand, but he noticed she still retained her throwing grip on the fork. She had dark circles beneath her eyes, as though she was tired. He couldn't blame her.

He held up her flip-flop. "I've come to return this. And to say thank you…" He took a cautious step toward her, offering her the footwear. He cleared his throat. "I also came to apologize," he said in a quiet voice.

She tilted her head, as though assessing him, then stepped forward, accepting her flip-flop. "That's okay." She dropped the fork into the tray.

Dave frowned. That's…okay? It was that easy? He was expecting shouting, ranting, at least a remonstrative finger waggle. "You're not—you're not angry?"

She nodded. "Oh, I'm angry, but I know you had good reasons, and you're already beating yourself up about it way more than I could."

He gaped for a moment, then his eyes narrowed. This didn't make sense. He'd expected her to react explosively—okay, and maybe the fork still buried in the door behind him went a little in that direction, but… "You're awfully Zen about this."

She stepped closer to him, her eyes dark with emotions he couldn't name. "It's not every day the Witch Hunter comes after me," she admitted. "And it's not every day the Witch Hunter admits to making a mistake."

He winced, then nodded. "It was a mistake. A big mistake. A mistake of epic proportions. What happened… shouldn't have."

She tilted her head, and her honey-blond braid slid over her shoulder. She gazed at him in open curiosity. "Who are you?"

"You know who I am."

"No, I know you're the Witch Hunter. What's your name, though?"

"Ah, that's right. We haven't been formally introduced." He inclined his head. "My name is Dave Carter."

Her brow dipped. "Oh."

"Oh?" She sounded...disappointed.

"I just thought your name would be more...exotic."

His eyebrows rose. "More exotic?"

She nodded. "Yeah. Not so plain."

"Plain."

"Uh, normal," she tried to clarify. Dave pursed his lips. Normal. His name was probably the only normal thing about him.

She looked at him carefully. "So, how does it work?"

He shifted. He'd never talked about it. He wasn't supposed to. The Witch Hunter was the blind justice of the Ancestors of witchcraft. His mother knew—he'd *had* to tell her. She'd been his elder, and needed to know why he wasn't going through the Degrees for their coven. He should have guessed his sister, Melissa, was eavesdropping at the time—or maybe he did and he'd still wanted her to overhear so that she would understand, and there was at least one person he could talk to. Some of the other covens in Irondell knew—the witch community wasn't as big as the werewolf or vampire tribes, so news got around. People were wary of him, though, and his occupation didn't inspire shared confidences. Most witches avoided him like the plague. But other than that, he mentioned it only when he was performing a hit, as he recited the ritualistic words that would send the witch beyond the veil.

"It's...complicated."

She arched an eyebrow. Well, he guess she at least deserved a little bit of an explanation.

"I receive the name when a crime is committed, and I go hunt." Simple, really.

She frowned as she glanced at his chest. "I saw…how." Her voice was soft, confused. "I haven't committed any of those crimes, though."

His eyes narrowed at her word selection. *Those* crimes. Did that mean there were other crimes she *had* committed? He was getting curious about those coins she'd mentioned on the beach.

"It's never happened before," he admitted.

She frowned. "How can you be certain?"

Cold horror washed over him at the prospect. "Because I wouldn't be able to continue," he said roughly. The thought he could have killed other innocents…it would crush him. Cripple him. He shook his head. No. If that had been the case, the Ancestors would have yanked his ass into the Other Realm. The punishment for a Witch Hunter to break the laws they've sworn to uphold would be extreme, to say the least.

She folded her arms and strolled over toward another door he only just noticed. "Soooo," she said slowly, "when a witch breaks one of the Three, they…brand you with that witch's name, and you go hunt? Like a guard dog? Sic 'em, Rex?"

He tilted his head. "Kind of…" he said slowly, hating the analogy, no matter how apt it seemed. She opened the door and entered what was a small kitchen, with a door leading to the backyard, and another that led to a small bathroom, and a door that led to what looked like an addition to the back of the house. Shop. Factory. Whatever the hell this place was. She crossed over to the stove and lit the stove, then placed a kettle on it.

"But how do you know you're going after a witch for

something serious? I mean, what if the Ancestors want you to just warn someone?" She reached up to a cupboard, and Dave's gaze flicked down to where her loose blouse rose above the belt of her skirt. He wanted to focus on the gold skin of her back and side, but his eyes widened when he saw the decorative panel at the back of her belt, with two metal prongs that looked suspiciously like the hilts of the blades she'd used on him. How about that.

He forced himself to concentrate on the conversation, and he narrowed his eyes at her words. "Do you feel like you've needed to be warned about something, Sullivan?" *What* was this chick into?

"Sully," she corrected him, then shook her head, her expression forced into something that almost looked innocent. "Uh, no. Not really. I just—I guess I never thought I'd ever have the opportunity to talk with the Witch Hunter, and I want to understand…how do you know you're doing the right thing?"

Wow. She cut straight to the heart of his current doubts. He wanted to shrug it off with some sort of general comment, but Sullivan—no, *Sully*—deserved at least the truth from him, in all its unadorned, vicious glory.

"When a witch breaks one of the Three," he said, referring to the Three Immutable Laws of Witchcraft—never draw on nature's power to provoke another to an unlawful act—never seek power through the suffering of others, and never draw on nature's power for personal gain at the expense of another's well-being, "I am delivered their name, and I see their crime."

She frowned. "You *see* the crime?" Her face relaxed into something he could only call sympathy. "That's got to be hard." She turned as the kettle whistled, and lifted it off the stove. She pulled down a tin and spooned tea into two strainers and popped them into the ceramic mugs she'd pulled from the cupboard.

He was glad he was wearing his sunglasses, and could hide is surprise as she made the tea. He hadn't told anyone about that before, and it was difficult to broach such a personal subject. He'd never expected to feel sympathy directed toward him over it, but she was right. It *was* hard. There were some things you just couldn't unsee. Some crimes—especially the kids, damn it. He swallowed as he shut down that line of memory. He'd seen his own kind do terrible, horrible, heinous things. He'd seen them do great things, too, but when dealing with the dregs, you started to feel like you were covered in the muck, and it was all you generally got to see.

He cleared his throat. "I see the crimes, so I know what they've done, and generally where I can find them."

Her hands halted, and she slowly turned to face him, her face showing her confusion, and perhaps a hint of nervousness. "What did you see me do?"

He reached for one of the mugs—he couldn't quite believe the woman he'd tried to kill the day before was calmly making him tea in her kitchen.

His lips quirked. Sully Timmerman was proving to be an unexpected intrigue, on so many levels. "I didn't see you."

She frowned, confused. "Then why come after me?"

He sighed. "Usually, I see the crime through the killer's eyes, and can be with them for as long as it takes to identify them, or their whereabouts. This time I got neither."

Her frown deepened as her confusion did, and he leaned against the doorjamb. "I saw what Sullivan Timmerman did. Not you, this…monster. I saw—" he hesitated. It was one thing for him to witness these horrendous acts, he didn't need to spread that taint to this woman.

Her brow eased. "It's okay. You can't surprise me."

His mouth tightened. "Oh, I think I can."

"I think I have a right to know what I was accused of, don't you?" Her tone was gentle, yet with a core of steel-like implacability. She wasn't about to be fobbed off with half-truths and generalizations. She wanted—and deserved—the facts.

"I see through the witch's eyes," he explained. "So I see what they do. I saw someone get stabbed, and some ritualistic markings, the drinking of blood…"

She shuddered. "Yeah, well, I didn't do any of that. What did this witch look like?"

Dave grimaced, then sipped his tea. "That's the problem. Usually I can stay with the witch until he or she looks in the mirror, or passes a window, and I can see their reflection. Usually I get to see the neighborhood, some more of the crime scene, enough to establish their location… This time I got bumped."

"Bumped?"

He took another sip, nodding. Once the dam broke, it felt easier to talk, easier to explain. There was something surprisingly relaxing about Sully Timmerman. "Bumped. He—or she—drank the blood, said a spell and bam, I was out of there."

"So you didn't get to see this witch's face, or where they were?"

"I saw an alley, I saw a sign on a building—Mack's Gym, by the way—and I had the name."

Sully's mouth pouted as she mulled over his words. "Mack's Gym is in the next town…" Then she shook her head. "But I don't understand. My name?"

He nodded. "Yep. Sullivan Timmerman." He frowned, then glanced down at the tea. "What's in this?" He was finding it too easy to talk.

"Oh, it's just a little lavender, lemon balm, a tidge of nutmeg…"

His eyes narrowed. "Antianxiety?" Most of those ingredients were relaxants.

She shrugged. "A calmative. I thought you could use it."

He had to admit, it worked. He'd come here with his gut roiling, concerned about how she'd receive him, whether she'd hear him out…whether she'd forgive him. But…how did she know? Realization dawned, and he put the mug down.

"You're an empath." It wasn't a question. Everything added up. She'd made him a poultice to ease his pain and help him heal, had made him as comfortable as possible on his bed of sand and had displayed an unexpected insight to his turmoil—accepting he had a job to do.

She stepped back, her skirt moving around her legs as she did so, her movement was so sudden. "What— what makes you say that?" she asked cautiously. Warily.

He eyed the increased distance that now separated them. He'd spooked her, somehow. He shrugged, trying to keep it casual. "Oh, just putting the pieces together. I don't know how many witches would patch me up, hear me out and make me tea after I've tried to kill them." She was a sweetheart. She'd tried to ease his pain, and ease his guilt.

She frowned as she crossed to the sink—putting even more distance between them. "That's quite a stretch. Maybe I'm just a sucker for a bad boy."

His lips quirked. As tempting as the suggestion was,

he doubted it. He edged a little closer, and put his own mug in the sink, managing to hem her in at the same time. Sully paused, her gaze on the mug he still clasped. "Ah, now that's where you're wrong, Sully," he said in a low voice, leaning forward. "I can be very, very good."

Sully lifted her gaze from the large hand that made her mug look like a kid's tea party toy, up the corded forearm, over the bulging bicep, the edge of the dark tattoo peeking out from beneath the sleeve of his fresh black T-shirt, and across the broad shoulder and torso to the strong column of his throat. She swallowed, hesitating, before lifting it farther. The man had a great jaw. Strong, defined, with just the right dusting of hair that made you want to reach and stroke it. Was he—was the Witch Hunter *flirting* with her? His lips curled up at one end, a sexy little smile that made heat bloom tight and low in her stomach. She couldn't see his eyes behind the dark lenses of his sunglasses, couldn't see whether he was flirting, teasing, or just making an observation. And she desperately wanted to see his eyes.

The fact that she couldn't was frustrating, and just a little unnerving. She could relax her shields, get a sense of what he was feeling, but that method was fraught with risks. Risks she'd learned long ago weren't worth it, and she should have the sense to know better.

She stepped back, clearing her throat. "I'll take that under advisement," she said softly.

He tilted his head, and she tried to keep her expression impassive. Aloof. That's what she was going for, here. Distant. Cool. He was the Witch Hunter, tracking down a murderous wi—she frowned.

"I want to help," she blurted.

His eyebrows rose over his sunglasses. "What?"

"There is a witch out there murdering in my name. I want to help you catch him. Her. Whatever."

He shook his head, backing up a little. "Sorry, sweetness. No can do."

Funny. He didn't sound apologetic at all. She put her hands on her hips. "I insist. You said Mack's Gym. That's local. You'll need someone with local knowledge to help you. I can do that."

He shook his head. "I work alone."

"And look where it got you," she said, gesturing to herself.

"Hey, that was an honest mistake," he said in faint protest.

"One that you should avoid making again," she said primly. "Let me help."

"Not happening."

She stepped closer. "Someone is using my name—"

"It could be just as much his as it is yours," he pointed out.

"I can tell you now, there is no other person in the county with my name," she informed him. "But this person even has the Ancestors confused," she told him, her tone serious.

This time Dave stepped closer toward her, and she had to tilt her head back to meet his gaze through his sunglasses. "The term is Witch Hunter—not hunters," he told her roughly. "We don't buddy up on a job. This is something I've got to do on my own, Sully. You haven't seen what this person is capable of. I have. I don't want you anywhere near him."

"But this is *my* name, Dave," she protested.

"And I will get him," he assured her, "and you will stay far away from this matter, and be safe."

She opened her mouth to protest further, then halted when he stepped closer and cupped her cheek. Sensation. Heat. Desire. Protectiveness. Everything bombarded her, leaving her trying to catch her balance. Her shields. It was like he could pierce her shields with just a touch, invading both her personal and mental spaces. She tried to shore them up, but no matter how many times she tried erecting them, his presence kept swamping her.

"I owe you one, Sully," he told her seriously, his voice low. "What I did, I have to make it up to you. I'm granting you a favor."

A flare of forthrightness, a heavy dose of resolve, washed over her. "A favor," she repeated.

He nodded. "I happen to take debts very seriously. I owe you."

Well, she didn't think he owed her anything, but if this was important to him, she wasn't above using it. Warm promise. Integrity.

"Great. Let me—"

He placed a finger on her lips, and again, sensations rolled through her, her senses awakening to him, overriding her personal shields. She could feel his determination, his dedication—and his resistance. And something else. Something… Oh. Desire. She trembled, feeling a reciprocal flare of attraction.

"I have to find this witch," he murmured, "and I will not endanger you. This favor I grant you is for your use, at a time of your choosing, but I will never let you use it to put yourself in danger. Do you understand?"

His voice was so deep, so low. His expression was grim, intent. She stared up at his sunglasses, stunned by the sincerity, the commitment behind his words. "Uh, yes." She whispered the words against his finger.

"You need anything, you call for me."

She nodded slowly.

"I'll come for you. This is my promise to you." He said the words like a vow, conveying a determination that was...well, knee-weakening.

He dipped his head once in acknowledgment. His finger trailed across her lips. It was as though every cell in her body awakened and paused in anticipation. He brushed his finger first over her top lip, then across the bottom, pressing it down gently. Her mouth parted, and he lowered his head, removing his finger as his lips pressed against hers.

Chapter 6

Oh. My. God. She closed her eyes as he kissed her. His kiss was sweet, tender, capturing her lips in a firm yet delicate kiss. She sighed against his mouth, and then his other hand rose until both of his hands cupped her cheeks, and he deepened the kiss.

Warmth, slow and seductive, curled inside her. She could taste him. Coffee and male, a sweet and savory concoction that had her tilting her head back, wanting more. He smelled magnificent, all woodsy—sage, juniper and neroli. His lips were soft, yet firm. Supple. His mouth moved over hers, dancing almost, with a grace and skill that stole her breath along with her caution.

He slowly raised his head, and he was so close she could see his eyes behind the dark lenses of his sunglasses. It was too dark to see any detail, but his gaze swept across her face, and then he stepped back.

"Uh, I'd best be going," he rasped, jerking his thumb in the direction of the door.

She nodded. She would have said something—anything, only her brain forgot to kick-start again from the sensory overload.

He backed toward the door. "I'll keep in touch," he said, his voice husky.

She nodded. Yep. She would have said it, too, but she got only as far as opening her mouth.

He walked back through her workroom, then paused at the door that led to her shop floor. He gestured beyond to the front door, his brow dipping. "You should beef up your security," he told her. "Maybe a perimeter spell."

She blinked. Uh, maybe…? Only it wouldn't be much use. Nulls. She half nodded, then shook her head as he departed. What?

She heard a motorbike start up outside, then sagged against her kitchen bench as she heard it roar away. She lifted her right hand and gently pressed her fingers against her lips.

The Witch Hunter had kissed her.

He'd kissed her.

Dave shifted on his bike as he rode through town. He was sitting just a mite uncomfortably. What the hell had possessed him to kiss her?

Well, she was attractive, in a fresh, girl-next-door kind of way. Sexy girl-next-door, though. And she was sweet. Too sweet for her own good, really. He shook his head. Tea. She'd given him a calmative tea because she'd sensed his turmoil at what he'd done to her. Who *does* that?

She was such a fascinating mix, though. Back on the beach, she'd given as good as she'd got. She'd matched him with her powers, and had fought him with a skilled strength that was impressive. And she was armed. He'd seen her belt. She seemed so sweet, so trusting, yet she carried twin blades, and had made him concerned for his ability to bear children. Sweet, but spicy. A contradiction of lethal innocence.

And he'd granted her a favor. He *never* granted favors. He was the collector of debts, and had a bank of favors owed to him from a number of members of Reform society, from vampire or werewolf primes—to light warriors. And he'd granted this witch a debt.

Maybe it was because every time he touched her, he lost time, lost awareness of everything save her. The scent of her, all floral and summery, her warmth, her gentleness—when she wasn't trying to unman him— her…care. She'd minimized his effect on her, because she could see, feel, sense—however it worked with an empath—the effect of his job on him, and sympathized, putting his needs above her own.

That humbled him. He sensed her shields, though. They were impressive, almost tangible blocks to getting to know the woman inside—and he really wanted to get to know that woman. He could usually get a sense of people when he touched them…good, bad, past, present and future—he saw some of each. He was selective with his clients for that very reason. He didn't ink up anyone with one of his spells unless they deserved it, or desperately needed it, needed his special brand of protection. Sully, though, well she consumed his senses at a touch, but those messages, those visions he normally received about a person were missing with her. The protective walls she'd erected within herself were stunningly effective, and it made him wonder why she felt the need to close herself off so thoroughly from those around her. It had to be exhausting, maintaining those protections.

He glanced about the town square as he rode around it. The diner still hadn't opened, but there was a cluster of people at the bottom of the steps. Even when the place wasn't open, it seemed to be the hub for the town people to gather and gossip. He recognized the waitress, Cheryl, who lifted her hand at him as he rode by. He gave her a brief salute in return, then turned at the end of the block. There was a bar at the far end of the marina, he'd discovered. He glanced at the docks. Most of the boats were out. He'd learned Serenity Cove wasn't so much a vacation spot for cruisers, but a working fishing port. The salt and brine was distinctive, and he drove around the weighing station and the fishermen's co-op, to the small parking lot of the bar at the end.

He parked his bike and set his helmet on the dash, uttering his security spell as he did so. That was one more thing he didn't understand about Sully. Her store was poorly secured. One flimsy lock on the front door that a teenager with a penknife could pass. When he'd visited her home, he hadn't sensed any blocks or shields there, either. As though she couldn't be bothered. He didn't know a witch who didn't layer their security with any number of spells. Some were innocuous, some had painful elements invoked for trespassers. Personally, he preferred the painful variety. He didn't have any patience for those who tried to steal or damage his property.

He walked into the bar, pausing when he stepped into the dim interior. At this time of day a couple of patrons sat in a booth, a couple more at the bar. A game of college baseball was playing on the television above the bar, and the thickset, middle-aged bartender leaned his palm on the bar, watching it.

Dave walked up to the bar and sat on a stool two down from another patron. The bartender looked over at him, an eyebrow raised in query.

"Beer, please," Dave said.

The bartender lumbered over to the under-the-counter fridge and pulled out the first beer his hand grasped. He grabbed a bottle opener from the counter, then slapped a coaster down and thunked the beer onto it.

"Thanks," Dave muttered.

"Well, if it isn't Sully's friend," a tired voice muttered from the stool two down from his.

Dave turned, then frowned at the familiar man until he recognized him. The sheriff, out of uniform. No wonder he hadn't recognized him immediately. It was like seeing your elementary school principal sitting at your dinner table. Out of place and damn uncomfortable.

"Tyler, right?" That was what Cheryl, the waitress, had called him, wasn't it? He purposely didn't address him by his title. The man was out of uniform, and Dave hoped this was an opportunity to get the man to open up about the murders he'd seen.

He gestured to the sheriff's nearly empty bottle. "Another one for my friend," he told the bartender.

Tyler's eyebrows rose, but Dave noticed he didn't decline the beer.

"How'd it go with Sully?" Tyler asked idly, although Dave suspected the man wasn't as nonchalant as he appeared to be.

The bartender clunked the new bottle down on the bar. "You know Sully?" he asked, and Dave almost saw curiosity flare, but then the crowd roared on the TV, and he turned his attention back to the game.

"Didn't quite go the way I expected," Dave admitted to the sheriff.

"Oh? No more spark?"

"Oh, there were plenty of sparks," Dave said, thinking of their power struggle on the beach. "I had this meeting all thought out in my head, and it didn't go at all to plan."

Tyler chuckled. "Hell, been there. But you're still here?" His expression was friendly, but Dave could see the interest in his eyes at figuring out the new stranger in town.

Dave nodded. "Yeah. I thought I'd stay a couple of days. Hey, what's with the diner? I went for breakfast, but it's closed, even though the sign says it's usually open today."

Tyler moved his now-empty bottle aside and reached for the new one. "Yeah, well, Lucy, the owner, isn't well."

Dave's eyes narrowed. He sensed there was more to that than the sheriff was letting on. The game on the TV hit a lull, with the teams changing over, and a news broadcast filled the ad break. Dave watched as the announcer read about the murder of a local woman. His arms muscles tightened when he saw a photo of the deceased woman. It was the elderly woman from his vision.

The bartender sighed, then looked at the sheriff. "Mary Anne? What sick bastard would go after an elderly woman in her home?"

Tyler nodded, his gaze flitting to the screen momentarily before dropping back down to the bottle of beer he held. "Well, Tony, you got the sick bastard part right."

Dave frowned. "Isn't that the second murder in the area in what, a week?"

Tony, the bartender, nodded. "Yeah. First one was her

son." He shook his head. "Seems like the family pissed off someone."

"So, the murders are related?" Dave asked casually.

Tyler tilted his head to stare at him for a moment. "Yeah, looks that way." He lifted his beer to his lips and drained the bottle, then stood. "Thanks for the beer."

Dave realized the sheriff was shutting down any further conversation on the topic. He smiled, masking his frustration. He knew the law weren't supposed to talk about open cases, but he'd hoped he could make the sheriff crack.

"Good luck with your investigation," he said.

Tyler hesitated, glancing over his shoulder. "We're going to get this sick bastard," he said quietly, his gaze meeting Dave's. Dave's eyes narrowed. Was that—was the sheriff warning him?

Tyler pulled at the door and disappeared into the daylight.

Dave turned back to the bar, his attention now on the bartender. "So, mother and son, huh?"

Tony tore his gaze away from the game that had now resumed on the TV. His gaze flitted to the door, then around the bar, and then he nodded, folding his arms on the bar.

"Yeah. Pretty sad. Gary was a great guy. Didn't come in here all that often, wasn't much of a drinker, but he was the kind of guy who'd always stop and say hi, or give you a hand if you needed one. He and Lucy were going to be married in June."

Dave winced. That woman was going to need some time to heal. He added her name to the list of folks affected by this witch's actions. "And the mom?"

Tony grimaced. "Well, I didn't have too much to deal

with her. She was a great crocheter, though. She'd make beanies for all the newborns at the hospital. My sister got one when her daughter was born. Meant a lot, to her, that kindness from a woman she barely knew."

Dave frowned. "It doesn't sound like they were the kind of people to have any enemies."

Tony snorted as he straightened from the bar. "Nulls always have enemies."

Dave's eyebrows rose. "They were nulls?"

Tony looked at him, surprised. "Well, yeah. They're all over the north end. That's why we're so into fishing, here. Tourism blows."

"Huh." Dave drained his beer, than pulled some cash out of his wallet, placing it on the bar. "Thanks."

Tony nodded, picking up the cash and strolling over to the cashier. "Anytime."

Dave strolled to the door, then hesitated. "Say, do you know a Sullivan Timmerman?"

Tony frowned. "Sully? Sure. Everyone knows Sully. Sweet lady."

"Uh, no, I mean another Sullivan Timmerman," Dave clarified.

Tony shook his head. "Nope. That would be weird."

Dave nodded. "Yeah, I guess it would be."

He left the bar, and straddled his bike. He frowned as he gazed out at the tiny harbor. Nulls. Why the *hell* would a witch want to kill *nulls*? The very nature of a null meant that the witch's powers were nullified in their presence. No werewolf could shift in their presence, no vampire could get their fangs on, no witches could cast spells...

He kick-started his bike and eased open the throttle

as he rode out of the parking lot. Maybe it had nothing to do with nulls, and everything to do with the victims?

He needed to find out more about Gary and Mary Anne Adler.

Sully stood next to Jenny as the preacher gave his graveyard sermon. She glanced across the open grave to Lucy. The woman leaned heavily on Cheryl, her face streaked with tears and pale with exhaustion. Even from this distance, Sully could see the deep bruise on her chin and along her cheek. Cheryl had told her the previous day that Lucy had been attacked from behind and had fallen heavily on the wooden floor. She hadn't seen her attacker, hadn't witnessed Mary Anne's murder, but had found the older woman's body when she'd regained consciousness.

Sully returned her gaze to the open grave, Gary Adler's coffin poised above it. His mother would be interred at the end of the week, as her body was still at the county coroner's, her autopsy only just recently completed.

"This is so sad," Jenny whispered. "A family wiped out."

Sully nodded. It was beyond sad, really. "It doesn't make any sense, does it?"

Jenny shrugged. "Depends which side of the fence you're sitting on. Some of the older folk remember the Reformation, and what happened with us. They say it's happening again."

Sully flicked a glance at her friend. "Seriously?"

Jenny nodded, just once.

Sully frowned as she watched Gary's coffin lowered into the grave. The late afternoon was fiercely hot, and bottles of water had been handed out among the small crowd. The funeral directors had erected a tent, and Sully wasn't sure whether it was better to stay under the tent and out of the sun, or to get some distance from all the hot, sweaty bodies and brave the furnace beyond the shade. And of course, everyone wore black.

She glanced at Jenny. Her friend had a point. Nulls had experienced a varied history. On the one hand they were reviled by the shadow breeds. Any shifter or vampire, or even witch, was reduced to being powerless and vulnerable in the presence of a null, which meant ordinary humans had seen the benefit in protecting them, and using them as a barrier against the breeds. They lived in the gray area between natural and supernatural. Not quite a shadow breed, but not an ordinary human, either. As a result, they were hunted by the shadow breeds in well-planned, ruthless skirmishes. During Reformation, they were given no territory, being classed as a subcategory of the human race. As such, they were often not treated as equal to any other race, shadow breed or not. Some of the crimes that had been committed against them were horrific, but with the recognition of a new hybrid breed just outside Irondell, there was renewed action to also recognize nulls as a race of their own.

In the meantime, no shadow breed would willingly go near a null community. That meant a lot of trade and tourism was restricted in the null-saturated areas. Humans walked the fine edge of losing business among the shadow breeds, and having protection from being prey to the breeds if nulls were about. To hear that the murder of two nulls—the first murders in the area since Sully had moved there—was possibly race-based was... disheartening.

Sully had gotten to know many of the nulls. They'd initially viewed her with mistrust. Why would she want to associate with them? She'd learned that apart from the block on her powers, there was something familiar about the nulls. They loved family. They had a tight-knit community, where each looked out for the other. They worked hard and partied harder, but they were just like any other human community—or witch, vampire or shifter, with one major difference. They just didn't get into power plays.

And that was probably one of the most attractive qualities, in her mind.

"Tyler will find whoever did this," she whispered to Jenny.

Jenny turned to her, her eyebrow raised. "We're not going to wait for the humans to help."

Her friend turned to walk over to Lucy, and Sully caught up with her. "What do you mean?" Sully whispered.

"Tyler's a good guy," Jenny whispered back, "but these crimes have targeted nulls. We have our own ways of dealing with this."

"Really?" Sully glanced around the mourners.

Jenny smiled. "I keep forgetting you're not a born null."

"Thanks." Sully frowned. "I think."

Jenny halted, scanning over Sully's shoulder. "Oh, hey, I see my brother. You go ahead, I need to go see him. Gary was one of his close friends."

Sully nodded. Lucy crossed over to the group of nulls that had stepped away from the grave to have a quiet talk. She turned back to approach Lucy, and it was as she was stepping up to hug her that she felt the little scratching at her shields. She was out of null range. But no, she should be able to manage.

She smiled sadly at Lucy and held out her arms.

Lucy stepped into them, sobbing softly, and Sully held her. She smiled briefly at Cheryl over Lucy's shoulder. The waitress looked almost as miserable as Lucy.

"I'm so sorry," Sully whispered into the crying woman's ear.

"Thank you for being here," Lucy said softly, hiccupping into her shoulder. "I'm so sorry about the cutl—"

"Shh," Sully hushed her. "There's nothing to apologize for. This is more important."

Lucy squeezed her tight, and Sully could feel the woman trembling in her arms. She could sense the grief, the heart-rending sorrow in her. It was muted, like an annoying pain knocking at her shields. Sully hesitated, then heard Lucy sob anew. She couldn't leave her like this. Nobody should have to go through this heartfelt agony. Lucy had lost two members of her family in quick succession in the most violent way. Sully could feel the woman fracturing in her arms. Her trembling increased, her breath grew ragged as her sobs grew harsher. Sully closed her eyes, then opened her shields a crack. She sucked in the pain, trying to absorb only some of Lucy's pain, but she could feel the grief of the fellow mourners clawing at her shields, peeling them back. She fought, trying to shed the talons that were shredding her walls. She slammed a barrier down, and Lucy's head lifted, surprise on her face. The woman hiccupped, then patted Sully on the shoulder as she turned to the next person lining up to offer their condolences, her composure once more slipping into place as she brushed away her tears.

Sully stepped back, and would have staggered if Jenny hadn't caught her arm. Her friend eyed her curiously. "Are you okay, Sully?"

Sully nodded, smiling tightly as the pain screamed inside her head like a banshee with her finger in an electrical socket. The nulls could stop her using her powers, but once she absorbed pain, they couldn't stop her from feeling what was already inside. And with them around, she couldn't dispel it.

Oh, God, so much pain. It was unbearable. Sully could feel it eating at her mental walls, coursing through her brain like a hot wash of acid. Even now, her vision was beginning to darken at the edges. She had to dispel the energy, but had to get away from the nulls to do it—and you never did a discharge of this magnitude where other humans might pick up some of the spill.

"I have to go," she rasped to her friend, and started to walk between the gravestones toward the parking lot. She had to get out of here. She was going to lose it. Even now, bile rose within her, burning her throat. She swallowed, trying to contain everything.

"Oh, hey, there's your boyfriend," Cheryl said.

It took Sully a moment to realize Cheryl was talking to her. She tightened her lips as she glanced about. Boyfriend? What? Sully saw Dave in the shaded corner of the parking lot, leaning against his bike.

He frowned, straightening from his bike as she hurried toward her car.

"Sully."

She braced her hand against the car, bending over as her stomach muscles clamped as though a vise was trying to squeeze her gut in half. Her hands shook as she delved into her satchel and finally found her keys. They jangled in her hand like a wind chime in a tornado.

Two hands clasped hers, removing the keys from her grasp, and then she felt a strong arm guiding her into the passenger seat.

"I'll drive."

Chapter 7

The voice sounded like it was echoing down a long tunnel. She blinked furiously, trying to see beyond the darkness that was now bleeding into her vision. Perspiration broke out on her upper lip and lower back, and she winced, bending low in her seat. She felt rather than saw Dave slide into the driver's seat, and within seconds the car was in motion, driving out of the cemetery and headed wherever the hell they were going—she couldn't see, and quite frankly didn't care.

She groaned, her jaw clenching as she rode another wave of intense pain. As though from a distance she could hear the scream of wheels as Dave sped along the coast road.

They'd been on the road for only a few minutes— maybe. She was beginning to lose track of time, but she thought—hoped—they were far enough away from the crowd.

"Pull over," she gasped. Oh, God, this was intense. The pain—she panted as she tried to ride the hot wash of agony.

"What? Are you sure?

"*Pull over.*" Her voice emerged as something low and guttural and quite unnatural. The car jolted and bumped as he steered it onto the shoulder, slowing down.

She opened the door before he'd quite stopped.

"Sully!"

She tumbled out of the car, falling to her knees on the gravel. Her fingers clawed over, and she dug her nails into the earth, trying to ground herself.

"Sully—"

She held up her hand in warning. *Don't come near me.* She couldn't speak, couldn't communicate other than that one abrupt, urgent movement. She crawled a foot, her stomach muscles wrenching, and she screamed at the excruciating heat that rose up from within, as though a ball of fire was exploding inside her—inside her gut, inside her brain. It was blinding light and suffocating darkness, it was fiercely hot and blisteringly cold, it was nothing and it was everything, all at once. She released the pathetic hold she had on her mental barrier, opened her mouth and retched up all that heartache, all that crushing sadness and consuming sorrow.

Over and over, the hot tide of negative energy roiled through her, and her stomach heaved, her throat burned and her eyes watered as she expelled Lucy's and the other mourners' grief in a hot black sludge that splashed on the ground and ran to rivulets, steaming as it soaked into the ground.

When she had no more to expel, when the last drops

had left her body, she wiped a shaky hand across her chin. She straightened on her knees and started to sag.

Strong arms caught her, and this time she was too weak to fight that coalescence of power, that collision of energies. His scent, sage, juniper and neroli, his warmth, and then an overwhelming tide of tenderness, concern and just a hint of awe. It embraced her.

"Come on, sweetness. Let's get you home."

Dave pulled into Sully's driveway and cut the engine. The sun was setting, streaking the sky with fiery pinks and tangerines as dusk crept in. He climbed out and walked around the back of Sully's car—a sky blue station wagon throwback that should have visited a wrecking yard years ago, from the looks of it. The gears had been a little clunky, too. He'd have to look at them for her. He opened the passenger door, and Sully's eyelids slowly rose.

She hadn't quite passed out, but she was close. Whatever the hell she'd done had clearly drained her. He didn't question the relief that she was still conscious, still breathing, after what he'd seen her do.

She grasped the upper frame of the door, as though getting ready to haul herself out. "Thanks for the ride—" her voice trailed off as he leaned in and scooped her up.

"Relax," he told her. She needed sleep. She felt so limp in his arms, so…spent.

"No, I can—" her head bumped against his shoulder "—walk."

He snorted. "Please. You can't even keep your head straight."

He cradled her as he strode up the steps and uttered a yield spell. The lock clicked and the door swung open.

Dave walked into her house, glancing about. A hallway ran from the front door of the house and doglegged at what he assumed was the kitchen. There was a room on either side, neither of which looked like a suitable place to set her down.

"Bedroom?"

Her head lolled forward, and she waved her arm down the hall. "Back."

He walked down and around the corner. The hallway had a small bathroom at the very end, a doorway that led to the kitchen on the right and a closed door on his left. He muttered a few words, and the door swung open as he approached.

Yeah, this looked exactly like what he'd imagine her bedroom would look like—if he'd wondered about it. There was a bay window that overlooked her garden, and sheer, gauzy white curtains that blew in the breeze coming in from the open sash windows. There was a window seat beneath the bay window that looked well cushioned, with pillows in what looked like delicate blue flowers that matched the other cushions with blue or green striped panels, and a navy knit blanket haphazardly draped on the end.

Her bed was queen-size, with an ornate white iron bedframe that surprisingly didn't look overwhelmingly feminine. He flicked his fingers beneath her knees and the powder blue coverlet pulled back enough that he could lay her on the crisp white cotton sheets. She subsided against the pillows, and she struggled against the heavy weight of her eyelids.

"Thank you," she whispered, as though she didn't have the energy for her full voice.

He smiled as he drew the coverlet over her body. So polite. "My pleasure."

She snuggled down, rolling over a little and sliding her hand beneath her cheek. She frowned, and he leaned closer.

"Sully, are you okay?" he asked softly, concerned by her expression. Was she in pain?

"Why are you my boyfriend?" she murmured drowsily. Her tone was breathy, but there was no mistaking the confusion.

"Uh…" Dave hesitated. Oops. He hadn't expected that rumor to still have legs. "Well—" His eyebrows rose at the faint snore. "Sully?" he said gently. Her eyelids didn't even flutter.

She gave another delicate snore. He tucked the coverlet in around her, knowing he'd dodged a conversational bullet, then leaned forward and kissed her forehead, a little surprised at the tenderness he felt. That was a first. "Sleep well, sweetness."

He stood over her for a moment, his brows pulled down in a frown. What the hell had she done? She'd hugged that woman, and then couldn't seem to walk or see straight. He reached out and lightly cupped her cheek. He couldn't see, damn it. No past, no future and certainly no clue as to what had happened to her at the funeral. She was like a vault, closed off to his visions. He removed his hand, his fingers trailing across her smooth skin in a gentle caress. He curled his fingers into a fist. He liked touching her.

He stared at her thoughtfully. He couldn't afford to like touching her. His hands—they'd hit. They'd hurt. They'd killed. Sully was—well, she was different. She was… His brow dipped in a slight frown. She was too interesting for his own good. She was sweet—when she wasn't throwing forks at his head—she was gentle and caring. He'd seen how she'd embraced that woman at the funeral. Just walked right on up and opened her arms to the woman. She'd supported her when the woman looked on the verge of collapsing. She'd seemed so strong, so calm—until she'd turned and walked away. And then he'd seen her face when her mask had slipped. He'd seen the pain, seen how her face had drained of color, and how her legs had seemed to wobble. But she'd kept that hidden from her friends. She was open and genuine, and yet impressively well guarded and cautious. So strong for her friends, and conversely, so vulnerable away from them. And yet, he didn't mistake this vulnerability for weakness. And that brought him back to where he'd started. She was too damn interesting for his own good.

He couldn't afford to explore the mystery that was Sully Timmerman. Not with what he did—and what he'd done… He was a ghost. Once he'd figured out what was going on here, and resolved it to the satisfaction of the Ancestors, he'd be going back to Irondell—until the next trip, the next hit. He had no business getting interested in Sully.

Dave crossed over to the window seat and toed off his boots. He made a nest among the pillows, and drew the throw blanket at the end over his legs. He leaned his head back against the inset wall, and gazed at the woman sleeping so soundly in the bed. It took a while, but eventually he fell asleep, too, watching over her.

"You told them we *dated*?"

Dave jolted awake, slightly disorientated. Coffee. Bacon. He hadn't had dinner. God, that smelled amaz-

ing. He straightened the sunglasses that had slipped a little in his sleep. He looked around, blinking when he saw
Sully standing next to him, arms akimbo, a frown on her
face as she glared down at him. His gaze swept over her.
Her hair was unbound, falling in loose waves around her
head and shoulders, all shiny honey and totally appealing.
She wore an off-the-shoulder peasant-style white top. He
couldn't see any bra straps. Was she wearing one? His
gaze drifted down. That thought had him waking up fast,
along with the realization that she was not in a happy
mood. His gaze snapped back up to hers.

But she was obviously back to her usual spitfire setting, which was a good thing to see. A damn good thing
to see, actually. His gaze started to drift south to her
chest again, and he forced himself to blink, look away.
Don't perv, you perv.

"What?" he asked, then yawned, mentally scrambling
to think past the bra situation and the bacon in the next
room.

"You told Cheryl we dated in high school. I've just
got off the phone from Jenny."

Dave blinked as he rose from the window seat. Ouch.
Apparently the window seat wasn't much better than the
sand the night before.

"Jenny? Who's Jenny?" He needed coffee to jump-
start this conversation properly.

"My friend, Jenny, who had an interesting chat with
Cheryl yesterday at Gary's funeral."

He closed one eye as he looked at her. "Cheryl is the
waitress at the diner, right?"

Sully nodded, her eyes narrowing.

He blinked again, then nodded. "Oh, yeah. She's nice.
Got a thing for the sheriff, I see."

Sully pursed her lips. "Everybody knows that except for the sheriff." Then she went back to frowning. "You told them I was an old girlfriend."

He stretched, then smiled as he started to walk to the door. "Don't sell yourself short, you're not *that* old."

She thumped him in the arm. Ouch. Okay, so she wasn't in the mood to be teased. Sully strode across the hall and into the kitchen, and made a beeline for the kettle that was beginning to whisper on the stove. She was barefoot, and he caught a glimpse of tanned calves and pink polish on her toenails. Her skirt flowed with each movement, but he was pretty sure she didn't know how it skimmed her hips and butt in a way that couldn't help but draw a guy's attention. Damn, he had no idea domesticity could look so damn sexy in the morning.

He settled himself on a stool at her kitchen counter and watched as she moved through the kitchen. Her clothing might be loose, but it still draped over her limbs, and he could make out the shape of her thigh, the indent of her waist, the swell of her breast... And he shouldn't be noticing that. Not with this woman. And right now she was upset with him.

"I told her that so I could find out where you were," he told her truthfully. "Back when I thought you were murdering people."

"The whole town is talking about it," she hissed. She pulled out two mugs and started pouring the coffee.

He tilted his head. She sure was fired up about this. She was so Zen about him trying to kill her, but having her name connected with his seemed to really tick her off. "Shelving the fact I may have told a little fib to find you, what's so bad about people thinking we used to date?" he asked conversationally. The more he thought about it, the more the concept interested him. Heck, when was the last time he'd *dated* a woman? Not a hookup, not a one-night stand, or a spontaneous, fun-minded bed-buddy, but a *date*, with planning, and a full meal, real conversation, aftershave...

She slammed the mug down next to him on the counter. "Because I would never date someone like you," she snapped.

He blinked, surprised by the little flash of hurt at the words. He schooled his features into calm disinterest. "Someone...like me?" he asked conversationally. His gut tightened with tension as he waited for her response.

Her mouth tightened, then she nodded. "Yeah. Someone like you." She grabbed a plate at the side of the stove and started serving up some scrambled eggs and bacon.

"What is that supposed to mean?" He abandoned all attempts at remaining casual as she thunked the plate down in front of him, followed by the cutlery she pulled from a jar at the end of the counter.

She turned back to serve up her own plate. "You're physically dominating, and you'll do or say whatever you need to in order to get what you want."

She walked around the other side of the bench and sat on the stool next to him.

He stared down at his plate. *Uh, wow.* He slid some scrambled eggs on his fork and shoved it in his mouth, even though he'd lost his appetite.

It wasn't like he could argue with her. He did use his body to dominate others, particularly when doing a job. And after what had happened on the beach, Sully would know that better than anybody. Problem was, he had to. No witch he ever faced *wanted* to cross the veil to the Other Realm. These people were criminals, murderers…psychopaths. If he didn't dominate them, they'd kill him—and many others.

And yeah, he would say or do whatever he needed to if it meant dispatching a witch in order to protect the vulnerable.

He swallowed his scrambled eggs, and reached for his mug. "Fair call." And he hated it.

She sighed. "It's just—I don't date, and now they think I do."

Dave frowned. "You don't date…ever?"

"Never."

"Why not?" She was attractive, sweet-natured, smart, strong—she'd held her own against him. Mostly. She had the body of a siren. His gaze drifted over the creamy skin revealed by her top, and again wondered about her underwear—or, hopefully, lack of it. She was gorgeous. Why didn't she date?

She shrugged. "It's a lifestyle choice. I have my work to concentrate on."

He cut up some bacon and chewed it thoughtfully. He could relate to that. Kind of. There was no way he, as a Witch Hunter, could have a significant other. He'd known that from the start, and had accepted that. But he couldn't deny it—every now and then he'd feel lonely, and would seek out company. Not as a *date*, though. But Sully—Sully wasn't a Witch Hunter. She didn't have to up and leave in the middle of the night, didn't have to fight to the death every time she went to "work", didn't have to try to give the impression of being normal instead of being all torn up inside, hating what had to be done. He didn't know why she didn't date, why she wasn't available for a relationship, why she wasn't looking for company, or just plain fun…and yes, he was very curious, but was in no position to be allowed to care. Either way, though, his story at the diner had unintended consequences, which is the last thing he wanted for her.

"I'm sorry. I'll clear it up with Cheryl when I see her." He looked at her briefly. Her cheeks were still a little pale, and there was the faintest of shadows under her eyes. "How are you?"

She met his gaze as she sipped her coffee. She placed her mug on the counter. "Better, thank you."

He turned to face her on the stool. "What happened?"

She averted her eyes. "Uh, not sure. Probably sunstroke." She nodded. "Yeah. It was really hot." She finished her breakfast quickly.

He frowned. "That's the first time I've seen someone with sunstroke throw up black gunk."

"Really? Oh, I've seen it happen," she murmured as she rose from the bench. He watched her as she walked around to the sink, concentrating fiercely on navigating her way through her kitchen. Sully Timmerman sucked at lying.

"Sully."

She halted at the sink, head down, then turned to face him. "Yes?"

"Is it because you're an empath?" he asked softly. He'd heard of them, but had never encountered one, before. Empaths were considered the witch version of truth seekers, those individuals occasionally born across the shadow breeds with the uncanny ability to sense emotion, and to gauge honesty and subterfuge. They were highly sought after in some cases—fantastic to use in civil litigation or high-value deals. In other cases, they were considered a threat, particularly by those who were trying to keep secrets or maintain lies. He knew one, Vassi

Galen, but she'd always kept her truth-seeking talents a secret. Maybe that's what Sully did, to avoid the risk of folks wanting to shut down the walking lie detector. He held up a hand. "It's okay, you don't need—"

"Yes." She nodded slowly. "Yes, it's part of being an empath." She shrugged, palms up. "When you do your stuff, you get a name branded across your body. When I do my stuff, I draw in other people's pain, and it can sometimes make me…ill."

"Are you sure you're okay?" He couldn't help his concern. She'd coughed up a bucket-load of steaming black goop, and practically passed out.

"Yeah. Once I get rid of it, I'm generally fine. Yesterday was hard to control, though. There was so much grief and heartbreak."

"And you drew it all in?" Hell, no wonder it looked like she was barfing up toxic tar.

She shook her head. "No. Not all of it. Lucy lost the love of her life, as well as the woman who pretty much adopted her as her daughter. She will feel sorrow, and she'll feel grief, and I can't take that away from her, because that's based in the love she has for those people, and I'd have to take away that, too. I took away some of the pain of it, that's all." Sully grimaced. "Only I can't necessarily cherry-pick who I help in that kind of situation. Once I crack the wall, anything can come through."

"Crack the wall?" His eyebrows rose as he looked down at her. "Is that what it's like?"

She thought about it for a moment. "Yeah, I guess it is. When you open that gate, the emotions come in. In a situation like that, it's like a…flood. With claws." She shuddered, then waved her hand. "But that's gone now."

She took a deep breath. "Thank you so much for driving me home." She frowned. "Why were you there?"

Dave looked at her for a moment. "Actually, that's a really good question," he said slowly. "I wasn't expecting to see you there." Over the past few days he'd tried talking to the first victim's neighbors, his work colleagues, people at the gym, but they were all pretty noncommittal, and for the first time he couldn't just bespell these people to tell him what he wanted to know. Darn nulls.

"I knew Gary, and Lucy is a friend. Naturally I'd go to his funeral. What about you?"

Dave frowned. "You knew Gary Adler?"

Sully frowned back at him. "Yeah. How do you—?" Her eyes rounded. "Oh. Good. Grief. You saw Gary die."

Chapter 8

Sully leaned back against the counter and looked up at him in horror. "Mack's Gym. Gary was a member. I didn't know where he'd died—Tyler didn't tell me that, but that would make sense." She closed her eyes briefly. Another realization dawned.

"Oh, heck. On the beach—you saw Mary Anne die." She felt the itch of tears in her eyes. Whoever had killed that nice little lady had done it in a way to bring a Witch Hunter down on him. She blinked, then looked up at him. "When I went to visit her that night—"

Dave frowned. "You went to visit her?" His voice was low and harsh.

"Yes, I'd heard about Gary, and thought I'd take Mary Anne and Lucy some tea—"

"You could have walked in on the killer," Dave exclaimed.

"No, her body had already been discovered, the sheriff was there—and why are you angry with *me*? It's not like I went looking for a killer—like you," she said, glaring at him.

Dave took a deep breath, then nodded. "You're right. You weren't to know, I just—I just don't want you hurt."

She blinked. "Oh." He sounded so…protective. He was taller than she, and his shoulders…she eyed his shoulders. There was so much strength there, in his broad chest, his muscled arms. His short hair was rumpled, his T-shirt a little wrinkled and the sunglasses shielded his eyes, yet for once she had no trouble reading his expression. He looked rough and sexy and just a little dangerous, with the soft curve of his lips when he let his witchy protective side out.

But she'd seen how protectiveness could be used to disguise control, and she wasn't going to be sucked in again. "But I'm an empath," she told him firmly. "I constantly feel hurt, and I know how to handle it. You don't need to worry about me."

His lips firmed. "I can't let anything happen to you."

"Anything else," she said, giving him pointed look. Then she sighed at the obstinate lift to his chin. "Look, it's very sweet, but I don't need a protector. What I do need is to figure out what's going on, here."

"*I'll* figure it out," he growled.

"Dave, please," she said, clasping her hands together. "Whoever did this, did it in *my name*."

Dave walked back a little and leaned back against the fridge, shaking his head. He folded his arms, and his biceps bulged with the movement. He'd caught some of the fabric of T-shirt with the movement, and it pulled out from his jeans, exposing just a little bit of skin, that fascinating marking framing his navel—oh, good lord, she was staring at his navel. She snapped her gaze back to those sunglasses. He looked sexy and strong and more than a little stubborn.

"Nope."

"Lucy was one of the first people I met when I moved to Serenity Cove," Sully argued. "She introduced me to a lot of the folks here, including Gary, who introduced me to my best friend, Jenny. He and his mother were super sweet to me. They brought me into their community, and that's where I—" Sully shut her mouth. Uh. That's where she met more of the nulls, and learned how they were all battling poverty, and how she came upon the idea to use the offcuts of her cutlery and weaponry to produce counterfeit coins. Gary had even helped her build the coin press.

Dave arched an eyebrow at her hesitation. "That's where you…what?"

"Really got to know these people," she said, then cleared her throat. "Uh, these people, they gave me a safe place, Dave, and now someone is killing them in my name."

Dave frowned. "What do you mean by safe place, Sully?"

She'd said too much. She bit her lip. She never talked about…before. Dave straightened from the fridge, his face grim as he walked a little closer. He dipped his head so that he was on eye level with her. She saw her reflection in his sunglasses—did he ever take them off?

"What are you running from?" His voice was low, and she could hear the curiosity tinged with concern in his tone.

She frowned. "No. I don't run from anything." She

didn't try to delude herself anymore, either. She'd worked damn hard over the last four years, and felt stronger than she ever had before. Hell, she'd been strong enough to hold off a Witch Hunter. No. She didn't run from anything, not anymore.

"When I said safe place, I mean for an empath. They shut everything down. With these people, I don't have to shield myself so much, I don't have to protect myself. *They* become my wall." She trailed her finger along the sink. "You have no idea what that is like, for someone like me. To not have to constantly watch for emotion, to always guard against everyone around you." Sully lifted her gaze to meet his. "So when someone starts killing these very special friends of mine, I want to help stop that. And you can't do this on your own."

Dave lifted his chin. "Of course I can."

Sully's eyebrow rose. "Really? How many nulls have talked to you about Gary? About his mother?"

Dave's lips pursed, and Sully's gaze was drawn to them. They looked…soft. Just a little plump—not stung-by-a-bee plump, but kissy-plump.

And here she was again, getting all woozy-doozy over the wrong kind of man. She cleared her throat. Focus. Think of Gary, and Mary Anne…

"Please, tell me what happened to them. Let me *help* you. What did you see?"

Dave sighed, his breath gusting over her bare shoulder. She trembled. She couldn't deny it, the sensation was…nice.

He held up a finger. "Fine. I'll tell you, but this is my gig. We're not partners, you're not doing any investigating, you're—" He hesitated, as though trying to find the right word. "You're a consultant."

A consultant? That wasn't going to work for her, but she knew when to pick her battles. She gave him a nod. Just one. Enough to make him think she actually agreed.

He reached past her and started to run some water into the sink, then reached for the detergent on the windowsill. "I see a blade in the heart, which is the kill action that gets the Ancestors involved," he told her. He started washing the breakfast dishes, and she grabbed a tea towel from the oven handle, and started to dry as he handed her the cleaned dishes.

"Then he—or she," he added, "removes the knife from the chest, and carves some sort of symbol into their wrist, squeezes some of their blood out—"

Sully looked up at him when he stopped talking. His mouth was curled in distaste. "Go on," she urged him. "I'm no shrinking violet."

He turned his head to look at her. This close, she could see the light of his eyes behind the lenses, maybe even his eyelashes. She saw his gaze drift over her. "You're not, are you?" He was making a comment, more than asking a question. He washed the frying pan and set it on the drainer next to the sink, and pulled the plug.

"He squeezes some of their blood out and drinks it."

Sully scrunched up her face. "Ew, gross."

"He—or she—says a few words, and then I get bumped."

Sully wiped up the frying pan and bent down to put in her pot cupboard. "And that's not normal?"

"No."

She frowned in puzzlement. "I wonder if he—or she…?" She looked at Dave. "You really don't know whether it's a man or a woman?"

Dave shook his head. "I really don't, and I'm an equal

opportunity hunter. The killer wears gloves and whispers the spell. Can't tell whether it's a guy or a chick, and I know chicks can be just as psycho-crazy as guys."

"Oh," Sully said faintly. "Good to know."

He turned to face her, and folded those big, beautiful arms of his again. She shook her head slightly. Stop staring at those arms. "Uh, so, we have a witch who has killed nulls. *Nulls*." She shook her head again. "I don't get it."

"Neither do I." Dave sighed.

"Maybe the witch didn't realize Gary and Mary Anne were nulls," she thought aloud. "Maybe the witch thought they were ordinary humans. I can't see what benefit he'd get out of killing a null—" She frowned, and tapped the sink. "Drinking null blood—that's going to reduce his powers. I don't get it. He must not have known."

"I need to find out more about the guy, and his mother. Who they came into contact with, who might have held a grudge—who stands to gain from their deaths…"

"We can talk to Jenny," Sully said, turning toward the door. Dave caught hold of her arm.

Fierce protectiveness, warm and snug, curled around her. Exasperation. Frustration. Curiosity. Damn it, he was doing it again, plowing through her shields as if they were made of tissue. Why couldn't she block this guy?

"Whoa, sweetness. *I'll* go talk to Jenny. I'll do it subtly. I don't want to go around announcing I'm a Witch Hunter, here to kill a witch. One—it would be around this town before I got out the door, and two—that's a conversation I really don't want to have with your sheriff."

Sully glanced down at his hand. "She won't talk to you," she told him.

Dave's lip's curled in a lazy smile. "I'll have you know some women find me charming."

She just bet they did. Smoking hot muscles, sexy smile, a handsome face and an overall impression of... experience.

"I told her we broke up because you cheated on me. My best friend won't give you the time of day unless I'm with you. And this *is* a small town. How many nulls do you think know about you now?"

His grip slackened, but not before she felt the flash of surprise. She continued on her way to the door. "You're not the only one who can tell a fib."

Dave shoved his hands in his jeans' rear pockets and tried to make himself comfortable against the wall. He hadn't even bothered to try the tiny little seats attached to the tiny little desks. Had he ever been that small as a kid? The kids were outside on a short break, and it was surprisingly relaxing, hearing the kids' chatter and laughter outside, a little muted, while he stood in the silence inside the room.

Okay, maybe not *that* relaxing. He lifted his gaze from the students' desks to realize Sully's friend was still staring at him. Coldly.

Well played, Sully. There was no way he'd be able to get this woman, or any of the nulls they'd passed on the way in who'd given him similar death stares, to give him the time of day, let alone any solid information on the victims.

"So you want to find out more about Gary and Mary Anne, huh? Why?" Jenny definitely wasn't sounding cooperative. He pursed his lips as he looked over at his new "partner".

Sully nodded, seemingly oblivious to the tension in the room. "We want to find out who did this."

Jenny frowned. "Why?"

Sully frowned back at her. "Why not?"

Jenny's eyebrows rose. "We're not used to others being interested in what happens to us."

Dave watched as Sully folded her arms. "Jenny, this affects all of us. A murder is a murder, no matter who the victim is."

Jenny tilted her head. "Sully, you have no idea how many nulls have been murdered in the past where it's been treated as though they were dogs being put down. Heck, Reform doesn't even recognize us as a breed of our own. We are a *subset*."

Dave winced. Sully's friend had a valid and sobering point.

Sully's frown deepened. "Have you ever felt like I've treated you like a subset?"

Jenny's eyes widened. "Of course not," she said hurriedly. "No, you've been so generous and helpful with all of us, especially with—"

"Nothing," Sully interjected, and Dave's eyebrow rose.

"Uh, nothing that I wouldn't do again," Sully quickly supplied, her cheeks blooming with heat. Dave's eyes narrowed behind his sunglasses. What had she done for them? What had she done that she didn't want him to know about?

Jenny's gaze slid quickly between Dave and Sully, then back to Dave, and she nodded. "Exactly." She tried to mask the confusion and curiosity about them, but apparently Sully's friend was about as good as Sully when it came to lying.

So Sully's friend knew whatever it was his sweet little partner was into. He shelved that observation for later.

"When someone hurts you guys," Sully said quietly, stepping up to Jenny's desk, "I hurt, because you guys are my friends. You're my family."

Dave found himself wondering what had happened with Sully's original family. She'd made comments about her First Degree classes, so she'd been brought up in a coven, but where were they now? And why had she left them?

Jenny smiled, although there was a tinge of sadness to it. "Thanks, Sully. That's so lovely to hear." The young woman turned to face him, and her eyes narrowed. "So why do *you* want to help?"

"Uh…" He wasn't quite sure what to say to that. Sully had shut down his one plausible excuse for being in town. He needed to set the record straight. "Look, about Sully and me—"

"He's trying to make it up to me." Sully's quick interruption made his mouth slack. What was she doing?

"Don't you think that's too little, too late?" Jenny commented.

Dave looked at Sully. What happened to setting folks straight? For right now, though, it would work for him. He could adapt. "I made a mistake," he said, and this time it wasn't so much a lie but a variation of the truth. "I need to make things right between us."

"So you're going to do that by…looking into a couple of null murders?"

"He's also got skills in this area," Sully added. "He's an investigator."

This time Jenny eyed him shrewdly, and he felt like he was being measured carefully.

"You mean, like a cop?"

Dave shuddered. "Not quite." Not at all.

"A private dick, or something?"

Hell, this was getting worse. He frowned. "Or something."

"Seems apt," Jenny muttered, and Dave noticed that Sully was trying not to smile and failing spectacularly.

Great. "Uh, Gary and Mary Anne—did they have any enemies? Did they owe money? Did Gary…cheat?"

Both women frowned at him. "No," they said in unison.

Jenny rose from her seat. "Gary loved Lucy. There was nobody else for him. Mary Anne—she was well respected in our community. Loved, even. Gary really tried to help with these kids, and everyone could see that. He was a nice guy, and didn't deserve what he got."

She glanced out toward the kids lining up in the schoolyard. "Look, I can't talk now, I have to go." She smiled at Sully. "Come over to Mom and Dad's for dinner. A few of us are getting together to remember the Adlers. We can talk, then." Her gaze slid to Dave. "You may as well come, too."

He nodded. "Fine." He would have loved to have talked more, but maybe this way he'd get a chance to talk with more of the nulls, and get a better sense of what these Adler folk were really like—and how they became the target of a murderous witch. He followed Jenny out to the door, but halted when she paused.

"If you hurt Sully again, I'm going to pulverize your nuts," she said in a low voice, then smiled brightly at the kids lining up outside the door. "Hey, guys!"

Dave's eyebrows rose as the fierce woman of less than a second ago morphed into a sweet kindergarten teacher as she walked out to the students. Sully stepped up behind him, and he turned to glance briefly at her. What was it with the women in this area? So nice, so…he kept coming back to the word, but he couldn't find one that fit better than *sweet*. So damn sweet. And so dangerous you had to guard your life, your gonads and your heart.

Sully raised her eyebrows when she saw him looking at her. "Is everything all right?"

He nodded as they stepped down toward the parking lot. Sully turned and waved as her name was called, and then stopped to catch a little red-haired boy who literally threw himself at her. She laughed as she set him down.

"Hey, Noah. How are you doing?"

"Good! Are you still coming to the festival?"

"I sure am! Don't want to miss those donkeys. Hey, how are your mom and dad?"

"Dad says he's going to catch you a big tuna!"

"And what does your mom say?" Sully asked with a knowing glint in her eye.

"Mom says we're having mac and cheese, then."

Dave's eyebrows rose at the comment, and Sully grinned. "Well, you tell your dad that if he does catch that tuna, I'll have to make you all my tuna and rice bake."

"Noah! Come on, we have to get back to work," Jenny called from hallway.

Noah sighed. "I have to go," he said, and Sully nodded.

"Yeah, but I'm pretty sure Miss Forsyth has some art planned."

Noah's face brightened, and he waved as he ran back to his class.

Dave watched the pupils wave at Sully as they walked back into the building. There was no hiding from the fact that these kids adored her. Her friend, Jenny, seemed decent, once you got past her frosty defenses and painful threats, and she was protective of Sully—like any good, loyal friend. The nulls respected Sully. That was…unusual.

He slid into the passenger seat of her beat-up car, and glanced over as she climbed into the driver's seat. "How did you get so cozy with the nulls?" he asked, curious.

She frowned as she started her car. "What do you mean? They're people. They're nice people."

"Yeah, but they're also a fairly closed community. They don't like outsiders."

"I guess they don't see me as an outsider then," she said simply as she drove away from the school.

"Hmm." He leaned back in his seat and watched the scenery flash by. How was it that a witch was able to be accepted by a null community? They normally avoided everyone with supernatural abilities, and the practitioners of magic did the same. He frowned.

"They don't know you're a witch, do they?"

She kept her gaze on the road. "I can't be a witch around them, so it doesn't really come into the conversation. I can't do spells, I can't do rituals, I can't practice magic near them, so when I'm with them, I'm not really a witch, am I?"

His eyebrows rose. "Wow. That's an interesting defense."

She frowned. "Defense? Defense for what?"

"You're lying to them."

She shook her head, flashing him a brief but pointed glare. "No. I'm not. I've never said I'm not a witch. In their presence, I'm just plain old me. Normal." She held up a finger as he opened his mouth to argue. "And that's me without any shields or artifice, so in reality, I'm more me when I'm with them, than when I'm not. Totally authentic."

He pinched the bridge of his nose, raising his sunglasses just a little. "Your logic is giving me a headache." He positioned his shades and stared out the window. She'd mentioned something similar before, about how she didn't have to block herself when she was with the nulls. And yet, she kept this one important, innate detail about herself from the community she said she trusted. But if she couldn't be a witch around them, like she said—was she really lying to them? Or just omitting a detail about herself that had no impact on them?

"Where to now?" Sully asked, interrupting his thoughts.

"The graveyard, please," he said. "I need to pick up my bike."

Sully nodded, then flicked him a quick glance. "Then what are we doing?"

"Well, I have to find a place to sleep," he told her. "I wasn't expecting to stay in town this long." He shifted in his seat. No, he'd fully expected to roll into town, kill Sullivan Timmerman and then roll on out again. "Can you recommend any places to stay?"

Sully frowned. "There's a motel down south, about thirty minutes' drive. Nothing much up north. We're not really a tourist mecca."

He frowned. Thirty minutes away. That was a little too far from the action. "Nothing closer?"

Sully drove carefully around the bends of the coastal road, then looked at him briefly. "I have a foldout couch," she offered.

His eyebrows rose. Staying with Sully…he could feel his body throb at the prospect, and tried to hose it down with rational thought. Sully was nice. And she didn't date—she wasn't the love-'em-and-leave-'em type of woman. She was a lady, and deserved so much more than the frolic-in-the-bedsheets that he was limited to offering.

But…she could give him access to the nulls, provide some local information in the tracking down of this killer.

And it would be pure hell living in the same house and not touching her. He eyed her hands on the steering wheel. Her skin was covered in small marks, a legacy of the craft she worked. They weren't the soft hands of a woman who did office work. They revealed a delicate strength, and a capacity for pain and perseverance. Almost like the dainty hands of a warrior, if that was possible. He wondered what it would feel like to have her hands on his body. He could feel himself growing hard at the prospect.

And that was exactly why he should stay the hell away from Sully, and her foldout couch. He couldn't afford to be distracted from his duty.

"Thanks, that would be great," he said, then glanced back out the passenger window. *Hell, here I come.* He tried to distract himself, and thought about what they'd learned from Jenny—pretty much nothing. He frowned.

"Why didn't you let me set Jenny straight about us?"

Sully's lips pursed as she focused on the road. "You heard her. There is a real us and them attitude there. If you don't want people to know who you really are, tell them something they'll believe. I couldn't think of another way for us to get them to talk."

He looked at her carefully. *If you don't want people to know who you really are, tell them something they'll believe.* That had just rolled off her tongue, as though she was talking from experience. She was talking about convincing people, not about telling them the truth. What other "omissions" was she guilty of? The difference between what he knew about his new "consultant", and what he didn't know, just got greater.

Sully Timmerman just got a whole lot more interesting.

Chapter 9

"A toast to Gary."

Sully sipped from the cup of ale she'd been handed. She was leaning against the wall near the living room door inside Jenny's parents' home, and the house was packed. People were still arriving, mainly men who'd just come in off the boats, and had done a quick shower and change before heading over. Food was set out on the kitchen table, and people were helping themselves, piling up plates before they sat or leaned against any available surface.

Sully peered around the doorjamb. Dave was just outside the back door, talking to some of the younger fishermen as they smoked cigarettes outside. They'd been wary of him, at first, but she could see they were beginning to relax around him. Even if he still wore his sunglasses at night.

She turned back to those gathered in the living room. Sully was content to listen to the stories the gathered folks wanted to share. Some were funny, some were poignant, but all showed the deep respect and love this community had for the murdered victims.

"So, you have a boyfriend, huh?"

The deep voice whispering in her ear made her jump, and she turned.

"Jacob," she said, half laughing in relief when she recognized Jenny's older brother.

He grinned. "Sorry, didn't mean to startle you."

He stepped back into the hallway, and she followed him, so that they could talk without intruding on the memories being shared within the room.

"How are you, Sully?" The tall fisherman tilted his head to the side as he looked down at her. "I didn't get a chance to talk to you at the funeral."

She waved a casual hand. "I think it was something I ate, combined with being in the hot sun. I'm fine now." And she was. She'd tried to bolster her shields before coming, but the null effect made her work unnecessary. Surrounded by nulls, none of her empath powers worked, and she didn't have to worry too much about shielding herself, even if she could. "How are you?"

"Dealing with the fact you've got a boyfriend," Jacob teased, although there was a slightly serious light to his eyes.

"It was quite the surprise to see him," she said truthfully, although she felt a little discomfort at perpetrating an untruth. "How's the fish?" she asked in an effort to distract.

Jacob shrugged, his blond hair glinting in the light. "Biting, but not busy."

Sully winced. The community were doing it tough,

and were hoping the fishing loads would increase. They'd implemented a sustainable fishing program, but that didn't seem to be paying off just yet. "Sorry to hear that."

Jacob glanced around, then leaned down toward her. "Hey, I hear Leo Campi is doing it tough. Dislocated his shoulder in a netting accident and can't work for several weeks. We're passing the boot around tonight," he said, pointing to the leather boot that Jacob's father, Jack, just passed to the person next to him, after stuffing some paper money into it.

Sully nodded. "I'll see what I can do," she said quietly. She had some silver that had been delivered the day before at the shop, and had some cheaper metals she could melt and press into coins. "They'll have to travel into Irondell to spend it, though. Too many coins circulating here will draw attention."

Jacob nodded, patting her on the shoulder. "Thanks, Sully. You're all right, you know?"

"She is, isn't she?"

Sully turned at the sound of Dave's voice. He stood just behind them in the hallway. The Witch Hunter smiled at her friend, and stuck his hand out. He hadn't removed his leather gloves. Sully's brow dipped. Huh. Funny, she'd only just noticed that. This man always wore his sunglasses, and with the exception of eating, he pretty much always wore his gloves.

"Hey, I'm Dave, the ex."

Jacob eyed the gloved hand for a moment, then shook it. He smiled grimly. "I'm Jacob, the current…friend."

Sully looked at both men who seemed to be engaged in some sort of staring contest. Both men were tall, with broad shoulders and an impressive physical presence, yet they looked as different as night and day. Dave, with his neat beard and dusty blond hair, and Jacob with his dark hair and hazel brown eyes. And both looked like they were sizing each other up.

"Hey, Jacob, I wanted to ask you—this is the first time I've been invited to this sort of thing," she said, trying to distract them both. "It's really powerful. Is this how you normally handle someone's passing?"

Jacob finally relinquished Dave's hand. "No, but Gary and Mary Anne were PBs, so it's a special night. For both of them to go…" He shook his head, his expression a mixture of sadness and concern. Then he frowned. "Jenny mentioned you two were wanting to help, somehow…?"

"Uh, Dave has some experience with this sort of thing," Sully explained.

Jacob's eyebrow rose. "With null murders?"

Dave shrugged. "Murder is blind," he said. "Shouldn't matter what breed, it should just matter."

Laughter rose from inside the living room. Another story had been shared about the Adlers. Sully could hear the clink of glasses and mugs as people toasted their departed.

Jacob looked at him thoughtfully, then folded his arms. He dipped his chin in the direction of Dave's sunglasses. "Do you have a vision problem?"

Dave smiled. "I think I see pretty good. Hey, you said the Adlers were PBs—what does that mean?"

Jacob glanced at Sully, and she shrugged. She hadn't heard of the term, either.

"PBs are purebloods," Jacob informed them. "They can trace their lineage back to before The Troubles." The man shrugged. "Shape-shifters have their alphas, vampires have their primes, covens have their regents and everyone has elders—we have our purebloods. Their lineage hasn't been tainted with shadow breed blood, or diluted by ordinary humans."

Sully blinked. It was interesting. The shadow breeds took a similar view of null blood tainting their blood-line, and muting their supernatural abilities…but there were many mixed-bloods throughout all communities. Still, this was a surprise. What else did she not know about these people she'd just spent the last four years with? "Huh. I never knew there was a hierarchy within the null community."

Jacob grimaced. "Meh. We respect them, and the pure-bloods definitely get a voice at the council, but we like to think it's your actions that define you as a person, not your ancestors."

"Interesting," Dave said grimly. Sully realized he was thinking about his own actions, and how closely linked it was to the Ancestors. For Dave, it really was a case of ancestors defining him as a Witch Hunter.

"Are there a lot of purebloods around?" Sully asked, curious about this new facet of the community she'd adopted.

"Some. There's more over on Stoke Island—it has the highest population of purebloods in the country."

"How is it that the rest of the breeds don't know about this?" Dave asked.

"In case you haven't noticed, the rest of the breeds don't give two hoots about us," Jacob said. "Besides, it doesn't really mean much. PBs are still normal like the rest of us. There's no added strength or ability. Just inherited blood."

Sully met Dave's gaze. "Interesting," they said in unison.

Dave followed Sully into her home. He'd driven his bike out to the null area, and Sully had taken her car,

so they hadn't had a chance to talk on the way home.
Now her expression was thoughtful as she turned on the
lights in her living room. He glanced inside the room.
There was an impressive bookcase on one wall with—
he squinted—gardening books? Mathematical theory?
Reform politics? Yeesh. He definitely wouldn't be bor-
rowing a book from her. He looked away from the bookcase. She'd already pulled out the sofa and covered it in
sheets and a blanket. She must have done it in the afternoon when he'd been out at the library, looking up any
stories he could find that mentioned the Adlers. All the
articles he'd located had been complimentary. His lips
quirked as he stared at the made-up sofa. There was even
a neatly folded towel on the pillow.

He looked over at Sully. "So, are you and Jacob an
item?"

He could see his question surprised her. He didn't
know why it did—he'd seen the way Forsyth looked at
Sully, and the almost protective, possessive glare he'd
sent in Dave's direction. You didn't need any magical
powers to see the guy had feelings for her.

"No, just friends," she told him. She scratched her
temple. "Did you think Gary's and Mary Anne's murders have something to do with the fact they're PBs?"

He looked away as he set his backpack down on the
floor. Her answer had pleased him, and he didn't want to
think too much on the why. He focused on what they'd
learned. "I don't know. Why would a witch want pure
null blood? It's not like they can do anything with it."
Ugh. He'd just spent the last two hours with a bunch of
nulls, and the knowing, the awareness, the darkness that
surrounded his natural ability like a cloak... Well, it was
enough to give a witch the heebie-jeebies.

Except for Sully. She seemed to enjoy it. Go figure.

"But it could explain why you get bumped out of your visions…?"

He thought about it for a moment, then nodded slowly. "Possibly." He frowned. "But it's *null* blood. Why consume it? What possible benefit would that have for a witch?" Just the thought made him want to gag.

Sully crossed over to the small end table that held her phone and a notepad and pen. "Can you remember what the witch drew on their wrists?"

"Yes," he said slowly, watching as she brought the notepad and pen over to him. "Why?"

"Can you draw it?"

He nodded. In two strokes of the pen he'd drawn the symbol he'd seen carved into Gary's and Mary Anne Adler's wrists. *X.* He showed it to Sully, who frowned when she glanced down at it.

"It's from the Old Language?"

Dave's eyebrows rose. "I'm impressed. You're familiar with the Old Language."

Sully gestured toward his chest, her cheeks heating. "I saw my name…"

"And you were able to translate it?" Okay, he was more than impressed. For all intents and purposes, the original language of the witches was dead. Learning it, deciphering it, was usually down to Witch Hunters and bored scholars wanting to challenge themselves. But the language was one thing. Learning the symbols, the ancient runes—that was another thing entirely. "How did you learn it?"

Her shrug was noncommittal. "Oh, it was just something I was interested in at one time."

A general interest didn't explain being able to decipher without a key, or instantly recognizing a rune for what it was. His sweet little cutler seemed to hide some pretty big secrets.

"Do you know what this rune means?" he asked her. She frowned, her attention caught by the symbol on the notepad.

"No, I don't. I might be able to look it up, though."

Dave's eyes rounded. "Look it up? How?" There were no computer databases for this sort of thing. No text books to consult. No dial-a-friend service. She would have to have—

Sully walked over to the bookcase, arms out. She closed her eyes, murmuring something so softly he couldn't hear it. The books on the shelves began to glow and shimmer, the defined edges blurring as they transformed into an entirely different library. Damn, she'd hidden it behind a camouflage spell—a damn good one if it fooled another witch. He'd had no intention of going anywhere near her books.

She held out her palm, and again murmured something. This time, though, he recognized the ancient language. She was asking for information on runes. His brow quirked. Who was she asking? He could feel the crackle in the air, the weight of power in the room.

A tome flew from a shelf, and she caught it, staggering back under the force. Her eyebrows rose. "Uh, thanks," she muttered.

"Who are you talking to?" He gazed around the room, then looked back at the bookcase.

She glanced up at him as she walked over to the end table. "The books, of course."

He nodded. "Of course." He looked down at the book

she held in her arms. It looked remarkably like—his heart thudded in his chest.

"Is that what I think it is?" he asked hoarsely, stepping closer.

"What do you think it is?" she asked as she set the tome down on the table. He looked down at it. No. It couldn't be.

"A coven grimoire."

Sully glanced at him for a moment. "Yes, it is." She tilted her head, her brows drawing together. "You act like you've never seen one before."

"I haven't. I'm not allied with a coven." Only those in the third level of a coven could even view their coven spellbooks. As a Witch Hunter, he had heard of them, but never seen one. Until now. Dave felt like his eyes were going to pop from his head.

"You have your coven's spellbook?" He had to ask again. It was incredible. These things were passed down from generation to generation, added to through the years… They were the living resource of a coven's history, their power, their alliances and enemies, the spells they'd devised and recorded.

"Not the current one. This is an old version," she said. "We had to make a copy to allow for new spellwork."

"And you have your coven's original? I thought these were protected, that a coven never let any of them go?"

She frowned. "This *is* protected," she told him. "It's with me."

"This is your coven's archive?" he asked in disbelief. A coven's archive was sacrosanct. It held the history, the good and the bad, the strengths and weaknesses, of a coven. The coven protected those references, and they were always honored as deeply private and confidential material. If you accessed a coven's archive, you could access and then exploit those weaknesses, or sabotage their strengths, or worse, steal from them. A coven protected their archive just like a werewolf pack or vampire colony protected their territory. Accessing a coven's archive without permission or supervision was a serious crime among the witches.

And only the most loyal and powerful witch within a coven was entrusted with the security and care of an archive.

Mind. Blown.

He looked down at the volume she held in her hands. "How old is it?"

Sully blew her cheeks out. "Well, that's a good question. This one's been handed down for several generations, it's hard to date it."

His jaw dropped. No. It—it couldn't be. The pages were made of vellum and what looked like—Dave clutched his chest. Honest-to-God papyrus. He pulled his leather gloves off and reached for the codex. Halted. Then took a deep breath and touched it.

Images swam through his mind, of a man painstakingly writing in the book, of passing it to his son, of a ritual within a ring of monolithic stones, of a woman clutching the tome to her chest as the howls of werewolves echoed through the forest, along with the screams of her coven. A young man stumbling along a riverbed, ducking and weaving as vampires chased him, while hundreds fought in the fields behind him. The Troubles.

That same man handing it to a pregnant woman, his face twisted in pain and anguish, an arrow sticking out of his gut. The woman sobbing as she bent to kiss him. "Gabriel…" she cried as he died.

Holy fu—. Dave whipped his hand away. He swallowed, then wagged his finger at the ancient book. "That—that's not possible," he said, despite the visions he'd seen that proved it was, indeed, possible. "That is not supposed to exist." Gabriel. Gabriel, a legend of The Troubles, who'd saved so many lives with his magic, who'd unlocked many of the secrets of the shadow breeds during the wars, and had helped devise spells and weapons to fight against them. This—this was Gabriel's grimoire.

"You're right. It's not supposed to exist."

Dave lifted his gaze to Sully. She looked remarkably calm for having the oldest book of witchcraft in modern times here in her living room. "Who *are* you?"

She frowned at him, perplexed. "You know who I am. My name is branded onto your chest, for crying out loud."

He tried to think. He really did, but the ramifications of this, of the very existence of this book long thought destroyed before the dust had settled on a new world order…

"Gabriel's grimoire. It was believed to have died, along with his line, during The Troubles."

"He had a family."

Dave held up a hand as he subsided onto the sofa bed. "Whoa. Stop. My brain is exploding. Are you telling me that his wife managed to pass it on to someone?"

Sully shook her head. "No, I'm saying that young woman passed it on down the line."

Dave took a deep breath. *Okay. Settle. This* will *make sense.* "What coven are you from?" he asked quietly.

Sully hesitated, then dropped her gaze to the codex on the table. "I'm from the Alder Coven." Her voice was so low, he barely heard the words.

"The Alder—" Dave closed his mouth. The Alder

Coven. Conspiracy theories abound about the infamous coven. It died out in the Roman invasion. They all perished with Atlantis. Pompeii. Or the Minoans, with the first reported shape-shifter. Hell, there was even the story of them being swallowed by flames in a city that burned after an earthquake. Then of course, came The Troubles. He didn't think anyone had connected Gabriel to the Adler Coven, though. Wow. He would have thought she was crazy. Crazy beautiful, but definitely a few sandwiches short of a picnic. Now, though, with the evidence right in front of him, he couldn't deny it.

"Man, you guys are good." He moved from stunned amazement to full acceptance and realization in the blink of an eye.

He rose, picked up the grimoire and gently but hurriedly placed on the shelf. "What the *hell*? You can't just whip something like this out whenever you like," he whispered furiously.

"Dave, this book is so protected—"

"You brought this book into a null area," he whispered harshly. "You bring a null into the house, and all of your protections don't mean diddly."

"No, this is different," she whispered, then frowned. "Why are we whispering?"

"Because you have Gabriel's grimoire in your living room," he whispered back as he turned to face her.

"Dave, relax."

"You can't tell me to relax," he exclaimed softly. "You have a mammoth book of ancient spells, Sully. Do you know how many people would *kill* for this?"

She frowned at him, then straightened her shoulders as she glared at him. "I am a member of the Alder Coven. I have sworn to protect this book with my life. Of *course*

I know how many people would kill for this," she said, her voice low and fierce.

"Then why show me this?" he asked, gesturing at the shelves. Now he would have to keep this secret to his dying day, and if his sister ever found out he knew and hadn't told her, well, she'd make sure his death was slow and painful. Hell, his mother—God, she'd have a field day with this. And then would plot until she held the tome in her own hands. Every witch he knew would want to get their hands on this, and every shadow breed in existence would want to destroy it.

This book was the source of modern-day spells, but covens only worked from bits of it. Nobody had the full resource.

Until now.

"How can you just pull this out, like it's so damn ordinary and mundane?" he asked, and had to shove his hands in his jacket, otherwise he'd act exactly like his coven elder mother on a rant at his rebellious sister, and gesture wildly.

"Because I trust you, Dave," Sully said.

He thought a blood vessel popped in his brain. "You *trust* me?" Okay, he hadn't meant to yell that at her, or make her flinch, but her words had surprised him. Stunned him. "You *can't* trust me. I tried to kill you, remember?"

"You apologized for that."

He clutched his temples. "You have to stop defending that," he told her. "You—you're so—so—" his brain scrambled for the right word.

Sully lifted her chin. "So what, Dave?" She arched an eyebrow.

He flung his arms out. "I'm trying to think up the right word, but all I'm getting is gullible."

Her blue eyes widened in surprise, then darkened with anger. "Gullible? You think I'm *gullible*?"

"No, but I can't think of the right—ah!" he snapped his fingers. "Naive. You're naive."

Sully blinked, as though trying to marshal her thoughts into a logical sequence. Good, because he'd hate to think he was the only one losing his mind over this.

"You trust too easily. I came up to you on the sand— a stranger, and you stopped and talked to me," he said, his thumbs pressing against his chest. "You were going to let me kill you, you've invited me into your home and you barely know me—" his eyes widened as a thought occurred to him. "What would have happened to the grimoire if I'd killed you?" he breathed, as the slow chill of horror crept over him.

"The grimoire would have gone to its new owner," she stated calmly. "There is a built-in hereditary spell."

For a moment he was distracted by all the protections and wards this book must have on it, but then brought his gaze back to the woman in front of him—the woman who could get herself into serious trouble for trusting too easily.

"You have to protect yourself better," he told her. God, the more he learned about this woman, the more he wanted to shield her. And that totally wasn't what he was used to. He was used to annihilating witches, not protecting them.

"Dave, you're the Witch Hunter. Our own version of law enforcement. Why shouldn't I trust you?"

"I kill people, Sully," he rasped, pain burning his throat. "I kill witches. Like you."

She shook her head. "No, not like me. You kill the evil among us, Dave."

He shook his head at the blind faith, the respect in her voice. He deserved neither. And that hurt. It hurt how much he wanted it to be true, and how far away from the truth it was.

"You don't get it. The Ancestors picked me because I can kill my kin and walk way," he told her. "I've had to, in the past." He shrugged out of his jacket, and then pulled his black T-shirt over his head. "Look at me, Sully."

He held his arms out, and then slowly turned around. "Every single one of these names belongs to a witch I've killed." His back was covered in the black tattoos. His biceps. And now the spot over his heart. It was getting so that he barely recognized himself in the mirror anymore. He sometimes had to force himself to stare at his reflection. Those names…each kill was burned into his memory. Those who had begged for mercy…those who had resisted and fought to live, or tried to kill him instead. He lifted his gaze to hers, and it was one of the hardest things he'd had to do. "You can't trust a monster like me, Sully," he rasped.

Her eyes were bright and luminous, as though she was fighting back tears. She took a tentative step forward, her hand out. She paused, then laid her hand on his chest.

There it was again, that clash of energy, that tidal wave of sensation, and then there was her touch. He closed his eyes at the contact, so light, so gentle and warm. He hadn't realized how much he'd craved a woman's touch—*her* touch. It was soothing, it was arousing, it was the very essence of a complex and complicated woman, and he wanted more—and hated himself for it.

"You may be a Witch Hunter," she whispered, and took a deep breath. "But I know you're not all bad."

He slowly opened his eyes. She stood so close, her honey-blond hair loose and luxurious around her shoulders, her blue eyes so full of sympathy, of tenderness. He felt like a brute next to her.

"I'm not all good, either."

She bit her lip, then moved her hand to cup his cheek. "You're good enough."

Her gaze dropped down to his lips, and his breath froze in his chest for a moment. She nodded. "You're good enough," she whispered. She rose up on her toes and pressed her lips against his.

He stood there for a moment, stunned.

Hell, if he wasn't a monster, he sure as hell wasn't a saint. He wrapped his arms around her waist, and slanted his lips across hers.

Chapter 10

She slid her arms around his neck as he gathered her close. So many messages, it made her dizzy trying to make sense of them all. Desire, so hot, so sharp, it took her breath away. Frustration. Loneliness. Self-recrimination. Arousal.

She'd meant to comfort him. She'd sensed his guilt and remorse, so heavy it was nearly suffocating. His gaze was hidden behind his sunglasses, but those lips, the set of his jaw… She'd wanted to reach out.

Now, though, there was no thought for comfort, for reassurance. Sully opened her lips to him, her breath hitching as his tongue slid against hers. His hands tightened on her hips, pulling her against him, and she could feel the hard ridge of his arousal pressing against her stomach.

Her hands trailed over his shoulders, his arms—oh, heavens, his arms. The man was magnificent. So strong and broad, so warm, so—

Dave flexed his hips against hers, and Sully thought she was going to combust. She slanted her head first one way, then the other, their tongues dueling, their breaths coming in shared, staccato pants.

His large hands slid beneath her loose top, and goose bumps rose on her ribs. She arched her back as his hands trailed up her back. She moaned. Heat, so much heat. Her heart thudded in her ears, and she could feel herself getting damp between her thighs. Her breasts swelled, and she pressed herself against him firmly. God, his chest was amazing. She ran her hands over the defined musculature of his torso. His skin was smooth, so sleek, so not what she expected. She could see some marks that weren't tattoos. Scars. But, astonishingly, the evidence of his strength, of his skill, just felt sexy against her fingertips as she caressed him.

Dave made a surprised sound against her lips when his fingers encountered the clasp of her strapless bra. She raised her eyebrows as she drew back, and he gave her a wicked smile. "I've been fantasizing about your underwear," he murmured, then took her lips again as his clever fingers undid the clasp.

He drew the garment away from her, and she shivered in his arms at the caress against her skin.

And then his hands covered her breasts beneath her top. She moaned, tearing her lips from his, her head tilting back as she surrendered to the sensation. He cupped the weight of her breasts in his hands, his thumbs strumming over her nipples.

So hot. Liquid heat slicked her thighs, and she pulled his head down, capturing his lips in a kiss that conveyed her own hunger. For him. For the Witch Hunter.

He growled softly into her mouth, then his hands

glided down to her butt. He caressed her there, clasping the fabric of her skirt and inching it up her legs. She slid her tongue against his, her breath coming in pants. She could feel the heat of his body, the cool against her legs, her nipples tight with want. Dave bent his knees. His grip tightened, and he lifted her up. Sully swung her legs around his hips as he walked her back to rest her butt on a shelf of the bookcase. She ignored the clatter, the tumble of magical texts falling to the floor.

She lifted her head to take a quick breath, then closed her eyes as she tilted her head back. He was hard against her. Everywhere. Hard. Hot. His hips rolled against hers, and she shuddered. Her thighs tightened around his hips, and he moaned, low and sexy, as he trailed his lips down the line of her neck.

So much heat. She heard him hiss in her ear, felt him shudder. Heat. Like, burning. She pulled back, and his neck arched, the veins in stark relief against his skin. He leaned back, his hips holding her in place on the shelf.

The mark on his chest glowed. Her name.

Realization hit. *Oh, God, no.*

"Dave," she gasped.

The mark brightened, and Dave clasped the shelf on either side of her, gritting his teeth as he sucked in a breath. His biceps bulged, his knuckles whitened and his thighs tensed beneath hers.

He was in pain. She could feel it. Intense, burning. Consuming.

"Sullivan Timmerman," Dave gasped, tugging off his sunglasses.

Sully gaped as his light gray eyes turned silver, and his expression went slack as he stared sightlessly at the shelves above her head, entranced.

Instinctively, she reached out to give him comfort, to offer him support.

Red. Fire. Scalding. Darkness. Running. Panting. Determination. *A woman, scrambling down the side drive of a house. She pauses at the chain-link fence, fumbling with the gate's latch.* Satisfaction. Gotcha. *The woman turns to face her, her eyes wide with terror.*

"No! Please, no!" She holds up her arms to ward off blows, but the knife strikes fast. Not to kill, just to stop her from running. Triumph. *The woman clutches her stomach, her face twists in pain. She gasps as she falls to her knees, and she collapses, cradling her stomach as the stain blooms across her blouse.* Cold intent. End it. *The knife flashes again, plunging into her chest. The confusion, the shock, the terror, gently wanes as the light leaves her eyes.*

Dave lowered her to the floor and stumbled back, breaking their contact. Sully's vision snapped into focus once more. She was back in her living room, leaning back against her bookshelf, her skirt gently draping down to her calves as Dave grimaced. He shook his head once, still caught in the violence of his vision.

His lips tightened. Then his lips turned down, and for a brief moment sadness crossed his features, before it was removed by determination and that same ruthlessness she'd seen on the beach. He blinked, and the light in his eyes flickered down to a light silver.

"Are you okay?" she asked. His chest didn't glow anymore, and she could see him in his eyes again, not some vacant glaze.

His chest, though, looked painful. The mark that had healed a little was now rebranded onto his skin. Her name.

Sullivan Timmerman had killed again.

"I have to go," Dave muttered, wincing as he reached for his T-shirt.

Sully raised a shaky hand to her lips, trying to fight back the tears.

"Aman—Amanda Sinclair," she said, then clutched her stomach. Oh, God. Her family…

"What?"

"Amanda Sinclair. The woman he just killed. That's her name," she said, then covered her mouth. Deep breaths.

Dave frowned. "You—you saw?" he asked, his tone baffled as he took a step toward her.

She nodded. "Touch, we were touching. Oh, my God, Amanda," The tears fell, hot on her cheeks. Her gut clenched, and she could feel the bile rising in her throat.

Dave's eyes widened in shock, then his features showed his dismay. "Oh, Sully. I didn't know—I'd never want you to see—"

"He hunted her," she cried, her hands twisting in the cotton of her blouse.

Dave stilled. "What?"

"He—he was hunting her. I could—I could feel it."

Dave looked from her to the door, and back to her. He reached for her arm, gently pulling her away from the bookshelf, and then turned and guided her to sit on the foldout sofa.

"I'm sorry, I have to go, I have to find him—we'll talk later," he promised, his face filled with regret. "Where does Amanda live?"

"Lived," she corrected automatically, shock putting her into a numb autopilot. The woman was now dead. Oh, hell.

He nodded. "Yes. Lived. Sully, where did Amanda Sinclair live?" he asked gently.

"Two streets down from where we were tonight. Number 6." Her response was automatic, the words falling from her lips as she replayed what she'd seen in her mind. Amanda had been so terrified. Another tear fell on her cheek. She'd never felt so helpless, so useless, watching the woman's murder.

He cupped her cheek, and tilted his forehead against hers. "I'm so sorry, Sully." Intense guilt. Remorse. Grief. He was full of it. For Amanda—and for her.

"No, this isn't on you," she told him, blinking back her tears. "I'll come with you," she said, and braced herself to rise off the sofa. The Sinclairs…she had to go to them.

Dave's hand on her shoulder prevented her from moving. "No," he told her firmly. "You're staying right here."

"Dave, I know the family," she told him urgently.

He nodded. "I understand. But I'm going to the scene of a murder, Sully. This guy—he might still be there. I don't want you anywhere near this."

Her eyes narrowed. "I can take care of myself, Dave." She'd spent the last four years making sure that was true.

His lips firmed. "You're strong, I'll give you that. But this guy has now murdered three people. I'm not willing to take the chance that you could be the fourth."

She opened her mouth to protest, and he cut off her words with a quick kiss. "Please, Sully. I have to do this, and you being there—it will be a distraction. I'll be wanting to make sure you're safe, and not focusing on the job." Dave straightened. "I have to go. But we'll talk when I get back. I promise."

"Your chest," she said in protest. Dave was pulling his T-shirt on over his as head as he walked toward the door.

"I've got a first aid kit on my bike," he said brusquely, and then left.

Sully sagged back on the sofa, and stared around the room. Dave's suggestion was definitely the safest course. His job was to hunt the null killer. The witch killing the people she knew and loved in her name.

"Screw it," she muttered. Dave expected her to sit quietly at home. She hadn't let a man make her decisions for her for four years. She wasn't about to let that happen again. Her friends needed her. She trotted out to the shed in the back garden to gather some supplies.

Dave drove up to the makeshift barricade on the street and surveyed the scene. A crowd had gathered along the designated perimeter, and deputies were out to direct traffic and enforce the boundary. Red-and-blue lights flashed down the street, casting colored flickers into the darkness. The sheriff stood near the driveway gate and was talking to a man who Dave could only guess was Amanda Sinclair's husband, judging from his devastated, grief-stricken expression.

Darn. With the sheriff and his deputies traipsing all over the area, he couldn't get any closer to the scene. Couldn't witch his way past, couldn't bespell people to tell him what he needed to know, couldn't become invisible or forgettable—not in null territory, anyway. This was a novel experience, not being able to use his powers to get what he wanted. Which was exactly what Sully had said before, wasn't it? She wouldn't date him because he was the kind of guy who did and said whatever was needed to get what he wanted.

And yet, they'd kissed. So maybe dating was off the table, but other stuff wasn't...? He frowned. The burn in his chest had subsided, but was still an aching reminder of what he was in Serenity Cove for—and it wasn't to get up close and all kinds of personal with an empath witch who seemed to know him way too well for his liking.

He kicked out the stand for his bike and swung his leg over. He removed his helmet, wincing at the pull on his chest. He'd slapped a nonstick dressing over the wound and used tape to hold it in place, but it ached, and his skin was pinched by the tape with each movement. He hung the strap of his helmet over the handlebars, then strode a little farther along the edge of the perimeter. He eyed the front of the house. The door was closed. His lips tightened. No sign of forced entry. He glanced over toward the gate. A sheet was draped over the figure on the ground. He backed up a little. The drive had a five-foot-high wooden fence down one side. She wouldn't have been able to scale it, not with her killer right on her heels. House on one side, fence on the other, her only option would have been to run down the drive toward the street. He wondered if that had been the killer's plan, or whether he'd just been lucky.

"Excuse me, sir."

Dave turned as the deputy stepped around the road-block, gesturing beyond him. Dave realized he was standing in the man's way and stepped aside, giving a casual wave of apology as the deputy passed him.

He turned back to the scene. Sully was right. Amanda Sinclair had been hunted down and killed. He glanced up at the night sky. The moon was a chunk of silver. A waxing gibbous moon. Enough light to stop you from tripping off the curb, but still kind of gloomy, especially in this neighborhood with no streetlights, he noticed, eyeing up and down the street.

A warm breeze ruffled his hair. He would have liked to remove his jacket, but with the law already here, he didn't think he'd be sticking around for long. A hand thudded down on his shoulder, and he turned, hiding the wince at the resulting pull of muscle and scorched skin.

Jacob Forsyth. Sully's wannabe-boyfriend nodded grimly at him. "I thought you left?"

"I turned back when I saw all the police cars on the highway," he lied. He couldn't very well say he'd received a magical vision from the Ancestors. That wasn't something folks readily understood or accepted—except for Sully, it seemed.

Jacob nodded, accepting his excuse at face value. He looked over toward the cordoned-off house, his expression dark and grim. "This sucks. Ronald found her when he came home from the Adler farewell."

Dave looked over at him. "She wasn't at the farewell?"

Jacob shook his head. "Nope. She was home with the kids."

"Kids were in the house?" Dave looked back at the house in horror. He hadn't seen the kids in the vision.

Jacob nodded, his lips tight. "Yeah. They slept through the whole thing." His answer was short. Abrupt. The man was visibly upset—no, maybe angry was a better word— at what had happened.

"But they're safe?" Dave's gut clenched with apprehension at the risk to the kids.

"Yeah, they're safe."

"Thank God," Dave muttered in relief. Jacob watched him closely for a moment, then glanced back up the street.

"When did you say you arrived in Serenity?" Jacob's tone was conversational, but the words cut like hot steel.

Dave met his gaze. "I didn't." He should have expected

this. "I arrived the morning of Mary Anne Adler's death."
Which meant he wasn't in the area for Gary Adler's
death, and he hoped that was enough to eliminate him
from Jacob's obvious suspicions.

"Murder," Jacob corrected.

Dave inclined his head. "Murder."

"Where's Sully?"

"She's back home," Dave said.

Jacob nodded. "Good. She doesn't need to see this."

Dave turned back toward where the sheriff was talking quietly with the husband. Jacob sounded protective.
Proprietary.

Not that he should care. He was here to hunt his witch.
If the witch moved on, he moved on. If he managed to
kill the witch, he moved on. If another witch committed
a crime, he moved on. He couldn't see a scenario where
he didn't move on. It shouldn't matter to him what Jacob
and Sully did. He wasn't here to interfere with Sully's
life—after what he'd done to her on the beach, he'd be
ensuring that Sully's life was a long and happy one. If
that meant a life with—*ugh*—Jacob, so be it.

Only, that idea was more irritating than the recurring
brand on his chest, and just as painful, if he let himself
follow that thought down the rabbit hole. He tried to tell
himself he had no business feeling annoyed at this man
trying to stake his claim on Sully.

But he was, especially when he still had the taste of
her on his lips.

He tilted his head as he eyed the sheet-covered body.
"Was Amanda Sinclair a pureblood?" he asked, curious.

Jacob stilled. He seemed to be considering his response. Then he leaned closer, and Dave lifted his chin
to meet the null's gaze directly. "I know you're a friend

of Sully's and all, and I know the noise you've made about helping us, but my bullshit radar is going full alert around you. You may have Sully convinced that you're here to help, but I don't know you, and I don't trust you. If you're wanting to get into Sully's good graces, figure out a different way, because this," the man said, gesturing between Dave and the Sinclair house, "is a pretty crap way of doing it."

Jacob turned and walked farther down the street, and Dave saw Jenny running up to her brother, her face distressed as she took in the scene.

Dave shoved his hands in his pockets, and turned to look at the few people nearby. Each time he made eye contact, they turned away. Jacob wasn't the only one who didn't seem to trust him. He wasn't going to get any answers from this crowd.

He sighed as he strode back to his bike. Tracking down this killer witch was getting more complicated by the day.

Sully quenched the blade in the tub of oil, watching as steam curled up from the surface. She withdrew it slightly, then dipped, repeating the process gently, moving her head out of the way of the small billowing flare-up when the vapors burned. When the blade had cooled, she placed it on the stone bench where the others lay, then raised her protective visor.

She surveyed her handiwork. Four blades. As soon as the metal blades were thoroughly cool, she'd do a hollow grind them on them, sharpen them and polish them, and then she'd cut out and fix the tangs inside the handles. She'd have four more close-combat weapons. When finished, these blades would have a forty-five-degree angle to the blade from the hilt that made it easy to draw them from whatever holster or sheath they occupied. She picked up one of the blades. The steel she'd used was composed of a greater iron alloy than usual, and then she'd give them decorative silver engraving along the blade. A kind of catchall against the shadow breeds. While the null's presence voided a shadow breed's supernatural abilities, it didn't stop the effect of injuries. With iron as the base metal, the blade had not only the physical aspects of creating damage, but any race sensitive to silver, or to iron, would still feel the effects of the metal. It was like a double-pronged attack by the wielder. Shadow breeds naturally had a greater muscle mass that put them at a slight advantage over ordinary human beings, whether they were nulls or not. This kind of blade did a little toward evening out the playing field.

Once the blades had cooled sufficiently and she didn't run the risk of shattering them, she'd engrave on them some simple spellwork, and bleed some molten silver into the designs. The spells would be voided if being wielded by a null, but if it was, say, a witch against a werewolf, or a human against a vampire, or even witch against witch, the spells would still engage—and cause significant damage. Her lips firmed. She wanted to get this witch, but if she couldn't, then she'd damn well protect her friends—protect them in a way she'd wished someone had protected her, all those years ago.

She rolled her shoulders, shaking off the tension, the dark memories. She'd worked through the night, and her neck and shoulder muscles were tired, her feet were sore and she'd definitely be feeling her biceps tomorrow. She reached over and turned off the burners for her forge. She'd added an extension to the back of her factory shop, creating a blacksmithing Shangri-la. It had taken her a few years, but she finally had a number of forges using different fuels, and anything she could think of in the creation of her cutlery…and weapons and coins. She could have made these blades at home. She eyed the other daggers, dirks and swords she'd also stockpiled that now were lined up neatly on one wall, weapons that she could create only here, in the bigger forge. In the past few days she'd made a whole bunch of arrowheads, and this time, she'd used her own unique broadhead style, with three blades angling out from the tip of the arrowhead. Excellent penetration, minimal deflection, maximum damage.

She removed her protective glasses, apron and gloves and started to clean up. She wrinkled her nose as she hung her leather apron up on a hook. Man, she was rank. She'd have to go home and shower before she did anything.

She put all her tools away, and then placed her new blades and their handles on a shelf running along the wall. She then pulled the sliding wall along its track until it settled into its position. She stood back and eyed the wall, then nodded, satisfied. It looked like a normal wall, and not the entry to her secret armory.

Once everything was cleared away, and the floor swept, she switched off the lights and locked the doors. She smiled as she turned to her car. Dave expected her to bespell her factory and shop. The problem was, in null territory, it didn't matter how many wards she layered over the access points, they were rendered useless here.

She yawned as she drove out of town and along the coast road toward her home. The ocean was on her right, and the sky was already lightening, the sun just beginning to edge its way over the horizon. It was early. Too early to call Jenny. She'd go home, have a quick shower and some breakfast and then—she yawned again. Okay, so it had been a while since she'd pulled an all-nighter in the forge.

She braked gently, eyeing the turnoff that would take her to the null neighborhood. She clenched the wheel. Poor Ronald. He and Amanda had just celebrated their four-year anniversary. She'd babysat their little darlings, Becky and Lily. She took the turn, and moments later was driving quietly down the main street. She stopped at the corner and looked down the street. Yellow crime scene ribbon fluttered in the warm morning breeze. Two deputies stood by their car, and another was using one of those wheely measure things as he walked along the driveway. The sheriff rose from where he'd squatted near the gate, camera in one hand as he rubbed his other over his face.

Sully eyed that gate. That's where it had happened. A flash of memory, Amanda's terror-filled eyes, her trembling hands. Sully blinked rapidly to dispel the vision.

A long night for the local law, too, by the looks of things. She eyed the house. Now was not the time to visit Ronald and express her condolences. She drove on down the street and took the next right, and then another right and then a left to head back out to toward the coastal road. A little while later she was pulling into her driveway and avoiding the motorcycle that was parked up near the side of the house.

She climbed out of the car, closing the door quietly, then climbed the stairs to her porch. She turned and gazed out over the headland. The sun was higher now, the sky bathed in fiery pinks, burning away the horrors of the night. Sully bit her lip as she again remembered seeing Amanda run down the driveway, only this time the memory morphed into her running, her stumbling along, trying to get away.

Of being caught.

Sully sniffed and turned her back on the beautiful view of a stunning sunrise over the ocean. She had stuff to do. Shower. Breakfast. Call Jenny.

She let herself inside the house, wincing as she tried to close the door silently, then cringing at the soft snick of the latch. Darn it. She hesitated. The house was quiet, save for a sonorous snore emanating from her living room. So Dave had returned. Her lips tightened as she remembered him commanding her to stay. That chafed. And she hadn't rebelled, either. She'd stayed away from the Sinclair home, from the null neighborhood. Damn it. She'd have to watch for that. She wasn't some guy's doormat anymore.

She slipped her flip-flops off and started to tiptoe across the foyer toward the hall. She peeked into the living room as she passed. Well, peeked and then stopped.

Dave lay sprawled out on her sofa, his feet dangling over the sofa arm at the end, one arm draped toward the floor. He made her lounge look like furniture from a dollhouse. The blanket laid pooled on the floor—it had been a warm night—and he lay there, with just the sheet covering him. Almost. His sunglasses were folded and placed on the end table by his head.

Her mouth grew slack. Holy mother of smoking hot men. His chest was bare, and she could see again all the Old Language lettering inked across his biceps, and down his rib cage and across his abdomen. A white square dressing was taped across his left pec, but it didn't quite cover his nipple. It was almost as if the Ancestors had used his musculature as a writing guide, and the markings enhanced the dips and bulges of his body. His sheet was—she swallowed—*just* covering his groin, and she could see his bare hip, and the curve of his butt cheek… She curled her fingers into a fist. *No touching.*

Warmth bloomed inside her. Damn, Dave Carter was one crazy hot Witch Hunter. She tried to look down the hall. She really did. Her lip caught between her teeth as she eyed his smooth skin, his broad chest with the—she frowned. Good grief. Had he used *duct tape* to stick his bandage down?

She shook her head. Men. She let her gaze travel down his body. The one leg outside the sheet revealed a strong thigh and muscular calf. Her heart thumped a little faster in her chest. She was perving on a guy who was sleeping, a guest in her home.

And she was not sorry at all. She eyed the sheet. It really was draped precariously. She tilted her head to the side. She wasn't sure if that was just a large rumple of the sheet or whether that was him…

She blinked. No. She should march herself down to the bathroom and jump into a nice cold shower. She nodded. Yep. That's exactly what she should do. She took a step back, and the floorboard creaked.

Her eyes widened.

Dave's eyes opened to slits, his silver-gray gaze meeting hers.

Chapter 11

Dave's lips quirked. Sully looked like she'd been caught with her hand in the cookie jar.

"Hey, good morning," he said, his voice husky as he started to sit up.

"No!" Sully said, her hand flashing up in that universal stop signal.

He froze. "What?" He glanced about, narrowing his eyes against the soft morning light. He couldn't see any threat. He looked back at her, bewildered. "What's wrong?"

"Uh, you might want to cover up," she whispered, gesturing in the general direction of his groin while keeping her gaze on the ceiling. Except for when she peeked at him. Twice.

His lips curved into a smile as he sat up. He didn't touch the sheet. Not that he was in any danger of losing it. His body had apparently recognized Sully before his brain kicked in, and his hard-on had hooked the sheet.

And then he realized she was wearing the same clothes he'd kissed her in. That loose billowy top with the strapless bra underneath. His eyebrows rose. "Are you just getting in?" He'd tiptoed in last night, thinking she was asleep down the hall in her bedroom.

Sully nodded as she glanced toward the end of the hall, then back at him. "Yeah. I couldn't just sit here, last night, so I went into the factory."

"The factory," he repeated, then frowned. "Your factory near town? With the lousy locks?"

She nodded. "Yep, that would be the one." Her gaze dropped to the sheet, and her cheeks grew rosy.

The room was gradually getting lighter, as the sun climbed higher, glinting through the bay windows, and he had to narrow his eyes against the glare.

"Sully, that could have been dangerous," he told her as he reached for his sunglasses.

She folded her arms, her flip-flops dangling from one hand. "You can't have it both ways, Dave. If it was too dangerous for me to go with you to Amanda's house because the killer may have been there, it should have been fine for me at my factory."

His lips tightened at her logic as he slid his glasses on. The dimming of the room gave him some relief, but he could still see Sully clearly. Too clearly. She was annoyed. Well, so was he. He'd slept here, knowing that he'd hear anyone entering through the house and could protect her. It was galling to realize he'd been protecting an empty bed.

"Sully, until I catch this guy, anywhere you go—"

She shook her head. "No, let's put this into perspective. So far, this witch has gone after nulls. I am not a null. There is no link between me and the victims, other than I know them, and in a town this size, so does pretty much everyone else. I'm going to go wherever I want, whenever I want—starting with visiting Jenny after breakfast."

"The guy kills in your name, Sully. The Ancestors gave me *your name*." He rose from the couch, frustration eating at him. He pulled the sheet with him to save embarrassment—not his, hers. Her eyes widened, but to her credit she kept her gaze fastened on his. "You say you only have a minor connection to these people, but we both know that's not right."

"You're right. My connection to these people is not minor. These people…" She gestured toward her front door, to the community beyond, "These people have become my family, my *home*." She turned to face him, and her expression was so sad, so frustrated, he took a step toward her before he realized what he was doing. He halted, clutching the sheet to his groin.

"I will do what I can to help them, to protect them," she said, her shoulders straightening. "So for the record, I will do everything within my power to stop this witch. Don't even think you can sideline me on this."

Her gaze had turned fierce, her blue eyes practically snapping fire at him.

This time he took that step, bringing him closer to her, and her gaze dropped to his chest. "Don't even think I'm going to let you risk your life here doing *my* job," he said, his voice low and rough. His job sucked. She had no idea the toll it took on a person, especially a witch, to kill another. It was that one little loophole—and every spell and rule had one. Witches were supposed to honor and protect nature and her creatures. Witches weren't supposed to harm another, but when they did, his ordained job was to harm them. And it sucked a little at his soul, each and every time.

She had to drag her gaze up from his chest, and he saw the moment his words sank in. Her eyes narrowed, and his chin jutted forward as he waited for her response, a response he could just see was going to be fiery.

"I am not about to let another man dictate what I can and can't do," she said, her voice sounding like it was pulled tight over sandpaper, all husky and coarse. "If you ever again tell me to sit and stay like a good dog, I will show you just how much of a bitch I can be."

He blinked. There was so much to unpack from those remarks, he was trying to figure out what to address first. Okay, the dog comment definitely had to be straightened out. He was horrified that's how she'd perceived his remarks, that he'd made a woman feel like that. "I'm sorry, Sully, I never meant to treat you, or make you feel like a—"

She smiled tightly. "I know you didn't, but when you command a strong, capable witch to stay at home and out of trouble, how do you expect it to sound?" She folded her arms, and he saw her breasts swell against the material of her top. He adjusted the sheet in front of him. They were having a serious conversation, for Pete's sake. He wasn't supposed to be distracted by her body.

Her gaze dropped to track his movement with the sheet, and a blush crept over her cheeks. So, he wasn't the only one battling distraction. Good to know.

She cleared her throat. "Would you have said it to me, if I was male?"

"Yes," he answered immediately. "Gender has nothing to do with this. If you were male or female, and I thought you were in danger from this witch, I would say the same thing—which is, let me handle this," he emphasized, leaning forward to meet her gaze. "If you're a witch, or a vamp or a shifter, this witch is capable of performing magic of some sort around a null. I've never seen that before—I didn't even know it was possible. We have no idea what this witch is capable of. We do know that he's killed two women as well as a strong, physically fit and capable man, so yes, guy or chick, I'm saying steer clear for your own safety."

He raised his hand to tuck a tendril behind her ear—and *pift*, there was that zing, that little clap of power that always happened between them, that awakened his senses on a cellular level, that heightened his awareness and made him feel like he was surrounded by a field of electricity with her. "Your safety is very, very important to me," he told her in a low voice.

Her gaze dropped from his eyes to his mouth, and her own mouth opened. She pressed her lips together. Swallowed. "It's just as well you're being sincere. A bit of a douche, but a sincere douche."

He smiled. "I've been called worse."

Sully nodded, then her gaze drifted down. He was tempted to lose the sheet, to sweep her up in his arms, step back to that damn sofa and make these sparks between them fly.

Sully gaped at him, then snapped her mouth shut. She jerked her thumb over her shoulder. "Shower. Me." She was looking at him. All of him. And there was a desire, a hunger in her eyes that was so naked, so blatant, he so damn wanted to reach for her then and there and finish what they'd started the night before.

He raised an eyebrow. "Is that an invitation?"

Her cheeks got rosier, and she shook her head. Just a little nervous shake. "I mean, I'm going to take a shower." She hurried down the hall, and Dave smiled.

"Pity."

Sully pulled up in front of Jenny's drive, and glanced over at Dave. He'd opted to travel with her this time, instead of riding his motorbike. She wasn't sure if it was for the sake of convenience—they were both going to the same place, so it made sense—or whether it was to keep an eye on her.

Protect her.

She swallowed. She'd spent way too much time in the shower this morning, thinking about Dave and that sheet. Or rather, Dave without the sheet. Even now her cheeks heated with the images that had flashed through her mind as she'd washed away the sweat and grime from her night in the factory. His golden skin, those markings that followed the line of his sculpted muscles, those amazing silver-gray eyes.

The man was gorgeous. He oozed a dangerous sensuality that seemed to bypass any of her personal controls and call to something deep inside her, something she thought she'd gained control over.

She'd wanted him to join her in the shower. Heck, she'd wanted to join him on that sofa, just like she sensed he wanted. She couldn't remember ever having such an intense physical reaction to a man. Sure, things with Marty had been physical—way too physical, especially toward the end. She thought she was past all that, or at least wary of it, with a logical desire to steer clear of that kind of allure. Dave, though, was…more. More man. More muscle. More presence. More power. She should be running in the opposite direction, especially when he got his alpha witch on and demanded she stand down.

When he'd touched her, she'd sensed him—again. She couldn't mistake his need to protect her, and it was so genuine, so sincere, it touched her. He was frustrated, and he was worried—for her. She couldn't sense any darkness to his need to protect her. It was pure, it was light and it was so damn seductive, she'd wanted to jump into his arms and give him what they both wanted. Whatever that may be.

Which, in turn, annoyed her. She'd spent the past four years proving to herself she didn't need to be with a man… She didn't need permission, she didn't need approval, or assistance, or support, or any little tie that would anchor her to a guy. No. She'd learned she was more than capable of standing on her own two feet, of paying her own bills, of developing her own business, honing her craft—establishing her own damn identity.

She didn't need to be told where she could and couldn't go, who she could and couldn't see, what she could and couldn't wear, and what she could and couldn't think, feel, say, do.

There was something about Dave, though, something that snagged at her, drew her in. She had to shut that crap down right now. Before she got sucked into another nightmare.

Sully turned her head to eye him. He looked deep in thought, staring through the windshield. He'd showered after she had—which involved more fantasizing on her part about his naked body under the stream of hot water. Steam. Soap suds. Muscles.

She cleared her throat, and he turned to look at her, his eyes shielded by the dark lenses of his sunglasses. He was wearing a navy T-shirt, and she could see one of his markings peeking out from beneath the edge of his sleeve. Name, not marking, she corrected herself. The name of a witch he'd killed.

See, just that thought should give her chills. She'd been on the receiving end of his murderous intent, after all. Yet, it didn't. She'd seen him in action, seen his ruthlessness, his power turned on another—her—along with a physical dominance that should have her ducking for cover. But... it didn't. Why was that? What was it about this guy that made her ignore all her safeguards, all those red flags she'd warned herself to watch out for and steer away from?

"You might want to let me do the talking," she said to him. He'd told her the conversation he'd had with Jacob. She was mildly surprised the nice, friendly guy she knew had so abruptly shut Dave down, but she was beginning to find out a lot of mild surprises from the people she thought she'd gotten to know so well.

Dave's lips tightened, but he nodded. He didn't like it, she could tell, but, well, what could he do about it? Nulls didn't like outsiders. It was only because she'd been able to make teas and ointments that made them feel better that they had welcomed her in, initially. And Dave—well, Dave didn't look like the tea-drinking type, let alone the tea-making type.

They got out of the car, and Sully squinted against the bright sunlight as she closed her car door. She wore a loose cotton top with thin straps, and the sun beat down on her bare shoulders. Today was going to be a hot one.

She slid the strap of her tote up her arm to her shoulder as she waited for Dave to walk around the car, and they crossed the street together. They were walking up the garden path to Jenny's cottage front door when they heard the scream.

Chapter 12

Dave bolted up the steps and across the porch, hand out to thrust open the door. Heart hammering, he could feel the skin over his pec muscle beginning to warm. More screams.

No. God, no. Not again, not here. "Jenny!"

He heard a clatter in the kitchen. His arms pumped as he ran down the hall, scanning the rooms through the open doorways until he raced around the bend in the hall.

"Jenny!" He heard Sully's cry, the sound of her flip-flops smacking the floorboards as she raced along behind him.

The door to the kitchen was closed. Dave didn't slow down, just bent his right arm in front of him and shoulder-charged the door.

The door gave way, whipping open as he barreled through. Jenny was on the floor, screaming, legs kicking. A guy straddled her, but froze when he heard the door. Dave roared. Instinctively he summoned his powers, only to feel…nothing.

Damn it. Nulls. The guy didn't even turn to face him, but rose and raced through the back door. Dave's skin stopped itching.

His gaze met Jenny's wide-eyed fearful stare. She was crap-scared, but physically all right. He didn't stop, but darted through the back door. He hesitated briefly, scanning the yard. There. The back gate hung agape, as though it had been slammed closed but not latched, and was slowly swinging back open again.

Arms and legs pumping, he ran through the gate, and caught sight of a dark leg and shoe as his quarry raced down the narrow lane between rows of houses, and then around the corner. Dave took off again, hands straight, his stride lengthening. So close. Finally. So. Damn. Close.

He skidded around the corner. Damn it. Another lane. There. Farther up, the guy was hitting the gravel pretty damn hard. He wanted to send a blast toward him, level the bastard with a powerful shove of magic, yet being in the heart of the null neighborhood, it didn't matter how much he tried to draw on his powers, nothing would come forth. Dave sprinted after him. The man turned and jumped over a low fence, and Dave followed, bracing his hands on the horizontal rail as he swung his legs over in a smooth movement, and then took off running across someone's back lawn. Well, dirt patch.

He ducked under the low-hanging branch of a magnolia, and ignored the cry of an older woman peering through her kitchen window.

The witch pounded along the driveway, then took a gradual curve across the front lawn, jumping over the fence like an athlete in a hurdle race. Dave sprinted, then inhaled as he leaped over the fence. He didn't break stride as he hit the ground running.

The witch raced along the street. *Look at me.* Dave's jaw clenched. The guy wasn't looking in any direction except straight ahead. Wasn't even checking if Dave was still in pursuit. All Dave could see was the back of the man's head. The witch hit an intersection and turned right, his hand raised to shield his face.

Dave pumped his legs harder, faster. Damn him. He was hiding his face. The witch ducked behind a tall fence, and it took Dave a couple of seconds to reach the spot. Dave skidded to a stop, glancing about wildly.

What? Where the hell had he gone? An old woman, stooped over so much that she could barely make eye contact with him, gave him a friendly smile and wave as she started to cross the street.

Dave went up to the fence, grabbed the top and pulled himself up to peer over it. He scanned the backyard. A dog lifted its head, then rose when he saw Dave. He barked.

There was no sign of the witch he'd been pursuing, and the dog would have sounded the alarm had someone tried to scale the fence and run through the yard.

Dave dropped to the ground, then glanced up and down the street. What the hell? He jogged from one driveway to the other, glancing down and around. Nothing. Nobody. He tried to summon his powers again, and frustration licked at him like a hot flame at the silence, the cool…the void.

He hurried in the direction of the old woman.

"Excuse me, ma'am?"

The woman slowed, and it took seconds for her to scan the street.

"Ma'am," Dave said again as he jogged up to her. It seemed to take a moment for her to realize he was behind her, and she shifted. Slowly. Little shuffling steps.

"Excuse me, ma'am, but did you see where that man went?"

She was hunched over, her gaze on his shoes, and it took her a moment to try to lift her head enough to meet his gaze. Dave leaned forward to save her the effort.

"What?" she asked, her white brows dipping. She raised her hand to cup her ear.

"The man," Dave repeated loudly. "Did you see where he went?"

"Man? What man?" Her rheumy eyes showed her confusion. She blinked at him, as though trying to understand him. Or remember him. Or…maybe just focus on him.

"Uh, the man—I was following a man round here," he said, gesturing toward the corner.

She shifted. Slowly. Little shuffling steps so that she could see where he was pointing. She blinked, squinting. "Where is he?" she asked him.

He took a breath. "I don't know. Did you see where he went?"

"Where who went?" she asked curiously, angling her head this way and that to peer up and down the street. She reminded him of a bird, with her hooked nose, small eyes and the tilt of her head, first one way, then another.

He sighed. She was nearly deaf and blind, and obviously hadn't seen anything. "Never mind. Thank you," he added. He looked around. The witch had disappeared. Somehow. "Here, let me help you," he said, offering her his arm. She smiled up at him.

"Why, thank you."

They shuffled across the street together, and he cupped her elbow as she stepped up onto the curb.

She nodded at him, then shuffled on her way. Dave turned back to the street, his hands on his hips as he tried to figure out how he'd managed to lose the guy. Lips pressed tight, he started to walk back the way he'd come, then started to jog. He wanted to get back to Sully—and to Jenny.

Sully's friend was going to have to talk with him, now—whether she liked to or not. He wasn't going to take no for an answer.

Sully looked up from Jenny as Dave thumped up the back steps and through the back door. Jenny startled, her tea sloshing in her mug, and Sully covered her friend's hands as they cupped the ceramic mug on the table.

Dave's large frame seemed to darken the kitchen, until he stepped farther into the room. His navy T-shirt sported a damp V-patch on the front, and perspiration dripped down the sides of his face and neck. He'd run hard.

He walked over to her friend and put his hand on her shoulder, bending low to meet her gaze.

"Are you okay?" he asked Jenny quietly. If it had been appropriate, Sully would have stood and hugged him. His tone was low, so gentle, with just the right amount of concern that was heartwarming, but still strong enough that Jenny wouldn't break down into tears—which seemed likely. Sully could feel her friend trembling, and she so wanted to take some of that fear, that residual terror from her. For the first time, she wished she could still use her powers with the nulls.

Jenny nodded, her eyes wide. "Yeah," she said, her voice hoarse.

Dave reached for a high-backed chair at the end of the table, swung it around on a leg and straddled it, his muscled forearms folded across the top as he looked directly at Jenny.

"Mind telling me what happened?" he asked in a mild voice.

Jenny nodded. She opened her mouth, then blinked. She frowned. "I don't—I don't know," she said, then looked uncertainly at Dave, then at Sully.

Sully reached for her shoulder. "It's okay, Jen. Take your time."

Jenny shook her head, her expression becoming distraught. "I—I don't know," she said, her voice rising in pitch. "I remember…" Her gaze drifted to Dave. "You," she breathed. "You, breaking through my door…"

Sully glanced over at the kitchen door. The section of the door where the doorknob was located was rough and splintered, and there was a long crack down the middle panel. From the moment they'd heard Jenny's scream from the front door, Dave had become a force of energy, barreling through the house, and not slowing down for something as trivial as a door. She had entered the kitchen only to see him race through the back door.

For a big guy, he could move like lightning.

And Jenny had been on the floor, shaken and trembling. Sully had made a quick call to Tyler Clinton, and then to Jacob, and then had tended to her friend.

Now, with a cup of tea in her hands, Jenny was beginning to calm, although her cheeks were tear-streaked, and her knuckles were white as she clasped the ceramic mug.

Dave nodded. "Yes, we heard you screaming," he told her. "What can you tell us about the man, Jenny?"

Jenny's hand went to her neck. "My throat is sore."

Sully nodded, smoothing her hand across her friend's back. "You were screaming, Jen."

"The man?" Dave prompted.

Jenny frowned, her gaze caught by a bruise on her wrist, and she turned her hand over to see how far it extended. "The man…" she repeated. She blinked, then looked at Sully. "I don't remember him," she whispered, tears forming in her eyes. "Why don't I remember him?" Her voice held a hint of panic.

"Shh, it's okay," Sully said, knowing it was anything but. "Take your time." Her gaze flicked to Dave, but his face was composed. Neutral. She smiled gently at Jenny. "What were you doing earlier?"

Jenny frowned, looking around the kitchen. "I—I'm not quite sure."

"Why aren't you at school?" Sully tried a different tact.

"Uh, the principal has to do a day each month or so in a class, and today she's teaching my class. She says it keeps her fresh, gives her a chance to see the syllabus in action. She's done it for the past six years." Jenny nodded. "It's a good thing—she can foresee some of the issues when the curriculum changes. So I'm home preparing lessons for next semester."

"Where were you preparing the lessons?" Dave asked.

Jenny blinked. "In—in my living room," she murmured. He rose from his seat and indicated the doorway.

"Would you mind showing us?"

Jenny nodded, and rose, leaving her tea on the table. She led them to her small living room. The coffee table in the center of the room was strewn with papers, and her large diary was opened up to a couple of months away.

Dave nodded, then glanced around the room. "Okay. Can you remember what happened after that?"

Jenny touched her hand to her mouth, then turned to the hallway. "There was a knock at the door..." Her hands trembled, and she pressed her fingers to her temple. "It's so murky. Why can't I remember?"

Dave reached for her hand, and cupped it in both of his. "It's okay, Jenny. We'll figure this out," he reassured her.

Sully watched as her friend seem to draw comfort from Dave's words. He pulled her gently into the hallway. "So, there was a knock at the door...you went to answer it?"

Jenny nodded, and Dave guided her closer to the door. "Can you remember what happened? You would have reached for the doorknob..."

He raised her hand, and Jenny whipped it out of his reach. She stepped closer to Sully, her face pale. "No."

Sully glanced at her. "No? Do you remember something, Jen?"

Jenny shook her head, folding her arms as she looked at her front door with trepidation. "No."

"It's okay, Jenny. He's not here anymore. He can't hurt you."

"Can you remember anything about him, Jen? His hair, his eyes...?"

Jenny caught her lip between her teeth. Sully watched the movement, dismayed. Her friend was so...timid, so afraid. On one level, she could understand—the guy had tried to kill her. But—this was *Jenny*. Her friend was normally so feisty and vivacious, and here she was, too scared to open her own front door.

Memories surfaced, of a similar time when her own heart would stutter at the slightest sound inside her city apartment... She reached for her friend's arm, trying to imbue support and comfort, and feeling nothing rise inside.

Jenny shook her head and took a step back, her gaze fixed on the door.

"Okay, Jenny," Dave said, and Sully was momentarily distracted by the smooth, soothing tone he used. He stepped between Jenny and the door.

"You can remember the knock at the door, you can remember going to answer it. Once you opened the door, what—"

The pounding at the door made them all jump. "Jenny! Jenny, are you okay?"

Sully's shoulders sagged when she recognized Jacob's voice. The doorknob turned, and the door swung inward.

Jenny screamed, collapsing to the floor sobbing, holding her arms up in front of her. "No, please, no," she cried.

Jacob stared down at his sister in stunned shock, and stepped toward her. Jenny screamed again, scrambling back on her hands and feet.

"No! Stop, get out!"

Jacob halted, his mouth agape. Sully glanced between Jenny and the brother her friend adored. Why was she reacting like this?

"Jenny—" Jacob breathed in dismay as flashing red-and-blue lights flickered into the hallway, and Tyler Clinton bounded up the stairs in his sheriff's uniform.

"No!" Jenny screamed, almost hysterical as she backed away.

Dave held out his arms between the siblings, inserting himself between them. "Jenny, it's okay," he said, soothing.

"It was him," she cried, stopping when she backed up

against a wall. Her head tilted, and she drew her knees up as though trying to back her way through the wall.

Sully frowned, looking over at Jacob. He looked so shocked, so hurt, so worried. She looked back at Jenny. Her friend was trembling, pale and teary as she tried to curl up and disappear.

Tyler frowned as he stepped inside the house, and looked between Jenny and Jacob. Sully knelt next to her friend, holding her arms out, and Jenny collapsed against her, sobbing. She lifted her gaze to meet Dave's. His expression was grim as he looked between the Forsyth siblings.

"What happened" Tyler asked curtly, surveying those gathered in the hallway.

Dave shifted his gaze from Sully to Jenny. "Good question."

Chapter 13

Dave followed Sully into her home and watched as she rubbed her neck. He closed the door behind them, locked it, then put a magical ward over it, just for the sake of it. Relief swelled through him as he saw the brief bloom of color, the intricate markings of his spell take hold of the door and its frame before disappearing from view. It had felt damn weird not being able to call on his powers when he was chasing the witch.

She turned to look at him. "Nightcap?"

"Hell, yeah."

She turned on the light to the living room, and he narrowed his eyes. She must have seen his reaction, because she turned off the lights, then waved her hand casually. The candles that were placed around the room sputtered to life, and he smiled his appreciation. She crossed to the white timber cabinet, and his eyebrows rose when she pulled out a bottle of Irish whiskey and two glasses. She poured a measure of the amber liquid into each and handed him a glass. She took a seat in the armchair, and he subsided on the folded out sofa.

"What an awful day," Sully muttered as she took a sip of her drink.

Dave nodded. It had been interesting, explaining to Sheriff Clinton about an intruder the victim believed had been her brother. But he'd chased that bastard, and it wasn't Jacob. Wrong height, wrong weight, wrong hair color—just wrong, wrong and wrong. Jacob had been removed from his sister's home to give her a chance to calm down, but with Jenny being a null, Dave had been unable to do any body or brain scans to figure out what the hell had happened.

"He blurred her memory," Sully murmured, incredulous. "She's a null, and he tricked her." Her lips tightened. "And to make her think it was Jacob—that's just plain low."

"While I think Jacob Forsyth is more than capable of being a dick, you're right, he wasn't the man I chased out of Jenny's kitchen."

He took a sip of his whiskey, enjoying the mild burn as it slid down his throat. "I just wish I'd gotten the bastard."

Sully tilted her head. "So, he just…disappeared?"

Dave nodded, and finished his drink. He didn't like failing—hated it, but he just couldn't figure out how the witch had done his vanishing act.

In null territory.

When he couldn't so much as muster a powerpuff punch.

Sully rose and crossed to her library, waving a hand across the front of the bookcase. Dave watched as the camouflage spell glimmered at the movement to reveal the tomes of magical spells and history.

Sully dragged her finger gently across the spines, and for a moment he was distracted by the graceful movement.

"What are you looking for?" he asked, and rose from the sofa. He placed his empty glass on the end table and crossed to her. She pulled out a book and passed to him, then scanned again, pulling two more volumes from the shelf.

"Something isn't adding up here," she said, as she crossed to the liquor cabinet and snagged up the whiskey bottle. "This guy has used my name—I don't understand that part, or why the Ancestors sent you after me. That's number one," she said, holding up the bottle. She poured another measure in his glass, and one in her own, then placed the bottle on the table.

"Number two, he's able to use magic. Around nulls. That doesn't compute. Nulls void any natural magic. Wolves can't shift, vampires can't fang out, witches can't cast spells."

Dave nodded as he sat down on the sofa again. "I know, that's something that's confusing the crap out of me, too," he admitted.

She nodded, then started to flick through one of the books she held as she sank into her armchair. "So, how is he doing it? There has to be something in these books that can help us figure this out."

He eyed her for a moment. He didn't need to ask her why she was doing this. He'd seen her with her friend. She'd been worried. Jenny had been distraught, clutching on to Sully as she'd given her statement to the sheriff. He and Sully had spent hours with the nulls, and he had even walked the neighborhood again, with some of the deputies, in case they could find some trace of the man who'd managed to enter Jenny's home through her front door, mess with her memory and almost kill her.

When Sully had been sitting with Jenny, he'd been trying to soothe Jacob. The one thing he and Sully had agreed on was not to mention the witch aspect. It didn't make sense—yet. They couldn't explain it, and Dave didn't want the sheriff looking at them as potential suspects and distract the man from pursuing the relevant clues—or interfere with his own objective of finding the witch and sending the bastard to the Other Realm.

Jacob, though, had had a difficult time accepting that his sister believed he'd tried to kill her, and was looking for answers—and Sully had wanted to give them to him, and Dave knew how hard it was for her to bite her tongue.

"They're PBs, obviously," Sully muttered absently as she scanned the pages in front of her.

Dave's eyebrows rose. "Really?"

She nodded, her honey-blond braid sliding across her shoulder. "Yeah. Jacob confirmed it. He told me the Adlers, Forsyths, Sinclairs, Drummonds, Maxwells and Tarringtons are the PB families in their community. A member from each family sits on the council."

Dave blinked. "When did he tell you that?"

"When you helped Jenny up, and I had to tell her brother she wasn't really losing her marbles," Sully said calmly. She winced. "Those were Jacob's words, not mine."

Dave's lips tightened. "So when Jacob told us about the PBs, he just happened to forget to mention he was one of them?" That was damn annoying.

Sully shrugged. "They'll tell us stuff when they trust us. We just need to work harder to earn their trust."

Dave frowned as he glanced down at the old and weathered book he held. "And in the meantime, more of them are in danger." It didn't escape his notice that Jacob Forsyth trusted Sully enough to divulge this information, after pretty much telling him to get lost the night before.

Sully played with her braid, and Dave found himself watching her more than reading from the book in his lap. She turned a page, and he forced himself to look down at the book he held. Yet in a moment, he found his gaze lifting to surreptitiously peek at her again. Her slightly crooked mouth was quirked, and a faint line had appeared between her eyebrows as she read through the spells and histories. For some, it took only a momentary scan. For others, she seemed to catch her lip, as though hopeful she'd found the answer, and then she'd press those sexy lips into a disappointed pout and turn the page.

She glanced up at him, distracted, and he glanced back down at his book.

"What about the Ancestors?"

He blinked at the question that seemed to come out of left field. "What?"

"The Ancestors," she repeated, then rose from her seat. She disappeared into her kitchen, and he heard the tap run in the sink, and then she came back into the living room carrying a bowl of water.

"Can you ask them?"

He put the book off to the side, frowning as she set the bowl down on the floor between them. She slipped her flip-flops off to the side, then sat cross-legged on the floor.

"Ask them what?" He leaned forward, bracing his elbows on his knees as he tried to figure out where she was going with this.

She met his gaze. "The Ancestors directed you to me. They were wrong. Can you ask them for help?"

Dave shook his head briefly, confused as he tried to work through her suggestion until it made sense. He eyed the bowl.

"It's the Ancestors, Sully. They've only ever given me the name, and I take it from there. There's no conversation. It's not like a phone call, where I can chat with them over it."

"Have you ever tried?"

He frowned as he lowered himself to the floor, eyeing the bowl. "You want to scry the Ancestors?" He crossed his legs. He'd never heard of that being done, so he had no idea whether it would work or not—or whether it would just piss off the Ancestors.

Sully shrugged. "It can't hurt to ask, right? This guy is doing stuff that we've never seen before. Surely they can give us a clue."

He gave her a doubtful look, and she responded with an expression full of exasperation. "This guy managed to give you the slip—and I've seen you in action. I even went invisible, and you still caught me. Aren't you interested to see how he managed to evade you?"

He shifted uncomfortably. Admitting to failure yet again was like running a cheese grater over his skin. Damn it, she had a point. He nodded, then settled himself comfortably. Sully did the same, and he closed his eyes, centering his awareness. Once he felt the peace, the warmth of relaxation, he slid his eyes open. He tried to extend his awareness, his senses, to encompass the witch in front of him, but her shields were in place yet again, blocking him off. His brow dipped briefly. It wasn't unusual for witches to combine powers in something like this, but Sully was completely closed off to him. He'd have to do this on his own.

Sully met his gaze, then dipped her finger in the bowl and swirled her finger to create a gentle whirlpool. She murmured a chant in the Old Language, and he shoved aside his surprise at her knowledge and skill, focusing on the water in the bowl that was beginning to cloud over as steam rose from the surface.

Sully kept chanting, and once he could decipher the words, he joined her. The water thickened, and Sully nodded at him. Dave closed his eyes, and using the Old Language, summoned the Ancestors, and asked his question—who was this witch, and where could they find him?

He removed his sunglasses, then opened his eyes. He could feel a coolness sweep over him, the gentle but dizzying sensation as his perception of Sully's living room, of Sully herself, slipped from view, and instead the steam enveloped him. At first it was gentle, its touch against his face whisper-soft, but the pressure increased, and the color faded from white to red. Murky shadows, dark and indistinct, danced around him, weaving and ducking, fading and reappearing. Flashes of light snapped and crackled around him, so bright it hurt his eyes, but he remained steadfast, eyes open, until the light dimmed into that *X* symbol he'd seen carved into flesh. Over and over, the symbol flashed around him, and then he saw a face emerge from the red mist. The features were fuzzy, and he squinted, but no matter how much he tried to focus, the features wouldn't sharpen, but would twist and morph as it got closer, bigger, growing larger the nearer it drew.

"Dave," Sully gasped, and Dave blinked.

The red mist dispersed with a soft hiss, and he had to blink again to snap Sully into focus. She was staring down at the bowl, her expression perturbed.

He glanced down. The clear water they'd started with was now thick and red, and the metallic scent was nearly overpowering.

Blood.

It was expanding in the bowl, creeping up to the lip. "There's so much of it," Sully whispered.

He reached for the bowl, sweeping it up as he rose to his feet and strode into the kitchen. He tipped the blood down the sink and ran the tap to get rid of the liquid that had splattered the sides of the basin.

Sully followed him, and he turned to face her. "Well?" she asked him, curious. "Did it work? What did you see?"

He frowned. "I'm not sure. Red cloud. That symbol, flashing over and over," he told her, his fingers spreading out like mini fireworks. "Then there was this face, but I couldn't see it, the features kept twisting and moving." He gestured to the now clean bowl sitting in the sink. "Then the blood."

She shuddered, and rubbed her hands over her arms. "There was so much of it," she whispered. "What do you think they meant?"

He shrugged. "No idea. I've never tried to contact them before, so…" He winced. "I don't understand their code."

Sully gestured to his chest. "So the Ancestors can freakin' spell stuff out, but use cryptic picture codes for the important stuff. Nice going," she muttered, glaring up at the ceiling, as though talking with them directly.

"That symbol is obviously important," he murmured,

and headed back to the books in the living room, then halted. He turned to her.

"You use your safeguards, even when you're at home?" Why was she so guarded? She certainly had the right— every witch could decline a sharing of powers, it was their prerogative, but it had still been a surprise. He'd felt a companionship with her, a camaraderie, a shared intimacy as they worked together to figure out what the hell was going on. Admittedly, the magical block had made him realize he'd taken that for granted, and now was uncertain just how much they could or would share.

Her expression was surprised for a moment, then understanding crossed her features. "Yes. I guess it's just reflex." She scratched her head. "I'm sorry, I didn't even think to try to link for the scry." She indicated the bowl. "It's been so long, I just instinctively do it by myself."

He turned to face her fully. "How long has it been, Sully?" Witches were funny creatures. Mostly, they gathered in covens, but there were plenty of outliers, and one could certainly reserve their right not to link. Sully, though, seemed too sociable, too connected with the well-being of others to be so isolated. He'd seen her with Jenny, the amount of times she'd reached out to touch her friend, and the frustration on her face when whatever she'd wanted to do to help her was blocked. He'd seen her comfort her friend, hold her, reassure her… She genuinely cared for others, and that kind of witch seemed conducive to sharing, to linking and bonding. It was almost as though she was fighting her own instinctive nature.

Sully shrugged as she stepped toward the living room. "Four, maybe five years."

He reached out and clasped her arm, halting her. His

ears popped, and the hairs rose on his arms and the back of his neck as their magical fields collided once again, awakening and enhancing his senses. He blinked, then swallowed, trying to ignore the physical sensations bombarding his body. He wanted to understand—no, needed to understand why a witch, why Sully, would bury herself in a place where she couldn't use her powers.

"Why?" he asked hoarsely.

She hesitated, and he wasn't sure if she realized her slow shift toward him. "I needed to," she said to him. "I needed...space."

It was that line. *I need space. It's not you, it's me...* he'd heard it a dozen times, and used it himself at least a dozen more. Realization, swift and unavoidable, hit him. "Who was he?" he asked. He slid his hand down her arm and loosely grasped her hand. It was meant to be comforting. Friendly. But her smooth skin beneath his touch was distracting.

She lifted her shoulders in a casual, dismissive gesture. "He was nobody important."

"He must have been, for you to hide yourself here for four, five years," he pointed out. He slid his thumb back and forth over the back of her hand, enjoying the feel of her silken skin.

She frowned up at him, her blue eyes darkening. "I'm not hiding, Dave." She gave a slight shake of her head in denial. Her gaze drifted to his chest, then down to where their hands joined.

His eyebrows rose, and he shifted toward her. "Oh, really? From what I can tell, you're the only witch in this area—"

"You can't know that for sure. This is null territory," she interrupted. "You could have a whole coven here, and they wouldn't be able to practice or reveal their talents. We wouldn't even know."

"Is that why you're here? To conceal your talents?"

"I—" her gaze dropped to his lips, and then she met his gaze again. "I'm not concealing my talents," she said in a near whisper. Her breath hitched, then released in the sexiest sigh, the sound curling down deep inside him, flooding him with a molten desire that had him hardening in his jeans.

How could she make that sound so damn suggestive? So hot? He tried to focus on the conversation, but felt he was losing that battle fast. "Are you sure?" He stepped closer, and brought her hand up to rest against his chest.

She swallowed, and he smiled when he heard the audible gulp. He slid his other hand beneath her braid, cupping the back of her neck. He could see her nipples tighten against the cotton of her camisole, knew he wasn't the only one affected by this attraction, this fascination between them.

"Show me," he whispered, leaning down to kiss the side of her jaw. He inhaled, and her scent, roses, vanilla and sunshine, hit him like a drug.

She rested her hand on his waist for a moment, her eyes dark with confusion. "Show you what?"

"Show me you, Sully," he whispered, his lips trailing down her neck. She angled her head to the side, exposing more of her neck.

"What—what you see is what you get," she murmured, then moaned when his lips found that delicious indent between her neck and collarbone.

His hand slid from where it cupped her head down her back, and he halted when he found her belt with the concealed sheaths, and the blades they contained. His lips curved against her skin. "Oh, I think there is more to you than meets the eye," he murmured, then raked his teeth gently against her shoulder.

She trembled, a slight quivering that set off an answering throb deep inside him, hardening his cock. She slid her arms up over his chest to twine around his neck, her nails raking through his short hair. Her fingers clenched in his hair, pulling his head back up.

"I'll show you me if you show me you," she whispered, then stood on tiptoe to kiss him.

Chapter 14

Sully parted her lips against his, and was rewarded when his tongue slid inside to tangle with hers. His arms enveloped hers, pressing her against his body. She could feel the strength of those arms, those muscles, against the sides of her breasts, could feel the hardness of his chest and hips against her, and could feel the throbbing hard length of him against her stomach.

She could sense his curiosity, his tenderness, as well as the tidal wave of desire and arousal. He'd asked her about her shields. Suggested she was hiding. With Dave, though, there was no hiding. There was no defense against his overwhelming presence, with *feeling*, and there was no way she could fight the burning attraction she felt for this man. It was hot, it was immediate and it was undeniable. And she didn't want to hide anymore.

Her hands trailed down the column of his neck, tracing the breadth of those massive shoulders, and trailing over the soft fabric of his T-shirt. She angled her head, and he deepened the kiss, sucking and nipping with a skill that had her desire pooling in her panties as she arched against him.

"Oh, sweetness," he moaned, kissing his way to her jaw and down her neck. Her head leaned back, and he pulled her tighter against him, leaning forward so that her world tilted. His hands slid down and cupped her butt, and he picked her up, turning to seat her on the kitchen counter.

Her legs wound around his hips, pulling him into the cradle of her groin, and she moaned when she felt him, hot and hard, against her. She tugged at the hem of his T-shirt, and he leaned back, hips still pressed to hers, and helped her pull the garment over his head. Her eyes widened at having his chest so close, and for a moment she was content to place her palms against his warm skin. The mark over his heart looked almost healed, and she traced it very gently.

"So much pain," she murmured.

He winked, grinning as he ducked his head. "Nah, just a tickle." He took her lips in a hard kiss. His hands played briefly over her shoulders before hooking the thin straps of her cami and tugging them slowly down her arms.

She shrugged out of the straps, sighing when he dragged her against him, her breasts mashed against him, and they both moaned. He kissed her shoulder, nipping at her gently, and she shuddered, her breasts swelling at the sharp but seductive sensation. She dragged her nails down his back as he kissed and licked his way across her chest while he slid his hand under her long skirt, dragging the fabric up her legs. She trembled as his hand skimmed over her knee, gliding up her thigh. Liquid heat pooled between her legs, and her pulse thudded in her ears.

He got to midthigh, then halted. He lifted his head, eyebrows raised. "You're full of surprises, aren't you?" he gasped, before taking her lips again. He fumbled with the leather strap of the sheath she'd strapped to her leg, and she laughed breathlessly.

"Sorry, I forgot that one."

He undid the tie, and she shuddered at the caress of leather against her sensitive skin when he tugged it away from her. He placed the sheath, with her custom-made push-dagger on the bench beside them. He chuckled.

"You are so dangerous," he murmured, gazing into her eyes, his hands rising to cradle her jaw. There was a humor, but there was also warmth, admiration and a little concern, all bombarding her with his touch.

She looked up at him, feeling the answering smile on her lips. "You have no idea," she whispered, then took his lips.

He sighed against her mouth, their tongues tangling. He lowered a hand to her chest, and she gasped, arching her back when he covered her breast with his warm palm. He pressed back, their hips rubbing against each other, and she could feel his hardness, separated by the folds of her skirt and the denim of his jeans.

Heat. Desire. Tight arousal. It hit her, and she wasn't sure if it was him, or her, or that they were just so perfectly in sync.

Panting, she reached for his belt, and within seconds she'd undone it, as well as his button fly. His hands gripped her body as she reached inside his jeans, and her lips curved against his when her fingers slid beneath his boxer briefs and found him.

He growled softly, and she gasped when he pinched her nipple, just enough to make her tremble with delight. It was as though the floodgates opened. She pushed at his jeans. He tugged at her skirt, and she felt his fingers slide under her panties, felt the brief tug of the cotton as the fabric gave, and then she moaned when she felt those fingers against her, then inside her.

He groaned, then took her lips in a kiss so carnal it stole her breath. He played with her, strummed her, and she shook as she used her feet to shove his jeans down his legs. She gasped when she felt the tension coil inside her. Her nipples tightened, as his tongue slid against hers, his fingers moving with ease inside her, and then his thumb found that secret little pleasure nub, and everything tightened, tightened, tightened, until she exploded. Sensations, so sharp, so crystalized, cascaded over her. He positioned himself between her legs and entered her smoothly.

She tore her lips away from his, crying out with the pleasure as he thrust. Over and over, the waves of intense bliss crashed. Swirls of colors, sparks, everything was exploding—around her, inside her, until he finally groaned his release, his head back, the cords of his neck standing out as he found his own pleasure inside her.

He slid his arm around her waist, pulling her up tight against him, chest to chest, heart to heart, as their panting subsided. He hugged her, and she could feel him. Inside her, around her, it was all warmth and tenderness, an intimate gentleness with the steel edge of determined protectiveness.

She'd never felt safer.

Dave blinked. Hair. Honey-gold hair. All over his face. He brushed it away, blinking some more, then shifted, drawing his thigh up against the warm curves enfolded in his arms.

Sully.

His eyes opened.

Sully. They'd made fireworks last night. He'd seen them. Lots of pops of colors, sparks... While he wasn't shy with women, and thought he could hold his own in the sack, he'd never quite experienced fireworks before with a woman.

He lifted his head slightly, shaking away the last of the tendrils that seemed to want to cling to him. She was asleep in his arms, her back to his chest, her butt resting—he sucked in a breath. Damn, she felt good in his arms.

They were on the foldout sofa, and sunlight streamed in through the bay windows. They'd tried to make it to her bed, but somehow got distracted.

Very distracted. Twice.

His lips curved, and he dipped his head to press a kiss to her neck. She sighed and smiled as she scooted closer. Her stomach growled, and Dave chuckled as he caressed the curve of her hip.

She turned in his arms, her eyes opening, and he pressed a kiss to her lips. "Good morning," he murmured.

She smiled. "Good mor—" she yawned, then blinked "—morning."

"Feel like pancakes?" He was ravenous, and her stomach was making all sorts of hungry noises.

She grinned. "Are you cooking?"

"Yep," he said, and gave her another long kiss. When he drew back she sighed and stretched, then nodded.

"Sure, pancakes sound wonderful."

Dave reached for his sunglasses and slid them on,

then rolled off the foldout sofa and snagged up his boxer briefs, hopping into them as he walked through to the kitchen. Within minutes he had a pancake mix going—they were his specialty—and started to set up the counter for breakfast.

Sully walked in. She was wearing his T-shirt, the navy blue bringing out the blue of her eyes. Her hair was a tussled tangle, her features soft and relaxed. The shirt hit her midthigh, and he paused for a moment, taking his fill of her. She had the longest, sexiest legs he could ever remember seeing in a woman.

He watched as she crossed to the fridge and leaned in to grab the juice, the T-shirt riding up a little to expose a hint of butt cheek. He swallowed. She was a beautiful woman. He glanced back down at his pancakes. They were bubbling. He flipped them, his gaze briefly diverting back to the domestic, disheveled goddess behind him, and was pleasantly surprised when the pancakes landed back in the pan.

He smiled as he got the plates ready for serving. They didn't converse as she got glasses and poured the juice. They worked alongside each other in companionable silence, and he smiled when she caressed his back as she passed. He pulled her back for a kiss, enjoying the feel of her against him, so scantily clad in his T-shirt. The pancake batter in the pan popped and fizzed, and he drew back, winking at Sully's grin as she backed away toward the pantry. This felt…nice. Normal. But a normal he'd never had before. A cozy kitchen, a sexy woman with a heart of gold and a body built for sin. He could get used to this.

He halted midscoop of the pancake. What?

He could not get used to this. He had a job that translated to here today, gone tomorrow. He had a home and business in Irondell, and a task that meant the Ancestors would always take priority in his life. There was no room for a woman, for a relationship, no matter how tempting playing house could be.

He flipped the pancake onto a plate and poured a ladleful of batter into the pan. Sully started to hum as she moved around the kitchen, and he saw her place a bottle of maple syrup on the kitchen counter, along with a basket of strawberries. She even did a cute little dance move when she thought he wasn't watching.

He focused on the pan, watching as the air bubbles popped on the mix. He liked this. He *really* liked this. It was so tempting, just to reach out and kiss her again, feed her strawberries in an indulgent, dreamy little episode of domestic codependency.

And that scared the ever-lovin' crap out of him.

He quickly served up the last of the pancakes. His job—his calling—wasn't something he could just walk away from. He figured once a Witch Hunter, always a Witch Hunter. Everyone assumed his tattoo parlor in Irondell was his main focus, but they were wrong. It was the sideline, the business that bubbled along when he wasn't hunting witches. Eventually, though, his luck would run out. Somewhere along the line, he'd face a witch who was faster, stronger, more powerful…and it would be he crossing to the Other Realm. And another Witch Hunter would be assigned the hit and carry on the duties.

This moment, this side trip down fantasy lane, was exactly that—a fantasy. And he didn't do fantasy. He didn't drift away on daydreams, wishing for what couldn't possibly be. What he did—well, it was a special low, dealing with the excrement of the witch world, but damn it, it was necessary, and he believed in it, believed in the necessity, and that the bad was done for the greater good. He shouldn't be here, cooking breakfast and stealing kisses. This fantasy, this illusion of a different life, was a recipe for a whole world of hurt—at his hands.

"Wow, they look great," Sully said, eyes widening when she saw the stack of pancakes. She smiled as she sat on the stool. "I'm famished."

He gave her a small smile as he sat down next to her. He picked up his cutlery, but sat for a moment, eyeing the food on his plate. He'd lost his appetite.

Sully frowned. "What's wrong?" She eyed the pancakes suspiciously. "What did you to them?"

His lips quirked. "They're fine. Tuck in." He cut out a bit of pancake and popped it into his mouth, his gaze resting briefly on the woman next to him. Sully deserved to be someone's priority. Not someone's booty call, not someone's "between jobs", but someone's first, last and always. He'd eventually hurt her. He'd let her down when he'd have to pursue another witch over spending time with her. Or worse, what he did for the Ancestors could wind up hurting *her*.

He stabbed more pancake onto his fork and shoved it in his mouth. Damn. This sucked. Domestic bliss was obviously some sort of weird mind-meld crap designed to make you assess your life decisions and cry.

Sully eyed him closely as she chewed, then swallowed. "Is everything all right, Dave?"

"It's fine," he said, then put his cutlery down on the plate. "No. No, it's not fine." He turned to look at her. "You and I—we shouldn't have…done. What we did. That." He gestured to the kitchen counter, and then the living room.

Sully's cheeks heated, and she glanced down at her plate. "Oh." She frowned. "You didn't...enjoy it?" She blinked, then waved her hand. "Don't answer that."

His eyes widened. "We did it three times. Yeah. I enjoyed it. A *lot*." Too much. "We just...shouldn't have."

Sully kept her gaze steadfastly on the glass of juice as she reached for it. "I see," she said. Her voice was low. Calm. Like, dead calm. He glanced at her. Her lips were pursed. Just a little, but that cute crooked little pout of hers was just a little more pronounced.

"No, I don't think you do, Sully. I have—"

"A job to do," she interrupted. She nodded. "I get it." She rose from her stool and placed her plate on the bench with just a little too much force.

"This—" he gestured to the kitchen, to her. "I can't do this. And I shouldn't have done that."

"Because of your job," she said, and folded her arms as she leaned against the doorjamb. "How does sex with me interfere with your job, exactly?" She tilted her head, and although her expression was curious, he could see the darkening anger in her eyes.

Sex. She'd called it sex. They'd made fireworks. It had been more than just sex. Hadn't it? Dave forced himself to focus on the question, and not the quiver of uncertainty that perhaps he was the only one who'd felt the impact of what they'd done, the magical coalescence of their power...

"I need to track down a killer," he told her solemnly. "I'm here having breakfast with you, when I should be out hunting that witch." He rose from his stool and leaned his palms on the counter—the counter where they'd first made incredible, firework-inducing love.

"That other night, when Amanda Sinclair was killed—

I should have been out there, hunting, not in here, kissing you."

She gaped at him for a moment. "Are you saying it's my fault Amanda Sinclair was murdered?" Her voice emerged as a hoarse rasp. She folded her arms.

He gaped. "No! God, no! No, not your fault—*my* fault. I should have been out there. I should have been looking. My fault, Sully, not yours." He pressed his thumb to his chest. "None of this has anything to do with you. It's all on me."

Her eyes narrowed. "Ri-ight," she said slowly, although her tone didn't quite suggest agreement. "So this," she said, unfolding one arm to encompass her kitchen, "this was all what? An *oops*?" her voice rose on that last word, and he winced.

O-kay. He'd screwed this up. Monumentally. And he'd managed to minimize the first real emotional connection he'd had with a woman in years. Ever. "No. Yes. Hell, sort of."

She gaped at him. Then she held up a finger. "Okay, first, the correct answer to that was supposed to be a hell, no."

"What we shared meant something to me," he said through gritted teeth. "And that is the problem. I'm not supposed to feel this—" he held up his palms, shrugging. "I don't even know what *this* is, that's how foreign it is," he exclaimed. "I'm supposed to up and go when the Ancestors call, and if we keep going down this—" and again he gestured, palms up "—then I won't want to answer the Ancestors' call."

She stared at him for a moment, and that cute little crooked pout of hers got more crooked, the tighter she pursed her lips. "I see."

His eyes narrowed. "See, I get worried when you say that," he said. "I think you see something that I don't mean."

"Okay, well, let me break it down for you," Sully said, her hands dropping to her waist. The position hiked up his shirt, exposing more of her tanned, toned thighs. "You are hiding from this," she said, and gestured between them. "You feel something, so you are running. You're using your vocation as an excuse to avoid a personal relationship. With…me. You don't trust. You don't trust me, you don't trust us."

His eyes rounded. "Trust?" He placed his hands on hips. "Really? Me? Trust issues?" He found he could only repeat the hot words, so surprised was he by her comments. He was sure he'd get around to forming some rational response.

"Yes. You. Trust issues. You didn't want to tell Sheriff Clinton about the killer witch. Reform law recognizes your authority as a Witch Hunter, Dave—just like they would a guardian enforcer hunting down a werewolf, or a vampire guardian hunting a rogue vampire. Tyler's not going to arrest you for enforcing tribal law on one of your own kind. But you don't want his help—because you don't trust him?"

Dave frowned and opened his mouth to argue, but she was already talking.

"You don't tell the nulls there's a null-killing witch coming after them, you don't want to trust them with the information and still allow you to hunt that witch down. And if I hadn't enhanced that white lie you told about us dating with the breakup factor, you wouldn't have allowed me to tag along in your investigation—because you don't trust me. I'm a witch who wants to help, and you don't trust me to do that. Now, you're starting to feel something, and you don't trust *us*. You want me to believe that all I am to you is some quick screw that you can't get involved with."

"Hey, there was nothing quick about us," he told her, and she shot him an exasperated glare. "And you're not completely wrong," he allowed, holding his hands up. "You're right. I don't trust the sheriff. Nice guy," he said quickly, "but once I approach him, I have to follow Reform rules, and they don't work, not for us. He'd want us to arrest the witch, and have him stand trial with Reform peers—who may or may not be witches, when we already have a higher authority who have made a decision. I trust Tyler—to do exactly what his job tells him he has to do, which doesn't align with what I have to do."

He sighed. "The nulls—I'm not sure about them. Someone is walking among them. Both Amanda Sinclair and Jenny opened their front door to this guy and let him walk right in. He's somehow been accepted by that community, and is able to walk freely among them, so yeah, you're right, I don't trust them. But you…"

He stepped around the counter. "I have never met anyone who is so damn trusting, and that scares me."

Her frown deepened, and he paused, searching for the right words. "You…you're amazing. You're so…big-hearted," he said, shrugging. It was the only word he could think for her. "You can't help yourself, you need to help others. You try to ease people's pain—I saw you with Jenny. You were so frustrated that you couldn't use your empath powers on her and ease her suffering—yeah, I saw that." He nodded at her shift in position, her disconcerted expression. "You tended to my wound, when I'd done everything that should have made you run in the opposite direction. You're wanting to hunt down this killer—to prevent him from hurting others. You're helping me, because I need it. I saw you at the funeral, Sully. When you take on the pain of others, you put yourself at risk. When I visited your shop, you made me tea."

"After I tried to skewer you with a fork," she argued.

He nodded. "Okay, granted. But that's my point. It's so easy to get past your defenses. You sense, therefore you trust, regardless of whether I'm worthy of that trust. You don't really know me," he told her, and he had to force the words out of his throat. "You don't know what I've done. You're right—I don't trust easily, but in my line of work, that's a survival skill, not a flaw." He ran his hand through his short hair. "Which is why I have to leave. The longer I stick around, the more danger I put us both in."

Her blue gaze was dark and solemn, and she sighed. "I would never, ever, beg or force someone to stay with me against their will," she said quietly. "You want to leave, leave." She levered herself away from the wall, and dragged his shirt over her head, and tossed it to him.

He caught it to his chest, still warm from her body. He looked at her, standing naked and proud, her shoulders back, her chin up. And no, he damn well didn't *want* to leave.

"I hope you find your witch," she told him sincerely. "Be safe."

She turned, walked across the short hall to her bedroom and closed the door behind her.

He turned in her kitchen, holding the warm garment to his chest, and stared at the abandoned plates on the counter, the sullied remnants of a glimpse of heaven.

He'd blown it. He blinked, then turned and walked down the hallway to the living room. He scooped up his

gear and was dressed in minutes. He looked around for
his jacket, and realized he'd left it in the back of Sully's
car the night before.

He glanced down the hallway, toward the bend that
led to Sully's bedroom. This was lousy. He didn't want
to leave her like this, thinking…thinking what? That he
thought she was just a brief dalliance? Or that he didn't
trust her?

His lips tightened. Maybe that was for the best. If
she knew how he felt, that he wanted nothing more than
to walk down that hall and crawl into bed with her and
never, ever leave—would that change the situation?
Would it make her feel better, or worse?

He closed his eyes, letting his senses drift down to
that bedroom at the end of the hall. He could sense the
peace and tranquility of her room, and he tried to sense
her, to comfort her. He gently searched for her essence—
a spark exploded in front of him, and he flew across the
room, flipping back over the sofa.

Ouch. He looked up from his position on the floor.
Okay. She was pissed. He could respect that. He'd knocked,
and she'd sent him flying. He got the message. Go away.

He rolled to his feet, pulling up his backpack as he did,
and strode out of the house. He shoved his backpack into
one of the panniers on his bike, then crossed to the trunk
of Sully's car for his jacket. He shook his head. Sully had
left the rear window down. The woman had no regard for
securing herself or her possessions. He reached in for his
jacket and tugged at the sleeve. It caught on the lid of a
long metal box in her trunk. He tugged harder, and the
jacket pulled free. The lid clanged open, and Dave froze
when he saw the contents.

What the—? He reached in and pulled the box closer,

frowning at the weight of the darn thing. He peered inside, his jaw dropping.

A supply of swords, axes, knives and arrows—along with a heap of deadly looking blades, gleamed in the light of day. A cloth bag sat in one corner of the box, and when he pulled at the fabric, he heard a clink, then saw the treasure of Reform dollars winking up at him. A lot of them.

He heard the soft slap of flip-flops on the veranda, and looked up at the woman, that sweet, naive, gullible woman, standing on the top step, hands on hips, as she glared down at him. He glanced back down at the mobile armory and cash stash in the trunk of her car, then back up at her.

"Who *are* you?" he exclaimed.

Chapter 15

Sully padded down the steps and across the yard. "I'm a cutler," she responded shortly, and reached for the lid of the box. First he'd dumped her—although they'd only had a one-night stand, so she didn't think that was the technical term for the one-night-wonder-lover walking out on her. Skunk, maybe. Now he was snooping through her stuff. Dave's large hand flashed out to catch the lid, preventing it from closing.

"This is not cutlery," he exclaimed, pulling out a stiletto blade.

"It's a knife," she pointed out.

"That's one hell of a knife," he remarked. He replaced the stiletto and removed one of her short swords. "Why do you have these in your car, Sully?"

She shrugged. "I made them."

"All of them?" he asked in disbelief, scanning the weapons. She tried to close the lid again, and he braced his hand against the lid, then delved his hand into the cloth bag and pulled out a fistful of coins.

"Where did you get this money?" he rasped.

"Weren't you leaving?"

"Where, Sully?" His voice was low, grim. Determined.

She considered lying, but decided against it. "I made that, too."

He dropped the coins, and closed his eyes as he pinched the bridge of his nose. "Oh. My. God."

She rolled her eyes. "It's not a big deal, Dave."

He removed his sunglasses, and his eyes opened to slits as he peered closely at her. "It's not?"

His voice was quiet, almost conversational. Reasonable. Receptive. And he'd removed the dark lenses that hid his eyes. He seemed open. Approachable. "No, it's not."

He lifted his chin in the direction of the box. "So, that's not really what it looks like?"

She paused, looking at him, then the box. "What does it look like?"

"Well, it looks like you're selling counterfeit cash and weapons," he said.

"No," she said. "I give the money away, not sell it, and I'm not an arms dealer." She thought about it for a moment. She did make weapons on commission, though. "Uh, technically, I might be an arms dealer, but only a little bit." She pinched her thumb and forefinger together to show just how little an arms dealer she was. The thought almost brought a smile to her face, but Dave's expression was so serious she didn't think he'd see the humor in it.

His mouth gaped open for a moment. "Only a *little* bit?" his voice emerged as a high-pitched whisper.

"Well, if I'm being completely honest—"

"Please—"

"I do make weapons for a price, but it's only on a commission basis."

"—don't tell me."

Sully blinked as his words sank in. "Oh."

Dave's shoulders sagged. "You told me."

"You did ask."

"I wanted deniability."

Dave slung his jacket over the rim of the trunk and
braced both hands against the car.

"You're not a cutler," he said, shaking his head.

"I am a cutler," she told him, then shrugged. "I also
make…other stuff." She leaned back against the car and
folded her arms. She'd quickly changed into a cotton
camisole and a skirt, and had come outside to make sure
he left—or so she told herself. It wasn't because she'd
wanted one last glimpse of the man who'd given her fireworks and made her feel safe.

Four years.

"Ah," he said slowly as comprehension spread across
his face. "These are the coins you were talking about,
when we first met."

She frowned. "What?"

"You mentioned coins on the beach, as though you
were surprised the Ancestors had sent me after you for
that."

"Oh." She vaguely remembered asking him about it,
and feeling confused and hurt that the Ancestors would
sic a Witch Hunter on her for such a trivial matter. "Yeah."
She eyed the way his biceps flexed as he gripped the
edge of her trunk window. She wasn't going to stare. She
wasn't going to think about them wrapped around her, or
the way she felt when she was in those arms…the passion,

the sense of protection. She had to remind herself he was on his way out. Leaving. Adios, amigo.

And she was going to be just fine. This was not a—she pressed her palm to her chest. God, she hurt. No, damn it. This was no big deal.

"Why?"

She blinked, his question bringing her back to the matter at hand. The serious matter at hand. She hadn't expected him to find her...stuff. Only a few people knew about her sideline business, and it was weird, having to explain it to the man she'd shared a bed with. Well, sofa. Kitchen counter. Whatever. This wasn't a conversation she'd expected to have. Especially not when she really wanted to go curl up in bed and cry.

"Why?" She eyed the drive. "I really thought you were leaving," she grumbled.

He turned to face her. "Sully."

She narrowed her eyes against the glint of morning light. "You want me to tell you?"

He nodded.

"Really?"

He nodded again.

"But Dave, I'd have to trust you with some sensitive information," she said, "and I'd hate for you to think I'm too naive and gullible." She glared at him meaningfully, and his lips tightened as he recognized his words thrown back him.

"Sully."

She levered herself away from the car. "No, Dave. You can't have it both ways. You accuse me of being too trusting, while you won't trust anyone, and then you demand me tell you what you want to know." She leaned forward. "Well, guess what? Trust works both ways, buddy."

She turned to walk away, but stopped when his hand gripped her arm. Not enough to hurt, but enough to turn her to face him. Worry. Genuine concern, flooded her. Damn it, he was doing it again, without even realizing it.

"Are you in trouble, Sully?" he asked earnestly.

"Not if you don't tell the sheriff," she answered honestly.

His exasperation, tinged with frustration, pricked at her, but she could still feel his very real worry. For her. No. He didn't get to do that. He didn't get to worry about her, or feel that warm concern for her, because that made this whole walking out thing really, really suck. But obviously, he wasn't walking out, not until he had some answers.

She sighed. "Look, you've probably noticed the nulls here are really struggling. The fishing season hasn't really hit the high mark, and we have families who are struggling to put food on the table. This," she said, jerking her chin in direction of the coin bag, "is just to get them by until the fish stock picks up. That's all. That's all it's ever been." She wasn't some criminal mastermind, for crying out loud.

His mild relief warmed her, and she pulled her arm from his grip. She didn't want to feel his emotions, didn't want to understand. She wanted to hold on to her anger from earlier. Because if she held on to that anger, the hurt couldn't touch her.

"The weapons?" he asked.

She paused as she considered her answer. "I like weapons," she answered in a low voice. They made her feel... safe. "And I think Jenny and others can use them, right about now."

Dave sighed, his lips firm. "I don't like this."

"You don't have to," she said, stepping away from the car. "You're leaving, remember?"

"Sully, I don't want to leave, I *have* to leave. Every minute I spend with you, everyone else is in danger from this witch, including you."

Damn it. She glanced down at her flip-flops. Buried beneath his need to flee she could see his annoying, frustrating, bloody-minded logic. It didn't mean she had to like it.

Four years.

The words kept repeating themselves over and over in her head. Four years since she'd been with a man, and when she finally surrendered, when she shared something of herself, he ran.

Rode a motorcycle. Whatever.

"Well, don't let me stop you," she whispered. She cleared her throat, then looked out past her front yard toward the headland. "I have things to do, too."

She could see him out of the corner of her eye. His expression was somber, his gaze an almost brilliant silver against his tanned skin and close-cropped beard. She wasn't going to meet his gaze, though. She didn't want him to see how shredded up she was inside.

Silly, silly girl. She'd gone and gotten hooked on a Witch Hunter.

"I'll, uh, get going, then." He stood there for a moment, waiting for her response.

She nodded. Her pose was casual, arms folded, but she could feel the tiny little arcs pressing into her skin as her fingernails dug into her biceps. She wasn't going to cry.

At least, not until after he'd left.

He turned and walked toward his bike, slipping his leather jacket on as he went. He got to his bike, then paused, his hand resting on the handlebar. Then he abruptly turned and stalked over to her. She straightened, frowning, and her eyes widened when his arms slid around her waist, pulling her in for a hot kiss.

Frustration. Anger. Lust. Sorrow. All bombarded her at his touch, his tongue tangling with hers. It was quick, but it was a whirlwind of emotion and passion that left her breathless when he lifted his head. He tilted his forehead against hers.

"I'm sorry," he whispered. He stepped away, and this time he didn't look back when he reached his bike. He slid his helmet on over his head, straddled his bike, and within too few seconds he was riding out of her driveway.

Sully stood where she was, shoulders sagging, by the trunk of her station wagon. She listened as the sound of his bike slowly diminished, to be taken over by seagulls, crashing waves and the sound of cicadas looking for their mates.

Tears blurred her vision. She had done so well. She'd avoided guys—especially the strong, dominant kind of guy. She'd managed to secure her heart, her safety, her *sanity…* She straightened her shoulders. No. She wasn't going to fall apart again. She wasn't going to surrender her peace of mind, her independence, her identity, to a man. Never again.

She turned back to the house. She hadn't been lying to Dave. She did have things to do, and a delivery to make. He was going to pursue this witch on his own. He'd made that clear.

Well, she hadn't said anything about stopping her own search for this bastard. This guy was hurting her friends, and she had every intention of stopping him—with or without Dave's help.

* * *

Dave smiled at the librarian who brought forth another old book from the archives and placed it with the others on the table at which he sat. "This is the last one, and contains the first census records since Reformation," she told him in a hushed tone. He glanced about. It must be a reflex for the woman, as he was the only person in the records section of the library.

"Thanks." He summoned forth a slight wisp of power. She was human, and there were no nulls in the library that he could sense. "If there is anything else you can think of that will show me the family trees of the nulls, let me know."

She smiled at him sweetly as she nodded. "If I think of anything else on null families in the area, I'll let you know." He watched as she walked away, her low heels making a slight clack-clack as she lowered her reading glasses. She tucked a strand of gray hair behind her ear as she crossed to the catalogs.

Dave opened the large-paged book. The pages were divided in columns, with neat, meticulous script detailing the names, ages and connections of the residents of Serenity Cove since the town was recognized as part of Reformation society.

He placed one hand on the pieces of paper the librarian had given him to make notes on, and another on the book. There were lots of pages, and more volumes to sift through. It would take him hours, if not days, to sift through all of this on his own.

A little voice whispered that he didn't have to do it on his own, that Sully wanted to help, and that she could get the nulls to reveal the names he was looking for.

He lifted his chin. Well, that would dangerous. For

everyone. He'd never had to rely on anyone else to do his job. Witch Hunters worked alone. He'd never had a partner work a hit with him before. Nor had that partner wanted to bring in a whole damn community to help, either.

No. He was on his own. It was better this way. Less... danger. To Sully, anyway.

He closed his eyes, summoning his powers. He murmured a reveal and transfer spell, and could feel the pages warm beneath his hand. He raised his hands from the surface, slowly opening his eyes.

Names on the page started to glow, and he watched as the glow drifted out of the book and onto the piece of paper. Names, dates and connections—they all imprinted on the paper, giving him a list of the purebloods in the area since the town's formation. The pages started to flip, faster and faster, as the names were pulled forth. More books opened, more glowing references. He sat back and waited until the last name landed on the paper, and then he murmured a genealogy spell. He watched as the names reconfigured on the page. Some names faded—individuals who had already passed away.

It took a while, and it was probably early afternoon by the time he had a list of purebloods currently residing in the Serenity Cove area.

He rose from the desk, then waved a hand at the books at the table, sending them back to their homes among the shelves, to save the little old lady at the desk some work. He walked up to thank her, but kept his mouth shut when he heard her snore. He walked out to his bike, opened up his pannier and removed his map of the area. He spread it out on the seat of his bike, then bent down and scooped up some dirt from the ground. Holding his clenched fist over the map, he glanced at the first name on the list, murmured a quick location spell, and let the dirt fall out of his hand in a measured funnel. Within seconds he had the address, and within a minute he was riding out of the Serenity Cove library parking lot.

Chapter 16

"Again," Sully instructed, then brought the wooden blade down toward Jenny's chest in a low-handed grip. Jenny blocked with her arm, pushed Sully's arm outward and stepped in close. Jenny hesitated, then frowned.

"I can't remember the next step," she admitted.

Sully reached for Jenny's other arm. "Your hand. Bring it up and into my armpit—" she stopped talking when her friend followed through with the movements, and was able to bring the practice knife in under her outstretched arm, just beneath the armpit. "Good."

She glanced down at the row of ten or so adults who'd accompanied Jenny over, and were now lined up in her front yard. Kids, including Noah and his sister, were sitting up on the steps of the front veranda watching, or else had taken their cue from the adults and were play wrestling. "Okay, let's do it again."

"So this is supposed to help us, huh?" Jenny said, as she faced off and started to go through the steps. From what Sully had seen, when she'd piggybacked on Dave's vision of Amanda Sinclair's murder, and from what she'd seen when she and Dave had interrupted Jenny's attack, the killer got his victim on their back on the ground, then delivered the death blow. She was giving the group of purebloods that Jenny had managed to convince to come over for defensive training some choreographed moves to fend off a similar attack that would get them into that kill position.

"Yep." She'd shown them a couple of moves, and was getting them to practice, over and over again. She could hear the clang of metal against metal out in the backyard. Jacob was showing some of the men how to use some of their fishing gear in defensive movements. Jenny was still wary around her brother, and so Sully and Jacob had decided it was best if he was out of sight, out of mind for this.

Jenny looked up at the sound of the mock fighting coming from around the back. "I wish I could remember," she said quietly as Sully slowly made her go through the defensive motions again.

Sully nodded. "We'll figure it out. But you do know that Jacob would never hurt you, right?"

Jenny hesitated, then nodded. "I know. On a rational level, I know. But there's something up here," she said, tapping her temple, "some glitch, and I keep—I keep having these flashes."

Sully narrowed her eyes. "What kind of flashes?"

Jenny performed the block, and a smooth shift to bring the knife up to mock stab her under the arm. Sully smiled and stepped back, assuming the attack position again.

"His face, but—not his eyes. It's…it's so weird." Jenny's lips tightened as she met Sully's gaze. "I'm a null. This crap has never happened to me before. It's not supposed to happen." She shook her head. "If I didn't know better, I'd say it's…magic." Jenny shuddered. "But then, never having experienced it, I wouldn't know. It's just wrong as all crap."

Sully blinked, then averted her gaze. "We'll figure it out, Jen." After how close her friend had come be being viciously murdered, Sully was even more determined to track down this damn killer witch.

"How the hell do you know this stuff?" Jenny panted as Sully repeated the attack, gradually getting faster and faster.

"I learned it a few years ago," Sully said, then held up a hand. "Okay, let's try something else."

She lay on the ground as the adults gathered to watch. "If you find yourself in this position, and your attacker is kneeling over you, this is what you do."

She gestured to one of the men, Sam Drummond, who tentatively straddled her. She handed him the wooden practice knife. "If he's bringing the knife down at you, he's got the advantage," she told the group. "Grab the wrist with the knife—you want to control that. Use your other hand to strike, preferably punch the throat," she said, showing them slowly a strike to the throat. "Wrap your hand around his neck, and bring him in close—"

"Close?" Jenny exclaimed. "Don't we want to get away?"

"Yeah, but he's got a knife, and close quarters are good. If you try to push him away, that's giving him more room to attack," Sully said, and showed them by gently pushing Sam back to arm's length. "See, here he can stab, strike, etc." She grabbed the back of his neck and pulled him down to her. "Here, he can't, he's too close." She pushed him back so that he straddled her once more.

"So, he's got a knife, and is bringing it down to you. Grab the wrist with the knife," she told them, wrapping her fingers around the thick wrist. "At the same time, strike at his throat." She demonstrated slowly and gently. "Then pull him forward, wrap your opposite arm over the back of his shoulder, like this, then under his wrist so that you can grab your wrist in a lock." She did the move slowly. "Then, turn his wrist up."

Sam grunted, and tapped the ground as he released his grip on the practice knife. The kids on the veranda cheered, and the adults made noises of surprise and appreciation.

"Then you can control the wrist like this," Sully said, levering Sam's wrist up, and she heard him hiss softly, and his tapping on the ground became fiercer. "You can wrench the shoulder, snap the wrist, move him off you," she said, demonstrating by using the vise-hold to direct Sam's gentle momentum off her body. "You can do various strikes, and run—or pick up that knife and finish him."

The gathered adults gasped, and Sully looked up at their shocked faces. Two of the women shared a look, horrified at the suggestion. Sully rose to her feet. "Guys, this person has killed three of your neighbors. Friends. In some cases, family," she said, eyeing Ronald Sinclair. "If he's coming for you, he wants you dead. Take him out before he takes you out."

Jenny gaped at her, then exhaled. "Well, uh, thanks, Sully." She brightened as she looked around at the others. "Hey, who's hungry?"

The adults nodded, and the kids on the veranda

cheered. Sully glanced back at them. Oops. She'd forgotten the kids were there. Not really a conversation you
wanted to have in front of the littlies…

She forced a smile on her face. "I have some salad fix-
ings. We could have a cookout. We just need some meat."

The children squealed, then jumped up and down.
Which led to a little bit of pushing, and then quickly de-
teriorated into a game of tag around the house.

"I've got some meat back home," Ronald said.

Sam rolled to his feet. "So do I."

"I've got some bread rolls," one of the women offered.

"I've got more salad—you'll need some more," Mrs.
Forsyth suggested. "We could pop home and be back
within the hour."

Sully smiled. "Uh, great. That would be great." She
blinked, looking at the group as they discussed what to get
for the spontaneous potluck meal. It seemed so…big and
hearty and wonderful, to have all these people get ready
for a large, communal meal. At her place. Like…family.

"Okay, I'll stay here with Sully," Jenny stated as Jacob
led more of the adults around to the front. They were all
sweaty from their exertions, and most of the men were
shirtless, Jacob included.

"I'll help with the kids," sixteen-year-old Rhonda
Maxwell offered, winking at her younger cousin, Noah.

"Me, too," Susanne Maxwell, Noah's mother, stated,
and Noah pouted, then ran off with his sister, with
Rhonda jogging close behind.

"Hey, did we hear something about a barbecue?"
Jacob grinned as he rested his foot on the bottom step
of the veranda and braced his hand against the railing.
Sully watched as Jenny forced a smile to her face, but

her knuckles were white as she hugged herself. Jacob's smile faltered when he saw his sister's awkwardness.

"You can come help me pack the car," his mother told him, patting him on the shoulder as she walked toward the street. Some of the purebloods had carpooled, but there were still too many vehicles to fit in Sully's drive. The overflow were parked on the grassy verges on the road beyond.

"I'll start cleaning the grill," Jack Forsyth stated, turning toward the barbecue pit Sully had built shortly after arriving in Serenity Cove. It included a basic grill and metal plate set on a low ring of cinder blocks, and was set in a sheltered corner of her yard that still allowed for a one-hundred-and-eighty-degree view of the ocean.

"I'll take the kids down to the beach," Rhonda sang out as the children ran out of the yard in the direction of the path and stairs that led to the beach below.

The group split up, and Sully led Jenny and Susanne through to her kitchen.

"Do you mind, Sully?" Jenny asked. "I mean, we've all just invited—"

"I love it," Sully interrupted, beaming. "This is great. I miss having family gatherings…"

"Where's your family now?" Susanne asked as she started opening Sully's cabinets. She made a triumphant sound when she located the wooden chopping boards.

Sully smiled, but it took a little effort. "We're all kind of spread out." She crossed to the fridge and started to pull out lettuce and tomatoes and anything else she could use to feed the hoard that was about to descend.

"So, what happened to your family?" Jenny inquired, her brow dipping in curiosity as she reached for a knife in the knife block. "I don't think you've ever told me."

Sully shrugged. "Nothing happened to them. I just... left."

"Why?" Susanne asked as she started to pull off leaves from the head of lettuce. "Wow, that sounded nosy, didn't it?" the woman said, chuckling.

"It's fine," Sully said. "I needed to move away, find my own feet. They're still around, but I don't generally see them unless there's a special event." She'd missed so many birthdays, so many weddings and baby blessings, coven gatherings... She forced a smile on her face. She hadn't let herself think about that, but now, with these people who were being so lovely and warm, so inclusive, she found herself thinking about her family, her coven. Thinking about them...missing them.

But she couldn't go back—she couldn't risk it, for their sake. Something clanged outside, and Jenny smiled. "Sounds like Dad's decided to give your grill a good going-over." She leaned forward. "So tell me, what happened with Dave?"

"Is this the boyfriend Noah was telling me about?" Susanne inquired, and Sully could feel her cheeks heat.

"Uh, he left me this morning." Sully focused on washing the tomatoes.

Jenny slapped the knife down on the board. "What did that son of a bitch do? Where is he? How badly do we need to hurt him? Bruise him up, or make it impossible for him to father children ever again?"

"No, no, it's—it's not his fault," Sully said hurriedly, although she was touched by Jenny's fierce loyalty. "He—he really wants to find the person behind all this," she said, waving her hand around carelessly. "So, he's off—"

"He's dicking around, isn't he?" Jenny muttered, then glanced at Susanne. "He's a private dick."

"Investigator," Sully corrected, then sighed. She could see his point about working without interference, but she still felt like she was not being completely honest with her friends, and hated it.

"Oh, no," Jenny said as she reached for one of the washed tomatoes.

"What?" Sully glanced at the tomato. Was there something wrong with it?

"You have that look," Susanne said, running the lettuce leaves under the tap.

"What look?" Sully frowned, looking between the two women.

"That look that says you've totally fallen all over again for the guy you dated in high school," Jenny said. She brought the knife down sharply on the cucumber, chopping off the end.

"No, I haven't."

"Well, you've done something," Jenny said. Sully's cheeks heated, and she turned away to open a cupboard door, ostensibly to find a bowl. Yeah, and that something had been wicked fun.

"Oh, my God, you did," Jenny exclaimed, and Susanne gasped.

"Whatever it was, from the look of that blush it had to have been good," Susanne said, grinning. "Or very, very bad."

"Guys," Sully pleaded.

"Oh, my God, you did, too!" Jenny squealed.

"Shush," Sully said, looking out the window. She couldn't see Jack Forsyth, but she certainly didn't want Jenny's father to hear the details of her sex life. "It's… over." She pulled the bowl out of the cupboard and placed it on the kitchen counter.

Susanne frowned. "Why, was it bad?"

"No! No, it wasn't bad."

"So it was good, then?" Jenny said, resting the base of her palms on the wooden chopping board.

Sully covered her face. "This is so embarrassing."

"That means it was very good," Susanne explained in a knowing voice to Jenny.

"And he left you?" Jenny asked, a slight frown of confusion on her forehead. She firmed her lips, then nodded. "Fine. Castration it is, then."

"Jen, it's not that simple."

"Yes it is. You can hold him down, and I'll show you how simple it can be."

Sully laughed. "Jen, calm down." She sobered. "We're just—he doesn't trust me as much as I want him to," she admitted quietly.

Jenny hesitated, then placed the knife down on the board. "So *he's* the one with the trust issues…?"

Susanne winced, then leaned her hip against the counter. "Ouch."

"What do you mean?" Sully glanced between her two friends.

"I mean," Jenny said, leaning forward, "you have enough weapons here to arm every man, woman and child in the greater Serenity Cove area, and you showed us some pretty lethal moves out there. That doesn't just come out of a vacuum, Sully. You've been holding out on us."

"What the hell happened to you?" Susanne asked quietly, and for once, her face was dead-set serious.

Sully opened her mouth, then closed it. How did she respond? There was so much she hadn't told her closest friends…

"Hmm, I'm thinking your Dave may not be the only one with trust issues," Jenny stated, then started to resume chopping the cucumber.

There was a knock at the door, and Sully held up a hand. "I'll get it," she said, hurrying toward the hall.

"This conversation isn't over," Jenny called after her.

"I'm already pouring the wine," Susanne sang out.

Sully sighed as she walked down the hallway. Her friends had a point. She'd hidden so much from them—but was she ready to let them in? Was she ready to tell them anything? Everything? And did Jenny have a point? Did her own lack of trust affect her relationship—such as it was—with Dave?

She opened the front door, and raised her eyebrows when she saw the deputy standing on her veranda. He clasped his hat in his gloved hands, and smiled at her.

"Hi, ma'am. I'm looking for Jennifer Forsyth, and I was told she was here…? The sheriff has asked me to stop by with some follow-up questions about her attack yesterday."

Sully's eyebrows rose. "Oh, uh, okay." She stepped aside, gesturing down the hallway. "Come in, she's in the kitchen."

She turned toward the hallway. "I'm surprised Tyler didn't just call," she said.

She heard an agonized cry and turned back. The deputy had stopped just inside her home, and had ducked his head as he clutched his face in pain. She hurried toward him. "What—" she reached for him, but jerked her hand back when he lifted his head.

His features twisted, his skin bubbled and then his eyes flashed rage at her. Her body processed the danger before her mind could quite grasp it. She turned to run, but he grabbed her hair and spun her around. His fist flashed out, catching her in the jaw, and her head smacked against the hall wall. Anger, fury and an evil that was suffocating, slammed into her. Dizzy, she brought her arms up, but his fist struck her again, and darkness crashed over her.

Chapter 17

Dave peered in through the front window. The house really was empty. He stepped back from the front door, and glanced down at his list. Susanne and George Maxwell, not home.

Just like the other purebloods he'd called on. Nobody was home. Anywhere. He glanced down the street. None of the Forsyths—and he'd tried Jenny first—were home. Neither were the Drummonds, or the Sinclairs. Maxwells, and a bunch of others… It was as if they'd all suddenly gone to ground.

He strode down the garden path and had almost reached his bike when his tattoo started to heat. He halted, and pressed his hand to his chest. *No. Please, no.*

"Sullivan Timmerman," he whispered, removing his glasses and staring blindly down the street.

His vision blurred, and then cleared. He was walking up behind a man. The man was stooped over, and using a wire brush on something he held, the grating noise masking the sound of his steps. He reached for the man at the same time he swept his leg out.

The man cried out in surprise as he was grasped, then tripped backward onto the ground, the grill he was cleaning clattering against cinder blocks.

Like lightning, he straddled the man, and Dave grimaced in horror when he recognized the shocked face staring up at him. Jack Forsyth. Bracing one hand against the older man's shoulder, the killer brought down his blade in a smooth arc.

"No," Dave rasped, bracing his hands on his bike. *Damn it.*

Jack's eyes rounded as the blade pierced him, and Dave's hands clenched into fists as he saw the life drain out of the older man's gaze. The killer reached for his wrist, and moved quickly, carving that *X* symbol into his wrist, draining the blood into that damn horn. The killer rose, turning away from the thicket surrounding them, and faced a house.

Dave's breath caught. He knew that house. The killer raised his horn in a silent toast, then drank its contents. He started to walk toward the house—Sully's house— and murmured those words that blackened Dave's vision.

Dave blinked and shook his head. Oh, God. *Sully.*

Heart pounding, he started his bike and roared down the street, his helmet still dangling from its strap over his handlebars.

Sully was in danger.

The tattoo over his heart began to heat again, and Dave gasped, leaning forward, accelerating out of the null neighborhood and onto the coast road. He blinked furiously, trying to dislodge the vision that was slowly creeping in over the road ahead. "Sull—Sullivan Tim—Timmerman," he gasped.

Sully lay still on the floor of the hallway, her face bruised. "No!" Dave roared, taking the curve of the road at a dangerous speed. The killer walked down the hall, and Jenny turned from the kitchen bench. Another woman was closer, one Dave didn't recognize, and she turned from peering into the fridge.

"Who was at the door?" Jenny asked, and turned back to sliding salad ingredients with a knife along a wooden chopping board and into a bowl.

The other woman smiled. "Sauvignon blanc or—"

The blade flashed, catching the woman in the chest, the smile slowly slipping from her face.

Jenny screamed, and the board she held fell to the floor. The killer worked quickly, laying the woman on the ground and carving the mark into her flesh, then draining her blood. Jenny darted past him, running for the front door. The witch sipped from the horn as he raced after Jenny.

"No," bellowed Dave, his muscles tensing, and he leaned forward, ignoring the high-pitched wail of his bike as it hit maximum speed.

The witch caught up with Jenny in the hall, tackling her to the floor next to Sully's still body.

Jenny screamed and lashed out with the kitchen knife she still held. The witch clasped her wrist, forcing it above her head as he brought his own blade down, and Jenny's scream ended in a gasp.

Within moments, the witch had performed his gruesome ritual with the mark, and was drinking from the horn. His gaze turned to Sully as he murmured those damn words, and Dave's vision again darkened, and he found himself staring at the asphalt of the road unfolding ahead of him.

Sully.

Hands gripping the handlebars tightly, his gut clenching, Dave focused his gaze on the road. He overtook a series of cars all heading in the same direction. One of the cars started honking its horn at him, but he ignored the sound.

He prayed. Prayed for Sully, making all kinds of promises to the Ancestors. He'd never look at a woman again, never get distracted. Keep her safe. He'd walk away, he'd never see her again, just make her safe. Alive.

He heard the squeal of rubber behind him, but didn't turn around to look. The turn for Sully's street was ahead, and he leaned into the turn early, taking it like a motorbike racer on a circuit, before screaming down the road to Sully's house. He turned into her drive and jumped off the bike, not even slowing down to stop it properly. He could hear the bike clatter as it fell, the screech of tires on gravel behind him, and ignored it when someone called his name.

He ran across the yard and up the stairs to the veranda. He shouldered the door open, then raced inside. He skidded on the floor to reach Sully.

"Please, Jenny." Sully was sobbing, clutching her friend's hand. She placed her other hand over the wound in Jenny's chest. Sully's shoulders where shaking, her face tear-streaked as she cried. She started murmuring, and Dave felt his own eyes burn with tears at the grief, the heartbreak in Sully's voice as she tried a healing spell.

A spell that would have no effect on a null.

Dave placed his hand on Sully's arm. "Sully," he murmured, trying to get the sound past the razor blades in his throat.

She shook her head, the tears streaming down her face. "No, let me help her," she cried, and crawled a little closer. Footsteps pounded on the veranda outside, and Dave looked up as Jacob halted at the front door. The big man had to clutch the doorjamb as he swayed, his face torn with grief and shock as he looked down at his dead sister inside.

"Jenny, please," Sully sobbed, and Dave grasped her shoulder.

"Sully, she's gone," he said softly.

"No, no, she can't be," Sully cried.

A scream, heartrending, full of grief and rage, echoed through the front yard, and Dave looked up at Jacob. The man had turned, and his eyes widened in disbelief. He took a step forward, and more screams, more wails were heard. Jacob took another step, then collapsed to his knees, his face twisted in anguish. He leaned forward, rocking on the veranda, a howl of pain erupting from deep inside him.

"Jenny, come on," Sully gasped, and squeezed her friend's hand in hers. "Let me take it, let me take it," she wailed. She stopped, squeezing her eyes shut, but no matter how much she concentrated, Dave knew she wouldn't be able to take on any of this pain. Not now. Not for Jenny.

"Sully," he whispered, pulling her toward him. "She's gone, love. You can't help her."

"No, no, no," Sully sobbed, and dropped Jenny's hand. Sully's hands clawed over, and she lifted her head and screamed. Her pain, her anguish, her frustration pierced his heart. Dave felt the hot lick of tears trailing down his own cheeks in the face of her despair, and rocked her in his arms.

* * *

Sully poured the steaming water into the mug, and blankly watched the chopped-up leaves and twigs swirl as though caught in a mini hurricane.

A storm in a teacup.

Sully placed the kettle back on the warmer, and took a seat at the table. The tea had to steep. Not for long, but she needed this tea to be potent. A trickle of perspiration ran down the side of her face. She glanced around the tiny little motel room. She'd turned off the air conditioner. It had made an annoying crank-crank-crank noise, and she'd shut it off before she'd screamed.

Her eyes skimmed over the ugliest coverlet she'd seen, its geometric pattern looking like a witch's vision quest on acid. The carpet may have been orange and cream at one point, but now looked brown. Gray. No, baby-crap brown and dead-fish gray.

Her home was a crime scene. She blinked at the tears that welled in her eyes. Correction. Three crime scenes. The tears fell slowly as she stared at the mug, steam curling up from its surface. She watched the steam as it rose, and sucked in her breath as the tendrils roiled, and she saw his face again, the bones moving underneath the skin, his flesh blistering as he stepped inside her home. She blinked. No. She wasn't going to think about that anymore.

She plucked at a loose thread of the long skirt she'd changed into. She'd had to change at her house. Tyler had folded her clothes, covered in Jenny's blood, and placed them separately into evidence bags. She'd given all the information she could to the sheriff. She'd sat through hours of grueling interviews, had flicked through photos…but she'd known it would be a pointless exercise.

Still, Tyler needed to feel like he was doing something, that he was taking action at tracking down this killer. She could understand that. She could give him that, at least.

An image of Jen lying bloodied and still on her hall floor filled her mind. Sully blinked slowly. She didn't want to see that anymore. Didn't want to feel that pathetic uselessness ever again. She'd reached for her friend, but couldn't feel her, couldn't sense her, no matter how much she opened her walls. She couldn't take away any of that pain, that fear and horror that must have preyed upon her best friend in the last moments of her life.

Her gut clenched, and her shoulders shook off a dry retch. Oh, God. *Jenny.*

Hot tears welled in her eyes, before trailing down her cheeks. Jenny. Jack. Susanne. They were all gone.

And it was her fault.

She reached for the mug, her fingers trembling. A knock sounded at the door.

"Sully."

She closed her eyes briefly at the familiar sound of that voice. Dave. She didn't want to see him. Didn't want to speak with him. Didn't want to look him in the eye and see the disappointment, the blame.

"Sully." The voice was louder, as was the pounding on her door.

She pulled the mug closer, but opened her eyes when she heard the lock disengage, the handle turn and the door open.

"Sully." He filled the doorway. So big, so strong. He wore his leather jacket, despite the heat outside. His sunglasses shielded his eyes, but she could guess at the accusation, the recrimination. She deserved it. Hell, she deserved so much more than looks of censure. From everyone. Dave. Jacob... She winced. Mrs. Forsyth.

"Go away," she said, her voice hoarse from screaming.

He stepped inside and closed the door behind him. "I'm not going away."

She cupped her cold hands around the warm mug but couldn't seem to absorb any of the heat. His words sank in, but slowly, like sharp little barbs hitting rubber walls. Some stuck, some didn't, but not quite penetrating the numbness surrounding her. For once, she could feel... nothing.

"You were going away," she said, her gaze fixed on the mug. "Jenny wanted to castrate you." She almost smiled, remembering the conversation, only she couldn't quite get her facial muscles to work. Nothing worked anymore.

Dave paused, then bowed his head. "Yeah, well, I would have deserved it," he said in a low voice.

He crossed over and lowered himself into the seat opposite her at the table.

"I don't want you here," she said in a low voice.

"Well, from what Jacob and Tyler have told me, you don't want anyone here."

She drew the mug closer to her. "I want to be alone."

"You shouldn't be alone, Sully. Not now."

She slowly lifted her gaze to meet his, and decided to ignore the pain and grief she saw etched into his face. "Yeah, I should."

"Sully—it wasn't your fault," he said roughly, leaning forward to rest his arms on the table between them.

This time her mouth did move into a smile, a bitter, self-hating smile that bore no joy or warmth. "But it was, Dave," she whispered. "I let him in."

Dave frowned, and looked down at the table. "Every-

one let him in, Sully. Gary let him in close. Mary Anne let
him into her home, so did Amanda... Jenny." He clasped
his hands together. "I don't know how he does it—"

"He's a skinshifter," she said, and tried to hug the mug
closer to her chest. Dave's gaze met hers.

"What?"

"He's a skinshifter," she said, and she moistened her
lips.

Dave's eyebrows rose, and he leaned forward some
more. "A skinshifter? How do you know?"

"When he—when he came inside, I don't know why,
but his facade started to drop." She shuddered. "Literally." She could see it happening again, the way his bones
seemed to dissolve, the skin bubbling... She flinched.
"He couldn't keep up the disguise." She glanced down
at the tea.

Dave sat back for a moment, stunned. "A skinshifter."

She nodded. Skinshifters were a special breed of witch.
They could rearrange their features, their physique, to
look like anyone they'd physically come in contact with.
They couldn't shift into a different species, though, like
a bird or a cat, only people. They were the chameleons of
witchcraft, and not very well liked. The only time you dis-
guised yourself was when you had something to hide, and
these witches had a questionable moral compass. They
passed themselves off as others. Sometimes it was a harmless form of mischief, but most of the time it was a form
of betrayal and deceit. As such, those witches born with
skinshifting abilities were generally outcast—the witch
equivalent to a werewolf stray or a vampire vagabond.
Tricksters. Imposters. Charlatans.

And in this case, a murderer.

"So that's how he got close to them," Dave murmured.

"Yes." She stirred the tea. "He looked like a deputy. I guess he couldn't pretend to be me with me."

Dave's eyes narrowed. "You say his disguise faltered when he stepped inside your home?"

She shuddered. "If by faltered it looked like his face was melting off his skull, then yes."

Dave rubbed his hand over his mouth. "I, uh—I put a ward on your door," he said quietly.

Sully lifted her gaze to meet his. "What?"

"Uh, the night before, when we got home. I put a ward on your door. A protection spell. You only have a very basic lock on your door, and I wanted to make sure you were safe."

Her lips twisted. "Those spells don't work when the source of dark intent is invited in," she told him.

"No, but they reveal dark intent," Dave told her. He winced. "I, uh, I'm so sorry. About Jenny. And…the others."

She shrugged. "You were right. I should never have gotten involved. I'm just an amateur hack when it comes to catching bad guys."

Dave shook his head. "No, you're not, Sully. This guy is strong, and he's smart." He rose from the table, crossed to the tiny kitchenette counter and picked up a mug. "Mind if I have some tea?"

"Yes," she said sharply, then realized how snappy she'd sounded. "I mean, there's none left."

"Oh." He turned back to the board she'd used to chop her ingredients, and she raised the mug to her lips.

He whirled back to face her, his arm flashing out, and an arc of power zapped from his fingers, blasting the mug from her fingers.

"What are you doing?" she asked shrilly, jumping to her feet.

He stepped up to her, his expression fierce. "Water hemlock? Oleander? What are *you* doing, Sully?"

"Go away, Dave," she cried, stepping away from him.

He grabbed her arm, and for the first time, she sensed nothing from him. He glared at her.

"Why? So you can try to kill yourself again?"

Chapter 18

Sully tried to pull her arm out of his grip, but Dave wouldn't let her go.

"What do you think you're doing, Sully?"

"Let me go," she said, her curled-up fist thumping him on the chest.

He shook his head. "I'm not letting you go, Sully." No. He wasn't going anywhere, he wasn't about to leave her alone, not like this. Maybe not ever.

"Jenny's dead," she hissed, and for the first time he saw a spark in her otherwise dead eyes. She thumped him again on the chest, and he met her gaze squarely. His lack of response seemed to anger her. She thumped him again. "Jack's dead." He remained silent. She thumped him. "Susa—Susanne's dead," she cried, then hit him again. And again. He stood there and let her hit him, again and again, relieved at her anger compared to the blank numbness he'd seen from her since she'd accepted that her best friend was dead.

"They're all dead," she cried eventually, sagging against him. He enfolded her in his arms, felt her shuddering against him as she sobbed. "It's my fault. I shouldn't have let him in," she said.

"Shh, it's not your fault," he murmured against her tangled hair.

"I let him in," she said, and kept repeating it as she leaned her forehead against his chest. "You shouldn't have destroyed my tea." Her knees bent, and he caught her.

"Come on, sweetness," he said, scooping her up and carrying her over to the double bed. He flicked his fingers and the coverlet folded back. He lay her down, then climbed over her to lie down next to her.

"You should have left me alone," she cried softly.

"I'm not going anywhere," he told her gruffly as he pulled her back against his chest. "Hate me all you like, but I'm not leaving you. Never again."

"They died because I invited that evil in," she whispered, and he levered himself up on his elbow so that he could see her face. He smoothed her mussed hair away from her face.

"They died because a witch killed them," he told her. "He's killed before, Sully. Odds are, he would have gone after them, sooner or later. They just happened to be at your home when he did."

"I brought them there," she wailed. "I brought them all there. I may as well have sent up a damn Bat Signal to the universe that the purebloods were at my home, come and get them."

He closed his eyes briefly at the devastation, the regret he heard in her voice, emotions that he was all too familiar with. "You aren't responsible for the bad deeds of another," he murmured, gently caressing the hair at her temple. "You were trying to help."

"You don't believe that," she said into the darkening room.

He frowned. "Why do you think that?" He didn't believe for one minute that she was responsible for her friends' deaths, and he needed to make her see it, before the guilt ate its way through her.

"You feel guilt," she said in a low voice. "I've felt it. You feel responsible for those witches you kill, and you feel responsible for those they killed. You carry that guilt with you."

His lips parted, stunned at her insight. "Uh…"

"You think you can take this from me?" Sully glanced at him over her shoulder, her eyes dark and solemn. "You think you can carry this weight for me? Make me feel better?" She shook her head. "You can't take this away from me. This is mine to bear. I did this. This is my darkness to carry, not yours."

He leaned forward so that his head touched hers. "This darkness, Sully…it will weigh you down. With me, it's different—"

"Why? Because the Ancestors gave it to you?" She shook her head. "That's a cop-out."

He sighed, stroking her arms. "You can't carry someone else's sins. It doesn't work like that."

"It works that way for you."

"But it doesn't have to work that way for you," he whispered into her hair.

"They were my friends," she whispered. "My family."

"And you loved them," he said, and hugged her just a

little tighter. "I understand. Believe me, Sully, I understand. But you have to let it go. The blame is not yours
to hold on to."

There was silence for a moment, and then her body
jerked, and he realized she was crying silently.

"Sully."

"I can't," she wailed. "I can't let it go. If I let it go, I
let *them* go, and I can't do that to them. I can't dishonor
them. I can't forget. *I* should be dead, not them. This is so.
Not. Fair." She whispered her words harshly, forcefully.

He closed his eyes, drawing her even closer, feeling each shuddering breath. She was so devastated, he
couldn't bear it, couldn't bear the guilt that made her want
to cross over to the Other Realm. He tried to reach out to
her, to draw in some of that pain, to exchange it for some
comfort...

He surrounded them with a light cover of warmth, of
well-being, tucking the essence around her like a cloak. He
took care, making sure he left no gaps, and was surprised
when he found it. The slight crack in her shield. He gently
pushed the warmth inside her. He heard her gasp, felt her
stiffen in his arms and saw the splintering of those walls.

He scooped her up close as she started to cry anew,
drawing on the pain and grief. His eyes itched, and he
sucked in his breath as the darkness creeped out. Into
him.

"What are you—"

"Shh," he whispered, concentrating on rolling the
darkness into ball, feeding the light into it and gradually dispersing it. He had no clue what he was doing, but
whatever it was, it felt right.

He sensed her relaxing in his arms, and her breathing deepened. He inhaled, slowly, relaxing against her

as the warmth spread over them both. He could feel her walls loosen, become more fluid, more flexible, allowing more light inside. She became still against him, so relaxed. He listened as she breathed, deep and regular.

He smiled as he, too, allowed himself to drift off to sleep, and for what seemed his first time in years, he experienced a true sense of peace.

She ran down the hall, her heart thumping in her chest. It was her hall—but…not. No. Familiar, but wrong. Where…? Wait. This was her apartment in Irondell. *No, not again.* She glanced over her shoulder, eyes wide with fear. He was behind her, the deputy with the melting face. She ran faster, but the hall kept getting longer and longer. She looked behind her once more, and stumbled when she saw his face blend into Jack Forsyth. The older man reached for her, and his features twisted, then slid into Susanne. Susanne stared back at her, saddened and disappointed, before morphing into Jenny.

Sully stumbled onto her knees, hands smacking against the tiled floor. She'd fallen in front of the mirror next to the door. She tried to look away, tried to turn back, to face Jenny, to tell her how sorry she was, but her reflection caught her gaze, held it.

Her mouth opened when she saw her own features start to swim, to slide down her face, and she would have screamed, only her jaw felt boneless, loose. She watched in horror as her face melded into masculine features, features she recognized and had prayed to never see again.

Marty.

Sully jolted awake, gasping.

"Hey, it's okay," Dave said, blinking as he reached for

her. "It's just a bad dream," he said, caressing her arm in an attempt to soothe her.

She shook her head and sat up. "No, no, I don't think it was," she panted, pushing her hair back off her face. She turned to look at him. "I think I know who's doing this."

Dave frowned. "What?" He sat up in bed, his biceps flexing as he braced his hands against the mattress and shifted his hips. His silver eyes still bore the shadows of sleep, and a little confusion. Adorable confusion. It took her a moment to get past the fact she'd been snuggled up against this man. And he'd kept his word. He'd stayed.

She didn't quite know why that was so important, but it was a fact that kept reverberating around her skull. He'd stayed.

And he'd…shared her pain. How—? What—? So many things were swirling around in her head, but she plucked the most pressing, the most urgent, out of the maelstrom.

"I think—I think I know who's doing this," she repeated, and threw off the coverlet. She rose from the bed—whoa, headspin—and then lurched for her tote bag, her skirt slowly untangling from around her legs.

"Sully, hold up," Dave said.

Sully shook her head, certainty filling her with determination. "No. I need my books. Now." A sense of urgency sparked inside her.

Sully made her way to the motel room door, but Dave beat her to it. His silver eyes—it took her a moment to really look at him—showed his concern, his bewilderment. "Sully, talk to me."

She met his gaze, still grappling with the shock. "Marty—Martin Steedbeck," she said.

"Who is Martin Steedbeck?" Dave asked, and opened

the door for her. He stood aside to let her pass, then followed her out to the parking lot.

"My ex."

"Whoa. What?"

Dave scooted around in front of her, his hands up. "Come again?"

"Marty Steedbeck, my ex-fiancé," she said, and then fumbled in her bag for her keys. Dave shook his head and guided her toward his bike. "But I need my books."

"I'll drive," he said, and removed a helmet from a pannier. He placed it on her head and connected her strap when her fingers fumbled with it.

They made it to her place in about fifteen minutes. It possibly would have been sooner, but Dave parked the bike near the turn and they ran down the street toward her home. It was past midnight, the darkest part of the night, and the stars were hidden behind clouds, disbursing a dull illumination, full of murky shadows and patches of gloom.

Dave held up his hand, and she halted behind him as they sheltered behind the hedge. A deputy stood by her gate, smoking a cigarette, and she could see Tyler through her living room window. Her front yard was lit up like a football field on a Friday night, and a technician walked out of the front door carrying a number of brown paper evidence bags.

"Can we go in?" Sully asked, and Dave shook his head, his fingers on his lips.

"No, it's a crime scene. It looks like they're about to finish up for the night," he murmured, eyeing the technician who placed the bags in a container in the trunk of a four-wheel drive vehicle, and then started to tug off his gloves. Dave guided her gently behind a bush, squatting down beside her. "We'll wait until they go."

"I feel bad about this," Sully said, eyeing Tyler as he nodded at another deputy, and then they started to walk toward the door. "Can't I just go and ask Tyler to let me go grab my stuff?"

Dave looked at her. "Do you remember talking with him yesterday afternoon?"

Sully glanced at him. "Sort of." A lot of yesterday afternoon was a blur. Evening, too.

Although she did clearly remember Dave blowing the bejeebus out of her tea.

"Your house is a murder scene, Sully. You're not allowed in for several days. You can't remove anything—and they still want an explanation for all those weapons."

"But it's my stuff," she protested in a low voice.

Dave shook his head. "No, at the moment it's evidence. So we wait." He patted the ground next to him. "You may as well get comfy."

He sat down, bringing his knees up and resting his arms across his knees. She followed suit.

He leaned closer, and she caught a whiff of his scent. That neroli did things to her, strange, wicked things. She eyed him. For once, he'd ventured out without wearing his sunglasses. His lips looked soft and relaxed, and his beard had gotten just a little longer, a little scruffier. His leather jacket was open, and his T-shirt was navy. Her brow dipped. Maybe dark gray. Perhaps black. Either way, his shoulders looked broader, and he looked tougher. His short hair and scruffy short beard made him look dangerous. Dangerously sexy.

She looked down at her flip-flops. She shouldn't be thinking about how sexy he looked in the dim light of the stars. Jenny flashed in her mind, sprawled on her hallway floor. She blinked. She was such a horrible person, noticing how good-looking her witch-hunting companion was the day three people had been murdered on her property.

"Mind telling me about this ex?" Dave inquired, his tone low but casual.

She winced. She'd hoped never to have to utter his name again, let alone discuss him in depth.

"It wasn't a healthy relationship," she murmured.

Dave looked at her. "Is he the reason you're hiding in Serenity Cove?"

"I'm not hiding," she argued, her voice low.

"Sully, these people you live among don't know you're a witch. You purposely stay where your powers are restricted, where no other witch will come near you because they'd be powerless…if that's not hiding, it's a damn interesting lifestyle choice that I just don't understand."

"It—it may have started out that way," she admitted, "but I stayed because I wanted to."

"Why?" Dave said, scooting around to face her. "What did he do to you?" His whisper was fierce.

She shook her head. "It was more what I let him do," she said, her eyes on her toes. She sighed. "Marty had… issues." God, just putting into words what had happened, what a monumental failure that relationship had been and how blind, or ignorant, or self-delusional she'd been, was so damn difficult—and humiliating.

Dave's eyebrows rose. "Why do I get the feeling that's an understatement of epic proportions?"

She nodded. "A little. Marty's father was a coven elder. His mother, though, was human. Marty's powers weren't very strong." She rested her chin on her knees. "And his father never let him forget it. The only thing he could really do was skinshift, and even that he wasn't very good at."

Dave leaned back to look up the street, and she followed his gaze. Tyler was now by the drive entrance, talking with the deputies. Dave turned back, and lifted his chin in a silent "go on" signal.

"So Marty started to drink. And when the buzz was dying there, he'd do drugs." She shook her head. She'd been engaged to a drug addict. She couldn't remember when she first noticed the little white lies…and then chose to ignore them. "At first, I didn't realize how much he was drinking when I wasn't there. He was very good at playing sober." She winced. "But the drugs made him… different." She hugged her knees tighter as the memories surfaced. "He'd wait for me to come home, and he'd get angry over the slightest thing."

She hugged herself a little tighter. Maybe it was sitting behind a bush, whispering in the dark while light blazed just a short distance away, reassuring but still hidden. Maybe it was Dave, and this sense of intimacy, of familiarity and friendship on a level that she couldn't remember experiencing before, or the fact that her best friend had died without knowing any of this about her, but for the first time in the longest time, Sully wanted to talk. It was like getting rid of some emotional dregs she'd held in way too long. She'd carried so much darkness with her, but whatever Dave had done earlier that night, it had shone a light on that darkness…illuminated it. Shared it. For the first time since she'd been hiding the reality of her and Marty's relationship from her family and coven, she felt ready to reveal.

"He was in so much pain," she said, shaking her head.

"And I'm an empath. I could help him. Like, *really* help him," she said, her hand moving in a smooth roll to emphasize each word. "I could take away his pain." Her chin dipped. "And I'll admit, in some sick way, I felt good about being able to help him." She paused. "But then he'd have more pain, and he needed me to take that, too. I almost think that among his other addictions, my taking away that pain from him, making him feel good, became an addiction in and of itself.

"He'd show me that he was trying, that he was doing some small measures to get better, like taking a different way home to avoid that bar, or showing me where he'd hide his stash so that I could check at any time…" The apologies, the promises…

She shrugged. "But then, he'd stumble again, fall prey to those insecurities, and I'd have to fix him—because the last time didn't work as good as it should have, or my fix didn't last as long as it should have, or I should have known that this would flare up and stopped it from happening… He had me convinced that it was actually my fault. I—I started to feel…useless. He would demand more of me, and would be upset and angry about it." She turned her head so she could look at Dave. "This sounds so pathetic, but he made me feel like I couldn't do anything right, and that—that just wrecks me."

"What do you mean?" Dave asked softly.

"I mean that I know now that he doesn't make me feel anything, I do. So I let him do that to me. That was on me," she said, and squeezed her eyes shut. That haunted her. That she'd fallen so low, and yes, Marty may have pushed her that far, but only because she allowed it. Which only made her feel worse.

"He'd get angry, and we'd argue." Her lips twisted in

an ironic smile. "I used to get hurt a lot by accident," she said. "He'd push, and I'd fall into that table, or smack into that door...you know, by accident. He didn't mean for me to end up smashing into the table and knocking myself out...it was an accident."

She swallowed, and Dave moved closer. "How did you get out of there?" he asked quietly.

She blinked back the burn in her eyes. She was not going to cry. Not over Marty. Hell, no. She'd wasted enough tears on that bastard.

"I don't quite know what set it off in my mind, but I finally figured out the reason he'd call me stupid, or useless, or powerless, or ugly...wasn't because I was actually those things, but because he was afraid of losing me." She held up a finger. "Oh, and when he threw me against a mirror. That may have had something to do with it, too." She still remembered the earsplitting crash, the pain as her head smacked the wall, her back broke the glass, the cuts as she fell to the floor amid the shattered pieces, all showing a warped reflection of her.

Dave sat there for a moment, and she didn't know if he was stunned, or disgusted, or trying to think up an excuse to run down the road, hop on his bike and ride as far away as he could get.

"I left—I ran out the door, with my shoes in my hand, and I ran."

Dave tilted his head. "That's why you make weapons." It wasn't a question, but a statement. A realization.

She nodded. She'd made a promise to herself, all those years ago, that she would never be in a position of weakness with a man—or a witch—ever again. "Yeah. I spent two years learning how to defend myself, how to protect myself... How to shore up my mental shields so that nobody could ever drain me dry again, and then I found Serenity Cove."

"With a null community," Dave finished for her. Sully nodded.

"Yep. You can't scry yourself up a witch if she's surrounded by nulls."

"But—" Dave indicated with his thumb over his shoulder in the direction of her cottage "—you brought your coven's books with you. That means your coven can't access their knowledge base. Why?"

Sully grimaced at the memory. "Marty was so damaged by his father, and was always wanting to prove him wrong—constantly. But he just wasn't that strong a witch. So he used his skinshifting abilities to pass himself off as me, and access our archive."

Dave gaped. "No," he said in horror.

She nodded. "Yes."

"What happened?"

"I found him before he could find the spell he was looking for. There was a fight—and like I said, his talents as a witch weren't as strong as others."

She'd kicked his ass, and protected her coven in the process.

Dave reached for her, his movement slow, as though giving her time to withdraw, or rebuff his touch. She did neither. He cupped her cheek.

"You are amazing, you know that?" he whispered. She closed her eyes, letting herself sense his emotions. The warmth of wonder and admiration. Sorrow and sadness. Anger—but not at her. No. It was tinged with a strong sense of protection. He pulled her closer. "You are the strongest person I know," he whispered against her lips, and kissed her.

She leaned into him, giving herself up to the kiss. His lips were gentle, tender and exactly what she needed from him right now.

The sound of car engines starting interrupted them, and they hunkered low as the sheriff and his deputies drove slowly down the street. Sully looked back at her house. Yellow crime scene tape was draped across her veranda and across her door.

Dave looked at her over her shoulder. "Let's go get you your books. Then you can tell me why you think your ex is killing nulls."

Chapter 19

Dave looked at the array of books strewn across the bed in Sully's motel room. She'd been very methodical in her approach at the house, and had selected volumes quickly. Then she'd performed a transfer spell that had removed the archive from her shelves to a place he didn't know where, and wasn't about to ask.

At which time she'd grabbed some personal items, including a change of clothes and weapons that the deputies hadn't found in their search. Getting the load home on the bike had been a minor miracle. They'd spent the hours since combing through the books. His stomach grumbled. He glanced at his watch. They'd missed lunch. And breakfast. Oh, and dinner the night before.

"I think we need a break." He reached for one of the books. So much...age. He wrinkled his nose at the slightly musty smell. Sort of like old people's stink.

"I think we've been approaching this from the wrong

angle," Sully said as she quickly flicked through some pages. "We know that nulls void any of the natural elements of a shadow breed—werewolves can't shift, vamps can't fang out, witches can't perform their spells…" she said, her hand rolling as she went through the litany. "But this witch has been able to work magic—when no witch working with the natural order can do so."

He nodded. He knew the limitations around nulls, had experienced it personally since arriving in Serenity Cove. That void made him feel almost naked. "I admit, it's one thing that's been driving me crazy, trying to figure out how he's been able to do the spells, bump me out of the visions, etc. I mean, how can a skinshifter even keep his facade around nulls?"

"Especially a skinshifter with limited natural ability," Sully stated. "I think he's drawn on unnatural elements."

Dave frowned. He'd seen the skinshifter carve into flesh and consume blood. "Do you mean blood magic?" Blood magic was a slightly more potent form of magic, and a witch had to be very careful—if their blood supply was killed in the process, it drew the wrath of the Ancestors, and a quick and painful trip to the Other Realm, courtesy of yours truly.

Sully shook her head. "No. From what I saw, he kills his victim, and *then* consumes their blood. I think he's using death magic."

Dave stilled. Oh. Hell. No wonder the Ancestors had called on him.

"The dark arts." It was so obvious, and yet, so damn reckless. Only those on a power thirst used death magic, better known as black magic, and it always—*always*— ended badly. Did this witch not realize that he would eventually pay for his sins? Either in this world or the next… Black magic had a kick to it. As long as you served the dark arts, it served you. One wrong step, though, and it could consume you. Hell into perpetuity. He'd prefer facing down the Ancestors in the Other Realm, thank you very much.

"I don't know why I didn't see it," she murmured, then chewed her lip—*look away from her lips*—before finally lifting her gaze to meet his. He whipped his gaze from her pretty, pouty mouth to her eyes. "Marty used to say that he wanted to find his happy place. When I asked him where that was, he said it was any place where he was the strongest witch—especially stronger than his father."

She shrugged. "I used to think this was a hypothetical what-if kind of conversation, and I'd say to him that even the strongest witch is vulnerable to nulls. He wanted to find a way to be powerful, despite the nulls." She held her hands up in a helpless gesture. "I never thought there was a way to counteract that."

Dave frowned as he flicked through the pages of the book. "You think he found a way to void the null effect." The idea was so extreme, so ludicrous, it was chilling that it might be true. The kind of "sure thing" you bet with a drunk at the bar and then laugh yourself silly as he tried to count out the logic on his fingers. Dave shook his head as he turned the page. He might need a beer or six for this. He glanced down at the page, then froze.

The X symbol was drawn on the side of the page, along with a spell written in the Old Language. Right there, in plain Ancestors-speak.

"Sully."

She looked up at the tone in his voice, then leaned over to look at the page.

"Oh, my God. You found it."

"I need to translate this," he muttered, reaching for the notepad and pen on the table by the bed.

She shuffled around next to him, her head close as he hastily scribbled. Her scent, rose, clove and vanilla, teased at him.

"No, wait," she said, placing her hand on his arm. "That's not liberation," she said, gesturing to the symbol. "That's sacrifice." He frowned, then realized she was right. He hastily crossed out the word and corrected, and then went through the rest of the spell, forcing himself to ignore that teasing, tempting scent.

It took a few minutes, but he finally finished the translation. He showed her the notepad. "Do you agree?"

She scanned the spellbook, and then the translation, line for line, then finally nodded. "Yep."

They both sat there for a moment, staring at the translated spell. "Holy crap," Dave finally murmured in awe. It was—it was—hell, he wasn't quite sure what it was. His brain was having trouble computing it.

"Yep," Sully breathed.

"The Gift," Dave said, his lips tightening. The marking the witch carved on the inner wrist of his victims— the pulse point—was a symbol used by the Ancients, the ones who predated the Ancestors. The symbol, directly translated, meant gift. This spell, though, added some further meaning. A transformative gift, a connection, with the addition of unification.

"He's tying the elements of the null blood—pureblood— to his through the unification spell," Sully said.

Dave nodded. "He's not fighting the null effect, he's accepting it. That enables him to control the effect."

"Like when he bumps you out of the vision," Sully

said, and Dave nodded. This was—this was incredible. Son of a bitch.

"So he uses their sacrifice under the guise of a gift, receiving the qualities and transforming it to become a part of a new…him." Dave met Sully's troubled gaze. "This means that he's warping his magic with a null effect. When others come near him, he nullifies their power and uses it to boost his own." His brow dipped. "An alpha elder." Like elders needed an extra creep-factor. His own mother would love this.

Sully shook her head slowly. "It's…it's ingenious."

"It's dangerous," Dave said. "He can effectively rob supernaturals of their power and convert it to his own, thus becoming the most powerful creature on earth." He frowned as he glanced down at some markings at the bottom of the page. What…what was that?

"But it's only temporary," Sully surmised, reading through the spell. Dave leaned closer to eye the markings, then counted them. Nine. Ni—ine. Three groups of—realization hit him.

"Holy crap."

"What?"

"If I'm correct, the effects can become permanent under certain conditions…" The blood chilled in his veins as he absorbed the meaning of the text.

"What conditions?" Sully frowned as she eyed the page, trying to find the clause.

"Sacrifices," he said, tapping his finger on the markings.

Sully nodded. "Yeah, well, we kind of figured that. He kills for the blood."

Dave shook his head. "No, he has killed six people so far. There are nine markings here."

"The law of three," she whispered, her eyes widening in realization. "Three groups of three—a threefold blood sacrifice."

He then pointed to the circle at the top of the page. "And a celestial event."

He glanced at his watch. When was the next celest—

"The harvest moon," Sully gasped.

Dave closed his eyes briefly. The witch was going after three more purebloods.

This year the harvest moon coincided with the fall equinox. With the day and night being of equal hours, the full moon would rise the closest after sunset, effectively the longest moonshine of the year. A natural phenomenon on steroids. Sheesh.

"So if he completes the blood harvest by harvest moon, he keeps his powers forever." Sully bit her lip.

"Son of a bitch."

"This is massive. We have to do something," she said hastily reaching for the book. "Does this mention anything about a counterspell? There has to be a counterspell—right?" She eyed him hopefully.

Dave shrugged, incredulous. "I didn't even know this spell was possible until two minutes ago. I have no idea about a counterspell."

"We have to do something. This means he's got to kill three more nulls, by moonrise in two days' time."

She started flicking through the book, her movements gaining speed. He tugged over another book and started scanning the pages. "Maybe we should—"

Her murmurs interrupted him, and he glanced over at her. Her eyes were closed, fingers splayed as she tried to encompass all of the books on the bed in her…discovery spell. Damn, she was good.

She growled in frustration, her fingers clenching when her spell turned up nothing.

Okay, so *mostly* good. Nobody was perfect, and you could only discover something if there was something to discover.

Her eyes opened, and he was struck by the panic he saw there.

"What are we going to do? I can't find a reversal."

He smiled. "We do what I do best."

"What's that?"

"Improvise."

"Please, we need to talk," Sully implored. Jacob stared down at her, his brown eyes dark with devastation. His gaze flicked to Dave standing behind her, then back to her.

"Sully, now's not a good—"

"I know." She swallowed. "God, I know. If it wasn't absolutely necessary, I would never come near you and your family ever again." Tears filled her eyes as that treacherous guilt ate at her like a gutful of chilies.

His expression gentled. "Sully, it's not your fault." He lifted his gaze to meet Dave's over her head. "It's not her fault."

Dave nodded, and she felt him place his hand on her bare shoulder. "I know. But you need to hear us out."

Jacob glanced over his shoulder, then stepped out onto the veranda of his parents' home. "I can give you five minutes," he said in a low voice. He shoved his hands in the back pockets of his jeans and leaned against the front wall of the house.

Sully nodded. She'd take whatever she could get, and be super appreciative of it. She turned to Dave, who pulled a scrap of paper from his jacket pocket and handed it to her. She caught her bottom lip between her teeth, and he gave her a reassuring nod. She turned back to Jacob, unfolding the piece of paper. Okay. Deep breath. She could admit that she'd lied, that she'd pretended to be someone she wasn't, that she was, in fact, a dreaded witch implanting herself secretly into the null community to hide her own ass from a psychotic ex. She hated what she was about to do, and was dreading Jacob's reaction. And his mother's. And everyone else she knew. Deep breath.

"We think we know why someone is killing nu—" she halted, "your family and friends." *Nulls* was a generic word, a catchall for the individuals she loved and mourned, and whom Jacob loved even more fiercely. But this was now very, very personal. For everyone.

Jacob watched her. "I'm listening."

She held out the piece of paper to him, and it fluttered in her trembling fingers. She could do this. She wasn't going to hide anymore. These people deserved more. They deserved better. And they'd lost far more than her peace of mind and comfort zone.

"He's carving this into them," she whispered.

Jacob glanced down at the symbol Dave had drawn on the paper. His lips tightened when he recognized the graphic. "I know. I saw it on my sister, on my father," he said roughly.

"He's carving this on them to steal the null restraint for the supernatural."

Jacob's gaze flicked up to meet hers. "Say what?"

"The man doing this—" she took a deep breath "—he's a witch. This symbol allows him to—"

She halted when she realized she'd be going into horrifically gory detail to him about Jenny's and his father's deaths.

"It allows him to use the null effect to cancel out any supernaturals around him," she said the words in a rush.

Jacob frowned. "I don't understand. If he's a witch, it doesn't help him."

"He's figured out a bypass," Dave said from behind her.

"How?"

Sully hesitated.

"He draws on the blood of his victims," Dave stated, and Sully sucked in a breath. His words gave an adequate description without sharing too much more. "He's figured out a spell that can help him absorb the effect without being affected by it."

Jacob frowned, shaking his head faintly. "How do you know this?"

Sully swallowed, then lifted her chin. "Be—because I'm a witch," she said in a whisper.

Jacob stilled. His gaze flicked between her and Dave, and back again. "Say what?"

"I'm a…witch," she finished in a hushed voice.

"A witch."

"Yes, a witch."

Jacob shook his head. "I don't believe it. You've been here for years, and you never—"

"I make remedies," she interrupted. "I know how to do that because I'm a witch, and I'm a student of nature."

"You make teas," Jacob argued. "Ointments. Like a doctor. Or a naturopath. That doesn't mean you're a witch."

Sully's mouth opened. She'd hidden the truth for so long, and it had taken much effort to come clean. She had expected yelling. Rebukes. Anger, betrayal. She hadn't expected not to be believed.

"Uh…" She glanced over at Dave. He shrugged his broad shoulders, a don't-ask-me look on his face.

"I am a witch," she said earnestly.

Jacob shook his head. She wasn't sure if it was in denial, disbelief or disappointment.

"I just didn't tell anyone," she said lamely.

"I don't believe you," he said, and looked at Dave.

"Oh, believe her." Dave smiled, but there was no humor in it. "For the record, so am I."

Jacob closed his eyes briefly, and when he opened them again, Sully saw the betrayal, the desolation in his eyes. And felt yay-high to a slug.

"You lied," he said in a harsh whisper.

She blinked back the tears his tone, his words, brought forth. "Yes," she admitted.

"You pretended you were normal," he accused her.

She opened her mouth. Paused. "When I'm with you guys, I am," she told him truthfully.

Jacob straightened and brought his arms forward to fold them across his broad chest. "You've lived among us for four years, Sully," he said, his voice low and harsh. "And that whole time you never hinted at what you really were." His lips pressed tightly together, and he looked out at the shadows lengthening down the street. "Did Jenny know?" He didn't look at her directly, but kept his gaze fixed on the middle distance.

This time she couldn't blink fast enough to stop the hot tears that spilled down her cheeks. "No," she whispered, ashamed.

Jacob's gaze slid to her, and her lips trembled when she saw the accusation in his eyes. "Liar," he rasped.

She flinched, then looked away. "I know. I'm so sorr—"

"Jenny's dead," he hissed. "My father. Susanne—we all welcomed you. We *trusted* you."

Sully squeezed her eyes shut, her heart clamping at the pain, the grief she heard in her friend's voice.

"There's more," she said, her voice catching. She glanced up at him. She had to tell him. She had to—oh, this was hell.

Dave's hand squeezed her shoulder, and she felt the comfort, the reassurance, the strength.

"The man doing this…is my—" her stomach clenched, and the muscles tightened in her jaw. "He's my ex."

Jacob's eyes rounded, and he stepped forward.

Dave drew her back behind him, shifting forward to stand toe-to-toe to Jacob, meeting his gaze directly. "Calm down."

Jacob's gaze narrowed. "Don't tell me to calm down," he said through gritted teeth. He glared at Sully over Dave's shoulder. "Is this guy here because of you?"

"I—I think so," she whispered.

Jacob swore and closed his eyes in pain.

"I'm so sorry, Jacob," she cried.

"Go." Jacob turned back toward the front door.

"But—"

"Sully, just…go."

Dave glanced over his shoulder at her, and his brows dipped. He turned back to Jacob.

"You need to hear her out."

Jacob turned on the witch, his expression fierce as he grasped the lapels of Dave's jacket. "I said g—"

Dave moved fast. Grasping the other man's wrist, he twisted his body—and Jacob's arms, and shoved Jacob's chest against the wall, the man's arm twisted behind his back. Sully gasped.

"This guy is not a friend of Sully's," he whispered harshly. "She left him for good reason, and she never believed he'd come anywhere near her. She risked her life to work with you guys, to help you guys, and from the moment I've met her, she's only wanted to keep you all safe. I know you're hurting, and I know you're angry. Calm down, and hear her out."

Jacob tried to struggle, but Dave shoved him back against the wall until the man stopped resisting. He looked over at Sully. "Go on." He nodded encouragement.

Sully took a deep breath. "He's coming after more nulls. He needs to kill three more purebloods to complete his spell."

Jacob stilled. She had his attention. "We believe we can stop him," she said, "but we'll need your help."

Chapter 20

Dave dabbed at the pinpricks on the wrist, then smiled at the tear-streaked face of the six-year-old red-haired pureblood. "All done, Noah. And you have a badass tatt to impress the girls when you're older," he said, and winked. He glanced briefly at the boy's father, and he smiled hesitantly back as he rubbed his son's back. Before tonight, he'd never tattooed a kid. Now he'd worked on four. Inflicting pain on kids was now on his "never do again" list.

The boy sniffed, and gave a tremulous smile as he glanced down at the white-inked tattoo. Dave reached for the antiseptic soap and gave the markings a gentle wash. Within minutes he'd taped the adhesive bandages to the boy's wrist. The tattoo was an ancient rune quaternary design, a protective shield. Simple, but effective.

"Does this mean I won't die?" the boy inquired tentatively.

Dave looked up at him, then raised his sunglasses to

the top of his head. This was the son of one of the victims—a woman who'd been killed at Sully's house. No wonder the kid was concerned. His mother had been murdered by this sick prick. "This means that you will forever have the witches protecting you," he told the boy in a low voice, his tone sincere. "This guy won't be able to come near you."

"Are you going after him?"

Dave nodded. "Yeah."

The boy frowned, worried. "Aren't you scared?"

Dave tilted his head, assessing the kid. He could appreciate that, living in such a tight-knit community as this null one, the boy had heard about the recent murders, and was scared—as well he should be.

But Dave had discovered he didn't like kids to be scared.

Dave lifted his chin in the direction of the boy's wrist. "That tattoo makes you pretty badass," he said, and lifted up his T-shirt to reveal his own markings. "These make me the king of badass."

The boy's eyes rounded, and he nodded. Dave dropped the garment, then grinned. "Get going." He gestured to the door, and turned back to clean up and put away his portable tattoo kit.

The bathroom door opened, and the kid ran out. His father followed, mouthing "thank you" to him as she went.

Sully peered around the doorjamb. "That was the last one. Can I get you anything?"

"Nah, I'm good." Dave answered as he gently placed the needles onto a little tray, and poured some bleach over them. He snapped the lid on the tray. He'd have to clean and sterilize them properly back at the motel room.

He carefully loaded the kit into his backpack and turned. Sully was waiting patiently, but it was the older woman behind her that drew his gaze. His eyebrows rose. "Mrs. Forsyth."

Jacob's mother smiled tremulously. "I just wanted to say thank you," she told him. He could feel heat fill his cheeks, and he cleared his throat.

"I wanted to say I'm so sorry about your husband, and Jenny," he said in a low voice. If he'd managed to catch him the day he'd first attacked Jenny, or any of the other times before, he would have been able to prevent the deaths of half of her family. Sully had it all wrong. It wasn't her fault her friends were dead. It was his.

He ducked his head as he walked past, but halted when Mrs. Forsyth touched his arm. He looked down at her. Her wrist also bore the adhesive bandages of one of his recent white-ink tattoos. She was so tiny, so frail. How the hell could such a petite woman spawn a giant douche like Jacob?

She smiled sadly as she lifted her hand to cup his cheek. "You're a good man," she told him in a low voice. Her smile broadened, although it was slightly shaky. "Even if you are a witch."

His lips curved briefly. She patted his cheek. "I know you had nothing to do with Jenny's and Jack's deaths. Neither did Sully." She reached her other hand out and grasped Sully's hand. "You both need to believe that."

Sully closed her eyes, her face pained. Mrs. Forsyth pulled them both in for a group hug. "It's not necessary, but if you need it, you have my forgiveness." She took a deep breath, then stepped back from them. "Now, you hunt that bastard down."

She patted Dave once more, hard enough to make him blink, then turned and shuffled down the hall.

He took a deep breath. That tiny little null had just given him more tenderness than his coven elder mother ever had. He frowned. It made him feel…weird. He shuddered. God, he was getting as sooky over these folks as Sully was. Yeesh.

He stretched his neck, then eyed the woman next to him. She wore the same weary expression he suspected he did. "Come on," he said. "Let's go."

They'd been at the Forsyth home for hours. Jacob had rounded up as many purebloods as he could find, but they knew there were still some who hadn't been inked—and that ink would mean the difference between life and death.

He'd been a little wary when suggesting this option for the purebloods. Tattooing involved injecting ink beneath the skin—resulting in a minor contamination of the blood. Most of the shadow breeds would have balked at tainting their bloodlines, but the nulls didn't seem to have an issue with it. And Jacob had been the first to accept the offer, showing his mother it didn't hurt "that much". Dave winced. He'd developed a basic design—something that could be done quickly so that more nulls could be protected in a short time, but also to try to limit the level of discomfort, especially for the kids.

Sully slid her arm around his and gave him a gentle smile. "That looks like it was tiring."

Dave shrugged. "Meh. I think that was a record for me." He'd worked quickly and consistently, and had managed to imprint the warded tattoo onto almost all of the purebloods in this area. He'd be coming back in the morning to work on anyone else who came forward. It was the Harvest Festival, with streets blocked off and stalls already being assembled. The nulls were determined to go ahead with the celebration. Which meant there'd be lots of purebloods walking the street fair, among many others. A skinshifter would be next to damn near impossible to locate in such a large crowd. All the witch would have to do is come into physical contact with a person, and he'd be able to take on their facade. It would be like having a haystack and looking for the needle—no, the ax—no, now the nail…

At least, if Dave was a skinshifter, that's how he'd do it. But with this protection ward tattooed onto the purebloods, they'd both tainted the blood supply with ink, which meant technically the purebloods were no longer pure of blood, but they also had a blocking ward to prevent attacks.

Take that, skinshifter.

They just needed to make sure they found all of the purebloods. If there were three left untattooed, this witch could still complete his spell. And that would make it incredibly hard for Dave to send him to the Other Realm. Sully claimed Mental Marty—his name for the witch, not hers—wasn't a skilled witch. He wasn't so sure he'd agree. He'd managed to come up with a really twisted plan, find an ancient spell and become almost undetectable in the process. It was like hunting and fighting a shadow—a shadow that had proven time and time again just how lethal he could be. Sully was so damn lucky she'd escaped him when she did.

He eyed her. Sully had dark circles under her eyes, and that crooked pout was just a little more pronounced, the lines a little more drawn, her complexion just a little more pale.

"You look tired."

"Gee, thanks."

He winced. Oops. "Sorry. But it's understandable." She'd had very little sleep since Jenny's murder, and had startled awake with nightmares. "Do you need to re-charge?"

Witches used nature to feed their energy. Finding a place to sit with exposure to the elements…sun, wind, rain, earth. Even moonlight helped. It was a chance to be still, to meditate and to become a little more present. After his inking marathon, he could do with a recharge, too.

She nodded. "That sounds great. I usually go the headland at the end of my street, but…" She shrugged, wincing.

He nodded. Her home was still classed as a crime scene, and she wasn't technically permitted access to it. If you followed the rules.

He didn't really follow the rules.

"Sounds great. Let's go."

Sully led him downstairs, but she halted when she saw Jacob coming out of the living room. The tall man paused when he saw them, his eyes on Sully. Dave stiffened. If this guy was going to threaten Sully—

The fisherman shoved his hands in his jeans pockets as he took a step toward Sully. He gazed sheepishly at her for a moment, then sighed. "Sully, I'm so sorry—"

"Shh," Sully said, shaking her head. "You've got nothing to apologize for."

"No, I do. You were Jen's friend, you're my friend. I shouldn't have said the things I did."

"You had every right to—" Sully's words were cut off when the big man swept her up in a bear hug.

"No, I didn't. I was being a royal dick."

Dave's eyebrows rose. Well, he wasn't about to argue with a royal dick.

Sully hugged Jacob back. "You've lost your sister and your father," she whispered. "And you're my friend. You can always speak freely with me, especially when I deserve it."

"But you didn't."

Jacob lifted his gaze, and met Dave's over Sully's head. Dave arched an eyebrow. He sure as hell wasn't going to give the guy a hall pass for being a royal dick. Sully had been so worried, so heartsick about telling the nulls the truth. And the big jerk had hurt her feelings when she was already feeling so much pain and guilt over the recent deaths.

But the big jerk had just lost his sister and family. He guessed if Sully could cut Jacob some slack, he could, too. He relaxed his features when he met Jacob's gaze. And then realized the man's hands were smoothing down Sully's back. Dave narrowed his gaze. Well, there went that warm and fuzzy moment. He narrowed his eyes as he met Jacob's, and this time it was Jacob's eyebrows who rose.

He gave Sully one more squeeze, then set her back. "Thank you," he whispered. "For everything."

Sully ducked her head and nodded as she stepped past. Dave made to follow her, but stopped when Jacob stuck out his hand. "Thank you," the fisherman said sincerely. Dave eyed the extended hand. Aw, darn. The royal dick was being halfway decent. He grasped the man's hand and shook it, giving him a nod, then he followed Sully out into the night.

He handed her a helmet, and within minutes they were

back on the coast road. The motel was on the other side of town, so passing Sully's home and pulling in at the headland was virtually on the way.

He slowly drove past the house. It sat, dark and silent, at the end of the street, the crime scene tape blocking off the drive fluttering in the night's breeze.

He pulled over onto the grassy verge, and waited for Sully to dismount before doing so himself. He removed his sunglasses and gazed out over the water. Light gray clouds drifted slowly across the sky. Stars glittered, and the moon cast a silver swathe across the water. The breeze was soft and still bearing the final warmth of a summer on the wane.

He sucked in a deep breath. Held it. Slowly exhaled. Salt and sweet blossoms. He glanced about. Yep. Sully's garden backed up to the fence.

"What do you think?" Sully asked as she sat cross-legged on the grass. He joined her. He could feel the night dew soaking through his jeans.

He looked out over the water. "It's beautiful," he said quietly. Even if he did have a wet seat.

They sat there for a while, soaking in the serenity. Dave's lips curved. No wonder this area was called Serenity Cove.

He tilted his head back, enjoying the feel of the breeze ruffling his short hair and the stretch of his neck muscles after the long day of bending over to ink up nulls. He watched the stars for a moment, then closed his eyes. He put aside his thoughts on Mental Marty, his very grave concerns that Sully's ex would find an unprotected pure-blood—or worse, get desperate when he couldn't, and strike out in a much more dangerous and lethal way. He put aside his thoughts on Jacob, of the teeniest spark of jealousy that had awoken when the man wrapped his arms around Sully… He put aside the torment of fulfilling another task for the Ancestors, and the self-doubt and guilt over the six people already killed by the target he had yet to dispatch.

He let nature have its way, let the calm and peace soak in, let the delight in a breeze against his skin take hold. He opened himself up, dissolving his mental wards, letting the energy gently roll in to fill his reserves.

He sensed a lightness, a warmth that was sweet and pure, with the cooling edges of worry and anxiety.

Sully.

Instinctively, he touched those cooler, darker edges with his own energy, feeding her reassurance as he drew in her worries to make them his own—and then realized what he was doing.

He snapped his eyes open and sat bolt upright. "I'm sorry," he blurted. After what she'd told her relationship with Marty, he could well understand her resistance to link with another witch, to have that witch consume anything from her, especially without her permission. They hadn't fully linked, but he'd forged a connection, one that hadn't been invited.

Sully sucked in a breath, her gaze fixed on the sea that glittered with silver diamonds under the moonlight.

"It's—it's okay," she said in a small voice.

"No, no it's not. You've never invited me in, and after hearing about Marty, I understand that. I—I didn't intend for that to happen."

She nodded, and her bottom lip disappeared between her teeth again. She tilted her head, and it was almost as though she was wanting to look at him, but trying to avoid him at the same time.

"You—last night you—" She sucked in a breath, and he watched as her breasts quivered beneath her cotton camisole top.

He whipped his gaze back to the sea. First he intruded on her mentally, and when she's trying to talk to him he's ogling her. *Bad form, Dave.*

"I don't know what happened last night," Dave admitted in a low voice, and this time it was him averting his gaze. "I just know that you were dealing with so much pain, more pain than I'd ever felt in a person, and…and I wanted to help ease it." He grimaced. He'd intruded on her then, too. Had no idea how he'd done it—he'd never done it before.

She remained silent, and he didn't know if she was mentally screaming "I hate you" and trying to map out her escape route. What she'd endured with her prick of an ex was on his mind, her vulnerability, the abuse of not only her generosity, but her body, her mind and her powers… and for a witch, that was a painful violation.

He raised his knee and rested his forearm on it. "I know—I know there's a protocol with power bonding," he said in a low voice. "I've bonded with other witches, like my sister, when it was necessary—and agreed to, but I haven't lived in a coven." He shook his head. "That's not an excuse, it's—it's that sometimes I'm ignorant of the process, and for some folks, I take shortcuts that can be…confronting."

It was a constant source of frustration for his coven elder mother—something he'd rather enjoyed doing, up until now—when someone he was beginning to really care about was affected.

Sully turned, and reached put her hand on his arm—and there it was. That little pfft of a power meld that he still couldn't get his mind around, but that awoke every single one of his senses and focused them on her.

"It's okay, Dave," she said, and gave him a tremulous but reassuring smile, and gave his arm a gentle squeeze. He felt an answering throb in his groin. Felt the want, the need for her, and battled it. He met her gaze, saw the tenderness, the interest. He raised his hand to cup her cheek. Her skin was so soft, so smooth, her eyes so dark, full of wariness, full of curiosity, and yet showing him a hunger he wasn't sure she intended for him to see.

But he did. He leaned forward a little, then halted.

He wanted her—desperately, but thoughts of Mental Marty, of what he'd done to her, bubbled up. He never wanted her to feel forced around him—for anything.

As though reading his mind, Sully moved. Tilting her chin up, she closed the distance, her lips pressing against his as she slid her hand up his arm and over his shoulder.

Dave closed his eyes, content to let her lead, let her set the pace, the level of intim—

Her tongue slid past his lips, and heat flooded him, tightening inside him, flooding his body with an arousal that was so damn gripping, so tight, it had him panting as he angled his head.

Without breaking contact, Sully rose up on her knees, her arms sliding around him, under his jacket. He shrugged it off to give her access—*oh, please, access*—and dropped it to the ground behind him. He raised his hands to her hips, guiding her as she straddled his hips.

He wrapped his arms around her, crossing them over her back as he pulled her against him. Sully sighed, her breath drifting across his lips as she tilted her head first in one direction, then the other, as though trying to find the best position.

He groaned at the teasing contact, and slid one hand up into her hair. He could feel the damp heat of her pressed against his groin and his cock stiffened. She moaned, her hips writhing against his, and he shifted beneath her, trying to get even closer, despite their clothes.

She drew back, tugging at his T-shirt. He brought her lips back to his, impatient at the loss of contact, and ripped his shirt from neck to hem, shrugging out of the scraps. She laughed huskily, and the sound had to be the sexiest he'd ever heard, that playful rasp against his neck.

She pushed him back, and he lay down across his discarded clothing. She made that sexy, crooked pout with her lips, and he raised a finger to trace her mouth. She captured his fingertip with her mouth, sucking on him in a way that almost made him delirious with need.

She pulled back for a moment, scanning his chest, running her hands over his body. He closed his eyes, enjoying the feel of her caressing her skin, until he felt her lips against his nipple.

Oh, wow. He bucked beneath her, and she chuckled throatily as she kissed her way down his torso. Her fingers fumbled with his belt and fly, and then suddenly she had him, all of him. He gave himself up to the intense pleasure as she took him into her mouth.

She tugged at his control, teased at his restraint, until he could feel himself swelling in her mouth. He reached for her and found the straps of her camisole instead. He

pulled gently at the garment; she helped him draw it up
over her head. He grasped her head, tugging her up to
him. He skimmed his hands over her back, dispensing
with the clasp of her bra, and the bra itself. Her skin was
so warm, so smooth, and he ran his fingers down her
back. His lips curved as he felt her shudder.

He pulled up her skirt, dragging at the lacy band of
her briefs until they skimmed over her bottom.

Sully moaned, shifting so that they could pull her
panties off, and then she straddled him again.

He looked up at her. Bathed in the silver glow of the
moonlight, her skin looked pearlescent, and he reached
out to touch his midnight goddess. She gasped when he
caught her breasts with his hands, and he fondled them.
She quivered, head tilting back, and her hair cascaded
down her back. She writhed against him, and this time
he could feel the molten core of her pressed against his
cock. God, he wanted her.

She caught her lip between her teeth as she quivered
above him. Looking up at her, seeing her body, the way
she undulated against him, was setting off a fire in him
that he needed to control, before he exploded. He grasped
her hips, rolling over so that she lay beneath him, and
she panted, surprised but smiling at the move. He gazed
down at her for a moment, and they both paused, catching their breaths.

He stared at her face, the gentle arch of her eyebrows,
those beautiful blue eyes, the straight nose and that
crooked, sexy smile. She was magnificent.

"God, you're beautiful," he whispered, and she smiled,
almost shyly.

"You're pretty gorgeous yourself," she whispered, her
gaze skimming his body, before her eyes once again met

his. In that moment, in that infinitesimal connection, something shifted inside him, something he couldn't name, but seemed to rock him to his core.

Slowly, he dipped his head and pressed his lips to hers.

Chapter 21

Sully closed her eyes, her arms twining around his neck. The kiss was tender, hot, slick and carnal, but yet she felt something, a weight, an impact that seemed to set her senses to overload and her emotions into a headspin. It was the perfect kind of kiss, full of emotion, passion and sensuality. Meaningful.

And so not what she was expecting.

She sucked in a breath as he pulled away from her, and kissed his way down her body. He carefully undid her skirt and belt—avoiding the daggers—and pulled the garment down her body, following it with his lips and tongue. She shuddered as the fabric slid down her legs, and then off her body. He shoved at his jeans, discarding them, and then was kissing his way back up her body until—

Her eyes widened as his lips kissed her. There. His hands stroked her, drawing out her reactions, making her tremble as the heat, the tension, coiled inside her. Oh. My. G—her neck arched when his tongue slid inside her, and she groaned, long and loud into the darkness. The stars above them were swimming as he laved her, over and over, until she was a hot, wet mess in his arms. He used his hands and mouth to wring extreme pleasure from her, and her back arched when that tension suddenly snapped, sending her spiraling into a cloud of bliss.

He didn't give her a chance to catch her breath. He crawled up her body, stroking her breasts, then biting and sucking on her breasts, until his hips found hers. He braced his arms on either side of her, his silver eyes meeting hers, and she gasped as he slid inside her. She brought her thighs up to his waist, and they both moaned at the change in angle, the deeper penetration. She reached for him, her breath hitching each time he withdrew, then slid back to the hilt. He covered her body with his, his hips thrusting, and she cried out as the passion once again swept over her, pulling her body taut with need.

He held her in position, hands grasping her shoulders as he slid home, and the heat exploded. She cried out, a sound snatched away by the breeze. Her nipples, her core, her very mind seemed to overload on sensation. She heard him groan as he thrust once more, his body hard and tight against hers, and then he, too, found release. Lightning crackled above them, and the air practically snapped with energy.

Heart thudding in her chest, she embraced him, trembling, as she tried to catch her breath, her reason, some modicum of control. She gazed up at the stars, and realized even her toes were clenched, and it took conscious effort to get her muscles, everywhere, to unclench.

"Oh, my," she panted, and he chuckled, setting off little rockets of sensation as he kissed her softly.

"Oh, my," he said, nodding.

He rolled onto his back and pulled her into his side, and they lay like that for a while, letting the wind play over their naked bodies. Dave stroked his hand down her arm, and she stretched against him, enjoying the contact.

"Well, that's one way to recharge," he commented, and Sully started to laugh. She definitely felt…renewed.

He pulled his T-shirt on over his head, then looked across at Sully. They'd arrived at the motel room in the wee hours of the morning, and had managed to catch a couple of hours' sleep. Which was hard when curled up to a soft, warm, luscious body like Sully's. Now, though, there was nothing warm, or remotely soft about the woman. Still plenty of lush, but as she strapped her weapons to that luscious body, he wasn't about to mention it.

She slid a dagger into her boot, and she was carefully drawing a long-sleeved blouse on over the interesting-looking contraptions strapped to her arms. He also noticed she wore her tricky little belt with the twin blades. The woman was a damn walking armory.

"Do you really think all that's necessary?" he gently asked her.

She eyed him, her expression set in an implacable expression. This woman before him was so far removed from the moaning siren in his arms from just hours before. She'd been like this, so grim, so focused, since she woke.

"Today—tonight—Marty will either finish off his spell and become the most powerful creature walking among us, or we will have killed that nutter."

He frowned, and stepped around the bed. "*We* are not killing him, Sully. I'm the Witch Hunter, remember. If you see him, you tell me. Don't go after him."

She tilted her head as she returned is gaze. "I don't want to see him. Just the idea that I will see him again makes me...nervous," she admitted. Then her chin dipped, and her stare became intent. "But I will do whatever I can to protect these people from him."

He didn't know whether to kiss her or criticize her. Sometime overnight, his sweet little Sully morphed into a fierce warrior woman. He eyed the leather pants, the boots, the black singlet with the gray overshirt. Her hair was pulled up into a braided bun on top of her head, and the severe style highlighted her cheekbones and drew attention to her bright eyes and that gorgeously crooked mouth.

He couldn't deny this whole badass vibe he was getting from her worked. He was a confident guy, he could admit when a woman turned him on, and right now Sully was ticking all the boxes. And that secretly worried him. He didn't want her anywhere near her psycho ex.

"This is why I'm here," he told her. "If you see him, let me know, and then let me do my job." He gestured to her outfit. "I don't want you to hurt yourself."

Sully's eyes narrowed. "Excuse me?"

He walked up to her. "These weapons—they're not toys. You could be in more danger from yourself with all these sharp blades than from anyone attacking you."

Her jaw slackened, as though she was lost a little for words. He sighed, and gestured to the guards strapped to her forearms. "Do you even know how to use these things?"

Her eyebrows rose. She thought about his words, then

gave him a small smile. "If you can take them off me, I'll leave them."

Dave cocked his head to the side, both annoyed and pleased with her challenge. "Really?"

She nodded. "Really."

He moved quickly, reaching for her right forearm. She moved so damn fast, her movements almost a blur as she flexed her wrists, and the pronged swords slid from their sheaths. She caught the handles, the blades moving in a wicked twirl as she easily evaded his grasp. He stepped after her, then hissed when he felt the flat of the blade smack his arm away. The blades twirled, and suddenly the tip of one was against the indent of his collarbone. He halted.

She eyed him coolly. "Yield?"

His eyes narrowed. "Never."

He dodged the tip, bringing his arm up to hit hers away from him. She turned, the blades flashing. He raised his arm to block her strike, and she hit him again with the flat of the blade. And then smacked him in the thigh with the second blade. He grimaced, and caught her wrist.

The world tilted, and he had a vague impression of the room flipping upside down, and then he landed on the floor, with a blade at his neck and one over his heart.

She arched an eyebrow. "Yield?"

He pursed his lips. That was…impressive. "Only if you show me that move," he said, and she grinned as she straightened.

"Let's get through today, first." She slid the pronged swords back into their sheaths, then extended her hand to him.

He grasped it, moving smoothly to his feet. "Fine. You…wear those." He gestured to the weapons she'd now hidden behind her long sleeves. He got the impression that she'd taken it extremely easy on him.

She nodded. "I'm glad we sorted that out."

She turned for the door, but he stopped her. "It's going to be okay," he told her. She smiled and nodded, but he knew neither of them were fully convinced. They were going up against a guy who could easily neutralize their powers, if the surrounding nulls didn't do it already. He grabbed his mobile ink kit and followed her out, his eyes on the leather-clad hips swinging in front of him.

Damn, but this look worked on her.

Sully stared at the street scene. The road had been closed to traffic, and people milled about, strolling from stall to stall. There was a fish market section down the end, and local farmers had brought produce. There was apple-bobbing, pumpkin-carving, clowns, wood-chopping, animals, bake stalls, food stalls...the scents and sights were like a colorful burst to the senses.

"I don't like this," Sully said, lifting her gaze from the crowd to the darkening clouds skidding across the sky. Talk about portent. The clouds had started to skid across the sky after lunch. A storm was coming.

Which was surprising, as the forecast called for a faux summer day.

She turned to Dave. He wore leather pants and a black T-shirt beneath his leather jacket, his dark sunglasses shielding his eyes. Tall, muscular...dangerous.

Badass sexy.

She ran her gaze over his body. Last night had been... wow. She had to admit, sex with Dave was...cosmic. Fireworks, lightning...she'd never experienced anything like that before with a lover. But there was something else, something more…like the buildup of a spell before the effect was visible. Full of magic, full of meaning and fraught with just as much danger. When this was over, though, she didn't know what was to come next, and that scared her. She'd lived her life quietly, safely, since leaving Irondell and Martin. Well, except for the two years she spent on the West Coast learning how to defend herself. But the four years since arriving in Serenity Cove had passed in idyllic peace and, well, serenity.

Dave had turned that all on its head. He'd threatened her—physically. And then had vowed to protect her. He challenged her, with every word, with every touch…he was able to get to the heart of her, the heart she'd successfully shielded from everyone. Until now. She was in very real danger of losing her heart to the Witch Hunter. She gazed around the crowd. And that was the problem. Marty had figured out a way to close down the Witch Hunter's vision. He'd figured out a way to nullify the null effect—which was pretty damned clever. He'd killed six people. He'd avoided the law, Dave and any number of nulls out searching for him. If they didn't find the other nulls before he did, they could be looking at a new world order by sunrise.

"There's Jacob," Dave said, raising his chin. Sully looked. Jacob was standing beside a chair and table set up, with a Free Tattoos sign. Dave grimaced. "Free?"

"They needed something to use as a cover," Sully said. Jacob had called them earlier that morning at the motel. He and his mother had convinced the mayor to let them set up another booth on the street so that Dave could tattoo the last of the purebloods under the guise of a market stall.

"But free?"

She smiled at the mock whine in his voice. "You're being very generous, whether you like it or not."

He turned to face her, his smile dropping a little. "I'm going to be at that stall pretty much for the rest of the day."

She nodded. "I'll be helping Jacob and his mom round up the rest of the purebloods."

Dave pursed his lips. "Don't stray too far. Stay with the crowd, no wandering off by yourself. This guy is using your guise to get close to these nulls, and I don't think that's by accident."

Her smile faltered. Dave was right. Marty had tracked her down, had tricked her friends to get close enough to kill him. Apparently her departure must have been a sore point for him. She nodded. "I understand."

"Good." Dave leaned forward and pressed a quick kiss against her lips.

"Dave!"

Dave startled at the call and drew back. They both turned. Noah was hurtling down the street, weaving his wave through the crowd.

"Hey, Noa—oh." Dave grunted when the kid ran into him full tilt. Noah clung to his legs, and Dave stooped down to hug him back.

"How's my little badass going?"

Sully winced at the language, but Noah laughed. "Great. How is the king of badass?"

Oh, my God. Now the kids were repeating it. She watched as Noah's father—George, Susanne's husband—shook his head as he approached, overhearing his son.

"The king is good," Dave remarked, then dropped Noah to his feet. He shook hands with George. "Hey, how you doing?"

George nodded. "We're…getting by." Sully could see the haunted look in his eyes, the dark circles and deep grooves. His wife's death had hit him hard. She ruffled Noah's red hair.

Dave looked down at the little boy. "Hey, do you want to come help me at the booth? Folks might be a little braver if they know you've got one of my tattoos…?" He raised his brow at George, who nodded in relief. "Thanks. I've got to go watch his sister in the pumpkin fairy production."

Sully blinked away a tear. Susanne was usually one of the stagehands for these things, working behind the scenes to get all the kids into costumes, soothe fluttery tummies and offer all sorts of encouragement. Noah's sister, Cherie, would be facing her first concert without her mom.

"Take your time, Dave and I can watch Noah," she told him.

George patted her on the arm. "Thanks," he said hoarsely, his eyes red, and hurried away before his son noticed.

Dave stretched his hand out to Noah. "Come on, LB, let's go get our ink on."

Noah scrunched up his nose. "LB?"

"Little Badass." Dave put a hand up over his mouth and mock whispered, "It'll be our secret."

Noah nodded. "Okay, KB."

Dave tilted his head. "KB?"

"King of Badass," Noah explained, his tone suggesting it was obvious.

Dave chuckled. "Yeah, that'll definitely be our secret."

Sully watched as the tall, leather-clad man led the little boy over to the booth. Noah was practically skipping.

Jacob greeted both of them, then went and got a stool for Noah to sit on as Dave set up his kit.

It was sweet, in a weird, testosterone-laden way.

She pulled a piece of paper out of her pocket and glanced at the list of twelve names. Mrs. Forsyth was already trying to locate the older purebloods, and as soon as Dave was ready for clients, Jacob would be out combing the crowd.

For now, it was her turn. She was on the hunt for purebloods.

Dave taped the adhesive bandage over the new tattoo and smiled at the twentysomething-year-old woman. She flicked her hair over her shoulder and eyed him.

"I'm thinking about getting a tattoo…here," she said. His gaze dropped to where she indicated. She was drawing her denim skirt higher up her thigh.

His eyebrows rose, and he gently grasped her wrist, stopping her from baring any more leg. "Uh, another time. It's best to let the body recover a little before going for the next tatt."

She pouted. He was sure she was trying to be flirtatious, but all he noticed was that her mouth didn't have that cute little quirk in it like Sully's did.

The woman sighed. "Fine. Maybe later, then?"

He gave her a noncommittal nod. "Maybe."

He turned away to clean and sterilize the needles, and looked up when Jacob joined him.

"How many is that?"

"Seven," Dave said, washing the needles in a solution before placing them in the pot on top of the camping stove Jacob had provided. It was rough, it was rudimentary, but the end result was sterilized needles ready to be used on the next pureblood null to make it to his booth.

Mrs. Forsyth had managed to locate the older pure-bloods, and Sully had tracked down three. Jacob had found two.

Dave leaned back to look behind Jacob. "Where's Noah?"

"Oh, he's right—" Jacob jerked his thumb over his shoulder as he turned. He frowned. "He was right be-hind me."

Dave closed his kit with a snap and rose. He lifted the cloth on the booth to look under. No Noah. He straight-ened to scan the crowd. "Well, he's not there, now."

Jacob paled. "I swear, he was right behind me."

Dave nodded, holding up a hand. "Okay. He's a kid. There could be lots of explanations, from deciding to go watch his sister in her concert to being distracted by a funny-shaped bird poop. Let's look."

Jacob nodded. "I'll go look around the stage," he com-mented, and strode off in the direction of the area desig-nated for performances.

Dave sighed. "Great. I'll take the bird poop." He walked around the booth, scanning the crowd. He wasn't going to panic. Sure, the kid was cute. Pretty cool, actu-ally. And tatted up with his own special ward. Noah was also full of curiosity, if his gazillion and one questions about tattooing, motorbikes, sunglasses, laser eyes, magic powers, leather underpants—how the hell that had come up, he still didn't know—and needles maybe turning into ninja spears for grasshoppers were anything to go by.

"Noah!" he called out the boy's name as he made his way through the crowd. The colors of the booths started to darken, and he looked up. Storm clouds were skidding across the sky.

Dave glanced about, his pace quickening. He didn't like this. He didn't like this, at all.

"Noah!"

Chapter 22

Sully glanced down at her paper. She, along with Mrs. Forsyth and Jacob, had managed to find eight out of the twelve remaining purebloods. Four were still outstanding. Marty needed only three. The paper in her hand darkened, and she looked up. Dark clouds, thick and voluminous, skittered across the sky, as though the Ancestors were angry and frowning down at everyone. She frowned. That cloud action was too fast to be natural. The night would arrive early.

Marty.

Damn him. She started to walk back toward Dave's booth. She waved to Cheryl, who was manning the Brewhaus Diner coffee stand. She noticed Tyler, in his sheriff uniform, standing beside it. She almost went up to him to ask him when she might be able to get into her home, but he was frowning as he tried to catch Cheryl's attention, and Cheryl was steadfastly ignoring him as she chatted to a young man who'd received his coffee but didn't seem in any hurry to move along.

Sully turned away. She'd have to catch Cheryl later for an update, but it looked like something had definitely changed between those two. She took two steps and halted. Was that Noah?

The red-haired boy was being led away from the crowd, toward the head of the walking trail that led down to Crescent Beach. He was being led by a woman wearing a long flowing skirt and a billowy top. A woman who looked a lot like Sully.

Sully blinked. No…

Noah tripped, and the woman turned to tug on his hand. Sully's heart seized in her chest, then started hammering.

"Noah!" She started to run after the pair, and stumbled a little when the woman looked casually over her shoulder. It was like looking into a mirror, or at a long-lost twin. The face staring back at her was her own.

Except for the eyes. Where Sully's eyes were blue, this woman's eyes were jet black. The woman spotted Sully, and her lips lifted in a smile. Then her features started to waver, and the boneless mass morphed into masculine features she knew all too well, and Marty scooped up a surprised Noah and started running.

"Noah," Sully screamed and bolted after them.

Dave stared around the petting zoo in frustration. Noah wasn't here, either. He moved his arm away from a donkey whose attention was becoming way too personal. Jacob hurried over to him, with George, Noah's father, close on his heels, his face pale with worry.

"I take he's not watching his sister's concert?" Dave commented.

Jacob shook his head, and George ran his hands through his dark hair. "Where is he?" The man's tone was panicked, his eyes wide with consternation. The man had lost his wife in a violent crime—Dave couldn't begin to imagine how he was processing the disappearance of his son.

"Is everything okay?"

Dave turned at the query. Tyler Clinton, in full sheriff's uniform, was eyeing George with concern. His normal reticence to involve the police, to involve others, disappeared. A little boy was missing.

"Sheriff, we need your help." Dave quickly informed him of Noah's disappearance, along with the fact that he may have been taken by a man who can change his appearance, by taking on the facade of anyone he came into physical contact with, and who was responsible for the recent murders in Serenity Cove.

To his credit, the sheriff took it well.

"You son of a bitch," Tyler hissed, eyes flashing with anger, his fists clenched. "You've known all this time—" he bit the words off, his gaze taking in George and Jacob. The sheriff pulled the radio from its holster on his hip and called for all available deputies to attend the festival in search of a missing six-year-old, believed to have been abducted. Then he pointed a finger at Dave. "You're with me. You withheld vital information to an ongoing murder investigation. That's obstruction."

The sheriff turned to George. "Do you have a recent photo of Noah? I'll need to distribute to the guys when they get here. We'll also make announcements from the staging area, and see if we can get everyone to help." He placed his hands on his hips, then looked at Dave. "Can this guy really play swapsies with his face?"

Dave nodded. "Yep."

Tyler sighed, then turned in the direction of the stage. "Let's get to it, then."

It wasn't long before most of the activities at the Festival were shut down—not because Tyler called for it, but because pretty much all of those attending the street fair wanted to help in the search of the boy. Tyler split the crowd into groups and assigned the groups areas to search.

Tyler beckoned him, and Dave followed him down the length of the street.

"You should have told me." Tyler's voice was low, and full of controlled anger.

Dave shot him a look. "Yeah, I can totally see how that conversation would have gone. 'Hey, Sheriff, your killer is a witch—I don't know who he is, or what he looks like, or why he's doing it, but I'll take it from here.'" Dave shook his head.

Tyler peered through the glass windows of a store. "You still should have told me."

"You were already suspicious of me," Dave reminded him.

"No, I wasn't."

"How many tourists do you ask when they're leaving?"

Tyler's lips curved as he looked back at him, eyeing the bike leathers. "You were never a tourist."

"But you see where I'm going with this. I have a job to do, too."

"You could have just told me."

"We witches don't air our dirty laundry." Dave looked

inside the window of the next store. Most of them were closed for the festival holiday. "Just like the wolves, the vampires, the bears..."

"So you were really going to kill your witch and leave me with an unsolved murder?"

"I'm a Witch Hunter."

Tyler grimaced. "No wonder people don't trust witches," he muttered.

"Hey, people trust witches," Dave protested. Tyler arched his eyebrow. "Mostly," Dave added, trying to be as truthful as he could.

Dave held up both hands. "Witch Hunter." He didn't like playing that card, would prefer to just drift in and out of a mission without pissing off the local law enforcement, but the reality is that he had a duty that, while focused on witches, had the recognition and enforcement from Reform authorities.

"The path of least resistance," Dave told him as they crossed the street. There was a break in the buildings, with what looked like a trail down toward the beach.

"So keeping this from me was to avoid an uncomfortable conversation," Tyler said, his tone dry.

Dave nodded. "Like this one? Hell, yeah." He squinted as he scanned the beach briefly. The wind was picking up, the temperature had dropped several degrees and the waves were crashing against the shore as though being hurled at the beach. He was about to move on when a figure running in the distance. Black pants, gray shirt.

Sully.

And she was bolting after something.

"Sully!" he cried out, taking the trail. His words were snatched away by the wind.

"What is it?" Tyler asked as he reached the top of the trail.

"Sully. Something's wrong."

Sully wasn't jogging leisurely along the beach. She was running at full pelt and was almost at the end of the beach where the headland started to rear out of the water. Dave took off after.

Sully clambered over the rocks. She heard Noah cry out, heard the fear in the little boy's voice. She hurried, her feet scrabbling over the wet stones slick with seaweed. The waves rolled in, smashing against the rocks, and she ducked under the spray.

She had to wait for a wave to recede before she climbed around a larger rock formation and stumbled when she landed on wet sand. A hole loomed in front of her, the entrance to a cave. The sand was drier up near the mouth of the cave, and she ran, plowing through the sand until she reached the cave and entered.

"Mar—"

An invisible force pushed at her, sending her flying against the rock wall of the cave. She landed heavily on the sandy floor, coughing as she tried to catch her breath.

Wicked laughter echoed through the cave, and she raised her head. The cave was huge, with various rock formations that created bridges and ramps within the space, so it was almost like a multilevel labyrinth, resident monster included.

She eyed Marty who was presently carrying a struggling Noah up a ramp. Had he—had Marty just magically blindsided her while carrying a null? His powers were getting stronger. Her shaking hands clenched fistfuls of sand. This was Marty. The guy who'd almost drained her dry, who had scared her so much, had hurt her so much, that she'd run from him. Not walked out. Not left. *Run*. All those years of training on the West Coast, all those hours of practicing with the weapons she created, all of that fled her in the face of the man she'd once trusted, and who had abused her so much. Memories, of him screaming in her face, of him pushing her, of her falling over furniture, against walls and doors, of glass breaking, cutting...they all surfaced, along with her sense of powerlessness, of the very real danger she faced with this witch.

"Let him go, Marty," she called out to him, and rose to her feet. She quickly bolstered her shields as she ran over to the base of the rocky ramp. The closer she got to Noah, though, the harder it was to maintain the protection.

Marty turned to face her. "I'm afraid I can't do that, Sully." He looked different. His skin was almost radiant, his eyes flashing. As though power itself was coursing through his veins, bringing with it a confidence and brashness she could never feed him. "I need him. He's the last."

Did that mean he'd killed already? She didn't think so. Each time she'd delivered a null to Dave at the stand, he'd seemed in good health and not reeling from the wound on his chest. Did that mean he'd captured the nulls? Is that why nobody could find the remaining purebloods?

"No, you don't." She started to jog up the ramp, and Marty whirled, his hand out.

"Stop right there," he told her. He reached behind him and pulled something out from the waistband of his jeans. Sully swallowed when she recognized the ceremonial knife she'd seen used in the vision to kill Amanda Sinclair. "Admittedly, I don't like using kids, but I'm working with a short time frame, here."

"You have to see this is crazy," Sully said, panting as she slowly advanced, arms up, palms out in a nonthreatening pose. Even she could see how much her hands were shaking.

Marty's eyebrows rose. "Crazy, huh? Crazy like a fox, maybe."

Noah squirmed, and Marty shook the boy. Sully took a couple of extra steps forward.

"I know what you have planned," she told him. "And it's clever, I have to admit—but it's so wrong, Marty."

Marty smiled grimly. "Only those in a weaker position would say that. To me, this feels very right—and long overdue."

Sully stepped closer again, and she had to lock her knees to stop from collapsing. Everything felt so unstable, so…shaken. "Why, Marty? Why are you doing this?"

Marty's smile turned into an unattractive twist. "Do you remember what you called me, Sully? Remember that day you ran out like a rat scurrying in a sewer…?"

Sully glanced at Noah. The boy was looking between them, his face pale, but his eyes—so like his mother's—showed a spurt of rebellion. She held out her palm in his direction, trying to make her warning to the boy to hold still look casual in the eyes of his captor. She'd learned that if you didn't move, didn't make eye contact, just burrowed down and let him vent, the storm would eventually pass.

"I remember begging you to stop," she told him quietly. "I remember you throwing me against that mirror."

Marty huffed. "Well, that was an accident," he told her. "You got me so mad."

She pursed her lips. So him throwing her up against a wall mirror was her fault? She shook her head. "You hurt me."

"When my father found out the Alder Keeper of the Books had cast me aside, he banished me from my coven," he rasped, and Noah cried out as the grip on the back of his neck tightened. "You called me pathetic."

Sully took a deep, quivering breath. "I realize that must have sounded harsh," she allowed. She couldn't agree with him, but she didn't want to outright challenge him, not knowing how he'd react.

His comment, though, brought a lot of things into sharp relief. He'd been cast out. For a witch whose powers were limited, he needed the safety of a coven to ward off threats. He would have been vulnerable. Alone. Although she thought that was a fitting outcome for this guy, she wouldn't have actually wished it on anyone. After living so long without her own coven, she knew how lonely, and how scary, it could be on your own.

Marty sneered. "You called me a pathetic vessel of puerile misery."

"I'd have to agree," a deep voice called out from behind her.

Relief flooded her when she recognized Dave's voice. She didn't turn, though, didn't take her eyes off Marty and little Noah.

Marty's eyes widened, and his hand moved. A fireball burst from his palm, and Sully ducked. She heard a grunt, a hiss and then a thud. She glanced over her shoulder. Dave was on the sandy floor of the cave below, and steam was rising from his jacket. Dave shot Marty an exasperated glare.

"Hey, watch it. This is my favorite jacket."

"Stand back," Marty shouted, and Sully turned in time to see him angle the knife toward Noah's throat.

She met Noah's eyes and saw a familiar terror, one she recognized from her own experience with this man. That day he'd pushed her down the hallway, and she'd fallen in front of the mirror… She'd seen her expression, seen the fear, the desperation…the depths she'd allowed herself to sink to. She saw that same fear, that same desperation in her friend's son. Something snapped inside her. Rage—but not fiery and unpredictable. No, this anger filled her like a cold, calm curtain of control.

She stepped closer. "You can't hurt him," she told Marty, her eyes on his.

"Oh, and who's going to stop me? You?"

She shook her head. "No." She lifted her chin in Noah's direction. "He is."

"He's a little badass," Dave called as he grasped the lip of the ramp and pulled himself up and over. He rose to his feet and winked at Noah. "Aren't you, buddy?"

Noah looked at Dave, then nodded faintly.

Marty smirked, then brought the knife down.

The blade halted about half a foot away from his body. Marty frowned and tried again. Again, he faltered, as though the knife encountered an invisible barrier.

Marty looked up at her and Dave, his eyes wide. "What have you done?" he rasped.

"You're not the only one who can draw symbols," Dave responded as he came up to Sully's side. "Only I'm better at it."

"He's protected," Sully told Marty. "It's over. You can't make your quota."

Marty shook his head. "No," he bellowed, his face blooming with the heat of his rage. He shoved Noah,

who screamed as he stumbled and fell over the edge of
the ramp. Dave launched himself over the edge, diving
for the boy. He caught Noah midfall and twisted so that
his body bore the full brunt of the landing on the cave
floor about twelve feet below.

Sully screamed, racing to the edge of the ramp to look
down. Dave wheezed, but he gave her a thumbs-up signal.
She turned around to see Marty running farther up the
ramp. The witch leaped across a divide to a rock ledge.
He scurried along to a tunnel opening and disappeared.

She hesitated, then Dave groaned.

"No," he gasped, his hand to his chest. He lifted his
gaze to Sully. "I'm warming up. He's got someone back
there."

She turned and ran, heart in her throat as she jumped
over the gap between ramp and rock ledge. She hissed
as her hands slammed into the rock wall, and she almost
bounced back. She clasped a rock bulge to prevent herself from plummeting backward into the cave. Taking a
deep breath, she scurried along the ledge, hugging the
wall until she reached the tunnel, and then started to run.

It was so dark. Sully braced her hands outward, using
her contact with the wall of the tunnel as a guide. A strangled scream echoed down the tunnel, and she sped up,
stumbling along until the tunnel opened up into another
smaller cavern. She skidded to a halt. A shaft of light
came through an opening in the roof of the cavern, almost like a natural skylight. The light was weak, though,
and growing dimmer.

A man lay cowering on the floor, Marty straddled his
body. His hands and feet were tied, and his yells were
muffled by his gag as he shook his head rapidly at Marty.
A woman lay on the ground nearby, her wrists and ankles

bound, tears streaking her face. Marty raised his hand and the blade gleamed in the weak light.

Sully reacted. She ran toward him, her hand pulling out one of her belt blades as she did. She raised her hand behind her ear and flung the blade.

Chapter 23

The woman screamed. Marty cried out in pain as the blade sliced across the back of his clenched fist, and he dropped his knife.

Sully leaped, her legs out in front, and caught Marty in the back with her foot. He tumbled off the man, and Sully landed heavily on the rocky ground, rolling with her momentum to gain her feet and spin around.

The null on the floor rolled rapidly away from Marty and kept rolling until he hit a boulder.

Marty reached for his knife as he rose to his knees, then his feet. His face was grim and full of anger as he faced Sully.

"You bitch," he said through gritted teeth. Sully put both her hands out, knees bent, waiting for his move. Marty started to laugh. "You think you can fight me?" He tossed the blade, letting it turn in his hand. Sully flinched at the nonchalance of his movement. "These are nulls, Sully. You have no power here."

Sully licked her lips, her gaze darting to the couple on the ground to the left. The man stretched his hand out and grasped the hilt of the blade she'd thrown at Marty. She brought her gaze back to the maddened witch in front of her. As long as she had his attention, he wouldn't realize the purebloods were cutting through their restraints.

She just had to keep him occupied long enough for them to escape…her, against the only witch to ever be able to use the null effect to his advantage. She swallowed.

"See, this is your problem, Marty," she told him, shaking her head as she sidestepped to the right. His gaze followed her—away from the bound couple on the ground. "You never got it."

He smirked, and she had to wonder what on earth she'd ever seen in this man who was becoming even more unattractive to her. "What's that, Sully?"

"You were always thirsty for magic, you always craved it and you never realized that magic isn't the only form of power," she said softly. She flexed her wrists, and her sai swords ejected from their sheaths, sliding along her arms until she grasped their hilts.

He grinned and his left eyebrow rose at the move. "You think you can take me on?" he asked silkily. "Do you forget all those times, Sully, when you were cowering on our living room floor, or beside the bed, quivering?" He spread his arms out. "That—that was power. And you always gave it to me."

Her eyes narrowed. "Well, I guess I'm taking it back."

She launched herself at him, and he brought his blade up. The clink and clank of blades striking each other filled the cave, little sparks coming off as the metals collided. Sully moved rapidly, spinning and ducking. A movement caught her eye. The couple had freed themselves, and were running toward the tunnel.

Her distraction cost her. She hissed when she felt the hot slice against her forearm. Marty had cut her.

He gave her a triumphant grin—until he saw the couple dart down the tunnel behind her. He shifted his gaze back to hers. "You bitch."

This time she smirked at him. "You have no idea."

She flicked her wrists, drawing her blades along her forearms in a defensive yet elegant move. His eyes narrowed and he came at her again, his blade flashing. Over and over, she blocked his strikes, the clash of metal ringing through the cave. He was forcing her back, his eyes wide with fury, his teeth bared.

She stepped back and halted. Her back was to the wall. Marty smiled.

Sully flicked the sai swords around to an offensive position, then started twirling them. She got faster and faster as she stepped forward, and Marty was forced to step back, unable to penetrate her wall of whirling blades.

"Martin Steedbeck," a familiar voice bellowed from within the tunnel. Dave.

She waggled her eyebrows at Marty. "Ooh, you're in trouble now."

"In accordance with Nature's Law, passed down by the Ancients, you have been found guilty, and for your dark crimes, the Ancestors call upon your return to the Other Realm, to a place of execution—"

Marty roared, lashing out with his feet and kicking Sully's knee out from under her. She fell to the floor, her knee landing hard on the rock surface. Marty smacked one sword out of her grasp, and grabbed hold of her other wrist as he stepped behind her, his knife at her neck. "Drop it."

He squeezed her wrist, and she could feel her fingers tingle. Her grasp relaxed on the blade, and it clanged as it fell to the stone floor.

Dave emerged from the tunnel. He stopped talking when he saw Sully on her knees, Mental Marty's knife to her throat.

"I don't recognize Nature's Law," Marty rasped, panting.

"It recognizes you," Dave said in a low, dangerous voice. He removed his sunglasses, sliding them casually into the inside breast pocket of his jacket. Son. Of. A. Bitch. He had to fight the natural instinct to go berserk all over the witch's ass.

The tip of the blade pressed under Sully's chin, and she had to tilt her head back to avoid it piercing her skin.

"Get up," Marty hissed to her. She rose to her feet, very carefully. One stumble, one awkward lean, and she could end up with a knife in her skull.

Dave's heart was in his throat. His fists clenched. He could still sense the nulls in the cave system, although their effect was weakening. Tyler was guiding Noah and the couple he'd almost cannoned into on the rock ledge outside. He'd told the sheriff to clear the area of nulls. If there were any nearby, they'd mute his capacity to fight this witch, and Marty would have the advantage.

"You're going to be fine, Sully," Dave said, trying to keep his voice calm and warm for her benefit, when he really wanted to bellow with rage at this witch putting the woman he loved at risk. He tried to convey all the hell he was going to visit on this witch with his eyes. "Don't even think about hurting her."

A clap of thunder reverberated throughout the cave. Sully glanced upward. The sky that she could glimpse at the end of the shaft was dark gray, and a flash of lightning jolted across the diameter of the shaft.

"Can you feel the power in the air, Witch Hunter?" Marty asked as he started to back toward the shaft. "That's *my* power. I created that."

Dave advanced, his shoulders moving in a way that made him look like a big cat stalking prey. Sully shuffled along with Marty, the knife at her neck silently urging her movement.

"But you can't complete the spell," Dave told him. Noah was protected. The other two nulls had escaped.

Marty shrugged. "Then I simply complete it between now and the summer solstice. I only need two more." He stepped up on a rock, and Sully hissed at the painful little prick under her chin. "Up."

"Sully," Dave's voice was low.

She gave him a shaky smile. "Trust me," she said in a tremulous voice. "It's going to be all right."

Marty laughed. "I don't think you're going to be able to make this feel better, Sully."

Dave frowned, his silver gaze full of concern. Sully was…calm. Alarmingly so. She slowly slid her hand to her belt. *Trust me,* she mouthed at him.

His mouth opened and his gaze flicked between hers and Marty's. Aw, hell. She could get herself killed.

He'd heard their fight through the tunnel, and he'd seen her display back at the motel. He'd been fairly confident she could protect herself—until she wound up with a knife at her throat. He wanted to blast Mental Marty.

He wanted to annihilate the bastard. That was his job. He did this alone.

His gaze met Sully's. She was pleading with him with her eyes. It wasn't like he didn't *want* to trust her, but… she was in a vulnerable position.

And she's armed to the teeth and knows more about personal safeguarding than he may ever learn. Damn it. He hated this. It was anathema to him, letting a woman— a woman in a vulnerable position—call the shots. But it was Sully. He had no idea what she was thinking, but she knew *something*…this was the woman who'd managed to hold her own against him, who could block an invasive threat to her mind and magic as easily as swatting a fly.

His frown deepened, but then he nodded. Just once. He kept his gaze on Marty. He could distract the witch, at least. "The Ancestors call upon your return to the Other Realm, to a place of execution, until you are dead. May the Ancestors—"

Sully's movement was graceful as she slid her blade from her belt and caught Marty's knife-wielding hand. She jerked it back, and Marty roared—and Dave winced— at the audible snap of bone. The knife fell to the ground, and she held his hand close to her body as she twisted and knelt. Marty flipped over her head, his feet flying through the air, as she used that same move on the man she'd used on Dave in the motel room. Marty yelled, his head tilting back as he cried out in pain. Dave ran forward, but the witch sat up, hands outstretched, and a wave of power rolled through the cavern. Dave was knocked backward, as was Sully. By the time he rolled over onto his back, Marty was hastily climbing the shaft toward the darkened sky above.

Dave bolted across the floor to Sully, who was just sitting up. "Are you all right?" he asked.

She nodded, then pointed at the shaft. "Go. I'm fine."

Dave sprinted across the cavern floor, leaping up over a boulder to grasp a bulge in the wall, and he started hauling himself up after the witch.

Sully stumbled to the bottom of the shaft. She wasn't anywhere near as fast as Dave, or that skunk, Marty. Her heart was pounding. Dave. All she could think about was Dave. Marty was strong. She could sense it in him. She would have tried to draw some of that power out of him, when he held her, but he would have sensed it immediately, and she couldn't get her magic on with a knife in the brain.

Her foot slipped and she gasped, clinging to the rock face. A ladder. A ladder would be really good about now. She kept climbing. The light was almost nonexistent now, and she was feeling her way up the rock wall.

Her arms were shaking by the time she got to the top and could feel the grass around the edge of the hole. She raised her leg, using it to lever herself out awkwardly. Panting, she looked around.

Oh. My. God. Clouds were swirling as though caught in a twister. Lightning flashed among the fiercely spinning clouds, illuminating the dark strands of a lethal magic. The sea at the bottom of the cliff showed white peaks as the waves roiled and rolled, as though caught in Mother Nature's washing machine. The wind was biting, and she had to bend forward to avoid being pushed back by its gale force.

Marty had tried to blast Dave with a ball of power, and Dave was currently holding it off. Streams of dark red fire were swirling toward him, but she could see they were slowly getting closer to him. She forced one leg in front of the other, her arms up to protect her face from the wind whipping at her. Her shirt cracked like a sail caught in a thunderstorm, and she could feel the fabric tear.

She had to help Dave.

As though sensing her, Dave turned his head, his silver eyes bright in the darkness. "Go away," he called to her.

She shook her head. She summoned her power, raising her hands toward Marty. He noticed her, and braced one hand in her direction. She reeled back under the impact of the blast, but managed to stop the dark fire from consuming her.

"Leave, Sully," Dave roared, his focus now on the witch.

Sully slowly crept forward, gritting her teeth as she tried to find her wedge through the wall of power Marty had thrown up. Marty was able to keep them both at bay, and his eyes brightened when he realized this. He was strong…too strong. Tears filled Sully's eyes at the realization.

She couldn't fight him off, not in a power struggle. His death magic was too powerful for her, and for Dave. A dark flame danced across her arm, and she screamed at the burn. Marty was going to kill them.

Dave shifted toward her, protective to the last. An idea hit her. She dropped her shields and mentally reached out for Dave. She felt his surprise, his confusion and then his acceptance. He reached back for her, and she grasped his hand. Marty started to fade in her vision as shards of light transferred between her and Dave. Blues, pinks, purples, the spears of light brightened. She sent Dave a mental image, and he squeezed her hand. Together they started to recite a spell, the Old Language glowing across her vision, like a magical teleprompter.

Marty frowned, wincing as his right hand started to glow. The force coming from him stuttered a little, then flicked on to high wattage, before stuttering again. Marty glanced down at his hand, turning it over. Sully and Dave continued to chant, but then spread their arms out, calling on the tempest around them, drawing in the elements—the wind buffeting them, the water crashing below them, the spark of lightning fire and the solid ground beneath them.

Marty's eyes widened when he saw the mark Sully had carved onto his hand when she'd thrown him in the cavern below. His gaze flicked to hers, and full comprehension dawned on him.

"No," he cried, trying to blast them away. Harnessing the power of the tempest, they rebuffed his attempt to incinerate them.

The mark on his hand glowed, and his skin began to blister. His face roiled, and he screamed in pain as his bones melted into another's features. First Jenny, then Susanne… Jack, Amanda, Mary Anne and Gary. Each time his face twisted, Marty screamed. He clutched at his skull, but the fire from within consumed him, his flesh melting as his bones turned to ash, plucked away in all directions by the wind.

Sully weaved on her feet, her hand gripping Dave's until they both fell to their knees. Sully dropped his hand, catching herself before she face-planted in the wet grass. Thunder roared, and lightning cracked, the blade of light spearing downward from the spinning clouds above.

The lightning hit Dave square in the chest, and he arched under the shock, his silver eyes glowing as the energy coursed through his body. Sully screamed as his lips pulled back, and for a brief moment his teeth glowed, his veins glowed, even his bones seemed to glow. And then the charge was gone, and Dave sagged to the ground.

"Oh, my God, Dave. Dave!" Sully hurried over to him, reaching for him carefully. She pressed her hand to his neck, her eyes closing when she felt his racing pulse, but even as she held her fingers against his skin, she could feel it start slow down.

"Dave, please be okay," she whispered as she cupped his cheeks. His eyelids fluttered, and it took a few attempts before he was able to force his eyes open. His silver-gray gaze met hers, and he gave her an exhausted smile.

"Well, that was shocking."

She laughed, her hands trembling, and she had to blink away tears of relief. "You are such a dick."

He lifted his shoulders.

"No, no, lie—"

He brushed aside her attempts to make him lie down, and she helped him sit up. She glanced up. The lightning was no more, and the clouds were no longer a whirling mess. They drifted slowly across the sky, revealing the night stars and the harvest moon.

"What was that?" she asked. Where had that lightning come from? Marty was dead. Incinerated. She didn't think it had been his hand that had called forth the spear of lightning.

Dave hissed, pulling at the neckline of his T-shirt and ripping it down the front.

Sully gaped. All of the markings on his body glowed on his skin, and then slowly faded, disappearing into smoke. All save one.

In the Old Language, emblazoned across his heart, was one name.

Sullivan Timmerman.

Dave gaped at his chest, then slowly raised his eyes to hers. "I—I think I just retired."

"What?" Sully gasped. She stared at his bare chest. His glorious, smooth, muscled bare chest, adorned with just her name. She smiled. All of those names, the proof of the Ancestors' hold over him, had disappeared.

Dave touched himself, then shrugged out of his jacket and the remnants of his T-shirt. He twisted about, turning his arms over. "They're gone," he breathed, stunned.

He looked up at her, and she smiled. "They're gone," he shouted, then clasped her head and brought her in for a kiss. She laughed against his lips, and collapsed against his magnificent chest. She smoothed her hands over him, testing for herself. The names were definitely gone.

Dave ended the kiss and rested his forehead against hers. His chest rose and fell with his pants, and she felt him shake his head gently against hers.

"You linked with me," he breathed.

She nodded. "I wanted to help you."

He closed his eyes in relief, in gratitude. "Thank you," he whispered, and kissed her sweetly.

Shouts drifted across the cliff top, and they both turned to the source. Flashlights were cutting swathes in the darkness, and Sully smiled when she saw the familiar faces of Tyler and Jacob, and Noah being carried by his father.

"Oh, look. LB." Dave slung his arm around her shoulders, and leaned in close to her ear. "I might be the king of badass, but you're the queen of whoop ass."

Chapter 24

Dave watched as the tall, dark-haired men emerged from the null council meeting. Both men had dark hair, both men had blue eyes, but both men were as different as night and day.

"Who are they?" Sully asked, curious. Dave slung his arm over her shoulders as the men approached, lazily inhaling her entrancing sent of rose, vanilla and…sunshine. She was wearing a pretty red summer dress, with buttons all the way from the V neckline to the hem. She looked so beautiful, so…feminine. He still marveled at the way she'd fought Mental Marty, and just how damn lethal she could be. She was smoking hot and fought like a ninja. He was in love.

"Friends," he said, finally answering her question.

One of the men shuddered, shaking out his shoulders. "I want out of here. It's weird," he muttered.

Dave's smile broadened. "Sully Timmerman, allow me to introduce Lucien Marchetta."

The lean vampire nodded at her, his smile quick and almost nonexistent. "Sully."

Dave gestured to the other man strolling toward him. He had a slightly more muscular build, particularly across his shoulders and in his arms. "And this is Ryder Galen. Ryder, this is Sully."

Ryder smiled and held out his hand. "Hi, Sully."

Sully shook his hand out of politeness. Cheers erupted inside the town hall, and her eyebrows rose. "Does someone want to tell me what's going on?"

A blond-haired woman skipped out of the hall, a wide smile on her face, and she caught up with the men, sliding her hand into Lucien's.

"And this lovely lady is Natalie Segova," Dave said, gesturing at the woman by Lucien's side.

"Marchetta," Lucien corrected, frowning. He glanced down at the woman by his side, and his frown disappeared, replaced by a genuine smile. "Her name's Natalie Marchetta, now."

"Hi," Natalie said, extending her hand. Dave's smile broadened. Natalie was a sweetheart, and her warm smile was contagious.

Sully shook the woman's hand, smiling back at her. "Hi, I'm Sully." His gaze stayed on Sully. She looked so relaxed, so…happy. He couldn't stop looking at her, and he could see out of the corner of his eye that Ryder was smirking at him. He would have frowned at the guy, but that would mean looking away from Sully, and well…he preferred this view.

There were more cheers inside, and Sully's brow

dipped in confusion. "Okay, now I'm really curious. What's going on?"

Lucien shuddered again. "I'm paying my debt." He arched an eyebrow at Dave. "We're even."

Dave nodded. "Yes, we are."

Lucien strolled over to a dark car and opened the passenger door for his wife. Natalie slid inside, and waved at them as Lucien climbed in, started the engine and drove off.

"Wait—did you say Marchetta?" Sully gasped as she finally recognized the name. "The vampires?"

"Well, technically Lucien and Natalie are hybrids. Ryder here is a light warrior."

"But, why are they all here? I would have thought vampires—sorry, hybrids—and light warriors would want to avoid Serenity Cove."

Dave shrugged. "I think Lucien Marchetta was overcome by a sudden desire to contribute to the community. The Marchetta Corporation has just established an investment program with the fishing co-op here."

Sully gaped. "Why?"

He grinned. "Because Lucien Marchetta owes me one, as does his wife."

"What did Natalie do?" Ryder queried calmly.

"She's researched the requirements for a request of recognition of the nulls as a breed on their own, and will oversee the submission process."

He enjoyed Sully's stunned expression. "Seriously?"

He nodded. "Seriously."

Sully turned to Ryder. "So…why are you here, if you don't mind me asking?"

Ryder smiled. "I'm also paying my debt. Dave mentioned that your closest medical clinic is over an hour away. My brother and I will help set up a clinic here for the nulls, and run the training programs for staff."

Sully turned and gaped at him. "You did this?"

Dave frowned. She was looking at him weirdly. "Not by myself—I had help."

"Dave, this will help them so much," Sully exclaimed softly.

He shifted uncomfortably. This is why he'd preferred to stay outside while the hybrids and the light warrior made their announcements. He didn't need the thanks, he preferred just quietly getting on with things and then disappearing.

The town hall doors were flung open, and Mrs. Forsyth scanned the street. She squealed when she saw them standing across the road. Darn. Was it too late to disappear?

"I'm out of here," Ryder said, and quickly jogged to his car.

Dave glanced about. His bike was down the block, and him running away would look fairly obvious to the little lady who was now hurrying across to them. He eyed Ryder's car enviously as his friend drove away. Darn, he could move fast.

"David, thank you."

He tried not to cringe outwardly as Mrs. Forsyth hurried up to him, her arms open wide. Only his mother called him Dav—

"David, you are so lovely," she said softly as she hugged him, and he had to lean down, she was so short. He patted her shoulder awkwardly. This was sooo uncomfortable. But nice, in its weird little way.

"It's nothing, Mrs. Forsyth," he said, embarrassed as Jacob walked out of the town hall, arms folded. The fisherman grinned when he saw Dave's discomfort. Dave shot a pleading look at Sully, who shrugged, grinning.

Traitor, he mouthed.

"You have to come over for dinner," Mrs. Forsyth exclaimed as she stepped back. Dave straightened and tried to make his disappointment look sincere.

"Oh, I wish we could, but Sully and I are on our way out today," he told her.

Mrs. Forsyth blinked. "You're leaving?"

He nodded, then grunted when Noah threw himself against Dave's legs.

"Don't leave, KB!" Noah cried, hugging him fiercely.

Damn it. He hadn't bargained on the kid. Something warm flared in his heart, and he smiled tightly. He wasn't going to get sucked in. He was the rolling stone that gathered no moss. The tattoo artist that could up and leave at the drop of a hat, the retired Witch Hunter who could disintegrate another, how could—

Noah looked up at him. "Please?" the boy begged. Those green eyes, that quivering bottom lip…those freckles. That warm spot turned into goop. Mushy, fluffy goop. Dave was touched, so touched that these people were welcoming him so warmly. He could understand how Sully viewed these people as family. He'd had more physical contact, more interaction with this community than he had any of the covens back in Irondell—including his mother's.

"We'll come back," Dave promised.

"You swear?" Noah demanded.

Dave grinned. "I swear."

A shadow fell over him, and he looked up. Aw, darn. The royal dick.

Jacob held out his hand. "Thanks," the fisherman

said. Dave accepted his shake, and winced as Jacob also thumped him on the shoulder. "For everything." Jacob's gaze slid to Sully, who was now talking to Mrs. Forsyth. "Take good care of her."

Dave nodded. "I will."

Then there was George, and Noah's sister, the sheriff and a whole bunch of others who wanted to come shake his—oh, wow, a hug. He nodded at Cheryl, the waitress, then stepped back toward Sully. He didn't miss the sheriff's gaze narrowing as he eyed the farewell.

"We should get going," Dave whispered in Sully's ear.

"Where are you going?" Jacob asked, squinting against the sun.

"Holiday," Dave informed them without giving too much information away, then waved as he and Sully managed to step away from the group. He handed her the helmet from his pannier, but hung on to it until she met his gaze.

"Are you sure you want to do this?" he asked, solemnly. It was a big move, for Sully. They'd decided to take a break—his first. Ever. Wherever they wanted to go, whatever they wanted to do…together.

She glanced down the street toward the small crowd gathered outside the town hall. She sighed. "You were right. I was hiding here. I love it here, but…you're right. This was my bolt-hole. I think I'm ready to travel, see some sights. Maybe even visit my coven." She nodded. "I want to do this."

He leaned forward and kissed her tenderly. "I'm looking forward to meeting your coven," he murmured. Then he grinned. "I'm also looking forward to introducing you to my family." He tilted his head. "Just don't mention your books."

She laughed as she slid the helmet on over her head. "I won't."

Her coven's archives were in a very safe place, and she'd pointed out to him that she could set up her factory…anywhere. They were going to keep things casual, see which way the wind blew.

He grinned. "Come on, sweetness. Let's go."

Sully stretched as Dave drove onto the grassy shoulder. He kicked down the bike stand and she slid off the bike as he cut the engine. She removed her helmet.

"Wow," she breathed, taking in the view. Chains of islands could be seen in the distance. "This is beautiful."

Dave made a sound of agreement as he removed his own helmet and straightened, his legs still straddling the bike. He crossed his arms over the helmet and lifted his face to the sky.

She took the time to appreciate the view—of him. His short hair ruffled in the light breeze. His sunglasses hid his eyes, but his face—it was probably the most relaxed she'd ever seen him.

"How are you?" she asked him as she walked toward him.

He looked at her. "I'm feeling great."

She gestured to his chest. "How do you feel about… the names?" They hadn't really spoken about anything in great detail. Nothing concrete about the future. Nothing concrete about a commitment—although this was the first time she'd up and left with a man. She wasn't quite sure how he felt about his change in circumstance, or what he wanted to do about his future…about them.

He shrugged out of his jacket, and then drew his T-shirt over his head. She looked about. They'd left the main highway about forty minutes ago, and hadn't seen a car since. Nor were there any buildings within view. This place, watching out over the ocean, seeing land in the distance... it felt like they were the only two people left in the world.

Dave glanced down at his chest. "It's...weird," he admitted.

"Weird, how? Like you've lost an arm, or something?" She couldn't begin to imagine what it would be like, having something that was such a part of you, that defined you, to a certain extent, suddenly disappear.

Dave shook his head. "No, not quite. More like an ache that you noticed you had, but only when it's gone."

She stepped close and ran her hand over his shoulder. "What do you think you'll do, now that you're not a Witch Hunter?"

His arm slid around her waist, and he tugged her close so that she was pressed along his side. Emotions fluttered at her. Attraction. Desire. Contentment. And something warmer, something deeper she was too afraid to identify. He removed his sunglasses, and his silver eyes stared at her intently. "I think I want to live a little, remind myself that life's not all about death." He leaned forward and kissed the corner of her mouth.

She sucked in a breath. "Oh?"

He nuzzled her ear. "Yeah. You taught me that." His voice was so deep, it practically vibrated in his chest.

She swallowed. "I did?"

"Yeah. You taught me...not to piss off a chick with a knife," he said, kissing along her jaw. Her nipples tightened in her bra, and she forced herself to focus on his kiss. *No! Words. Focus on his words.*

"Oh?"

"Yeah. You also taught me...that nulls are kind of

nice. Even the ones called Jacob." He ran his lips down her neck, and she trembled.

"Uh, okay…"

"But mostly you taught me that I don't have to do this alone. Any of it." He lifted her over the bike, so that she straddled it, facing him. The skirt of her dress hiked up with the movement, baring her thighs. He pulled her close, and she wrapped her legs around his hips. He cupped her cheek.

"Sully, I don't care what I do, or where I go—as long as it's with you." His stare was so solemn, so full of promise. "Whatever my life holds, I want to share it with you."

She blinked, overcome with the weight of his words… A weight that, if uttered by another man, at another time, would have felt crushing, but here, with this man, right now, it felt…right.

"You've taught me a few things, too," she murmured shyly.

His eyebrow arched, and he gave her a wicked look that heated her from the inside out. "Oh, I'm listening."

"You taught me that not all men in sunglasses are douchebags," she said, and his lips curved. Amusement, light and teasing, tapped at her. He leaned forward and kissed her, long and slow. He pressed her back, and she found herself lying back against the bike. "Uh-huh," he said, a soft, husky sound of encouragement.

"You taught me that leather can look good on, but much better off," she said, trailing her hand over his bare chest.

Desire. Hot. Hard. Gripping. It flooded him, and it flooded her. Her fingers trailed over the tattoo above his heart, her nails lightly scraping his nipple. She smiled when he swallowed, and then closed her eyes as he kissed his way across her collarbone.

His fingers slid beneath the neckline of her dress, and she felt the top button pop out of its loop.

She opened her eyes, staring up at the blue, cloudless sky. "But mostly, you taught me that I had closed myself off, that I didn't have anyone to truly share myself with, to talk with, to laugh with..."

He raised his head, his gaze meeting hers.

"You taught me that it was okay to trust again, Dave," she told him earnestly. "You taught me that a man could be safe." She smiled. "You taught me something that I hadn't even realized about myself...that I'd become a shadow, closing myself off to everyone. You taught me to open up, again."

He kissed her hungrily. "I love you," he whispered, kissing her over and over again. She arched her back, pressing her breasts against his chest, feeling his cock harden in his jeans. His fingers slid to the next button, and the next, and he peeled her dress open.

"I love you, too. So much," she said. She pulled back her mental walls, letting in his light, letting in the warmth of his love and feeding it back to him, firmly establishing their link. He groaned, caressing her, kissing his way across her chest. His hands slid under her, unclipping her bra and pulling it down her arms and off. She fumbled with the zipper of his jeans, sighing when she could feel the heavy, hard weight of him in her hand.

He drew back, just a little, his expression raw. "I will always be there for you, Sully. You're my everything."

"And you're the light to my darkness," she whispered against his lips, then kissed him, her tongue sliding in to tangle with his. The lace of her panties pulled taut across her hips until the fabric gave, the soft tear causing her to shudder as her desire turned her core into a slick channel.

She guided him inside her, and she moaned with pleasure as his length slid inside. When he was buried to the hilt, paused, then withdrew. His thrusts were long and slow, gradually quickening. She held on to his arms, and he grasped the handlebars. She moaned, the delicious friction of his body against hers, inside hers, sent her tingling. His eyes met hers, and they moved against each other, panting, linked physically, magically, emotionally, until it was too much, the pleasure, the sensations and sparks exploded around them. Sully cried out as she orgasmed, and Dave shouted his pleasure, out there in the middle of nowhere, bare to each other.

Dave swallowed, and Sully laughed with delight, experiencing a freedom, and a lightness of heart she'd never felt before.

Dave grinned and pressed his forehead against hers. "I give you my heart, sweetness."

She grinned back as she stroked her hand over the one tattoo that still marked his body. "You'd better. It's got my name on it."

He put his hand over hers, holding it there. "This is permanent, you know."

She wasn't sure if he meant the tattoo, or if he meant their commitment. Either way, she agreed. She nodded. "I know."

He leaned down, and they kissed, under a clear blue sky—with not a storm cloud in sight.

* * * * *

Jane Kindred is the author of the Demons of Elysium series of M/M erotic fantasy romance, the Looking Glass Gods dark fantasy tetralogy and the gothic paranormal romance *The Lost Coast*. Jane spent her formative years ruining her eyes reading romance novels in the Tucson sun and watching *Star Trek* marathons in the dark. She now writes to the sound of San Francisco foghorns while two cats slowly but surely edge her off the side of the bed.

Books by Jane Kindred

Harlequin Nocturne

Sisters in Sin

Waking the Serpent
Bewitching the Dragon
The Dragon's Hunt
Seducing the Dark Prince
Kindling the Darkness

KINDLING THE DARKNESS

Jane Kindred

For the freaks who suspect we could never love anyone...and just need someone to save us from ourselves. (With thanks to Aimee Mann, who expressed it so eloquently.)

Chapter 1

A timeless monument to spiritual devotion—and a 1950s architectural marvel that somehow managed not to insult the majesty of the burnished sandstone buttes into which it was wedged but to grace them—Sedona's Chapel of the Holy Cross wasn't where you might expect the gates of hell to open. But open they did, for a few brief moments on one gorgeous midnight last spring. On Lucy Smok's twenty-fifth birthday, to be exact. Funny thing, though, about opening the gates of hell to let something in: stuff got out. And it was Lucy's responsibility to round up the wayward "stuff" that escaped and put it back in. Cleaning up after Lucien. As usual.

Not that it was really his fault this time. It was their father who'd traded her twin's soul to the devil. And when Edgar Smok died, the bill had come due. Lucien's transformation into an infernal being had opened the gates until his descent to rule the nether realm closed them. In that brief interim, the path between the nether realm and this one had been a two-way street.

Dozens of hell beasts were now running amok.

The one she'd tracked this evening—or rather, early this morning—wore a female skin suit: a haggard-looking twentysomething waitress at a greasy spoon, dishwater-blond hair slipping out of a limp ponytail and into her eyes as she took Lucy's order. She was such a cliché that she had to be infernal.

Lucy had tracked the fugitive with a little help from the thousand-year-old Viking who happened to be dating Lucien's sister-in-law. Leo Ström was the chieftain of the Wild Hunt, and the instincts of the Hunt wraiths under his command functioned like a metaphysical GPS, homing in on any vicious killers in the area. As much as Lucy hated the idea of them, connections among the not-quite-human came in handy for her present mission. And Theia Dawn, Lucien's wife, had an entire family of not-quite-human connections. The Carlisle sisters, who claimed the demoness Lilith as their ancestor, seemed to attract it.

Lucy had other means of finding infernal fugitives, of course. As the CFO of Smok International and its subsidiaries, Smok Biotech and Smok Consulting—as well as its acting CEO in Lucien's absence—she had access to the world's most sophisticated database for tracking and logging unnatural creatures. But the fugitives from hell weren't in any database, and those that hadn't made themselves obvious through their sheer audacity in attacking humans right out of the gate, so to speak, were extremely good at blending in with the human population and keeping a low profile.

The stop at the coffeehouse had been serendipitous. After losing the trail, Lucy had taken a break to refuel, and the little downstairs café was the only thing open this early in the morning. She hadn't been sure until the waitress brought her order. A telltale flick of the woman's tongue at the corner of her mouth accompanying a rapid eye blink had given her away as a reptilian demon. Anyone else would have missed it. The demon saw Lucy's recognition in the same instant, eyes widening with alarm.

Before it could make its escape, Lucy grabbed it by the wrist and pinned its hand to the cool wooden tabletop.

"Let go of me." The eyes narrowed to reptilian slits with an unnerving clicking sound, like a muted camera shutter.

"You're out of your element."

The demon bristled, a reptilian reflex beneath the borrowed skin. "And you're about to discover how far you are out of yours."

Lucy smiled darkly. "You'd be surprised how far my element extends." She'd been banking on the fact that the demon wouldn't want to make a scene in the middle of a brightly lit coffeehouse with a small but decidedly human audience. She hadn't counted on the demon's desperation.

A hissing sound provided an instant's warning before the demon spat, giving Lucy the chance to duck and dodge, narrowly missing a face full of demonic acid. Unfortunately, the evasive action also loosened her grip, and her quarry was off in a flash.

Lucy catapulted over the counter into the short-order kitchen in pursuit of the creature, startling a busboy and a tired cook. The demon flung the busboy across the kitchen as a distraction, but Lucy wasn't here to pick hapless busboys up off the floor. She was here to stop a hell fugitive.

She leaped over him and followed the demon through the back door into the alley. It had given up its pretense of humanity, shedding its skin and leaving the corpse of the unfortunate woman it had been wearing in a heap among the trash bins as it dropped onto all fours and scuttled through a crack between two buildings.

Lucy spared a glance back up the alley to make sure she wasn't observed before using the advantage of her own unnatural blood to scale the back of the building and race over the top. Inheriting some of Lucien's curse came with a few perks. She leaped down onto the unlit street just in time to block the demon's egress as it crept out. The demon reared up on its hind legs in surprise, poised for an attack, as Lucy drew her gun—she'd brought her favorite, the Nighthawk Custom Browning Hi Power 9 mm—and aimed between the thing's inhuman eyes. The skin it had shed evidently wasn't the corpse of a human after all, but a sort of shifter's shell, as evidenced by the demon wriggling to redon the same form like a translucent skin coat, albeit a slightly fresher version. It was an obvious ploy to appeal to Lucy's humanity. Always a mistake.

"Please." The demon held its human-appearing hands in the air. "I have babies at home. I'm a single mom."

"Oh, for God's sake." Appealing to her womanhood was an even bigger mistake. Lucy palmed the slide to chamber a round. "Hope you kissed them goodbye."

Before she could pull the trigger, something barreled into her from her left, knocking the gun from her hands and her to the ground. Her Russian martial arts training kicked in automatically, and Lucy flipped over and onto her feet before her attacker could grab her, swiping his leg with a roundhouse kick from a crouch and incapacitating him with a one-two punch to the neck as he fell. When he hit the ground, Lucy leaped on top of him and dug her fist into the hair at his forehead to slam his head back onto the concrete. He managed to block her as she swung at his jaw simultaneously, trapping her arm inside his with an elbow jab toward her throat. They were deadlocked.

Lucy glared down at her attacker, sizing him up. A dark hood framed salt-and-pepper hair and a tightly compressed, disapproving mouth in a tan face offset by a sharp, muscular jaw. For a middle-aged man, he was in damn good shape. Not an ounce of fat on him.

"That was an escaped fugitive whose rescue you just came to, G.I. Joe. Thanks to you, a violent predator is in the wind."

"From where I'm lying, you seem to be the violent predator." He let go of her arm, and she let him yank his hair from her fingers. "I'd like to see your badge."

Lucy snorted with derision and rose to collect her pistol from where it had spun against the corner of one of the buildings. "I don't have to show you anything."

"Maybe I'll just make a citizen's arrest, then."

Lucy let out a sharp, humorless laugh. "I'd like to see you try."

The demon's rescuer rubbed the back of his head with a grimace as he got to his feet and observed her for a moment with a frown of mistrust. "Exactly what did that one-hundred-pound woman do that's so dangerous?"

Lucy checked her clip. "Killed at least five people last week, for starters. I tracked her here from Flagstaff, where she left a trail of bodies. Two of them kids. I won't go into detail, but let's just say she's got an appetite for skin."

Midlife G.I. Joe frowned and shook his head. "You've got the wrong girl. She's been working at the Mine Café for a month. Hasn't strayed beyond a ten-mile radius since she got here."

"How would you know?"

"I make it my business to know when someone extra-human is in my neighborhood. And this one's harmless."

So he'd peeked beyond the veil. Lucy studied him. Seemed human. Didn't necessarily mean he was. "My sources say you're wrong."

"Well, your sources are mistaken. I'm part of a neighborhood watch—of a sort—and I'm telling you this girl can't be your perp."

Lucy holstered the gun in her shoulder strap. "You think I'm law enforcement?"

"Not ordinary law enforcement, obviously. But yeah. Aren't you?"

"Let's just say I'm a private contractor. I track things that don't belong in this plane. And I tracked an infernal flesh-eater here."

His eyes had narrowed in a glower at the words *private contractor.*

"Maybe you tracked something here, but it wasn't her." He pulled up his hood as it began to drizzle, warm skin tone reduced to a craggy monochrome silhouette under the flickering sodium streetlight. "And we don't need any private contractors stalking our citizens. The town of Jerome takes care of its own."

"I don't really care what you 'need.' There's a killer on the loose, and I intend to take it down. Wherever it attempts to hide out."

He glared down at her, trying to use his height to dominate. "If I see you in Jerome again, I'll consider you hostile."

Lucy gave him her best death stare through the now-pouring rain. "Why wait? You can consider me hostile right now." She turned and strode away before he could form a retort, heading through the downpour back toward Main Street, where she'd parked her car.

As she wound down the two-lane highway, the beat of steady autumn rain against her windshield was already slowing, and the sun had made a dismal appearance through the dull steel of cloud cover in the five minutes it took to reach the bottom of Cleopatra Hill. The town of Clarkdale ahead of her was the first sign of civilization—if you could call it that—in the Verde Valley Basin. After that, the somewhat larger sprawling suburban town of Cottonwood laid claim to the title with a population of twelve thousand. Not that her current base, Sedona, was really any bigger, but it felt like a larger town with its hip vibe and nonstop stream of tourists who came for the metaphysical ambience and stayed for the real magic of sun and stream and stone.

After filling up at the Clarkdale Gas-N-Sip, Lucy headed for the restroom outside the convenience store, unwinding her knotted braid and separating the soaking hair into three dripping plaits as she rounded the building.

She sensed the presence in the bushes before it leaped, but there was only time enough to meet its force with a full frontal attack of her own. The creature snarled and went for her throat as she aimed for its solar plexus. She was taking a guess at where that was, but her left fist landed solidly while she followed up with a right to its jaw. Sharp teeth grazed her knuckles—luckily, she was

immunized against lycanthropy—but the blow to its gut
had slowed it down.

While its footing wavered for an instant, Lucy drew
her Nighthawk Browning and emptied four rounds into it
point-blank. It made a sort of furious yelp and snarl and
took off so swiftly she couldn't follow. More angry than
wounded, it seemed. Which was impossible. She hadn't
gotten a clear look at what kind of wolf it was, as it had
been mostly fur and blur, but the snout was clearly lupine and the upright frame humanoid. Four Soul Reaper
bullets should have incapacitated it almost immediately.
It should be writhing in its death throes on the ground in
front of her right now.

Though it wasn't the impact of the bullets in Lucy's
gun that killed infernal creatures. It was the poison inside. "Soul Reaper," Lucien had nicknamed it, because
it obliterated anything not human from within the host
flesh, and if any remnant of a human soul happened to
remain within the infernal, Soul Reaper sent the remnant to hell.

After cleaning up in the restroom, Lucy paid for her
gas and hit the road, grateful that no one else had been
outside the Gas-N-Slip. She was bone tired—by her
count, she'd been up for nearly twenty-four hours—and
ready for a hot shower followed by a stiff drink and bed
by the time she got home.

She glanced down at her bloody hand as she unlocked
the door. It was a little bit more than a graze. Immunization or no immunization, she had to take care of the bite.
With a growl of her own, she went inside, gun firmly in
both hands while she made a quick survey of the place.
It had become a habit. When she was sure the villa was
empty, she took off her jacket and slipped the shoulder

holster off and tossed it on the couch along with her piece. She'd meant to find something more permanent and less ostentatious than a villa at an exclusive resort once she'd decided to stick around after Lucien's departure, but apartment hunting took a back seat to rounding up hell beasts.

After cleaning the wound, she decided on a bath instead of a shower. Baths weren't really her thing, but every muscle ached at this point, and Epsom salt was a thing she believed in.

As the tub filled, Lucy wrapped her arms around her knees and rested her forehead on them, replaying the wolf's moves and her own, analyzing what she might have done better. Merciless postmortem had been ingrained in her from Edgar's training since she was a kid. She'd let down her guard because she was tired. Mistake number one. Vigilance was mandatory. But for the most part, she'd followed protocol. It was the creature that was the unpredictable element.

What the hell *was* that thing? How could it have kept moving with four Soul Reaper bullets in its chest? It *was* infernal. It had to be. But it moved faster—and it was larger—than any garden-variety werewolf she'd encountered. And it had seemed somehow less…furry.

The tub had filled, and Lucy shut the water off and leaned back against the built-in headrest. It really was a hell of a tub. She hadn't paid much attention to it when she rented the place, since she'd only intended to use the stand-alone shower. But it was deep enough and wide enough for her to stretch out both arms and legs and let them float in the silky water without touching anything.

Eyes closed, she ran through the encounter in Jerome with the same critical review. The reptilian-demon waitress wasn't in the Smok registry, so, killer or not, it was definitely a fugitive. But was it possible it wasn't the killer she was tracking? What were the odds more than one hell fugitive would be hanging out in Jerome, Arizona? The artsy haven carved into the side of Cleopatra Hill in the Arizona Black Hills, a former copper mining boomtown that had turned its colorful history into a touristy cash maker as an active "ghost town," had a grand total of less than five hundred permanent residents.

The vigilante—which was what G.I. Joe likely was, given his skulking around in a dark hoodie in the middle of the night on his "neighborhood watch of a sort"—had been adamant that the waitress wasn't Lucy's killer. Not that Lucy was going to take his word for it, but he hadn't struck her as a liar, whatever else he was. He genuinely seemed to believe the girl was harmless. And he claimed he'd been watching her for a month.

Maybe he was just a perv who liked watching young women. But he hadn't given off that vibe. And he hadn't made any typical masculine overtures toward Lucy, who was just a few years younger than the waitress appeared to be. Honestly, it had kind of annoyed her. She was used to being noticed by guys his age—just hitting their midlife-crisis stride and hyperaware of any younger woman in their vicinity to project their insecurities onto and gauge their own desirability. Not that she *wanted* middle-aged dudes creeping on her, but it was almost suspect when they didn't.

So what was this guy's deal? Middle-aged but in almost-military shape, living in tiny, artsy Jerome in the middle of nowhere keeping tabs on its "extra-human" population? Maybe *he* was a fugitive. Lucy opened her eyes. Maybe he was *her* fugitive.

The phone rang from the living room. She'd left it in her pocket when she stripped out of her wet clothes. Lucy sighed and climbed out of the tub.

She got to the phone after the call had rolled to voice mail, and she listened to the message on speaker while toweling off. An older woman spoke a bit hesitantly, as though her request was awkward. She spoke on behalf of "the council," which wanted to contract Lucy's services to investigate a werewolf sighting. In Jerome. So much for taking care of its own.

Chapter 2

Whoever this "council" was, they were clearly desperate. Lucy called the woman back to verify the job's legitimacy before agreeing to take it. Despite the unorthodox call to her personal phone, they'd been referred to Smok Consulting through the proper channels. They were anxious to meet with her this morning, in an hour, wanting to take care of the problem before too many residents—or more likely, tourists—became aware of it. This "werewolf" was probably the fugitive she was tracking. She could kill two hell beasts with one stone.

Lucy pushed down the exhaustion. She'd stayed up this long. Might as well go for two days. She couldn't remember when she'd last eaten—she'd left a gorgeous plate of hash browns cooked into a giant pancake, plus a sweet side of bacon, at the coffeehouse—but there wasn't time for a proper breakfast. Maybe she could grab coffee and a muffin somewhere in Jerome before meeting her contact.

Lucy sighed. As much as she'd resented Lucien's attitude about Smok Consulting's work, it had sure seemed easier handling these kinds of jobs with two people. Maybe he hadn't been entirely useless.

The road to Jerome, once she'd left Sedona and driven through the flat stretch of valley beyond Cottonwood and Clarkdale, was straight up the escarpment separating the Black Hills from the valley. One thing Lucy hated was driving slow, and driving up between the stacked limestone retaining walls that hugged the mountainside meant driving slow.

Arriving in Jerome with fifteen minutes to spare, Lucy parked in front of an artsy-looking shop in the bottom of a restored Victorian on lower Main Street near the Ghost City Inn, an old miners' boardinghouse turned B and B. A wrought-iron sign hanging over the door declared the shop was Delectably Bookish. She wasn't sure if it was a café or a bookstore, but she thought she smelled coffee brewing inside. She opened the door, pursuing the scent. It looked like a reading room, with comfy mismatched chairs and couches strewn among tables beside stacks of hardback books—and, hallelujah, a shellacked wooden counter at the back bearing an espresso machine and a case of pastries and treats.

Lucy made a beeline for it. Coffee was definitely brewing. But there was no one in sight.

"Hello?" She leaned over the counter, peering into the back through a beaded-glass curtain. "Anyone back there?"

Nothing.

She was running out of time, and she really needed that coffee. She'd been awake for almost thirty hours at this point. "Hey, *hello*? You've got a customer out here."

In frustration, she tossed a five-dollar bill on the counter and grabbed a lemon poppy seed muffin, stuffing a bite into her mouth while she went around the counter and helped herself to a cup of coffee. There were no paper cups. She'd have to bring back the cappuccino cup after her meeting.

Lucy sipped her coffee as she headed back around the counter and nearly dumped it on herself as she looked up. At the bottom of the staircase that led from the book stacks to the second floor of what she assumed were more book stacks, a ruggedly handsome middle-aged man stood watching her, arms folded—and they were seriously impressive arms packed tight into a white T-shirt—a scowl on his tanned face. It was her G.I. Joe vigilante.

"Find the cash register all right? I hope that pesky drawer didn't give you any trouble. It sticks sometimes."

"Cash register? No, I—just needed a coffee. There was nobody here. I left money on the counter."

"Jerome isn't your personal hunting ground. You might want to learn some manners before someone mistakes you for a thief and treats you accordingly."

Heat rushed to Lucy's face. "Yeah? Well, you might want to be a little more responsive when a customer is waiting. In the real world, baristas don't get tips when they ignore people. Maybe you shouldn't be taking bathroom breaks when you're supposed to be working."

"Maybe you should learn to read." His head tilted toward the words printed in large gold lettering on the outside of the glass panel on the door. "We open at noon."

Lucy tried to maintain some dignity, the stupid muffin crumbling in her hand as she set down the coffee cup. "Why the hell is the door unlocked if you're not open?"

Barista G.I. Joe studied her for a moment, his expression giving away nothing. "We generally trust our neighbors around here. This is the first time I've ever been robbed."

"Robbed?" Lucy picked up the five-dollar bill and waved it at him. "I paid you. But you know what? Forget it. Keep the coffee and the muffin. And the damn change. Maybe you can buy yourself a functioning lock."

She tossed the muffin and the money on the counter and stalked to the door, willing down the prickly heat in her skin threatening to top off her humiliation with a furious blush. She made it all the way to the door—and then pushed instead of pulled.

His soft laughter as she adjusted her grip on the handle followed her out.

Lucy wasn't easily flustered. Years of practice being the "good" daughter under Edgar's strict rules and dealing with supernatural rogues, paranormal entities and therianthropes—or shape-shifters, in layman's terms—of every description had made her preternaturally calm under pressure. Everything was to be kept inside. A Smok wasn't supposed to react with emotion but with a cool head to defuse the most unpredictable situations. And she certainly didn't get embarrassed. What was it to her if some petty wannabe-vigilante barista chose to call her a thief just because he couldn't be bothered to man the counter at his day job?

Normally, she'd have already forgotten the encounter. Maybe it was the lack of sleep—and caffeine—affecting her, but her blood was boiling, and she couldn't shake it off. She wanted to go back and punch the guy in the mouth.

Lucy gritted her teeth and entered the landscape-dominating Civic Center building on Clark Street that housed the town hall, an odd mix of classical architecture and Mission Revival that defied the small-town-Victorian aesthetic.

With a few minutes to spare, she stepped into the bathroom to make sure she was presentable. Charcoal-gray pin-striped suit immaculate, white shirt crisp, nothing out of place. After tucking a few stray hairs into the loose braid that hung down her back, she touched up her Blood Moon lip stain—the dark, dramatic hue was the one concession she made to traditional femininity; the over-the-top color went beyond sexual appeal, making an aggressive statement that made her feel in control—and headed upstairs to her meeting.

The door to the meeting room opened outward—like a respectable door. Lucy pulled it open and stopped on the threshold in disbelief. Among the three council members sitting at the table was Barista G.I. Joe.

His dark brows drew together into a disbelieving scowl that matched the one she was no doubt displaying as he met her eyes. "You have *got* to be kidding."

The elderly woman who'd risen from the seat next to him at Lucy's entrance glanced from him to Lucy and back. "Do you two know each other?"

"No, we don't," said Lucy before he could answer. "We just had a misunderstanding about coffee."

"I see." The woman reached a hand across the table. "I'm Nora Peterson."

Lucy stepped forward with a nod and shook Nora's hand, trying to ignore the unfriendly glare emanating from beside her. "Lucy Smok."

Nora indicated the chair opposite her. "Please have a seat."

As Lucy sat, she reevaluated her initial assessment of

G.I Joe's age. Prematurely graying hair had made him seem older at first glance. He was definitely on the nearer side of forty.

She smiled politely at Nora and the other council member, avoiding the glowering eyes. Even though they were compelling. And an intense deep cinnamon, just a shade darker than amber. Not that she noticed.

"I didn't realize the town council would be here. Generally, people like to keep these matters hushed up."

Nora tilted her head. "The choice of meeting place may have been unintentionally misleading. We're not exactly the town council. We're more like…the paracouncil." She gave Lucy a slight smile. "We're a volunteer group. But we've taken it upon ourselves to manage incidents that fall outside the normal operations of the town. With the council's blessing. Unofficially."

Lucy took out her phone to take notes. "So they do know about these paranormal occurrences."

"Everyone knows." The man on Nora's other side shrugged. "Jerome is a small town. It's hard not to know things. We just don't talk about them. Except for the ghosts, of course." He smiled. "They're sort of our livelihood."

Lucy nodded, uncertain whether he was being facetious. "I see. Thank you, Mr.…"

Nora clucked her tongue. "So sorry, Ms. Smok. This is Wes Mason."

Wes reached over the table to shake Lucy's hand, his dark skin weathered and rough. "How do you do?"

"And Oliver Connery." Nora indicated Barista G.I. Joe.

Lucy turned to him with a bland, polite expression. "Mr. Connery."

He rose to shake her hand, maintaining a similar expression in return. "Pleased to meet you, Ms. Smok." The handshake was firm but not too firm.

Lucy sat back in her chair. "So you said there's been werewolf activity?"

"We assume it's a werewolf," said Nora. "We haven't personally gotten a good look at it."

"You're sure it's not coyotes or stray dogs? And you're certain it's only one?"

"I think we all know the difference between a dog and a werewolf." Oliver Connery wasn't quite as unflappable as he'd pretended. The other two members of the council glanced at him, as if the defensive tone was out of character. He seemed to realize it and dialed it back. "We've spotted tracks matching the profile of wolves that disappear into human footprints. Normally, this wouldn't be cause for alarm. Most shape-shifters just want to be left alone, and we believe in a live-and-let-live philosophy."

"That's not consistent with my experience, Mr. Connery." Lucy calmly met his eyes. Now she was in her element. "Rogue shape-shifters are never benign. Every one I've dealt with has caused chaos and destruction."

"Your experience? Forgive me, but you can't really have much experience. I'm a little surprised, honestly, to find that someone so young is the CFO of Smok International. Or that the CFO herself would take this job."

Lucy fixed her gaze on him. "I've been deeply involved with the company operations—both the biotech side and the paranormal-consulting side—since I was fifteen, and I started working as a consulting agent when I turned eighteen. I spent the last five years traveling Europe and the eastern states as Smok Consulting's premier field agent before my father turned the business over to me prior to his death. And I am telling you—from *ex-*

perience—that shifters who aren't actively managing their conditions and integrating with normal society are dangerous."

Oliver opened his mouth, but Wes spoke first. "Ordinarily, I'd agree with Oliver, but this is a different breed. We've never encountered any so malevolent. It's been responsible for at least three vicious attacks in the area—official reports are attributing the deaths to a rabid mountain lion, but we have eyewitnesses who claim to have seen a large, misshapen wolf. That's why we've called you in. This is bigger than we can handle. We took a vote." He glanced at Oliver a bit apologetically. "It was two to one in favor of bringing in professional help."

"Well, you've made the right decision." Lucy spared a cool glance at Oliver. "This is my area of expertise."

Oliver's strong jaw was tight. "I'm not sure I care for your use of the word *normal*, but despite my reluctance to bring in an outsider—whose motives are purely mercenary—I concurred with Nora and Wes's assessment that this isn't ordinary. If it's a wolf, it's like no wolf I've ever encountered."

"You can't have encountered many, Mr. Connery. Smok Consulting tracks this kind of activity closely, and we have no previous evidence of any werewolves in Jerome, Arizona."

"You assume every werewolf in existence announces itself to you."

Now, *that* was an odd thing to say. Perhaps Oliver Connery had experience after all. Personal experience.

"You assume all the unnatural creatures in our database are aware that they're in it."

One dark brow, in stark contrast to the silver in his hair, twitched.

Nora made an effort to regain control of the meeting. "So how do you usually approach these matters? Despite the fact that people are aware of certain odd goings-on in Jerome, we do want to maintain some discretion."

Lucy nodded. "Absolutely. I'd like to start with a list of all reported sightings, including times and dates and any physical contact. And then I'll survey each of the sites, interview any eyewitnesses who are willing to come forward and get to work tracking the creature or creatures down."

"I'm not sure how many eyewitnesses will be willing to talk to you." Nora and Wes shared a look. "But I'll give you what I can." She rose and shook Lucy's hand again. "We're very grateful for your help. In the meantime, Oliver will take you to the location of the most recent sighting so you can examine the physical evidence."

Lucy paused as she rose with the others. "Oh… I wouldn't want to put you out, Mr. Connery. I'm sure I can find it on my own."

"Please, call me Oliver. And I'm sure you can't."

"You doubt my abilities?"

"I don't have any idea what your abilities are. It's not about your abilities. It's just that it's not something we can simply write down and give you directions to."

One of her abilities was being able to kick the asses of men twice her size. She supposed she could put that ability to use if she had to. Again.

Lucy shrugged. "Well, if it won't inconvenience you." She nodded to Nora and Wes as they headed out into the hallway before she turned to give Oliver a pointed look as he came around the table. "I suppose you have someone to cover your shift?"

"My shift?" He stopped in front of her, forcing her to look up.

"Aren't you working at the coffee shop?" She smiled darkly. "You did say it opened at noon."

Oliver chuckled, hooking his thumbs into the back pockets of his jeans. "I don't work there."

Lucy frowned, the usual potency of her practiced icy stare diluted by having to look up. "Then what were you doing there?"

"I live upstairs." He smiled back at her as if they were having a perfectly friendly conversation. "I own the place."

"Oh."

"So that coffee and muffin you stole come directly out of my profits."

She didn't normally lose her temper, but there was something about this guy that totally pushed her buttons. "I paid for the food!" Her fists were clenched at her sides as she resisted the urge to punch him in the face. The urge was strong.

His eyes were laughing at her, crinkled at the corners. "A large coffee is two fifty, and the muffin was four seventy-five."

"Four seventy-five for a *muffin*?" Lucy yanked her wallet from her inside pocket and pulled out another five and shoved it at him. "That's two seventy-five you owe me, then. I'm not leaving a tip for such poor service."

Oliver stared down at the bill as if he wasn't quite sure what to do with it or how to respond to her, thumbs still firmly in his pockets. When she continued to hold out the money, he took it at last and tucked it into the pocket of the flannel shirt he'd put on over the T-shirt since she'd seen him in the shop. It gave her the impression she must have caught him getting dressed.

Lucy cleared her throat deliberately. "My change?"

That dark eyebrow twitched again. "I don't keep a cash register on me. I'll just consider this an advance on your next muffin." He rolled up his sleeves and reached to open the door, and Lucy took a broad step past him to get it herself.

As she pushed it open and went through, he chuckled once more behind her. "I see you figured out how doors work."

Chapter 3

Oliver studied Lucy Smok's profile as she followed his
directions and drove toward the Gold King Mine & Ghost
Town attraction just outside the town proper. When he'd
clashed with her the night before, he was focused on her
militant intrusion into his world, her unwarranted attack
on poor Crystal Harney, an "undergrounder" who was
just trying to get by.

Crystal belonged to a certain class of the not-quite-human who were shunned by those who ran in elite circles
like the world of Smok International. Oliver had seen his
fill of vulnerable undergrounders being victimized and
demonized among the paranormal-aware community, and
he'd vowed to watch out for them when he could, since
no one else would. Lucy's arrogant insistence that Crystal was a killer rubbed him the wrong way, the sort of attitude he'd seen from law enforcement types all his life.

Then, today, when Lucy had appeared in his shop after

raiding his kitchen, Oliver took her for a spoiled brat. In the dark and the rain the night before, he hadn't noticed how young and slight she was, and it was hard to reconcile the two versions of her. But discovering she was Lucy Smok, the high-powered twenty-five-year-old CFO of Smok International the council had brought in to deal with their problem, had thrown him for a loop. How all three things could exist simultaneously in one compact—and highly opinionated—person was difficult to process.

She was also one of the most visually striking women he'd ever seen.

Pale aquamarine eyes and porcelain skin contrasted sharply with almost-ebony hair, and the deep red lipstick she wore—like the stain from a beet—enhanced the effect. The paleness of her eyes made her seem like a dangerous wolf. He might have suspected her of being a shifter herself if she hadn't been so adamantly bigoted against them. She also possessed a sharp cockiness he didn't see in most women, the kind of confidence a woman would need, he supposed, to run a multimillion-dollar corporation—especially at such a young age.

He kept coming back to that. Because, beyond her puzzling contradictions, he was having trouble reconciling his own powerful attraction for a woman almost ten years his junior. It wasn't the image he had of himself. Later in life, ten years wouldn't matter so much. But a man in his midthirties chasing after a woman in her twenties was just embarrassing. Not that he was chasing after her. He didn't chase. And he wasn't interested in any kind of intimate involvement. He was done with that. But the attraction was undeniable.

It was almost visceral, like he'd been waiting for her, his senses pricking up in anticipation as if his body recognized her. And not in a sexual way—though he couldn't deny there was that, too—but with a sense of familiarity, of knowing, that he couldn't explain and didn't particularly care for. Her scent seemed made for him, a blend of cardamom and amber, something both earthy and exotic at once. And he didn't think she was wearing perfume.

"Now where?"

Oliver blinked. "What?"

She glanced over at him, annoyance drawing her ebony brows together. "Where do I turn?"

They were at the crossroad where Jerome-Perkinsville Road split off in two different directions, one toward the rustic museum of antique mining machinery and the other up into the hills.

"Oh, sorry. To the right. You can pull over by the gate."

Lucy turned a bit too swiftly, tires kicking up dirt and gravel, and drew up in front of the rusted barrier chaining off the private road. "It says No Trespassing."

"We're not going in. We're just heading up the forest road a bit. We could drive in farther, but I don't think your car is made for dirt-road driving." Her expensive convertible two-seater looked like it was designed more for show than for sport.

He noticed the dress boots with a two-inch block heel under her tailored suit as she stepped out of the car. She was even shorter than she seemed. He could probably pick her up and carry her under one arm like a caveman claiming his mate. Not that he approved of cavemen scooping up and claiming women. Or that he considered her a potential mate.

Oliver swallowed and reined in his idiotic thoughts. Sometimes it seemed like his brain took pleasure in going off on tangents that would make him uncomfortable. At any rate, how such a slight-looking woman could possibly be one of Smok Consulting's premier field agents was beyond him. Going after someone small and defenseless like Crystal was one thing. And Lucy obviously had some kind of martial arts training. She'd briefly overpowered him with the element of surprise on her side. But what was she going to do when she tracked one of these things down? Call animal control?

Lucy was eyeing him with a mixture of impatience and annoyance. "Well?"

"This way." Oliver strode past her, hands in his pockets, up the dirt and gravel road, not waiting to see if she'd followed. Her expensive, unscuffed boots crunched on the gravel behind him. They weren't going to be unscuffed for long. He led her around the bend, where he veered off the road and headed downhill over the remains of old mining spoil, only to realize she was no longer behind him.

He turned to find her standing at the top of the hill with her arms folded, watching him. "Too steep for you?" he called up to her.

Lucy uncrossed her arms and rested her fists on her hips. "Mr. Connery, is there a point to this little trek?" Her ability to project was impressive. She must have had stage experience.

"It's Oliver," he yelled back. "And yes."

After regarding him with suspicion for a moment longer, she finally headed down the side of the hill with a sigh—extremely sure-footed on the damp earth despite the boots that didn't look like they were made for hiking. It occurred to him as she came closer that perhaps it looked like he was leading her out into an isolated area for nefarious purposes. He'd forgotten to put himself in her shoes—not that he'd fit them—which was a large part of his meditative practice.

"Sorry about that," he said when she reached him. "I should have told you what we were doing. This is where we tracked the creature after it was spotted lurking around the Ghost Town. The lupine tracks disappear here, to be replaced with human footprints."

She looked where he was pointing, and Oliver stepped aside and moved off a few paces to let her examine the area without him hovering behind her. Lucy sank into a crouch, perfectly balanced on those thick-heeled boots, and took out her phone to snap some pictures before straightening and walking around the prints to get some shots from another angle. After walking farther down the hill to follow the now-human prints for a ways, she turned and headed back up.

"I see what you mean. The animal tracks aren't standard wolves. I've never seen any quite like that. Certainly not that size. But those are definitely human prints leading away from them, with no sign that anyone else was out here until they appeared." She glanced at Oliver's footwear—a much more utilitarian pair of old brown work boots. "Except you, evidently. And now me, of course."

Oliver tilted his head and studied her, amused. "You think I'm the werewolf?"

"Are you?"

"Would I tell you if I were?"

Lucy shrugged and headed back up the hill. Oliver followed, and they walked in silence until they reached her car and got in.

"I'm not," he said as she started the engine.

"Not…?"

"The werewolf. For whatever my word is worth to you."

"Exactly as much as any man's is worth."

He had the distinct impression that meant "zilch."

She turned the car around and pulled back out onto the paved road. "Besides, I don't think we're dealing with a werewolf."

"Oh?"

"Lycanthropic transformation isn't instantaneous and smooth. The creature would have struggled and fallen, and the human shape would have been on all fours before the footprints began. There's no sign of any transition at all with these tracks. It's as if the creature simply chose to be human at that moment."

"What kind of shifter could do that?"

Lucy was quiet for a moment before she answered. "None that I know of. So where to now?"

"Haunted Hamburger."

She looked over at him. "Haunted...what?"

"Best burgers in town." He smiled. "I think I owe you a meal."

The outdoor seating overlooked the entire Verde Valley—the hundred-mile views the restaurant boasted of along with burgers, brews and "boos." The distinctive red-rock formations that defined the Sedona landscape, made blue and soft by distance, marked the horizon like the rim of another world. Lucy gazed out across the panorama while they waited for their food, wondering how much of this territory might "belong" to the creatures she was hunting.

"It's a pretty great view, huh? The ghosts seem to like it here, anyway."

She turned toward Oliver, who was sipping his porter. "Hmm?" Lucy glanced at the valley once more. "Oh.

Yeah, it's nice. I was just thinking about the direction this thing might have gone. The tracks we looked at must have been made within the last few hours since the rain stopped."

"That's right. We got the report of the sighting about an hour after I caught you harassing one of our citizens."

Lucy ignored the bait. "And what makes you think the tracks were made by the same creature responsible for the 'mountain lion' attacks?"

"Because similar tracks were seen at the sites of those attacks. And a kid was found close to that spot yesterday with his throat torn open and his intestines missing."

The same MO as the beast she'd been tracking from Flagstaff.

Oliver grimaced as the burgers arrived. "Sorry. I wasn't planning to talk about that while we ate."

"Why not? Isn't that why you brought me to Jerome? I didn't come for a social visit."

"No, of course. And to be clear, *I* did not bring you here. I was outvoted, if you recall. But don't you ever take a break?"

Lucy shrugged. "I'll take a break when they do." Which seemed like it was going to be never. She dug in to her burger, having forgotten how hungry she was until now. "So, where were the other attacks?"

"A hiker was killed in Deception Gulch near the old mine at Hull Canyon, and a couple of campers were torn to shreds near Woodchute Trail. And there was one more sighting recently at Hogback—the Old Miners Cemetery just south of town. But no contact there."

"So it's staying close to Jerome." Lucy washed down her burger with a sip of root beer. "I wonder why."

Oliver gave her a wry smile. "Some people like it here."

"No, I'm sure they do. I mean, why, specifically, would it gravitate toward a small town with limited hunting and few places to hide in an area that's neither urban nor wooded. Werewolves tend to prefer hunting grounds near large groups of people where they can blend in and stalk at night, or they isolate themselves and hide in undeveloped forestland and hunt small game. But this one—if it is indeed just *one*—has gone a few miles out, perhaps to hide, but then returned to the center of Jerome, where it made a brazen kill that it could have been caught at."

"Maybe it isn't afraid of being caught." It was an unsettling idea.

While they both concentrated on their food, Lucy pondered where to start her hunt.

After a moment, Oliver set down his burger and took a drink of his porter. "So, how do you intend to catch it?"

"I don't intend to catch it. I intend to kill it."

His hard jaw was set even harder. "So you're judge, jury and executioner."

"That's right. That's what people like you pay me to be. What did you expect me to do, put it in a zoo?"

"Doesn't your biotech company develop drugs to help shifters lead 'normal' lives?"

"We have certain promising pharmaceuticals in development but none on the market yet."

"Isn't that your brother's bailiwick? You both inherited the company, didn't you?"

Lucy breathed evenly. "Lucien has a lot of responsibilities that keep him from the day-to-day operations. But yes, Smok Biotech is Lucien's particular area of interest, and the anti-lycanthropy project is one that he's spearheaded."

"There are rumors about him."

Her hand remained perfectly still around her glass, and she kept her expression neutral. "Rumors?"

"That he's actually at some swanky rehab center in California, and his addiction is being quietly covered up."

She made a dismissive sound and emptied her glass. "Lucien isn't an addict. Rest assured, the company is in very capable hands. My brother just happens to be a rather private—and busy—person. You can spread *that* around your rumor mill." Lucy set her napkin on the table and pushed her plate away. "I'll take a drive out to Hogback and see if I can spot anything unusual. In the meantime, a sketch of the creature would be useful in determining what we're dealing with. Did you get a detailed description from any of the eyewitnesses?"

"I'm afraid not. We have fairly limited resources at our disposal. But I do have this." He took out his phone and displayed the photo, turning it toward Lucy on the table. "The eyewitness at the Gold King Mine got a picture of it before it took off. I'm afraid it's not very clear."

Lucy studied the blurry image, like a photo of Bigfoot through the trees, only this was a large, dark, doglike shape on its hind legs, its muzzle caught in midsnarl. As unclear as it was, there was something unsettling about the image. The creature seemed fully aware it was being photographed, as if it was posing for the camera, the snarl a ghoulish grin.

And it was a dead ringer for the thing Lucy had shot this morning.

Chapter 4

Lucy studied the photo on her phone while she waited for dark. It was blurred—as her glimpse of her attacker this morning had been—but she was certain that if it wasn't the same creature, it was one of its kind.

After seeing the picture, she'd changed her mind about the sighting in the cemetery. What this creature wanted was prey, and it seemed to prefer getting as close to populated areas as possible. It was likely to try again closer to town. And the creature that had attacked her this morning was intelligent and had sought her out on purpose. She needed to begin thinking the way it would.

Most likely, it knew she was here. And it was probably proud of its kill. It would return to the site of its latest victory to gloat, knowing she'd be there.

As dusk fell, she got out of the car and walked down the embankment where they'd seen the tracks before climbing up the other side of the hill into the area marked

No Trespassing. Full dark had hit. It was a new moon. But Lucy had no trouble seeing in the dark. Her cycle was perfectly aligned with the lunar month—and with PMS came the weakening of the drug that suppressed her condition.

Lucien's anti-lycanthropy compound had come in handy after their twenty-fifth birthday ushered in the transformation. There had been just one little problem with Edgar's calculations when he'd sold his firstborn son's soul to the devil: he hadn't figured in the fact that Lucy and Lucien represented a rare occurrence of opposite-sex monozygotic twins—genetically identical except for an extra X chromosome—and the curse had affected both of them. Lucy's change was only partial, but partial was enough. She'd become sufficiently practiced that she could use her infernal enhancements when she needed them, but Lucien's compound kept her from being a slave to them. It was "shift control." And like birth control, it only effectively balanced her hormonal cocktail about twenty-one days out of the month, leaving her vulnerable to accidental transformation during that critical week.

Lucy scanned the darkness for movement. She didn't have to wait long. Along the perimeter of a tailings pond—the slurry from leftover mining waste—something was skulking. It crouched on all fours, stepping out slowly into view, before rising on its hind legs to face her, letting her know it saw her, too. If it was the same creature, it showed no sign of being injured. And this time it laughed. The unnerving sound carried unnaturally, echoing across the hillside, and Lucy made the mistake of reacting, a slight recoil, a barely perceptible shudder. In that split second of reaction, the creature sprang into motion, striking her as it pounced and rolling with her over the ground with its claws slashing.

She couldn't reach for her gun from this angle. She should have had it ready. Her reflexes and instincts were shit when she was this tired.

Lucy scrabbled left-handed for the knife in her boot while defending herself from the creature's claws with one arm, her fingers closing around the handle just as the massive jaws clamped onto her left shoulder. With a primal shriek, she grasped the knife firmly and punched upward with it between her attacker's ribs. The thing howled with outrage and stumbled back, sheer hatred in its eyes.

It was readying for another attack, but this time Lucy was prepared. The shriek and the punch had been impelled forward on the strength of the infernal component in her blood, and as the creature came for her, she jerked the shifting bones at her shoulder blades to unleash her wyvern wings and leaped into the air to meet the creature's advance head-on, talons extended as they grew from her nail beds.

Weakened by the knife in its gut, it couldn't match her ferocity, and a final kick to the knife itself drove it in deep. The furious creature snarled and howled again at the dark of the moon before turning tail and loping away into the brush. As it disappeared among the foliage, she saw the distinct shape of a fully clothed man.

Ordinarily, she'd have flown after it, but she'd reached the limits of her second—or maybe third—wind. With the rush of adrenaline fading, Lucy wobbled on her feet, wings and talons retracting. The compound was still working for the most part, but she'd have to get another dose soon or risk transforming at an inopportune moment—and being unable to shift back on her own. In the meantime, she needed to clean up her new wounds and get some goddamn sleep.

Climbing back up to the car took a monumental effort. Lucy leaned back in the driver's seat and closed her eyes just for a moment. When she opened them, the stars visible through the windshield had shifted significantly. The clock on the dash read two in the morning. Her muscles ached, and her shoulder was killing her. She touched her fingers to the torn cloth over the bite; it was soaked with blood. There was no way she was going to make it home like this. And she knew the address of exactly one person in Jerome. He'd said he lived in the building his shop was in, which meant the upstairs must be his residence.

Lucy drove back to Main Street in Jerome and managed to find parking in front of Delectably Bookish once more. Her head swam, and the ground dipped and swayed as she got out of the car. Lucy gripped the post beside the entrance of the shop to steady herself and pounded on the door.

A light came on above, followed by the lights in the shop a moment later. Oliver Connery appeared, shirtless, salty hair askew and glaring furiously out of those cinnamon-brown eyes as he unlocked the door.

"What the hell is—" He stopped, staring openmouthed as he took in her appearance. "Jesus. What happened? Come inside." Oliver put an arm under hers and led her in to sit on one of the couches. "The werewolf?"

"I'm even more sure now that it's not a werewolf." Lucy rubbed her brow with the back of her wrist. "It's incredibly fast and resilient—and strong—and it shifts with the wind, like it just decides when it wants to be human."

Oliver had gone to the café counter to grab some towels, and he returned with them, shaking his head as he pressed one to the shredded shoulder. "I knew this was a bad idea."

"I assure you, I'm perfectly capable of handling this thing now that I know what I'm up against." She was sure of no such thing, but she wasn't about to listen to more of his criticism of her age and experience. Or implicit criticism of her sex.

"So you didn't kill it."

Lucy grabbed the towel from his hand. "It wasn't for lack of trying. You need to get over this idea that all lycanthropes are misunderstood people who need to be given a chance. This thing is a monster."

"That isn't what I meant." Oliver frowned down at her. "You're going to have to take that suit off. We need to disinfect the bite, and you're probably going to need stitches." He held out his hand. "Come with me."

Lucy bit back another retort about being fine and not needing any help and instead took his hand to let him pull her up from the couch. Because as much as she hated to admit it, right now, she was not fine.

Upstairs in the bathroom of Oliver's apartment, Lucy peeled off the torn suit and blood-soaked white shirt—both of them ruined by her transformation before the creature's teeth had even sunk in—and sat begrudgingly on the covered toilet to let Oliver clean the wound and sew her up. "I can do that myself," she complained between gritted teeth. "I know how to stitch up a wound."

"Oh, for God's sake, stop trying to impress me. I get it. You're experienced. You're tough as nails. You're a total badass."

"I'm not trying to—"

"That wasn't sarcasm." Oliver glanced up, his cinnamon eyes dark with concern. "I am impressed. I'm also very worried about this bite. If it's a werewolf—"

"It's not a werewolf. And... I happen to be immune."

Oliver's dark brows drew together. "Immune?"

"One of the perks of owning a biotech firm that specializes in parapharmacology."

"I see. I don't suppose that particular pharmaceutical is on the market for ordinary folk?"

"It's part of a limited trial."

Oliver's jaw tightened, but he said nothing else.

As he tied off the stitches in her shoulder, Lucy became acutely aware of the fact that she was sitting here in his bathroom in her bra and underwear while he was wearing nothing but a pair of flannel pajama bottoms. One of the other aspects of her heightened senses at this point in her cycle was unusually intensified sexual desire.

After putting the first aid kit away, Oliver glanced up and seemed to realize her state of undress, as well. "Let me get you a robe." He slipped out of the bathroom and returned with one in blue-and-black flannel that matched his pants.

"Thanks." Lucy rose and attempted to slip her left arm gingerly into the sleeve and nearly pitched forward into him.

Oliver steadied her, instinctively avoiding her arm and shoulder, instead catching her about the waist. His hands nearly circled her. Lucy looked up into his intense russet eyes. There were similar-colored highlights in the salt-and-pepper hair, and what she'd thought of as a tan was a matching cinnamon-bark undertone in his skin, evenly warm...everywhere.

Her spine twitched as she resisted a full-body shiver. This was no time to indulge her overactive wyvern hormones. It would be a disastrous mistake. She breathed in his scent—a damp, dusty smell like the desert after rain when the creosote bushes released their resin. She could swear she felt one of her ovaries dropping an egg.

"No, no. Hell, no." Lucy pushed his hands away and pulled on the rest of the robe, tying it with a jerk. Her hands were sweating.

Oliver blinked and took a step back, his expression mortified. "That wasn't a move. I was just trying to make sure you didn't crack your head on the basin."

"I know it wasn't a damn move. I wasn't talking to you."

He blinked again. "Who…who were you talking to?"

Lucy's head was starting to throb. She groaned and clutched it in both hands, unconsciously rubbing the spots at her hairline where a pair of ruby dragon horns had protruded just hours ago.

"Are you all right?"

Lucy shook her head and regretted it. "I need to go home."

"You can't drive in this condition."

"Don't tell me what I can do."

Oliver sighed patiently. "Your injuries aside, when was the last time you slept?"

"I don't sleep."

"You don't *sleep*."

"I don't have time. I catch a power nap when I can." The truth was that she couldn't sleep at this time of month. And she really had to stop smelling his desert-dusty-rain smell right goddamn now.

Lucy pushed past him and headed for the door. She wasn't sure if it was chivalry or indifference that kept him from trying to stop her as she advanced into the hallway weaving like a drunk. She stumbled and landed on her ass on the carpet runner at the top of the stairs. *Good move. Idiot.*

Oliver stood watching her, arms folded, from the doorway of the bathroom. "Would you like the double bed or the queen?"

She let out a low growl of defeat. "Can I just sleep here? Maybe put a grave marker on it and call it done."

He laughed, his right cheek dimpling in a way that made her want to growl more. "I'll get you a blanket." He crossed to the linen closet and took one out. "Of course, the queen room is right here if you prefer."

Lucy followed his glance to the open doorway on the other side of the bathroom. A high, fluffy-looking bed with a down coverlet posed invitingly beneath a sloped ceiling. "Why do you have so many rooms?"

"It's just three bedrooms, actually. But I've been planning to turn it into a B and B since I bought the place and took over the bookstore. I'm thinking of calling it Bed, Book and Candle."

"Nice." The bed really did look enticing. "Maybe I could catch a few winks." She got to her feet, steadying herself against the wall, and accepted the blanket. With a questioning look, Oliver offered his arm. She wasn't sure what would happen if she touched his bare skin right now, but she knew it wouldn't be good. "Thanks. I think I've got this." Somehow, she managed to pull off a semblance of normalcy, making it inside the bedroom and closing the door before she collapsed gratefully into the downy oasis.

She was almost asleep after all when something she'd been aware of in the back of her mind came to the fore. Oliver's bare chest had been notable for more than its exquisite form. He had four puckered scars, impact craters with jagged starred edges that looked distinctly like the kind made by bullets. It meant nothing, probably. Maybe he'd been in Afghanistan or Iraq. But they had the pale pink color and sheen of a recently healed injury. And they were placed almost precisely where the shots she'd fired into the hell beast would have landed yesterday morning. And lycanthropes were known for rapid healing.

Chapter 5

Lucy was gone in the morning. Oliver hoped to God she'd gotten some sleep. His sleep, on the other hand, hadn't been good. He couldn't get her off his mind. For an instant last night, when he'd caught her from falling, she'd looked at him with what he could have sworn was naked desire. It had shocked him. And the next instant, the look had been gone, leaving him wondering if he'd imagined it.

He worried the ring on his right hand with his thumb. Vanessa's ring. She'd been gone for more than five years, but he still couldn't take it off. Transferring it from the left hand to the right was the most he'd been able to do. It reminded him not only of his loss but also of his part in it. He was responsible for Vanessa's death.

Oliver imagined what she'd say to him. *You can't take credit for the failures and ignore the successes.* But the raid that day had been more than a failure. Darkrock had no business going into an unsecured nest without doing the proper reconnaissance first. And Oliver had gotten cocky, imagining that despite the disadvantage of not knowing how many vampires were holed up in the meth lab or how organized the vamps were, he had what it took to handle whatever they found. Darkrock had sent him, so Oliver had gone.

Vanessa had been his partner, in life and on his Darkrock team. Their team was first, positioned in a side alley near the den, and Oliver and Vanessa had scaled the fence into the weeds and garbage. Oliver had kicked in the back door while the other members of the team made a frontal assault. They'd expected a handful of meth addicts sharing needles and sharing each other's depleted blood. They'd expected any vampires, at least, to be sluggish with the daytime hour. What they hadn't expected was an ambush.

A very sophisticated operation had been overseeing the nest—a nest of donors, not vamps. They'd fed Darkrock an anonymous tip about the place, one that seemed reasonable on its face. It was a known hangout for meth heads, and meth heads were often mixed up in the trafficking of blood. Because of that symbiotic relationship between addicts and vampires, a house full of addicts often ended up breeding a house full of low-rent, weak vamps. And those that remained donors had only a short shelf life, so the siring vamps would move on once the supply dwindled.

When Oliver and Vanessa and the rest of the team had busted into the house, they'd expected to round up the victims and vamps with little resistance. Instead, they'd been set upon by very healthy, bloodthirsty vampire lords. One of them had Vanessa before Oliver even knew what had hit them, and the rest of the team was dead. The vampire lord holding Vanessa had smiled at Oliver, reading his mind, knowing what Vanessa was to him, before taking a drink.

Oliver slammed his fist down on the counter, jarring the coffee cups. He didn't need to go down that road again. That was a dead end. In more ways than one. As he got the coffee started for the morning, his phone vibrated on the counter beside him, skittering across the slick shellac. He was on call for the Jerome Volunteer Fire Department this week, and they were calling him in.

After shutting down and locking up, he headed over to the firehouse, expecting some cat in a tree or a kitchen fire at the burger place, but a two-alarm fire was in progress at the newly built storage facility off State Route 89A on the road down the mountain toward Verde Valley. Oliver's crew was assigned to search and rescue while the first crew fought the blaze. The storage units were brick and metal, but the summer had been dry, and maintenance hadn't been kept up to clear weeds and brush from around the facilities. And some clever asshole had thought treated wood-shingle roofing would be a good idea for a storage facility on a mountainside. In a town that had burned down more than once.

Since most of the units were locked up, scanning for occupants was simple enough, but after calling in the all clear on his section, Oliver caught movement out of the corner of his eye. He thought at first that he'd seen a coyote or a stray dog, but it had withdrawn into the shadows among the trash bins at the back of the rear units where the yard ended in a high cement fence. An animal might have been skittish around humans, but animals weren't generally good at hiding—particularly when they were trapped near fire.

"Hey," he called. "Anybody back there?"

Silence answered, but there was movement behind the bins.

Oliver moved closer cautiously. If it *was* a trapped animal, it could be dangerous. And if it was a person, it could be an arsonist. Why else would someone hide nearby during a blaze? He switched on the flashlight on his shoulder strap as he stepped around the industrial bin, illuminating the dark corner. Huddled beside the bin, a wide-eyed, sandy-haired youth stared up into the beam of his light, frozen in terror.

Instinctively, Oliver knew the boy was "family." It was the term he used in his head for Jerome's not-quite-human residents. And just as instinctively, he knew better than to call this in. No one helpful was looking for this boy.

He made sure his radio was off before crouching down to the boy's level. "Hey." He kept his voice neutral, his body relaxed. "I'm Oliver. You need some help?"

The kid's eyes widened a bit farther, as if he hadn't expected kindness. He shook his head, lowering his eyes under Oliver's continued scrutiny.

"You hungry?"

The dark eyes darted up once more, the answer obvious in them, though the boy didn't speak.

Oliver took a protein bar from his pocket and offered it to him. After glancing past Oliver as if to see if this was some kind of trick, he snatched the bar from Oliver's hand and tore it open, gobbling it down in two bites. As the boy looked up hopefully for more, Oliver took inventory of the dirty T-shirt, torn jeans and bare feet. The kid had been living on the street—or in the wild—for a while.

The boy jumped and scrambled back at the sound of Oliver's radio crackling with an announcement from the team leader that the fire was contained.

"It's okay," Oliver assured him. "Everybody's going to be leaving soon. I won't tell anyone you're here."

Looking only slightly less mistrusting, the kid nodded.

"So you can understand my language, yeah?"

Another nod.

"Can you speak it?"

No answer.

"Okay, forget about that for now. Do you have a name?"

The kid blinked at him, understanding but clearly having no words. Whether it was because he didn't have a name or simply couldn't speak at all, Oliver wasn't sure.

"Can I give you one? Just to make it easier for me to talk to you." When the boy didn't shake his head, Oliver pondered it for a moment. "How about Colt?" He reminded Oliver of one, skittish and wild.

The boy considered it and seemed to recognize its meaning, as a shy smile spread slowly across his face, and he nodded.

"Okay, Colt. I have to go right now, but I'm going to come back in a little bit. Will you stay here and wait for me? I can bring you some proper food and some water, give you someplace warm to sleep—but I'm not going to take you anywhere, don't worry," he added as Colt looked alarmed at the last bit. "I'm not going to bring anyone, either."

Colt's demeanor relaxed to his previous level of vigilance, and he hugged his knees, resting his chin on them with a slight, wary nod.

Oliver's radio went off again, his partner wanting to know where he was.

He straightened and responded before nodding to Colt once more. "Be back in a bit."

As he arrived at the front of the lot, a little zing of dismayingly pleasant recognition went through him at the sight of Lucy Smok conversing with one of the other firefighters. When she turned her head as if feeling his gaze on her, he smiled. And then felt like an idiot. What the hell was he smiling about? They weren't friends. He tried to look nonchalant and let the smile fade naturally. Lucy's expression made it pretty clear that he'd only succeeding in pulling off "idiot."

She took in his uniform as he came closer and managed a perfect Spock eyebrow lift. "So now you're a firefighter, too?" The words sounded like an accusation, like she thought he was messing with her.

"It's a volunteer fire department, and I'm a volunteer. So, yeah, I guess. I mean, yeah." *Jesus.* Why was he on the defensive all of a sudden? Something weird had happened last night. With that one little look from her as he'd kept her from falling, he'd lost his own mental footing with her.

The eyebrow was still halfway up. "Okay." She seemed to be waiting for him to say something else.

Oliver cleared his throat. "What brings you here?" *Jesus.*

"The fire. I got a tip that someone had seen a wild dog out here right after the fire broke out. I thought I'd check and see if our..." She paused and glanced at the crew packing up around them. "If there was any connection to the case. Did you see it?"

Oliver had been watching her lips move, the dark lipstick she favored mesmerizing, and he'd forgotten to listen to the words she was saying. "Sorry, see what?"

Lucy gave him that inscrutable look once more. "The wild dog."

He shook his head, and even as he said no, a certainty struck him in the gut. Of course he had. Colt.

"Well, it sounds like it wasn't big enough to have been…the animal in the other reports, but your chief says this fire looks suspicious. Definitely arson, but I'm getting another vibe. Like the origins don't make sense. No incendiary devices, no clear starting point, just combustion out of nowhere. Which is right up my alley. With Smok Consulting, I mean."

"Smoke." He was just blurting out dumb-ass shit now. So they sounded the same. Smoke/Smok. This wasn't news.

Lucy squinted at him. "Right."

"Well, I've gotta run. I'll see if I can get any more details about the cause." Halfway to the truck, he paused and glanced back. "How are those stitches? You look rested."

"I… It's fine. Yeah, I did. Get some rest." Now Lucy was stumbling over her words, too.

He tried not to smile. "Okay, I'll check in with you later?"

She nodded, and Oliver climbed onto the truck, avoiding looking at her as they pulled out of the lot, because looking at her made him feel warm. God, he was completely regressing to an adolescent state.

He shook himself mentally, remembering that Colt was waiting for him.

He gave it an hour before heading back in his regular clothes, a few boxes and a small rolled-up carpet loaded into the back of his pickup. The storage facility attendant didn't bat an eye. They hadn't had any direct interaction when he was here in uniform, so Oliver hadn't expected him to, but he still felt guilty, like he was doing something illicit. Which, of course, he was. But not because of the fire. At least, he hoped it wasn't because of the fire.

He asked for a unit in back, saying he didn't want his stuff to smell like smoke, and the attendant accommodated him without question. The unit was just two down from the trash bins where he hoped Colt was still waiting.

After unrolling the carpet on the floor of the unit and moving his boxes into it, Oliver unpacked the inflatable mattress and pump and set it up before heading to the trash bins. At first glance, he thought Colt had taken off, but the boy scrambled out from between the bins and the wall after evidently seeing that it was Oliver. It had probably taken Colt a moment to recognize him out of uniform.

"Hey, Colt. So I brought you some stuff, and I've put it in that storage unit over there, see?" He walked back to the opening between the rows and pointed, waiting until Colt moved forward cautiously to see where he was pointing. Oliver held out the key. "You can use it if you want. It's not meant for living in, but you can stay here overnight if you promise to stay out of sight if anyone comes around. Can you do that?"

Colt stared at the key and eyed the open door again warily.

"Come on. I'll show you what I brought." Oliver walked back to the unit, and in a moment, Colt followed, skittish and scuttling, moving in short bursts. He had definitely learned to stay out of sight in however long he'd been on his own.

Inside the unit, Colt gaped at the bed and blankets, but was even more impressed by the cooler of food and cold water Oliver directed his attention to.

"There's more water in here." Oliver showed him the box. "And some hand wipes. And there's a lantern that works on batteries. There's also some stuff to read if you want it. I don't know if you read."

Colt was already busy tearing into the sandwiches and fruit in the cooler. In a few minutes, he'd settled on the little bed, eating his lunch and looking with curious interest at one of the comic books Oliver had taken out of the box. It looked like the makeshift hideout was a hit. Now he just had to figure out a longer-term plan. And determine exactly what Colt was—and whether, as Oliver suspected, he was the cause of the morning's fire.

Chapter 6

Oliver Connery was up to something. If that was even his name. He'd had a guilty look on his face the entire time Lucy had been talking to him. And what better cover would some kind of paranormal arsonist have than being a volunteer fireman?

She loosened the top two buttons on her shirt as she sat in her car outside the Civic Center building after picking up the list of eyewitnesses Nora had finally compiled. For November—or was it December now? That might explain all the irritating lights and decorations she kept seeing around Jerome—it was awfully warm. Except it wasn't the weather. It was her damn wyvern thermostat.

Lucy swore softly. "A fireman? He's a goddamn *fireman*. Firefighter. Whatever." But "man" was the part her stupid hormones were focusing on, for sure. He'd been suited up in a heavy bunker jacket and loaded down with gear. It wasn't like he'd been shirtless and posing for a "Hot Firemen of Jerome VFD" calendar, for God's sake. But she'd already seen him shirtless. "Dammit." She didn't need this. She should just stop by Polly's Grotto in Sedona tonight, pick up some dumb, harmless satyr with an overactive libido and get her itch scratched.

Except that itch increasingly wanted to be scratched by Oliver Connery. Who was probably a fire-starting were-beast.

She'd phrased it that way in her head to remind herself of the dangerous territory she was heading into and shut off her train of thought, but her libido immediately responded with another spike of temperature. *You know you want a fire-starting were-beast.*

"I do *not* want a fire-starting were-beast!" Saying it aloud didn't help. She was never going to be able to concentrate on these eyewitness interviews if she didn't do something about this nonsense. It was only three o'clock—a little early for drinking, but Polly's had the distinction of being a sort of free-floating alternate dimension. There were always a few patrons inside from other time zones. Lucy could take care of business and be back in Jerome by full dark to hunt.

She stopped by the villa to change into something that would be easy to get out of and back into—a knee-length shift in black stretch velvet—and took her hair out of the braid before heading to the Grotto. Any hope of slipping in under Polly's radar was dashed almost as soon as Lucy arrived.

"That time of the month, is it, darling?"

Lucy gritted her teeth as she turned from the bar where she was waiting for her drink. Polly was sporting lavender locks this evening—and a silk sheath dress in the same color that was so transparent it ought to have been illegal.

"I'd say the same to you, except I'm pretty damn sure you're on the prowl all the time."

Polly blinked matching lavender eyes, an amused smile tugging at her lips. "So you're admitting you're on the prowl, then. That's refreshing. Until your accidental transformation when Lucien ascended—or rather *de*scended to the throne, to be precise—I had the impression you were a bit of a cold fish."

Lucy snorted. "I thought you were the one who was a fish."

Polly looked offended. "I am not a *fish*. Sirens are not *fish*."

Lucy's drink had arrived. She put her money on the bar and picked up the highball. "Honestly, Polly, I don't care if you have a mermaid's tail and scales or slippery shark bits. I didn't come here to socialize with you. I'm on a job tonight, and I have about thirty minutes to—" She felt her skin flush as she realized what she'd been about to say.

Polly laughed. "I have just the boy for you. It *is* boys you like?" She grabbed Lucy's hand before Lucy could move it out of reach and dragged her through the misty club to a set of booths in a dark corner.

"Finn, meet Lucy."

From one of the shadowy booths, a figure peered out—and instantly seemed to create his own bioluminescence. Lucy swallowed. Finn was about as far from human as a creature could get while still maintaining a human appearance—but what an appearance. The glow seemed to be coming from inside his pale green skin. He looked like a ghostly Channing Tatum.

Finn rose and smiled. "Pleased to meet you, Lucy. Won't you sit down?"

Lucy turned toward Polly and murmured, "What am I dealing with here?"

"Finn is a kind of deep-sea undine," Polly said without attempting to be discreet. "An electric mer-eel, if you will. He has a unique talent." She pushed Lucy into the booth. "Why don't you two kids get to know each other?"

Lucy glared at Polly's back as the siren turned and flitted away, trying to retain her dignity as she sipped her drink. "Sorry. I don't know what Polly was thinking—" Lucy's words cut off on a gasp as Finn took her hand while he slid back into the booth. His touch was like a light surge of current that traveled up her arm and over her skin in a tingly ripple. It was as if he'd instantly licked her all over then traced it with a violet wand.

"Is that all right?" Finn's voice was sensual and soothing. "You're unusually receptive. I normally have to ask first before a pulse is received."

"A...pulse?"

"My energy seeks to fulfill desire. Every time I breathe, it sends out a pulse."

Another one went through her. "Oh, shit." Lucy set her drink roughly on the table, sloshing gin and tonic over the rim. "Oh. Wow."

"And the pulse is translated by the receiver into whatever he or she is in need of."

He smiled and exhaled, and Lucy nearly had an orgasm.

But Finn's smile faltered. "Ah, I'm sorry." He looked a little sad as he let go of her hand. "Your need is more specific."

"What...my...specific?" She tried to regain her composure and resist the urge to snatch for his hand like a kid in a candy store grabbing for a sweet.

"Your desire is for an individual." Finn sat back. "If you want my advice, I wouldn't seek to fulfill it elsewhere, and I wouldn't try to resist it. It's not good for your health—physical or emotional—to bottle that up. If he reciprocates that desire, there's no time like the present." He smiled, and the smile seemed to set Finn's skin glowing in a slightly warmer hue.

Lucy downed her drink and cleared her throat. "And if he doesn't reciprocate it?"

Finn's gaze flitted over her with a little shake of his head. "I'd find that hard to believe."

After thanking Finn, Lucy made her escape. Polly winked at her from the bar as Lucy slipped out the door.

She collapsed into the seat of her car once she'd reached it. *What if he doesn't reciprocate it?* What the hell was she thinking? She was *not* going to throw herself at Oliver Connery just because her wyvern hormones had fixated on him. They weren't the boss of her. And they'd subside on their own in a few days if she could just keep her shit together.

Her phone, which she'd tucked into the waistband of her underwear, buzzed, and Lucy nearly jumped out of her skin. *Jesus.* Who needed a…whatever Finn was… when you had a vibrating phone? On second thought, Finn had been decidedly more satisfying. Just not…satisfying enough.

It buzzed again, and Lucy hitched up her skirt and yanked out the phone and answered. "Lucy Smok."

"Are…you okay?"

Oliver's deep voice rumbling against her ear made her wet. "Of course I'm okay. Why wouldn't I be okay?"

"You just sound a little funny. Sorry. I wanted to let you know that we've had another sighting."

Lucy sat up straight. "During daylight?"

"Sort of. It was in one of the mine shafts."

"Did it attack?"

"No, some tourists caught sight of it and got the hell out of there. They're here at my shop now. Do you want to come interview them?"

"I'm in Sedona, but I can be there in forty-five minutes."

It would take too much time to head back to the villa for a change of clothing, but she kept a "go bag" under the seat, a habit from her days of globe-trotting for Smok Consulting.

Lucy stripped off the dress where she sat, ignoring the looks from a couple who'd pulled into the space next to her, and wriggled into the garments she'd pulled from the bag: a pair of soft faded jeans and a comfortable shirt from her alma matter that she liked to travel in. After trading her heels for a pair of white slip-on sneakers, she was on her way. Dusk was just settling over Mingus Mountain as she made her way up.

Oliver did a double take when he came to unlock the door. This was a decidedly different look for Lucy. In a pair of well-worn jeans and a gray rugby shirt that said University of Oxford, she was wrapping her loose hair into a makeshift knot at the nape of her neck as she stepped inside. Her beet-stain lipstick was even more striking with the casual clothing.

"They're in back, having some hot chocolate." Oliver nodded toward the Hendersons sitting on the couch by the counter. "They were pretty spooked, but they've calmed down some."

Despite her uncharacteristic attire, Lucy introduced herself to the couple with her usual cool professionalism. "I'm Lucy Smok. Can you folks tell me what you saw?"

Mrs. Henderson held her mug between her hands as she looked up. "We found one of those old mine shaft openings out near the park. You're not supposed to go inside, but we just wanted to take a quick look around, and I think we...woke...whatever it was."

Her husband continued. "I thought it was a dog, but it was huge, like a wolfhound. Shaggy."

"And it smelled terrible," Mrs. Henderson put in.

"I figured it must be a stray, and I took a step toward it...and its eyes shot open." Mr. Henderson shuddered. "They weren't...right. We hightailed it out of there, and thank God it didn't follow."

"Tell them what you heard," Oliver prompted.

Mr. Henderson hesitated. "It's going to sound ridiculous."

"It spoke," said his wife.

Lucy had been looking slightly bored and annoyed at the pedestrian encounter, but she perked up at that. "It *spoke*?"

"It's crazy, I know. But I swear—"

"What did it say?"

Mr. Henderson studied Lucy with surprise. "What did it say?"

"You said it spoke. I assume you mean words. What did it say?"

"Sorry. I just didn't expect you to believe us. I mean, Mr. Connery was very understanding, and—"

"What did it say?"

He swallowed. "It said, 'Give my regards to the...the Queen of the Damned.'"

"It had to have been someone in a costume," Mrs. Henderson cut in. "I mean, it was very convincing, horrifyingly realistic, but of course it must have been a person."

Lucy was quiet, obviously thinking intently.

Oliver pushed himself away from the chair back he'd been leaning against. "We really appreciate you letting us know about this, no matter how odd it may seem. Ms. Smok is absolutely the best person to figure this out."

Lucy gave him an odd look.

The couple rose, recognizing that their exit was being announced, and Mr. Henderson shook Oliver's hand. "Thank you, Mr. Connery. Ms. Smok. I'm not sure how much we helped."

"You've been a great help," Oliver insisted as he walked them out. He turned around after locking up and shuttering the door to see Lucy sitting on the couch, staring at her hands poised on her thighs. "Did that mean something to you?"

Lucy's head shot up. "What the hell could it possibly mean to me?"

Oliver tucked his hands into his pockets as he neared the couch. "You just looked pretty startled."

"I was shocked that it would speak to a victim."

"But maybe they weren't intended to be victims. Maybe it was sending us a message."

"Or me, you mean. You think I understood the message."

"Do you?"

Lucy's eyes narrowed. "It means I need to get out there and find this damn thing." She rose decisively. "It's getting dark. I'm going to go check out this mine shaft. Where is it?"

"That thing tore your shoulder open last night. You need to let it heal."

"I told you, I'm fine. I'm a fast healer." She tried to walk past him, but he sidestepped in front of her.

"Let me take a look at it. You should have gone to a hospital today instead of rushing off to wherever hunting things."

"As a matter of fact, I saw my doctor. She took a look and said it was fine. She approved of your stitching skills."

"Is that so? Then you won't mind if I verify that you're healing."

If Lucy's eyes could start a fire, he was sure they would be doing it now. "Are you serious?"

"Very."

Lucy glared at him for a moment. "I'm trained in Systema. Russian martial arts."

"I'm familiar with it. I'm pretty sure I can take you."

"*Take* me?" Lucy's stance seemed to turn instantly rock hard and immovable, a promised threat emanating from her, though she hadn't moved. "I seem to recall you ending up on the ground under me the last time you tried." After a split second's pause, her skin grew flushed. With anger, presumably. But he was getting a weird vibe.

"I wasn't actually challenging you to a fight."

"You just said you could take me."

"You brought up your Systema skills. Which seems pretty strange, because all I suggested was that you let me look at the stitches and see how you're healing. Is there some reason those are fighting words to you?"

Lucy let out a slow, deliberate breath, as if trying to

breathe out her own anger—a gesture he was familiar with. "No, I suppose not." They stared each other down for another few seconds before Lucy unexpectedly crossed her arms in front of her waist, grabbed the hem of her shirt and whipped it up and over her head. She turned her bandaged shoulder toward him. "Well? Take a look. I haven't got all day."

Oliver stepped closer and peeled back the edge of the bandage. The skin was healthy looking. No redness or swelling. Little bruising. And soft. Really soft.

He drew back his hand with a jolt as though he'd touched a hot stove. "You're right. It looks good. Glad to see it."

She turned to face him, the T-shirt still balled in her fist. "Now let's see yours."

"Mine?" Oliver had to check himself from reflexively covering his crotch.

"You have some interesting scars. They looked fresh."

"Scars?" Oliver tried to keep his voice even, his expression believably puzzled.

"On your chest. From bullet wounds."

"*Bullet* wounds?" If he pulled this off, he deserved an Oscar. "I think your sleep deprivation may have gotten the better of you last night. It's understandable if you were a little confused."

"Was I?" Lucy's fists went to her hips. "Then take your shirt off and let's see."

"This is silly."

"It's a little weird that you won't just do it if I'm being silly."

Oliver blinked at her. "Maybe you should just put yours back on."

Lucy swore and yanked the shirt over her head, shoving her arms into the sleeves with two sharp jerks. "Quit stalling and take your shirt off, Oliver. Or I'm going to assume my suspicions are correct."

"And what suspicions would those be?"

"That you're something I should be hunting."

"Oh, for God's sake." His temper threatened to spike. He hadn't meditated yet today. Oliver pulled off his T-shirt and held his arms out at his sides. "Satisfied? No bullet wounds." He tried to keep his breathing steady as she stepped toward him, her nose scrunching with disbelief.

Lucy's fingers settled lightly on the pale thin line beneath his bottom right rib, and Oliver drew in his breath sharply. "What is this?"

"A scar from an accident I had a while back. If you think that's from a bullet wound, you need your eyes examined."

She glanced back up at his chest. She hadn't moved her hand except to relax it against his side. "I was sure I saw them." Lucy shook her head. "Maybe it really was sleep deprivation." She raised her eyes and met his gaze, her thumb stroking absently along the scar.

Oliver looked down at her hand. "What are you doing?" He'd meant for it to sound slightly accusatory, disapproving, a little annoyed. It came out sounding rough and low and hopeful.

"I don't know."

Her thumb was still tracing the scar, and he grabbed her hand. "Well, stop." He moved her hand away from him, which seemed to take a monumental effort. But he hadn't let go of it. It was like her skin was a magnet.

"I don't like you." Lucy's voice was equally throaty. "You're pompous and..." She seemed to be grasping for adjectives. "Full of yourself."

"Those are the same thing."

"See?"

She'd surprised a smile out of him. "I don't like you, either." His delivery was utterly unconvincing.

"Then let go of my hand."

He was barely holding it. "You let go." She didn't.

Whatever was happening here was a bad idea. His rational mind knew it. He didn't do romantic involvement. Or sexual. He should have meditated this morning. He should let go of her hand and put his shirt back on.

He put his other hand on her waist. *No. No, that is the opposite of letting go. Definitely do not kiss h—*

Oliver swore silently at himself as their lips came together.

Chapter 7

Lucy switched off her brain and let the hormones take over. Oliver was swearing softly against her lips, and she didn't think he was aware of it. It was sexy as hell. As if by silent, mutual agreement, their clasped hands released at the same moment—two seconds too late— and Oliver cupped her face in his hands and deepened the kiss as Lucy put her hands on his chest and stroked the hard terrain, moaning appreciatively.

When her hands moved down over his abs and traced the V of his obliques, Oliver let go of her mouth and cradled the backs of her thighs to lift her off the floor so that she had to wrap her legs around him, hooked behind his ass, and walked her swiftly backward to drop her into a plush, roomy armchair next to a pile of books.

Lucy unbuttoned his jeans while Oliver lifted her shirt from the back. He tugged it over her head as she finished unbuttoning him, and she let go for a second so he could draw the shirt away. His erection pushed against the briefs exposed at his fly, and Lucy tugged down the shorts and freed him while he unhooked her bra.

Oliver groaned as she encircled his cock in her hand, warm and hard like an eminently satisfying stick shift, and stroked upward, letting the bra strap slip off her other arm before trading hands to remove the other and toss the bra aside. She brought her right hand beneath the left. He was easily a two-fister. He swore a little again as he unfastened her jeans and tugged them down. Lucy lifted her butt to let him take them off, kicking off her sneakers, and wrapped her legs beneath his ass once more, using them to jerk him toward her.

Oliver pulled her hands away, locking his fingers in hers, and held her arms against the back of the chair as he dipped in to kiss her once more. The slick heat of his mouth and his tongue made her want to taste his cock.

"Stand up," she murmured against his lips, letting her legs drop.

Oliver paused. "What?"

"Just stand up straight for a minute." She wriggled forward on the seat, and he must have thought she was just trying to get more comfortable because the little strangled yelp as she swallowed him was more surprise than pleasure. But his soft grunts and groans—along with more delightfully muttered expletives—quickly turned into the latter as he gripped the arms of the chair. God, she needed him inside her. She needed to hear those little bursts of sound at her ear as he burst inside her.

Lucy released him and pulled Oliver down toward the chair, wrapping her arms around his neck and putting her mouth to his ear. "Do you have a condom?"

Oliver blanched. "Oh, shit. I don't... I don't think so." What kind of guy didn't have condoms?

She nodded toward the jeans balled up on the floor. "In the little wallet in my back pocket."

With a raised brow, Oliver extricated himself and dug in the pocket for the wallet, which was really more of a coin purse, containing two condoms and two applicator-free tampons. Part of her go bag supplies. Because you just never knew.

Lucy watched him don one of the condoms while she stripped off her panties and teased a finger into her pussy, getting herself ready. Hell, whom was she kidding? She'd been ready for almost twenty-four hours. With his pants still on, Oliver scooped Lucy out of the chair and sat in it himself, pulling her onto his lap and onto his cock. Lucy moaned with relief. Oliver kept his movements inside her slow and sensual, focusing on pleasuring her with his hands, one at her breast and one at her clit, until Lucy was squirming and pushing herself deeper onto him, her moans louder and more plaintive.

When she reached her arms over her head and back around his neck to bury her fingers in the hair at the nape of his neck, he finally let go of all restraint and drove himself into her deep and hard. She knew he was coming when he started swearing against her temple, like a stream of X-rated endearments, and his expert fingers at her pussy brought her to climax just moments after. It was as though they'd been racing to a frantic finish before either of them could back out of the game, and Lucy relaxed into him with happy little noises, whimpers of contentedness, relieved to have made it to the end.

Oliver wrapped his arms around her and kissed the side of her neck. "Still don't like me?" he murmured after a moment, and Lucy laughed out loud. It felt good to laugh; she wasn't in the habit. It felt comfortable. As did his arms hugging her. It was almost as much a relief as having him inside her. Almost. Oliver kissed the underside of her jaw. "You didn't answer."

Lucy grinned. "I like certain parts of you a great deal."

"Just certain parts?" Oliver sighed. "Any in particular?"

Lucy smacked his arm. "Now you're just fishing."

"Just name one part." He gyrated his hips under her. "One big one."

She laughed again. "Your ego."

"Ha. Touché."

Lucy relaxed in his arms and closed her eyes for a bit, almost falling asleep, until her eyes shot open as she remembered where she was. She glanced toward the door and let out her breath with relief. He'd lowered the shades and locked the door after the Hendersons left.

"What's the matter?" His voice was sleepy, too.

"I had a moment of panic thinking everyone could see us."

"Nah, just the ghosts." Oliver grinned. "We could probably get more comfortable upstairs."

Lucy yawned and shook her head reluctantly. "I should be getting back to work. You're not paying me to…" She paused, realizing how awkward that sentence was about to be. Because he was her client. Whom she'd come on to—and whose bones she'd jumped—while in the middle of a very serious job. She scrambled off his lap and snatched up her scattered clothes, trying not to look at him as she yanked them on. What the hell was wrong with her? She'd let her hormones take complete control. This was so unprofessional. This was so *pathetic*.

"Lucy."

She jumped at the sound of his voice and glanced up reluctantly while she braided her hair. Damn. There were two really good reasons not to have looked at him. That rock-hard body glistening with sweat and those deep cinnamon eyes watching her with disappointment. Or was that three reasons?

"You're just going to take off? That's it?"

Lucy sighed. "Your council hired me to do a job, and people's lives are on the line here. This was a mistake." She cringed internally even as she said it. He'd take it the wrong way. Or the right way. "I'm sorry."

If the sexual release hadn't left his body feeling blissed out, his rage would have gotten the better of him. Not at Lucy, but at himself.

Oliver cleaned up bitterly, everything that had been relaxed and loose moments earlier once more tense and tight. "Mistake" was right. He'd just ended five years of celibacy for an ill-advised twenty-minute romp with someone far too young for him. He should have checked himself, knowing his age and life experience tilted the power balance between them toward him, no matter how much professional experience she had or how tough she acted. And he'd betrayed Vanessa's memory.

He glanced down at the ring, toying with it between the thumb and forefinger of his left hand. He hadn't allowed himself the weakness of giving in to sexual desire since her death. He didn't deserve to be alive—let alone indulging in hedonistic pleasure—when Vanessa was dead.

For a long time, every meal he'd eaten, every breath he'd taken, had felt like a betrayal. With his daily meditation, he'd finally moved beyond that, but he didn't indulge his passions, like decadent foods and spirits. And he certainly didn't indulge in sexual intimacy.

And with Lucy Smok, of all people. Someone who made a living persecuting the paranormal.

Damn. He could still smell her. She was all over him, like she'd marked him. He was never going to be able to sit in that chair again.

Oliver went upstairs and undressed with angry jerks. He needed a shower. He needed to wash her out of his brain. But all he could think about under the almost-scalding water was how soft her skin was and how she'd sounded as she came. And how pale her naked body looked against his, contrasted with the rich darkness of her hair where it tumbled against her neck out of its makeshift knot, while she'd writhed in his lap.

Jesus, this was bad. He'd lost his mind. He had to end their association. Let Wes and Nora deal with her on this case. He was done. If she came pounding on his door in the middle of the night with battle wounds, he wouldn't answer. There was an emergency room in Cottonwood. If she was such a badass, she could get herself there.

But when insistent knocking woke him hours later, Oliver jumped out of bed and hurried downstairs to open the door anyway.

Lucy stood on his doorstep. Not bleeding. Not injured. Just Lucy, in her jeans and Oxford rugby shirt and a black leather jacket, bloodred lips in a pallid face and pale blue eyes boring into him, like the Queen of the Night.

"I don't know what I'm doing here."

He tried to breathe normally. "Are you coming in?"

"No. Maybe."

Oliver took her hand and pulled her inside and kissed

her with her back against the door until their mouths ached. When they came up for air, Lucy wriggled out of her coat with a swift, sexy shrug and went for his belt buckle, but Oliver stopped her.

"Upstairs."

Lucy nodded and let him lead the way, both of them taking the steps two at a time, and they were half-undressed by the time they reached the bed. She'd braided her hair again, and he unbraided it while he sucked on her neck and nipped at her throat, and the dark hair spilled across his white pillow like clouds of dark paint in water while he rocked and thrust and drove himself inside her for almost an hour. She came twice before he finally did—once underneath him and once on top—and he was almost sorry to come because he had to stop fucking her. Almost.

Oliver collapsed onto his back, exhausted and dripping with sweat. He hadn't had an aerobic workout like this in ages. Lucy curled up against his side and promptly fell asleep. He didn't realize she'd done so until he'd been talking for ten minutes—about politics and the messed-up state of the world and about being a widower and how he hadn't been with a woman since and how he was constantly questioning himself and his values and feeling adrift in his own mortal frame. After he'd asked her twice why she'd decided to come back and she hadn't answered him, he finally realized he'd been talking to himself. Thank God.

He played with her hair where it snaked across his chest. It felt like silk. Oliver curled it around his fist and smelled it—crisp and cool, like cucumber or avocado— and wondered what she used to keep it so luxurious.

It was too cold to lie here unclothed, as much as he

would have been content to look at her being naked and still, her body for once without its uneasy coil of tension and mistrust. He pulled the comforter up from the foot of the bed and covered them both.

When he woke—more rested than he could remember having been for a very long time—he found himself alone.

Chapter 8

Lucy huddled on the floor of her car in the parking lot outside the villa and cried until she was too exhausted to keep doing it, despite the fact that it hadn't provided her with any kind of release. People always said, "Let yourself cry. You'll feel better." It was bullshit. Crying always made her feel a thousand times worse. And this wasn't how a Smok comported herself.

A Smok didn't sleep with clients in the middle of a case—or with anyone while on the job, for that matter. And a Smok certainly didn't cry about it like a teenage girl in her car for an hour at six o'clock in the morning. She'd gone soft and weak and useless. And she couldn't even really blame it on the wyvern hormones, because she'd gotten her period this morning, which meant the past two days of out-of-control desire had been *after* her hormone levels dipped.

And the underside of Oliver Connery's right rib cage

had sported a fading scar from a knife wound yesterday afternoon that had disappeared by this morning. Just like the scars from the bullet wounds that she knew she'd seen had faded in less than a day. And every one of those wounds was identical to one she'd given the hell beast. She was fucking her client. And he was the murdering hell beast she was hunting. So *that* was fun.

Lucy sat in the car for a while longer, trying to get herself together and stiffen her resolve. She needed to take down that hell beast tonight, whether Oliver was aware of his alter ego or not. It didn't matter how she felt about Oliver. It didn't matter how decent a person he seemed to be. His infernal form was a dangerous monster, and it was Lucy's job to remove dangerous monsters from the earthly plane and send them back to hell.

It was ironic that she'd criticized Lucien for years for his secret campaign to rid the world of as many unnatural creatures as he could before he became one. It hadn't been part of the Smok Consulting business plan at the time to eliminate supernatural predators. Their loyalty was to their wealthy clients who paid handsomely to have paranormal events kept quiet. But now that Lucien was effectively out of the picture, the circumstances that had taken him out of it had made his former hobby Lucy's number one job.

Regardless of why, she had to get this thing done. Now. Which meant she had to figure out how to kill it. Soul Reaper bullets hadn't worked. Maybe Lucien's special exploding-tip arrows that delivered the Soul Reaper serum directly into the bloodstream would do the trick.

Lucy set up for the hunt, familiarizing herself with the arrows and testing the draw of Lucien's crossbow. After last night, she knew she didn't have to look for

the hell beast. The hell beast would find her. Satisfied
that her weapons were battle ready, she headed into the
bathroom and ran the water for a soak in the tub. It was
becoming a habit. Her muscles still ached from her two
encounters with the beast—and now she had the added
tenderness from last night.

She stared at herself in the bathroom mirror as she
undressed. He'd left a mark on her neck and another on
the side of one breast—and one on her inner thigh. She
closed her eyes, trying not to remember the moment he'd
given her that last one, flipping her over after the first
time she'd come and licking her pussy while she lay on
her stomach before he fucked her from behind. He hadn't
seemed the least bit interested in coming himself, just
wanting to find as many ways as he could to pleasure
her so he could prolong the experience.

Lucy opened her eyes and focused on her disheveled
hair. He'd kept running his hands through it, wanting it
loose and long. Who the hell was he to decide how she
should wear her hair? The long waves seemed like a symbol of her unprofessionalism, her foolishness in letting
herself get carried away by her own selfish desires instead of keeping her head in the game. She yanked open
the drawer and found the scissors, and with a hank of
hair in her hand, she lopped it off at fist length. With a
few violent motions, she'd chopped off the rest, jagged
and crude. Lucy stared at the wild mess. The scissors still
clutched in her fist tempted her to do worse.

She hadn't done it in years, but the temptation to cut
herself had never been stronger. To maybe just keep cutting until she severed an artery. The tub had finished filling with steaming, fragrant water. Just a couple of nice
matching cuts, and then step in and lie back and relax.

Lucy gripped the blades of the scissors until her hand was shaking. With a wordless scream, she swung her fist in an arc across the bathroom vanity and swept everything onto the floor, cosmetics and bottles of facial cleanser and liquid soap and lotion—all of it scattering across the bathroom rug and shattering on the tile. She dropped the scissors and opened the cabinets and the drawers in the vanity and emptied everything, smashing and screaming until she'd punished everything she could reach besides herself. The urge was still strong as she stood among the wreckage and looked up at her reflection once more.

Her eyes were reptilian. She'd partially shifted. Lucy forced out her wings with a howl of pain and fell on her knees, wrapping her wings around herself. What the hell was she anymore? She wasn't infernal royalty like Lucien, she was earthbound and half human and nothing mattered, and she was so fucking tired. Mr. Henderson's words came back to her, the alleged taunt from the hell beast—*Give my regards to the Queen of the Damned.* It couldn't have meant her. Maybe her sister-in-law. Maybe it was time to try to contact Lucien and Theia and get help.

Lucy let out a choked laugh. Maybe it was *really* time to get help. "Siri, call Dr. Delano." She hadn't expected the mic to pick it up. It was more of a joking plea to the universe. But her phone replied cheerfully from the pile of broken glass and powder, "Calling Dr. Delano."

She scrambled for the phone and shut it off, but not before Fran had answered. The phone rang immediately, Fran calling back, and Lucy hit the button to decline it. She probably should have just answered and pretended it was a misdial. But now Fran knew something was up.

The knock on the door came while Lucy was floating in the immense bathtub, her tucked wings keeping her from going under. Fran let herself in when Lucy didn't answer. *Dammit.* She'd forgotten she'd given her a key. Lucy plunged her head under the water and came up just as Fran arrived at the doorway.

She took in the scene and Lucy's appearance and shook her head. "Sweetheart. Why haven't you been taking your meds?"

"Sweetheart" wasn't what Fran usually called her. Their familial relationship went unspoken. Fran had abandoned her babies after trying unsuccessfully to live with Edgar, and she'd signed a nondisclosure agreement promising never to reveal that she was their mother. She worked for Edgar, just the company and family doctor, as far as they knew—kind but impersonal. But Lucy had figured it out from the way Fran reacted when Lucy was assaulted by a high school boy who asked her out on a date when she was thirteen. It was Fran who'd taken care of her, angry and tearful in turns as she got the story out of Lucy. And it was Fran, Lucy was certain, who'd paid someone to break the little asshole's arm, because Edgar had never found out.

"The pills don't work the same since the transformation. They slow me down."

"That's part of what they're supposed to do. The transformation speeds up your metabolism in ways that aren't entirely healthy. I adjusted your meds to work with the anti-transformative compound. Which I see you haven't taken this month, either."

"I was about to, but… I don't know what I'm doing anymore. The fugitives just keep coming, and now there's a hell beast stalking me. And I can't kill it. And I think I slept with him."

Fran sighed. "Lucy. Honey, come out of the tub. Let's get you warmed up, and you can tell me all about it. Have you eaten?"

"I don't know."

Fran kicked the shards of broken glass out of the way and set a bath mat on the floor, holding her hand out to Lucy. "Come on. You're going to eat something."

Reluctantly, and mostly because she really was getting a bit chilly at last, Lucy took Fran's hand and climbed out, accepting the bath sheet Fran wrapped her in.

After taking a mild sedative to help suppress her shift, Lucy put on a robe and sat cross-legged in front of the fire while Fran made coffee and whipped up eggs and bacon and fluffy cinnamon toast that she'd evidently brought with her—because Lucy's fridge sure as hell didn't contain any unexpired food.

Fran brought the plates to the living room and sat with Lucy on the carpet. "So what makes you think you slept with a hell beast?"

"He has the same scars—and then he doesn't."

"He?"

"Oliver Connery. He's a client—I know, don't even say it."

"I wasn't going to say anything."

"He's part of some paranormal Jerome town council—Oliver owns a bookstore and café there. They called me in because of werewolf sightings, which turned out to be the same thing I've been hunting. It's big, and it's vicious, and I'm not sure what it is. And I've shot it with Soul Reaper bullets and stabbed it, and nothing even slows it down." Lucy took a bite of toast. "And he's a volunteer firefighter."

"The hell beast is a firefighter?"

"Oliver, I mean. But he's also the damn hell beast, so, yeah. Firefighter hell beast. Can I pick 'em or what?"

Fran poked at her eggs. "You're sure he's the beast?"

"How else would he get those scars?"

"Maybe it's a coincidence. Hear me out. It just seems highly unlikely that this beast would have been hidden all this time, hanging out in Jerome living the life of an upstanding citizen, no reports of attacks until hell happens to be left open and a bunch of demons spill out."

Lucy ran her hand through the damp, shaggy wreck of her hair. "But I saw the scars, and they healed in a day. He's enhanced in some way."

"So are you."

"That was hardly my choice."

"Lucy. Honey. It is almost never anyone's choice. Maybe you should ask him."

"Like he's going to tell me the truth. He lied about having the scars in the first place. And he's lying about something else. I just don't know what. He claims to be some kind of self-appointed 'protector' of inhuman creatures in Jerome, and he's got some kind of law enforcement or military training." Lucy's fingers caught in her hair, and she swore as she yanked them out.

Fran set down her coffee. "Okay, we're going to fix that right now. You have a board meeting this afternoon—"

"Oh, shit."

"And you are Lucy Smok, steel-spined CFO of Smok International."

Lucy laughed as Fran pulled her to her feet by both hands. "I don't think that's correct."

"That is how people see you, my dear, and I know how important it is to you to present a sharp, professional image. You're like your father in that regard. Your appearance is part of your arsenal, so let's make it precision weaponry."

Lucy sat in a kitchen chair in front of the mirrored bedroom closet doors and submitted to Fran's grooming. The damage was bad. Lucy had hacked within inches of her scalp in places and left other ragged locks hanging. Fran turned it into a softened version of a men's business cut, close to Lucy's head and a little long above the ears, with a side part offset by a curve of eye-level bangs on the right. With a bit of hair wax to smooth the sides and emphasize the point at the nape of her neck, it looked both sophisticated and a little funky.

"Wow, Fran. I had no idea you were a barber *and* a doctor." Lucy ran her hand over the final product. "How Wild West of you. Thank you."

Fran smiled. "I think it suits you." She brushed the loose hair from Lucy's neck and took the towel from around her shoulders to shake it out in the bathroom. When she returned, she watched from the doorway as Lucy added some wax to the bangs to sculpt them into a wave that matched her hair's natural inclination. "Was there something in particular that led to this? I mean, I'm glad you didn't do anything worse, but attacking your hair is pretty specific."

Lucy's cheeks went slightly pink. "It was because he liked it. I know. It's stupid. But I just felt like such a fool, letting myself get caught up in, in being…" Words were eluding her.

Fran gave her a fond, somewhat reproachful smile. "Human? You're allowed, you know. You've been working yourself so hard, trying to do everything on your own at Smok. For that reason alone, I may never forgive Edgar. You deserve to have some pleasure once in a while. Did you at least have a good time with him?"

The heat in Lucy's cheeks became more pronounced.

Fran grinned. "That good, huh?"

Oliver waited as long as he reasonably could to check on the boy. He'd given Colt the key, so if the kid had locked the unit and taken off, he'd have no way of getting inside to verify. His initial knocks on the metal door yielded only silence, but a quick tug on the handle showed that it was unlocked.

He knocked again, not wanting to violate Colt's privacy. "Hey, Colt? It's just me, Oliver. I'm alone. I brought you some more things."

A slight rustling followed from inside, and in a moment the door slid upward a crack. Oliver pulled it up halfway and ducked inside. Over his dirty clothes, Colt was wearing the sweatshirt Oliver had left him in one of the boxes. The boy scuttled into the corner, still untrusting.

Oliver set the bag of dry goods and fruit next to Colt's bed. Luckily, he'd thought to bring more water, because from the looks of the empty bottles scattered about the floor, Colt had drunk nearly all of it.

"Sorry I didn't think about the bathroom situation. I take it you managed to slip inside the office and use theirs?"

Colt shook his head and pointed outside. Whatever worked.

Oliver glanced at the empty bottles once more. That was a lot of water for a kid who couldn't weigh a hundred pounds soaking wet. "Mind if I sit down for a minute?" Colt didn't seem to, so he sat. "Can I ask you a question? And I want an honest answer."

The boy hesitated, looking suspicious, before nodding reluctantly.

"Did you start that fire yesterday?"

Colt's eyes widened, and his gaze darted back and forth as if he was looking for a chance to bolt.

"It's okay. I just need to know. You won't get in trouble."

Colt scooted back against the wall and hugged his knees, staring up at Oliver with a haunted expression. After a moment, he gave a sharp nod and lowered his eyes.

Oliver sighed. "I'm going to guess it's something in your nature. That's why you're drinking all this water."

Colt looked miserable. He probably thought his brief good luck had run out.

"I'm also going to guess this form you're showing me isn't your natural state. That you aren't human."

Colt's face fell, and he slumped against the wall, letting his legs slide to the floor stretched out in front of him.

"I don't care about that, Colt. I just want to make sure you're safe and that you don't accidentally cause anyone harm. I'm sure you're already aware of how dangerous it is for people like you. That there are people who'd see *you* as the danger and try to hurt you." Like Lucy Smok. "And I don't want that to happen. It also isn't safe for you to stay here indefinitely. It's not healthy, for one, and you're likely to get caught sooner or later. I am *not* throwing you out," he hastened to assure the boy. "I just want to figure out what the best solution is for you. Do you have family? Others like you?"

Colt slowly shook his head. It was a mystery how he'd gotten this far on his own. Whatever family he'd had once had probably been hunted. By someone like Lucy. But Oliver couldn't justify leaving the boy on his own, no matter how self-sufficient he might be. He was a child, and he deserved to be cared for like one, human or not.

"I might know some people who could help you. People like you who are different, maybe in different ways than you, but good people. But it may take me a few days to figure out who the right people are and to track them down. Would that be okay with you?"

Colt's expression was fearful, eyes searching Oliver's face intently, as if he might be able to see in it the people Oliver was referring to. He shook his head uncertainly.

"Okay. I won't do anything you don't agree to. But I still want to find someplace better for you than this. I'm going to talk to the people I know, but I won't tell them where you are. I'll just see what I can find out and come back and tell you what I've learned. Is that okay?"

Colt was still uncertain, his anxious expression trying to convey something Oliver was missing. He'd been hiding when Oliver found him, and he'd probably been living in hiding for a long time.

"Colt…is there someone looking for you? Someone you're afraid of?"

The vigorous nod was unequivocal.

Chapter 9

Maybe Fran was right. Maybe Oliver would have a good explanation for the scars and the rapid healing if Lucy just asked him about it. And maybe Lucy was the queen of England. But after last night, maybe she owed Oliver the question. If he lied straight to her face, that would be an answer, too.

In the meantime, there was one way she could find out more about him. Smok International had access to more intelligence than most government agencies. It wasn't just unnatural creatures they kept track of. She'd start with exactly *who* he was. *What* he was might be more complicated.

Before the board meeting, she initiated the search with her research department, and by the time the meeting was over, the preliminary report was already on her virtual desk. He *had* been in the military, under the name Oliver Benally—a Navajo surname; if it was his real name, he obviously had an Anglo parent. He'd served four years in the Marines before being recruited by an organization Lucy was unpleasantly familiar with: Darkrock Security.

It was a paramilitary contractor that specialized in supplying forces deployed in response to paranormal events. Edgar had contracted some work to them once, cleaning up a series of rogue blood farms—vampire operations where humans were kept as long-term feeders against their will—but Darkrock's methods and ethics were questionable even by Edgar's standards. In the years since, Smok had refused to work with them.

So what was Oliver doing in Jerome running a bed-and-books-and-coffee joint and volunteering to fight fires—while advocating for demons and shifters as if they were simply misunderstood? It seemed to go against everything Darkrock stood for. Unless Oliver was undercover and still working for them. That would explain the assumed name. And in that context, his "paranormal protector" role took on new significance. He might be exploiting the creatures he claimed to defend for Darkrock's own twisted purposes.

Whatever the reason, he'd definitely hidden his identity well. If it hadn't been for Smok's on-staff clairvoyants, the research department might have missed it altogether. As Benally, he'd been reported dead.

Armed with her new information and her crossbow, Lucy drove back to Jerome after dark. Before heading to the mine shaft to smoke out the hell beast, she lingered in front of Delectably Bookish. She could go inside and confront him now, demand to know whether he was the hell beast. But if he was with Darkrock… How could he be both a Darkrock operative and a hell beast? Despite her distaste for Darkrock's business model, she breathed a little sigh of relief. Of course he couldn't be the hell beast. Darkrock wouldn't hire an inhuman creature.

She paused with her hand on the door handle. Darkrock wouldn't hire one…but it might create one. That was the one line Edgar had refused to cross. He might have looked the other way at Darkrock's abusive practices, but the company also engaged in live capture. They were known to experiment on their captives to see exactly what made them tick, and rumor had it their ultimate goal was to create their own custom hybrids as soldiers for hire.

Lucy's grip relaxed on the handle. It made a horrible kind of sense. He was hiding out in a small, deliberately created paranormal community off the larger community's radar, pretending to be a friend and protector. A hitherto unknown breed of wolf shifter that could phase in and out of animal and human form at will arrived in the area, coincidentally timed to be mistaken for one of the fugitives released from the gates of hell. Oliver displayed the same wounds Lucy had given the beast—and healed them overnight.

He was secretly still working for Darkrock. And they had created him.

Goose bumps rippled across Lucy's skin. Darkrock had long been interested in a partnership with Smok Consulting despite being frustrated by Edgar's refusals. Their public relations rep had reached out to Lucy shortly after she assumed control of the company, wanting to discuss how they could work together in the future, but Lucy had instructed her assistant to let them know in no uncertain terms that nothing had changed at Smok with Edgar's death. His policies would survive him.

What if they'd decided to get at Lucy another way? What if it hadn't been mere happenstance that Lucy had hunted the hell beast here, of all places, and had run up against Oliver Connery that first night? She'd thought the beast was targeting her. She had a sinking feeling she'd been more right than she knew.

She started the car and pulled back onto Main. If she was right, Oliver wouldn't be home anyway. He would be waiting for her in one of the lesser-known mine shafts. The incident with the Hendersons had obviously been for Lucy's benefit, designed to lure her to it. The mine shaft near the park where they'd spotted it was too obvious a place for the hell beast to be lurking.

Lucy parked at the base of the dirt road that led into the mountains, the spot where she'd fought it before, and hiked uphill, using a special GPS app Smok International had developed to find access points to some of the abandoned mine shafts in the hills. After surveying the area pinpointed on the app, she found the telltale footprints she was looking for leading to an opening hidden among the rocks. Lucy loaded up the crossbow, viewing the tunnel through the night vision scope, and headed in.

The wolf prints were only in sets of two, as if the beast was walking upright. Lucy followed them along the mine cart rails perhaps half a mile into the shaft before they stopped abruptly and became human footprints. Was Oliver himself waiting for her? A deep twinge of wistful body memory recalled the intimacy she'd shared with him not twenty-four hours ago. What kind of sick bastard would play a game like this? It was the ultimate bait-and-switch of seduction.

Lucy stopped and laughed at herself. She was talking about a hell beast. Of course he was a sick bastard.

A noise in the dirt to her right stopped her laughter instantly. She crouched and turned the scope toward the sound. A brief glimpse of the swiftly moving form of a man was all she caught before he rushed her, faster than any human she'd ever encountered, and knocked the crossbow from her grasp. Without the scope, she was blind. She should have opted for night goggles. The beast paced and circled her, now closer to the ground and growling low in its throat. It had shifted once more.

With her Nighthawk Browning in her hand, she tried to track it. If she missed, who knew what the bullet might glance off? She needed to aim into the depths of the mine, catching the creature when it was framed by the passage walls instead of in front of them. A brush of fur made her jump, and Lucy shot in the thing's direction, but it was already gone. She was sure the little growl that followed was laughter.

It was toying with her. And it was obviously every bit as sentient as she was.

"What do you want?" Her words seemed to thud into the dirt around her, as if no air flowed through the tunnels.

The laugh-growl came again from behind, and the creature leaped on top of her before she could spin and get off a shot, knocking her facedown and grinding her into the dirt and rusted tracks. Its weight was considerable, and it had her pinned. The gun was just beyond her grasp. She could feel the creature's hot breath on her neck. And she could also feel it transform, effortlessly, from wolf to man.

"What do I want?" The whispered words sent a chill down her spine. "I am Death. I am the Pit. I want to take you into my mouth."

Lucy shuddered as a hot tongue slicked across the back of her neck.

"But I am having fun here. Such a charming playground this world is. So I'm in no hurry." He made a breathing sound behind her that was more like a dog's panting than human breath. "And you have something of mine that I want first."

Lucy tried to keep her voice casual. "What could I possibly have of yours?"

"Don't play coy. The thing you've hidden from me. The thing that escaped."

"What thing? What escaped?" She struggled to breathe under his weight. "From where?"

He laughed with the growling, unnatural cadence of the wolf. "From hell, of course. Your obligation to your foolish rules is to send such things back, but instead you've put this one somewhere I can't find it. And I want it. It's my right." He breathed damply against her ear. "I want to feel its tender neck bones beneath my teeth as the hot blood of its carotid artery spills into my mouth." He licked her once more, and Lucy used the uncontrollable shudder to move her hand closer to the gun.

She almost had it, fingers curling to close around the metal, but his hand came down on hers, and he shoved the weapon away. But to do it, he'd moved his body just enough to free her arm, and Lucy punched swiftly back and up with her elbow, hitting him right in the throat. It bought her just enough time and space to scramble for the gun as he reacted with a surprised, furious guttural outburst. Lucy grabbed the weapon and fired into his shoulder, and he jolted backward with the impact, his head striking the shaft wall. She fired again as she rolled onto her back. No longer close enough for her to see his outline in the dark, her shot went wide.

"I will have what's mine!" The words came out in an inhuman bark. He'd shifted again.

Lucy fired blind toward the sound. It was a waste of bullets. He was already gone. By the time she'd found the crossbow and quiver after fumbling around in the dirt, any chance she had of pursuing it was gone, too.

She swore as she got to her feet, the sound this time echoing through the tunnels where they split off in different directions. She'd managed to have as close an encounter with its human form as she was going to get without becoming its next victim, and she hadn't been able to tell if it was Oliver. She was also furious that it had once again eluded her. She'd never fought and failed to kill the same creature three times in a row.

The walk back to the opening of the shaft was warm and dusty despite the temperature outside and the cool air underground. It was the anger and the energy she'd exerted along with the lingering adrenaline. Plus a bit of anxiety threading through her pulse from being in an enclosed space below the earth. It was the stuff of nightmares, and if she hadn't been following the only exit back over her own tracks, the anxiety might have overwhelmed her.

Outside under the open sky, she was able to breathe again. There was no sign of the beast, not even footprints leading away this time. Lucy sat on a boulder and stared up at the stars. There had to be a way to kill this thing. But right now she was just lucky to have gotten away without being killed by *it*. Orion had just cleared the horizon, its easily identifiable pattern in the sky somehow always comforting and grounding. The hunter with his bow. She clutched the crossbow and shook it in the air in solidarity. And made a silent vow to Lucien in the underworld to finish this.

As she walked back to her car, she wondered what

the hell beast thought she'd hidden from it. It had obviously meant something living, another creature that had escaped from hell during Lucien's descent. But why would one hell beast want to kill—or more to the point, feed on—another?

Lucy stopped dead on the trailhead as she reached the spot where she'd parked her car. With his back against the driver's-side door, Oliver stood with folded arms.

She decided not to tip her hand if he was really the hell beast. "What are you doing here?"

"I figured this was where you would go after what the Hendersons told us last night. I wasn't sure how else I could find you, since you haven't answered any of my texts."

"My phone is always off when I'm hunting. It's distracting."

"And did you catch anything tonight?"

Lucy lowered her head as she approached the car, not wanting to meet his eyes and give herself away. "No. It was a bust."

"Funny, you look like you've been rolling around fighting something—" Oliver paused, and Lucy looked up as she reached him to find him staring at her with a furrowed brow. "What happened to your hair?"

Her hand went to the back of her scalp reflexively. "I cut it."

"Why?"

Lucy glared. "Why shouldn't I? It's my hair."

"I'm not saying you shouldn't. I just wondered." He studied her face as if he was trying to get used to it. "It's very different."

"Yeah, well, I didn't do it for you." She reached around

him to the handle of the door he was blocking. "Can you please get off my car?"

Oliver pushed himself away from the door but stood where he was. "Are you mad at me?"

"Why would I be mad at you? I hardly know you."

He flinched, as if she'd thrown water in his face, and his expression hardened. "I thought we kind of got to know each other a little bit last night."

"We had sex, Oliver. We fucked. I'd hardly call it a bonding experience."

Wordlessly, Oliver stepped aside to let Lucy get in and drive away.

It was up to Oliver to keep the Jerome undergrounders safe while Lucy was on the prowl. She'd been frustrated in her attempts to stop the creature, and he wouldn't be surprised if she went looking for other "fugitives" to make up for it. His instincts were usually correct. At least as far as her bloodlust was concerned. His instincts about her primal, sexual lust were obviously way off. His attraction to her was as strong as ever. Stronger. Which was all the more reason for him to hit the streets tonight—if you could call Jerome's two main connecting drives and their handful of tributaries "streets"—and occupy his mind with something else.

He'd also promised Colt that he'd talk to his underground contacts about a safe place for him, even if the boy wasn't quite ready to go to one. None of his daytime contacts through the council had been able to offer him anything useful, and he didn't dare reveal enough to let them know he was trying to help a young runaway of dubious origin. That left the shadow people, undergrounders who kept to themselves and only ventured out at night. For most of them, it was because they were nocturnal beings; for others, it was the safest time in a sleepy little artists' town.

He made the usual rounds, walking up to Clark Street from the back of his property to Haunted Hamburger and Wicked City Brew and across the little park steps to Main Street past the Spirit Room under the old Connor Hotel and Paul & Jerry's Saloon—the sum total of Jerome "nightlife." Paul & Jerry's and the Spirit Room were the only establishments open past 11:00 p.m.

Oliver nodded to the regulars inside Paul & Jerry's and stopped in front of the fenced-off ruin of the old Bartlett Hotel on the other side of the gallery beside the saloon. The empty brick skeletons of its remaining rooms beyond the easily scalable ironwork bars made it an attractive place to squat for people who weren't quite human. Oliver blended into the shadows and stood watch until he saw signs of activity within the hotel's remains.

A young half vamp he knew—sired by a vampire who'd abandoned her before sharing his blood to give her invulnerability and the community's protection—materialized inside the iron bars.

She leaned against them, crossing her tattooed arms as she stared straight into him. "If it ain't the old man."

He nodded to her. "Hey, Eva. Though I'm not sure I care for that characterization. You're older than I am, as I understand it."

"And you look about as old as I ought to."

"That's...charming to know." He hoped she wasn't chronologically over forty. She looked eternally seventeen. He wondered if they liked the same music. Might be something to ask her some other time. "Listen, I was hoping I could get some information from you."

Eva bristled. "What kind of information?"

"About a safe house for a—someone who may be in a bit of trouble."

"Well, the latter's a given. Why else would they want a safe house? But I don't think I can help you."

"Why not?"

"We've got enough trouble right now. There's a feral shifter started hunting around here, and some kickboxing bitch tried to take out Crystal the other night."

"Yeah, I know. But if somebody really needed help…"

Eva sighed. "You talking about a kid?"

"Might be."

"I've seen that kid. He's not our kind. He doesn't belong here."

"That's what the normals say about all of you."

"Spoken like a 'normal.'"

He couldn't argue with that. "I'm not sure where he came from, but he can't survive out here on his own for much longer."

"Why don't you take him in?"

"I run a business out of my home. He'd be hard to explain."

"Not my problem."

"Yeah, I gotcha." Oliver shrugged. "I figured it was worth a try."

Eva had lit up a cigarette while they spoke, and she took a drag on it and breathed in the smoke through her nose. "I've heard about some chick in the valley who'll hide folks for a price. Some kind of nymph or dryad or something. She also has the dirt on anyone in the community. Name's Polly."

Oliver nodded thoughtfully. He'd heard of Polly's Grotto in West Sedona. "Thanks. Maybe I'll try her."

"Don't forget about the price, though. From what I hear, she ain't cheap—and she has zero use for human currency."

On second thought, maybe Polly would be better left as a last resort. Not that he had a lot of options. Oliver opened his mouth to thank Eva, but she was gone, leaving her cigarette smoldering in the dirt.

A quick scan of the otherwise deserted street gave him the reason. An unmarked black van with tinted windows had parked on the opposite corner. He felt his blood freeze. It couldn't be. It was Darkrock's signature "inconspicuous" mode of transport.

Chapter 10

Maybe they were just here looking for people like Eva. He'd hoped to keep the underground community off their radar, but with the public sightings of the wolf, he supposed it had only been a matter of time.

Oliver picked up the cigarette to avoid calling attention to the disappearance of the person who'd been smoking it and took a drag, trying not to cough with distaste. It had been years since he'd smoked—to impress friends when he'd been young and stupid—and he'd never really been a fan. He started walking away from the Bartlett, keeping tabs on the van out of the corner of his eye. It followed. Slowly. And obviously. They were here for *him*. How the hell had Darkrock tracked him after all this time?

Oliver tossed down the cigarette, feeling sick, and ground it out with his heel, pulling his hood close and shoving his hands in the pockets of his sweatshirt as he picked up his pace.

It was pointless. They knew who he was. The window slid down as the van pulled up alongside him.

The driver leaned his arm on the window frame. "Well, well. Chief Benally, in the flesh."

Oliver paused and stared ahead down the sidewalk. He shouldn't take the bait, but it wasn't like he was fooling anyone at this point. He could run for it, but he'd be on the run forever, and everything he'd built in Jerome would have been for nothing.

He turned slowly on his heel and faced the window. "Don't fucking call me Chief."

Artie Cooper, his flat-top crew cut the same as he'd had for a dozen years, grinned and turned to his passenger. "Ya see, Finch? I told you it was ol' Chief." He stuck his hand out the window, expecting Oliver to shake it. "Great to see ya, man." Cooper and Finch had both been in his unit.

Oliver kept his hands in his pockets. "What do you want, Artie?"

"What kind of greeting is that?" Artie withdrew his thick arm with a put-on frown. "Is that any way to talk to an old friend?"

Finch leaned across the seat to peer out, the light from the streetlamp falling on his dark skin. "It really is you." He seemed genuinely surprised, and actually looked pleased to see Oliver. "Well, goddamn. I thought you were dead."

He was beginning to think he might be. "Nah, you know me. I'm not that easy to kill."

Finch laughed. "What are you doin' here, man? I thought Artie was pulling my leg."

"Cap says he's running a damn artsy-fartsy inn or some shit."

"It's a book-café and B and B. Or it will be."

"Aw, shit!" Finch broke out into incredulous laughter. "Shut the fuck up."

Oliver shrugged. "So what do you want, Artie? I take it Captain Blake sent you to spy on me for a reason."

"Who's spying? We're just looking for a cup of coffee. It's supposed to get below freezing tonight. Why don't you lead the way to your place and we'll get caught up?"

Reluctantly, Oliver directed them to Delectably Bookish, though he knew they were aware of where he lived. As they made themselves at home, Finch investigating the book stacks with frequent exclamations of amusement, Oliver opened up the counter in back, making coffee for the three of them.

"I can't get over this." Finch accepted the coffee Oliver brought him and took a seat in the armchair that Oliver and Lucy had occupied just yesterday. Oliver made a concerted effort to put that out of his head. "Ollie Benally, puttering around with books and bedsheets in a little tourist trap in Arizona like an old man."

"I needed a change."

Artie stood drinking his coffee, significantly less amused. "You know you're still under contract."

"You can tell Blake that I'll be happy to buy out the rest of my term at whatever fair price Darkrock determines."

"It doesn't work that way. You made a commitment, and Darkrock expects you to honor it."

Oliver folded his arms. "You know I can't do that. You know why I left."

"You made one bad call."

"One bad call that cost Vanessa and two other men their lives."

Artie studied him. "Interesting thing is, it should've cost you yours. We're all curious how you walked away from that inferno."

"Because I was the one who burned that shithouse down." Oliver could feel his pulse pounding in his temple. "Vanessa and the others were dead. We'd been ambushed. So I threw a CS canister into the nest and got the fuck out."

"And we all felt for you, man, but that's the job. You knew it going in. Vanessa knew it. She was prepared to face the danger every time we went into a hostile situation. Every time, you take a chance you aren't coming back."

"Yeah, well, that's the deal. I'm not coming back. I'm done."

Artie set his cup on one of the tables. "I think you're aware of what's been going on in the area. Some vicious monster's been having a field day, leaving bodies in its wake. We understand it's here. And we need you to help us find it."

"What makes you think I can find it?"

"Because you've got yourself a little help, don't you?" Artie smiled. "Very attractive help, in the form of one Lucy Smok of Smok Consulting."

Oliver tried to keep his expression neutral. "A local group hired her to hunt the thing, yes."

"And you belong to this local group."

Oliver didn't answer.

"Well, I'll tell you what, Benally. We'll give you twenty-four hours to decide how you want to do this. If this Smok girl is everything she's rumored to be, she should have this in the bag. It's your job to make sure she captures the creature alive. Darkrock has plans for it."

"For God's sake." Oliver tried to tamp down his mounting outrage. "Do you have any idea what you're dealing with here? This is nothing you've ever seen before. Lucy's gone up against it twice now, and she still doesn't know what it is, but from what I can tell, it's nearly killed her both times."

"So it's *Lucy* already." Finch grinned. "Nice."

"From what you can tell?" Artie frowned. "Are you saying you didn't see it yourself?"

Oliver cleared his throat. "She's not big on keeping me in the loop. Both times, I've just seen the damage after the fact. I've tracked it, but I haven't seen it personally." He paced away from them, realizing they were already sucking him into Darkrock's orbit. "This isn't what I do anymore. And Darkrock's making a huge miscalculation if they think this thing is something they can just capture and put to their own use. It's intelligent and malevolent. And very powerful." Somewhere in the past two days, he realized, he'd come around to Lucy's point of view. The creature needed to die.

"Which is precisely why Darkrock is interested in it. This is an unprecedented opportunity to catalog a new species. Rumor is it can change form at will. That kind of ability could prove extremely useful. Revolutionary, in fact."

"It's not going to be terribly useful if it kills everyone in the facility. If you can even tranquilize it long enough to transport it there."

"You just let us worry about that. You make sure Lucy Smok doesn't kill it first. We want you to stick to her like a rat in a glue trap. No more of this 'after the fact' bullshit. The Smok enterprise has gotten in our way before. If she destroys this thing before we have a chance to study it, Darkrock leadership isn't going to be happy. There's talk of eliminating that problem."

"Is that a threat? If I don't take care of Lucy, Darkrock will?"

"It's whatever you want it to be, Benally. If the prospect of something unfortunate happening to Lucy Smok seems like it's a threat to you, well…that's for you to figure out, isn't it?"

And just like that, he was in again. Even if he managed to disappear, he'd be leaving Lucy at Darkrock's mercy. Not to mention the undergrounders. And Colt.

As soon as Artie and Finch had gone, Oliver headed back out on his "beat."

His earlier instincts proved to be right. As he circled back around toward the Bartlett, he caught sight of her watching from the shadows across the street. He'd probably made a mistake keeping close. He'd only drawn her attention to it.

She saw that he'd seen her. Even though he couldn't see her face in shadow beneath the hood of her jacket, he knew she was staring straight into him, as if she had night vision. There was something about her that seemed slightly to the left of human, now that he thought about it. Could Smok Biotech be doing the same kind of work Darkrock was? Was Lucy biologically enhanced?

"What do you think you're looking at?" Her voice carried across the empty street. Oliver almost laughed. It was such a film noir kind of moment. The femme fatale watching him watching her. The dialogue straight out of a movie from the 1940s.

"You tell me," he murmured. And he was certain from her posture that she'd heard him.

Lucy took her hand out of the pocket of her leather

jacket over the dark hoodie—she was holding a cross-bow in the other—and crossed the street. "A little late for you to be out prowling, isn't it?"

"I wouldn't call it prowling. Is that what you're doing? Prowling?"

Lucy's eyes were inscrutable within the hood. "I'm doing the job your council is paying me to do."

Oliver wanted to be objective about her. There were too many variables he wasn't sure of. What Smok International was about. How Lucy might be enhanced. Whether she meant real harm to the people he'd come to think of as "his" undergrounders. But Darkrock's implied threat had gone straight to the heart. She meant something to him. Already. And Darkrock knew it. They wouldn't have been able to manipulate him without that knowledge.

"Maybe you'd like some help with that."

"Help?"

"This thing seems to be pretty elusive, even for you. Maybe the two of us together would have more luck."

She was quiet for so long that he almost asked her if she was okay. "I thought you wanted to give it therapy."

Oliver burst out laughing. "Therapy?" Where had that come from?

"You were pretty adamant about shifters being these misunderstood creatures that didn't mean anyone harm."

"I never said this thing didn't mean anyone harm. It's pretty clear that it does. That's why we called you in."

"So you're prepared to do things my way? You're not going to get in the way when I try to kill it?"

Oliver had walked right into that one, because keeping her from killing it was precisely what he had to do. "Have you considered that maybe it can't be killed? I mean, you said you hit it with lethal force and it just kept going. Did you hit it tonight?"

"One shot, yeah. I didn't get to use my arrows." She indicated the crossbow at her side. "They're Lucien's actually. They may be more effective than the bullets." She looked thoughtful for a moment. "Maybe I could use someone to distract it long enough for me to get off a shot."

"You mean someone to act as bait."

Lucy shrugged. "Sure. Call it bait."

He couldn't quite figure her out. Was she mocking him or offering to work together? Either way, he needed to buy some time to come up with an alternative to killing the beast that would make sense to her.

Oliver studied her. "So, do you still not sleep?"

Despite her otherwise relaxed body language, her fingers curled and uncurled around the barrel of the crossbow in an unconscious gesture of conflict. "Why?"

"I'm wide-awake, and I have a feeling that's not going to change in the next few hours. I thought we could discuss some strategy over coffee."

She gave him another of those noncommittal shrugs. He took it for agreement.

At the shop, he realized he'd left the coffee cups sitting out from Darkrock's visit. As he scooped them up, he felt Lucy's eyes on him, but she didn't comment. While he started up the coffee maker, Lucy sat on one of the ottomans. The crossbow was still clutched in her hand.

Oliver glanced up from the counter. "You expecting to need that in here?" He nodded at the weapon.

Lucy looked down at it. "I suppose not. My case is in the car." She set it on the couch next to her. After a moment of watching him brew the coffee, she finally pulled back her hood. The shock of her cropped hair struck him all over again. It highlighted a change in her since yesterday that he couldn't put his finger on. She'd been stoic and hard to read before, but it was like she'd gone deeper. They'd been intimate—extremely intimate—and afterward she seemed to have revoked a level of trust.

The coffee was ready.

Oliver poured two cups and brought them on a tray with cream and sugar to the table next to Lucy. "I wasn't sure how you took it."

"Black."

Of course she did.

As he sat on the edge of the couch opposite, Lucy watched him over the rim of her cup. "You had company tonight."

He stiffened. Had she been watching him? *Oh, right.* The dirty cups. "Yeah, some old service buddies dropped by."

"You were in the service?"

"Marine Corps. *Semper Fi.*" He raised his cup in a salute.

"How long ago was that?"

His mouth twitched with a sardonic smile. "Are you trying to guess my age?"

"Why would I want to guess your age?"

Oliver drank his coffee, starting to regret that he'd suggested this. But there was a reason he had. "So, about the creature, I know you're set on killing it, but maybe we should rethink that, given how hard it's proving to be to kill."

"So therapy, then."

He smiled despite himself. "Not therapy. But doesn't Smok have some heavy-duty drugs that could knock it out first? We could hunt it like big game, hit it with the trank, then track it and wait for it to go down."

Lucy leaned forward on the ottoman, resting her elbows on her knees, the coffee cup still in her hand. "Is that what Darkrock wants you to do?"

Goddamn. Oliver swallowed a mouthful of too-hot coffee. How did she know about Darkrock? Unless...

He set down his cup carefully. "It was you. You told them where I was."

"Told whom?"

"Are you kidding me right now?"

"You expect me to believe Darkrock didn't know where you were?"

"I don't expect you to believe anything. I *would* like to know what you know about it, however. How did you learn about Darkrock?"

"I'm the CFO of Smok International. Of course I know about Darkrock."

"I meant..." Oliver paused. Was Darkrock part of Smok's operations? Had Smok, in fact, created it? Could they be simultaneously working for Lucy and working against her? "How long have you known who I am?"

"Since this morning. I ran a check on you through my research department. Standard operating procedure." Standard operating procedure after she slept with someone?

"And your research department shared that information with Darkrock."

Lucy's jaw was tight. "We don't share anything with Darkrock. If your people found out I was looking into you, it's because of their own flags on such searches. It's not like we're using Google."

"They're not *my* people."

"Are you denying that you work for them? You just admitted you were Oliver Benally. And they were obviously the 'service buddies' who dropped by tonight. Was that before or after you stalked me?"

Oliver got up and paced away from her, trying to employ his breathing technique. "I haven't worked for them since 2012. Since…" He turned to face her, thumbing the back of his ring. "Not since my wife was killed."

Chapter 11

Lucy's stomach dropped, and she straightened, resting her cup on her thigh. "Your wife?"

"We worked together at Darkrock. The last mission we worked was a disaster. Some vamps took out every member of my team. Including Vanessa. That's when I left the operation." Oliver's expression was grim. "I should have left earlier."

"I'm sorry." Lucy's eyes were drawn to the ring he was playing with on his right hand. It was a wedding band, and she hadn't noticed.

"Not as sorry as I am." He seemed to realize he was playing with the ring and moved his hand away, smoothing his palm along the hair at his temple.

"So you just walked away."

Oliver shrugged. "You don't exactly walk away from Darkrock. I burned down the vamp nest and let people think I'd died in the fire with the rest of the team. And they had no idea I was still alive until today. So…thanks for that."

She studied him, trying to decide whether this was part of his cover. Maybe the whole story had been invented for this very eventuality. If it had, he was an excellent actor. His eyes looked haunted. Whether the rest of his story was invented or not, she decided there had definitely been a Vanessa.

Lucy dismissed an odd little twinge at the idea that he'd loved someone so deeply that he still wore his wedding ring. What was it to her? Nothing. *He* was nothing to her. If anything, he was a threat to her. Which did nothing to dissuade her body from tossing her brain a little reminder of how intimately it now knew his. She needed to focus on the problem at hand. Despite what she'd told him, if Darkrock knew she'd run a search on him, it probably wasn't because of a flag. Her research department's searches were undetectable. Which meant she had a mole at Smok Biotech. The prospect was chilling.

"So you're not working with Darkrock."

There was a slight hesitation before he answered. "No. And they aren't too happy about it." He was holding something back.

"Do they know about the creature I'm hunting?"

"I have to believe they know something about it, but the subject wasn't discussed."

"And you just happen to have come up with the idea for us to team up and try to subdue it instead of killing it right after they came to see you."

"You know I was never a fan of killing it. But I'm becoming a fan. I just don't know if it can be killed, based on everything you've said. If only we could figure out exactly what it is and where it came from."

Lucy had been thinking the same. She wasn't going to make any headway with the hell beast until she had more information about it. And the only way she was going to get that was from Lucien. The problem was reaching him. Only Theia could bring him out of the underworld, and Theia spent most of her time in the underworld with him. It was time to talk to the Carlisles. If anyone knew how to reach Theia, it would be Theia's sisters.

Lucy set down her coffee. "I might know someone who could give us some answers. I'll see if I can track them down." She stood and picked up the crossbow.

"Right now?" Oliver looked surprised. Had he actually thought she'd come over here to have sex with him again? Unbelievable. A couple of orgasms—admittedly above-average ones—and he thought he'd be irresistible to her. He had delusions of grandeur.

"By the time I get back to Sedona, it'll be almost four, and I need to get cleaned up and put on something more suitable." She'd worn jeans again to hit the mine, and she was beginning to feel like a schlub.

"So you're really not going to sleep."

"With you? No."

She'd left him speechless for the moment, but he recovered by the time she reached the door. "I wasn't offering."

Lucy spared him a look over her shoulder before she went out. "Yeah, you were."

Oliver stared at the closed door. *Damn.* She was something else. He couldn't help smiling to himself, as infuriating as she was. It was just as well. He had business to take care of, too. Now he had two reasons to visit Polly's Grotto. To find someplace for Colt and to find out what

Polly might know about the connection between Smok International and Darkrock. Because he was convinced there was one.

He headed upstairs to shower, pausing as he undressed to peer closer into the mirror. There was a fresh mark on the skin below his left shoulder. A knot of scar tissue from a close-range bullet wound. Lucy had gotten off one shot—in the beast's shoulder. It was just as well she hadn't stayed the night.

As he'd expected, the Grotto was still open from the night before when he arrived. Apparently, the 2:30 a.m. last call didn't apply here. Oliver wasn't sure what the protocol was for getting the hostess's attention, but he didn't have to wonder for long. Something about him had already put him on her radar.

As he hovered by the entrance, a little overwhelmed by the underwater theme of the place and its fluttering blue-and-green light patterns that moved in waves across the walls and patrons alike, a partially shifted were-tiger approached him.

"My mistress requests your presence in her booth." The voice was deep and raspy through the tiger's larynx.

Oliver followed the were-tiger's glance to a woman in a sequined green gown, with hair that looked like seaweed spun from pure gold that somehow floated about her head despite it being not in water but in air. She lifted her champagne glass to him with an inviting smile.

He made his way to her booth, where a second glass was waiting for him. "I take it you're Polly."

"And you are positively delectable. Welcome to my grotto, son of Gwyn."

"Sorry, son of whom?" Maybe they'd mistaken him for someone else after all. "The name's Oliver Connery."

Polly twirled her hand in the air as she sipped her champagne. "Who cares? The more important question is what are you? And the answer to that, of course, is something nobody expects."

He was beginning to think this wasn't her first bottle of champagne. "I was told you might be able to answer a question or two for me. I'm prepared to offer a fair price for—"

"My ears!" Polly set her glass down and pressed her hands to the sides of her head, screwing her eyes shut. "You have absolutely no manners. Were you born in a bog?" After a dramatic pause, she peeked at him and moved her hands carefully away from her head. "I provide information for people who need it. Grateful recipients bestow me with *gifts*."

"My apologies."

"You said a question or two. The second, I suspect. The first, I'm absolutely in the dark about. I might even give you two answers for a single gift because I'm so curious about what that first question might be and because I'm in a generous mood." She reached across the table and squeezed his left biceps. "And you are just scrumptious. So what's question number one?"

Oliver was having trouble keeping a straight face—and keeping the heat out of it. "I'm looking for a safe house for a boy. A boy who fears for his life."

Polly raised a golden eyebrow. "Aren't there agencies for that sort of thing among the mortal world?"

"There are. But he's evidently not of the mortal world."

"I see. So he's a danger to others, no matter which world. And you want to foist him off on one of our kind rather than deal with him yourself."

"Uh…that's not exactly…" It was, though. Oliver sighed. "Shouldn't he be with his own kind?"

"You tell me, son of Gwyn." Polly laughed at his be-mused expression. "At any rate, I'm afraid you're on your own with that. I'm not running an orphanage. Now, on to your second question. You want to know about a certain raven-haired beauty and her connections. Am I right?"

"You are, in fact." He wondered how she could know that. "Specifically about her company's connections with a group called Darkrock."

Polly's expression went from flirtatious to threaten-ing, and she leaned toward him, her hand sliding down to his forearm in a hard grip. "Let me tell you something about Smok International. I happen to be old friends with the new CEO, and he would never tolerate those insidi-ous mercenaries. As for his sister, I can't speak for whom she chooses to associate with, but I would be very sur-prised to find her in league with such an underhanded operation. She *is* the chief financial officer, however, and I'm absolutely baffled by all things monetary. Perhaps if there's enough money in it, she might compromise her principles. But it *would* be a compromise. And for future reference, do *not* mention that name in my grotto again."

"I…see. My apologies. And thank you for being so candid." Not that he was entirely sure what she was get-ting at, but it seemed she was at least trying for candid. "What do I—What would be an appropriate gift to show my appreciation for the information?"

Polly's hand was still on his arm, and she squeezed his wrist with a mock expression of remorse. "Goodness, you're adorable. I ought to feel bad accepting a gift for telling you next to nothing." She smiled brightly. "But I do like a good gift." Polly tilted her head at him. "Perhaps in your case, a kiss would do."

"A kiss? That's it?"

"Darling, if you do it right, a kiss is everything." She leaned close, expectant.

What could it hurt? Oliver leaned in to meet her lips. They were surprisingly cool and damp. Not cold, by any means, but lower than normal body temperature—and salty, like she'd been swimming in the ocean. A prism of color seemed to swirl over her skin, flowing outward from her lips where they met his, and the color encompassed her hair, which shifted through multiple hues like a color-changing LED candle. She made the kiss a great deal more intimate than he'd planned before pulling away and breathing in deeply with her lips parted and a smile on her face. He had the distinct impression she was breathing something *out* of him.

Polly put her fingers to her lips and extracted what looked like a perfect pearl from between her teeth, holding it up in the dim light. "Marvelous. Aren't you just the sweetest thing?" She dropped the pearl into her champagne glass and took a sip, the pearl glowing golden at the bottom. "I feel like I owe you a little more for such a lovely gift. Perhaps I'll answer the question you didn't think to ask."

Oliver was still fixated on the pearl and wondering where the hell it had come from. "What question would that be?"

"This is not to go beyond this room, you understand. Not to be whispered to anyone else. Least of all those nasty little friends of yours."

"Of course. And they're not my friends."

"Lucy Smok has a number of weighty responsibilities—

incredibly weighty for a woman of her age, though she seems well equipped to handle them. And one of those responsibilities is protecting her brother, Lucien."

"Protecting him?" This was getting interesting. Perhaps he was about to get confirmation of the rumors about Lucien's drug addiction problem. Or worse, maybe Lucien was mentally unfit to manage a multinational corporation.

"Lucien presides over more than just Smok International. He also presides over the underworld."

Oliver's brows lifted in surprise. "You mean mob connections?"

Polly laughed and touched his hand lightly. "You're delightful. Not the mob. *The* underworld. In local parlance, he's the reigning Prince of Hell."

Oliver blinked at her, not sure he'd heard correctly. "The Prince of…"

"Hell. Or at least the underworld of medieval Christian interpretation. It's more complicated than that, but let's just say he presides over a great many things—*beings*—that don't belong in this world. By way of comparison, take a look around you. There are lots of people here who aren't human. But they do belong in this world. Things that cross over from that world to this, however, can be far more dangerous than those inhuman creatures who choose to prey on their human cousins."

It was a little much for Oliver to take in. "I'm not sure what this has to do with Lucy."

"It has everything to do with Lucy. She shares Lucien's blood. She may have avoided his inheritance—his place on the throne—but she's not entirely unmarked by the cursed strain. And her role as an infernal public servant is the guardian of the gates."

He barely had time to absorb the word *infernal* before he registered the latter half of the sentence. "The gates? Of hell?"

"If that's what you want to call it."

"What I want to call it? You're the one who's talking about hell."

"You're cute, sweetie, but I'm starting to get bored now." She emptied her champagne glass, the pearl still glistening at the bottom, and stared at him pointedly. "You're welcome."

It took him a moment to realize he was being dismissed. "Oh. Well, thank you very much for taking the time to answer my questions." Oliver rose, and Polly ignored him, reaching over the side of the booth to greet someone the were-tiger had brought by.

As he left the grotto into the surprising light of day, Oliver realized she hadn't really answered either of his questions. She'd just given him more.

Chapter 12

Lucy tried Theia's number just to cross it off her list. As she'd expected, the number was unavailable. Theia was about as out-of-range as you could get. The next best means of reaching Theia was her identical twin, Rhea. The call rolled directly to voice mail. Rhea had obviously gotten tired of Lucy using her as a go-between. That left Ione and Phoebe, the two older sisters. In Lucy's experience, Phoebe was the most approachable, even if her husband was a bit overprotective.

Phoebe answered on the first ring. "Hi, Lucy. Theia's still out of range."

Lucy was evidently becoming predictable. "I know. I've tried her number. And Rhea's. I just really need to get in touch with Lucien. It's not about the company," she added. "It's…infernal business."

Phoebe was quiet for a moment. "You don't mean some kind of infernal deal? If someone needs help with a shade or a ghost, Rafe and I are happy to offer our aid, but I'm not comfortable helping you get people to sign away their souls."

"No, it's not about getting more people into hell. It's about what's gotten out."

"Gotten *out*?" There was a pause and a muffled side conversation. "Hang on. I'm putting you on speaker. Rafe is here with me."

"Hello, Lucy."

"Rafe."

"What's this about something getting out of hell?"

"Do you remember when Carter Hamilton kept the gates open before Lucien descended?"

Phoebe groaned. "Not that bag of dicks again. Tell me he isn't back."

"No, he's safely locked away."

"You mean when Hamilton was trying to absorb hell's power," said Rafe.

"Exactly. He delayed Lucien's descent before you and Leo showed up to help. And during that delay, the gates were open both ways." Lucy realized this was the first time she'd admitted this to anyone. It felt like her own personal failing, somehow. Because she'd been susceptible to Carter's necromancy, he'd been able to control her through a step-in shade to lure Lucien into his trap.

"And things got out," Rafe said.

Phoebe cut in. "What kind of things are we talking about here?"

"Demons of various assortment. Hell beasts, in short."

"Hell beasts?"

Lucy tried to keep from sounding curt. "I can't go into all the kinds of things that are relegated to the underworld right now, but there are some things that are relatively benign and others that are absolutely antithetical to this world."

"How long have you known about this?" Rafe asked.

"Pretty much since the gates were opened. And I've been tracking them down and returning them, which is why you haven't heard about it. But there's one thing I haven't been able to catch."

"Why didn't you let anyone know?" The irritation was unmistakable in Phoebe's voice. "We could have been helping you."

"Because it's not your job." Lucy cringed at the harsh way that had come out. She hadn't wanted to snap—particularly when she was asking them for help—but her fuse was just too short right now for her to be civil. "This is what it means to be a Smok. You may not agree with our methods, but it's the job your ancestor saddled us with. Madeleine Marchant's last act was to curse our family with the responsibility for managing hell."

"Maybe Philippe Smok shouldn't have denounced her as a witch and had her burned at the stake." Phoebe was always quick with a comeback.

"Point taken. But regardless of how it came about, it *is* our responsibility, and we take that responsibility seriously."

"Some of that responsibility is Theia's now, too," Phoebe reminded her.

"Which is why I'm hoping you can help me contact her."

"She's been away for a while, so I expect she'll be surfacing before too long."

"I can't really wait for her to surface. People are dying. Is there anything at all you can think of? Maybe a spell Ione could do?"

"I don't think it works that way. Why not just have Polly open her infamous door for you like she did for Theia when Lucien first descended?"

"I have a policy of not being indebted to my brother's ex."

"Even if people are dying?" Rafe pointed out. Maybe he was right. If it was her only option, what was a drop of blood or a tear for Polly's trinket collection next to saving lives?

"Maybe," she began.

But Phoebe interrupted. "There might be one thing."

"Yeah?"

"Theia's been known to dream-walk."

"Dream-walk?"

"She's entered Rhea's dreams a few times while she's been below, to check in on her and pass on information."

"And Rhea can do this, too?"

"Well…not exactly. But she might know how to attract Theia's attention in a dream so that she'll enter it herself."

It sounded like a long shot, but it was better than being beholden to Polly if she didn't have to be. "Could you call Rhea for me? I think she's blocking my number."

"I can do better than that." Phoebe said something muffled, as though she'd covered the mic. "Rhea just walked in the door. Hang on a minute." The phone went silent as Phoebe put her on mute.

When the sound returned, the phone no longer had the echoey quality of being on speaker. "Hi, Lucy. It's Rhea. Phoebe says you need to get in touch with Theia. How do you feel about a semipermanent tattoo?"

"A what?"

"An inkless tattoo. It causes some scarring, but it usually fades in less than a year."

"And why would I want that?"

"Because I assume you wouldn't want to permanently mark yourself with the symbols that would get Theia's attention in the dreamscape."

What Rhea proposed was a series of archetypal symbols that she would tattoo without ink onto Lucy's skin. The images were commonly used in dream interpretation, which Rhea thought Theia would be drawn to while Lucy was sleeping. Apparently, a tattoo had worked once for Rhea when she'd been trying to reach her twin. As a tattoo artist, Rhea was constantly adding ink to her skin, so permanence hadn't been an issue for her.

The idea of using scarification on her body even temporarily wasn't something Lucy was wild about—and tattoos were definitely not her thing—but it was almost certain to fade, especially if she didn't bother the wounds. Unlike tattoos with ink, inkless tattoos used as semi-permanent body modification called for the opposite of meticulous follow-up care, since scarring was the goal. So if she did the careful follow-up, she would minimize the scars.

It seemed likely to be less permanent than bargaining with Polly. Lucy agreed. Rhea penciled her in for the end of the day at her tattoo shop. Lucy would have preferred to do it immediately, but Rhea insisted on honoring her existing appointments. It was just as well, since the second step of this communication method required going to sleep. Something that might prove more difficult for Lucy than getting a tattoo.

Rhea's Viking chieftain boyfriend was there when Lucy arrived. The two of them always made a striking picture together, his tall, brawny physique somehow perfectly complementing her diminutive spunk.

He gave Lucy a pointed look. "So that child-killing demon I pointed you toward—that was a hell's gate escapee."

Rhea's dark brows drew together in consternation as she pushed a wayward spike of bleached blond streaked with blue out of her eyes. "You helped her find a demon? When was this?"

"Four days ago. She said it was routine."

"I didn't actually say it was routine." Lucy shrugged off her overcoat and handed it to him. "I said it was right up your alley. It's a killer, and you track down killers that belong in hell."

"Náströnd."

"Same difference."

"I'm not so sure about that."

"At any rate, your instincts were a little off. I ended up going after a reptilian diner waitress who apparently has never hurt a fly." Lucy paused. "Well, probably definitely a fly. But nothing bigger."

"That doesn't sound right."

Lucy shrugged. "Anyway, the hell beast I was looking for found *me.*"

"What is this hell beast?"

She had to fight not to roll her eyes. "That's what I'm trying to find out by contacting Theia. I need more information from Lucien."

Rhea stepped between them and steered Lucy to the back room. "You can grill her while I work, Leo. We need to get this started."

Leo followed them in to hang Lucy's coat on the coatrack and leaned back against the counter as Rhea prepped Lucy's skin. "Do you mind if I observe?" He glanced at Rhea. "You're not going to need her to disrobe, are you?"

Rhea glanced up with a patient smile. She was prepping Lucy's forearm, and Lucy had worn a T-shirt. "No, Leo. I can get to her arm just fine." Leo Ström wasn't the sharpest crayon in the box. Good thing he was so easy on the eyes.

Lucy drew back her arm. "Maybe the arm isn't the best idea after all." She didn't relish having to make sure she kept it covered for a year. She pulled her shirt up to the band of her bra. "Can we do it here, below the navel?"

"Might be a little more uncomfortable if you're sensitive there."

"I'm not sensitive anywhere." Lucy glanced at Leo. "And you can stay." Anything for a little distraction, as far as she was concerned. She could handle pain just fine, but having dozens of little needles jabbing into her skin repeatedly wasn't exactly her idea of a good time.

She and Rhea had settled on the simplest possible symbols that could convey the meaning Lucy sought, things that would call to Theia's subconscious: the Lilith mark, a crescent moon with a simple cross descending from it that both Theia and Rhea had tattooed on themselves as descendants of the demon goddess; a serpent twined around an apple to represent Lucien as the archetype of the devil; and two overlapping infinity symbols to signify twinship. With Rhea's magical ability to read tattoos like tarot cards, she could impart more details than just the symbolic meaning as she created them, a sort of reverse reading for Theia to unravel.

Getting tattooed turned out to be more uncomfortable than Lucy had imagined. She'd heard people talk about the endorphin rush, but hers never kicked in. It was only afterward that Rhea mentioned the lack of lubrication from the inkless needles being a possible factor in the level of discomfort.

Leo's pestering helped to keep her mind off it. "The information I gave you from the Hunt was that the killer you were seeking had traveled to Jerome."

"That's right." Lucy tried not to react as Rhea went over a particular spot on top of her pubic bone for the third time.

"Sorry." Rhea gave her a sympathetic shrug. "Without ink, I have to make multiple passes to make sure the scarring will be deep enough."

"I thought we didn't want it to scar."

"Not long-term, no. But the lines have to be solid and deep enough for Theia to be able to pick up the image. Otherwise, it just looks like scratches."

"So the creature wasn't in Jerome?" Leo prodded.

"No, it was, but it wasn't the only one. Apparently, Jerome is a secret haven for paranormal outcasts."

"Well, there are no other killers. You asked me to point the way to a killer." That was good to know, anyway. Maybe Oliver wasn't so far off about the community he was protecting. "You didn't send the diner waitress to hell, did you?"

"No. I was interrupted."

"But you found the killer eventually. Or it found you."

"Yes."

"But you don't know what it is."

Rhea took her foot off the tattoo machine pedal and poked Leo's calf with the toe of her shoe. "Leo, will you leave her alone?"

"It's fine." Lucy looked up at Leo while Rhea returned to her work. "I've tangled with it three times now. I've never dealt with anything like it before. It looks like a huge wolf, but it's like no werewolf I've ever encountered, and it's able to shift without effort."

Leo frowned. "And you're sure it's from hell? Because it sounds a bit like Fenrir, the monstrous wolf brother of the serpent Jörmungandr." He drew up his sleeve and flexed his arm, making the knotted serpent tattoo around his right biceps undulate.

"Leo, stop posing," Rhea said without looking up. "She's not interested in your snake."

"It told me it was from hell," said Lucy. "Or at least, that it's hunting something that escaped hell, and it's not of this world. If I manage to reach Lucien, hopefully I can find out more definitively."

Leo nodded thoughtfully. "Let me know what you learn. I'd be interested to know what has those qualities."

Rhea released the foot pedal and lifted the needles off Lucy's skin. "All done."

While she cleaned up, Rhea gave Lucy instructions on how to use the tattoos. "It'll be easiest to reach Theia if you're experienced with lucid dreaming, but as long as you keep her name in mind as you fall asleep, you should make contact even if you lose track of the dream thread. She'll be able to pick it up from the tattoos."

"The dream thread?"

"It's like a story. If you're directing the story, the flow of the dream follows the thread you spin. Maybe a better way to think of it is as a tapestry. The picture takes shape on the tapestry as you weave the thread. All you need to do is give it your intent, that you need to reach Theia so you can speak to Lucien."

Lucy wasn't experienced. She barely even remembered her dreams. But Smok Biotech had developed a drug just for the purpose of lucid dreaming. It had the added benefit of being a powerful sleep aid.

"What do I owe you?" she asked as Rhea started to close up shop.

"Nothing. Lucien's family, and that makes you family. And I don't charge family."

Lucy thanked her awkwardly, never quite sure what to do with unearned generosity. Before heading home, she drove up to the lab in Flagstaff and picked up a sample of the dreaming compound.

It was almost midnight by the time she was back home and ready to try it out. She lay staring at the ceiling in her bedroom, convinced the sleep aid was faulty. Maybe she was just immune to them. Her wyvern hormones had wreaked havoc with her metabolism. *Think of Theia*, she reminded herself, and yawned. What was the point of thinking of Theia if she never fell asleep?

Something flicked at her ear, a moth or a mosquito that had gotten in when she opened the door, and Lucy brushed it away only to hear what sounded like a sigh beside her.

Warm breath exhaled against her ear, and something whispered in the darkness, "Shall I huff and puff and blow your house in?"

Lucy sprang from the bed and turned on the light, but nothing was there. All this stupid drug had done was make her hallucinate. And the raw flesh on her belly where Rhea had tattooed her was starting to burn. She pulled up her shirt to take a look and gasped. A bright orange glow began to trace over the lines as if molten lava were flowing through them. Instead of the images Rhea had tattooed, however, they were rearranging themselves and forming new lines, spelling out in a stylized script, *Veni, vidi, vici—I came, I saw, I conquered.*

Had Rhea's magic animated the tattoos somehow? And what did the glowing letters mean?

They began to change once more. *I huffed, I puffed, I blew your house down.* What the hell?

She realized she was reading the words even though they ought to have been upside down and backward from her vantage point. Lucy went to the large bathroom mirror. They were readable there as well, as if they weren't in reverse.

"Of course they aren't in reverse," her reflection said to her in a tone of irritation she was all too familiar with using. "You're dreaming."

"I'm dreaming." Lucy let the shirt fall back over the glowing tattoos. "Holy shit. It worked." Now what was she supposed to do? Weave the dream thread. What tapestry was she trying to create? What was the story she was trying to tell? She was already losing track. Lucy used the burning sensation of the tattoos to ground herself for a moment and think. She needed to find Theia and ask her to bring Lucien home so she could find out what the hell beast was.

Her reflection disappeared from the mirror in front of her, leaving her in the dark. Something growled behind her, and the hairs rose on the back of her neck.

There was just one problem with this lucid dream. The hell beast was in here with her.

Chapter 13

The bathroom disappeared, and Lucy was running through a dark, overgrown forest, with the hell beast's warm breath at her back. She managed to stay just ahead of it while it panted and snuffled behind her on all fours, but the grade changed, the forest sloping uphill, and Lucy tripped and caught her shirt on the thorns of a briar as she threw her arms out to steady herself. As she yanked the fabric away from the thorns, the hell beast leaped and knocked her onto her back, standing over her with its tongue lolling in a grotesque grin.

"Did you really think you could outrun me?" He shifted into human form in the blink of an eye. Lucy's heart sank. It was Oliver. She hadn't wanted it to be him. Oliver licked her throat and grinned down at her. "You're supposed to say, 'My, what a long tongue you have, Grandmother.' And then I say, 'The better to eat you out with, my dear.'"

"You're disgusting."

"Am I? You're the one who threw yourself at a hell beast. You knew it was me."

"I did not throw myself at you."

"I notice you're not contesting the second half of that assertion. You sought me out, not because you wanted to do your job, as you keep insisting, not to return me to hell, but because you wanted hell itself inside you. You couldn't be the mistress of hell. You're always going to be second-best, second-rate, the second sex. That one little pesky chromosome, and Lucien stole it all from you."

"What do you know about it?" She'd never told him anything about Lucien. "Get the hell off me." Lucy kneed him in the groin and rolled out from under him as he doubled over onto his side. She scrambled to her feet, but he grabbed her by the ankle and yanked her back down to the ground. Taking advantage of the fact that he was still compromised by the pain radiating from his groin, she kicked upward with her free foot as he tried to climb over her, landing a solid kick to his jaw while she brought her fist and forearm to the back of his elbow. The joint made a nauseating pop as she dislocated it.

His face transformed into the wolfish snout as he roared with pain and fell back. Lucy got to her feet and stood over him. This wasn't the hell beast. As confident as she was in her own abilities, she'd been no match for it physically in the waking world. She was letting her own subconscious get the best of her when she should be concentrating on the dream thread.

"You think you have this whole dream figured out, don't you?" the Oliver-wolf growled. "The problem with you is that you think you're smarter than everyone else."

"That's not a problem, you ass. It's just true. And right now I'm getting in my own way. I'm not here to psycho-analyze myself. I'm here to talk to Theia Dawn."

The rest of Oliver transformed into the massive shape of the wolf, eyes glowing red, salivating as it rose onto its haunches and came toward her. "I am Death. I am Sex. And I am going to devour you."

Lucy stood her ground. "Good luck with that. I'm just going to wait here for Theia."

The hell beast paused in its low, stalking stride and began to convulse, its underbelly splitting down the center as if a sword had sliced it, and a female arm and leg emerged from the wound. Lucy watched with slightly nauseous fascination as Theia climbed out of the empty carcass.

"Lucy!" Her sister-in-law threw her arms around her but seemed to remember in short order that Lucy was *not* the hugging type and let go. "What are you doing here? I thought I was dreaming of Rhea, and the whole wolf thing confused me, because Leo has a wolf-dog aspect, but it's nothing like this."

"So you thought you'd do a classic Red Riding Hood entrance."

Theia grinned. "Like it?" She brushed a little bit of wolf viscera from her checked skirt. The naturally dark chestnut bob that made her look as different from her twin as it was possible to be and still be identical peeked out from beneath a classic red hooded cape.

"Very nice."

The grin faded, and Theia hooked arms with Lucy beneath her cape, walking her away from what now looked more like a cartoon corpse. "But you wouldn't have gone to these lengths to reach me if something wasn't really wrong. What is it? What's happened?"

"I need to talk to Lucien. The breach Carter Hamilton took advantage of when he was trying to absorb hell's power has had unintended consequences."

Theia nodded. "Lucien has been having a hell of a time—pardon the pun—keeping the books straight. We've noted all the creatures you've sent back, and it's very much appreciated."

"There's one so far that I can't handle—the one I was dreaming of just now—and I need to know how to kill it."

Theia slowed and glanced back at the hell beast. "A werewolf?"

"It's not an ordinary werewolf. It shifts form without effort, and Soul Reaper bullets don't do a thing."

"You've shot it?"

"At least four times point-blank."

"That's not good."

The menacing woods landscape Lucy had dreamed up was starting to lose stability around them, unraveling at the edges. The wolf's body was gone, and trees were disappearing.

"You're waking up," said Theia. "I'll see you soon." She skipped away down the disappearing path in her red hooded cape.

Lucy opened her eyes and found herself on her bedroom floor. In her struggle with the Oliver-wolf, she'd apparently fallen right off the bed. After a moment, she realized the sound of knocking had woken her. Someone was at the front door.

She picked herself up and smoothed her hair with a glance in the hall mirror before opening the door to find Lucien and Theia on her doorstep.

Lucien gave her his lopsided James Spader smirk that he

didn't think anyone knew was carefully cultivated. "Theia thought you might be hungry after all that dreaming."

Theia held out a basket covered in a red-and-white-checked towel.

Lucy looked under the towel as she let them in. "Cupcakes and lattes. That's a modern twist on the fairy tale."

Theia grinned. "It was all we could get on short notice."

"How did you guys get here so quickly?"

"It wasn't that quick. Did you just wake up? It's been several hours since you left the dream."

Lucy shrugged. "I guess I needed the sleep." She took the basket to the kitchen table and passed out the lattes, taking a cupcake for herself.

Lucien sipped his coffee as he sat, studying Lucy for a moment. "Something's different. Are you wearing makeup?"

Theia shoved his arm playfully. "Stop teasing. It looks great, Lucy. When did you cut it? It was still long in your dream."

Lucy's hand went to the back of her hair self-consciously. "Yesterday. I just got tired of washing it."

"Ah." Lucien nodded sagely. "That's what's different. You've stopped washing your hair."

"Very funny, Lulu."

"Don't call me Lulu. I'm the King of Hell."

Lucy raised an eyebrow. "Oh, you've been promoted, I see."

"Only his ego," said Theia. "So, Lucien, tell her about the list."

Lucy sipped her latte. "The list?"

"I've been keeping a list of all the hell fugitives still at large," said Lucien. "There's nothing like the thing you described to Theia. There's a pack of hellhounds missing, four of them, but they're juveniles. They wouldn't be able to cause this kind of trouble. In fact, they're usually quite gentle unless someone's directing them to attack. And I'm pretty sure even a regular bullet would do some damage given how young they are. Four Soul Reapers and it walks away? Not a chance."

She'd gone to all this trouble of sitting through an uncomfortable tattoo and scarring her skin and subjecting herself to an untested psychotropic drug for nothing.

Lucy set down her cup forcefully. "Then what the hell is it?"

"Don't get bitchy. I came all the way from hell to try to help you. But I need some more information if I'm going to be able to figure this out. Tell me everything you know about it. Everything it's done so far."

Lucy described her encounters and the incidents reported in Jerome but left out her suspicions about Oliver. "I thought maybe the Soul Reaper serum would work better with the crossbow, so I took that with me yesterday to the mine, but the thing moves too fast for me to line up a shot."

Lucien's head shook as he swallowed a sip of coffee. "I don't think the arrows would be any more efficient than the bullets, to tell you the truth." He scratched his head, considering. "I would almost think this thing isn't physically in this plane if it weren't for the fact that it's obviously having physical effects on the living."

"Why do you say that?"

"The way it shifts when it chooses to and appears where it wants to when it wants to—it's almost like this thing operates purely on will."

"You mean a projection," said Theia. "Like Carter's

little trick of crashing Phoebe's wedding last spring and his stunts in luring you to the Chapel of the Holy Cross to take advantage of your transformation."

Lucy frowned, watching the paper cup as she rotated it slowly on the table. "You don't think Carter could be behind this?"

"Projecting his will from the underworld?" Lucien shook his head. "No. That isn't possible. And if this thing is interacting with the physical world, then the method of magical projection Carter was using before wouldn't apply."

Lucy ate a bite of her cupcake, pondering how much more she wanted to tell him. "What about Darkrock?"

His eyes narrowed. "What about them?"

"Could they have manufactured something like this?"

Theia glanced from Lucy to Lucien. "What's Darkrock?"

Lucien's jaw was tight. "They're opportunists. Paramilitary contractors that specialize in the paranormal." He studied Lucy. "What makes you think they could be involved?"

"I had a run-in with a guy who claims to be ex-Darkrock, but I have a feeling he's not so ex. He's on the secret Jerome town council that hired me to track the creature. When I found out about his involvement with Darkrock, I got to thinking…what if they created it and released it at the same time the gates were open?"

"How would they have known the gates would open?"

"Carter," said Theia with a sigh.

Lucien nodded thoughtfully. "It's a possibility. I'd be surprised if their research had progressed to the point where they could do that kind of gene manipulation—

and frankly, I'd be a bit disappointed that Smok Biotech hadn't beaten them to it."

"Lucien." Theia glared at him.

"I mean the ability, of course. Not that we'd do it."

"But they experiment on the creatures—and people—they capture," Lucy reminded him. "So if anyone were to have progressed to that point, it would be them."

Theia shuddered. "That's horrifying."

"That's why we don't do business with Darkrock," Lucien snapped. He grabbed Theia's hand and gave it a reassuring squeeze as soon as he'd done it. "Sorry. I just loathe their business model. They're despicable." He nodded at Lucy as Theia stroked his fingers with hers in an irritating newlywed PDA. "I'll try to find out more about what kind of creature might be capable of all this and get back to you—through Theia if I'm not able to get away myself. In the meantime, see if you can find out more about this Darkrock guy. If Darkrock is behind this, his role in bringing you to Jerome is very concerning."

Lucy nodded, focusing on her latte so her face wouldn't give away anything more about him. "I'm already on it. And thank you—both—for coming when I needed you." Something in her face or her words must have betrayed her anyway. Lucien knew her too well.

"Theia, can I have a minute with Lucy before we go?"

Theia smiled quizzically. "Sure. I'll just take a little walk around the complex and give you guys some time together."

Lucy tried to look nonchalant as Theia stepped outside. "What's up?"

Lucien frowned. "Lu. This is me. What happened?"

"What?" She gave him an irritated squint. "Nothing happened."

"Then why did I find a message from Fran on my phone when I arrived this morning?"

Lucy groaned and dropped her head forward on her crossed arms on the table. "She swore she wasn't going to tell you anything."

"She didn't. But you just walked right into that one."

"I hate you, Lucien," she said into her arms.

"That sounds a little more like you, but it's too little, too late. So out with it. Does whatever happened have something to do with your new look?"

Lucy raised her head. "You don't have any idea what you left me with, do you?"

"What I left you with?"

"The Smok legacy. Madeleine's curse. For you, it was a onetime deal. This isn't your true form in this plane. It's only with Theia that you can walk around in human skin."

"It's not exactly a party being a monster in the world of the living, babe."

She fixed him with a piercing look, letting her eyes shift. "You don't say."

Lucien's face registered surprise. "I thought Fran had you on a management regimen with the anti-transformative. Are you still shifting?"

"She does, but it's cyclical. Monthly, to be precise. And my hormones are all messed up, and I jumped a guy I barely knew, and he's Darkrock, and I think…" She stopped just short of saying she thought he was the hell beast. "I don't know what I think anymore."

"You…wait. You slept with the guy from Darkrock? The one who lives in Jerome?"

Lucy growled in answer and lowered her head to her arms once more.

"And what does this have to do with your hair?"

She stayed silent for a moment until frustration hurled it out of her. "I hacked it all off because I'm a *horrible* person, Lucien, and it was less drastic than cutting myself."

"Lu." His hand rested on her shoulder, and Lucy shook him off. "You are not a horrible person."

"Oh, come on. I'm the CFO of Smok International, and I've spent my life convincing people to sell their souls for some temporary peace, and I'm self-centered and arrogant, and I hate people. And they hate me."

"Lucy. That's not true. You do not hate people."

An unexpected ripple of laughter escaped her. "You suck, Lucien."

"I know. It runs in the family. Will you please stop talking to the tabletop and look at me?"

With a sigh, she straightened and met his eyes.

"I know you want everyone to think you're some cold, unapproachable bitch. That's the persona you've built, and that's fine. You don't have to let people know you. But when you start buying into the fiction you project to everyone else, you're not doing yourself any favors. Take it from me. I had everyone so convinced I was a lazy, arrogant asshole that I almost became one until Theia saw through my act. You and I didn't exactly get a lot of positive reinforcement or affection growing up. But we are decent human beings—even if we aren't entirely human." Lucien sighed. "Look, I know I'm not going to convince you to like yourself with a little pep talk. But at least cut yourself some slack. And take your damn meds."

"Ha!"

"And incidentally, I think the haircut looks great."

"Fran fixed it."

"Will you promise me something?"

"What?"

"Don't do anything Fran can't fix."

Chapter 14

Regardless of Lucy's existential crisis, Oliver knew more than he was saying, and Lucy intended to get some answers out of him this morning. After Lucien and Theia departed, she took her time rebuilding the physical presentation of her "public persona." Lucien was right that she needed to come off like a cold, unapproachable bitch. Given her age—and her sex—it was the only way to be taken seriously in her role, whether as corporate mogul, soul negotiator or infernal exterminator. To that end, she needed the proper attire. The sloppy jeans-and-T-shirt look had been an outward sign of her slipping control, and her tailored suits were the opposite.

She'd been wearing them since her senior year in high school, refusing to wear the little pleated skirts and knee socks of her school uniform. She had also refused to buy women's suits, because somehow when the word *woman* was added, it was no longer a business suit but a "pantsuit," as if pants were understood to be a form of playing dress-up as a serious person—in other words, a man—and straying from the proper feminine attire in a way that wearing pants without a matching jacket wasn't. Women's suits also had useless pockets and cheap stitching and idiotic cuts. Instead, Lucy commissioned all her suits from a bespoke men's tailor.

Oliver wasn't in when she arrived—some young blonde Lucy had never seen before was working the counter—and Lucy offered to wait. Her professional look evidently convinced the girl at the counter that whatever business she had with Oliver, Lucy must be too important to waste time sitting in a coffee shop waiting for him. Lucy was about to tell her not to worry about it when the girl told her where Oliver had gone.

"He had some boxes he needed to drive out to his storage unit, if you want to try to catch him there. I'm not sure how long he'll be or if he's coming straight back."

"Is that the facility over on Dundee Lane? Where the fire was the other day?"

"It must be. That's the only one around, unless he has a unit in Cottonwood."

It seemed a little odd that Oliver would suddenly be spending time at the storage facility. He'd been acting peculiar when she saw him there, and it wasn't just because she'd encountered him unexpectedly in firefighter mode.

Lucy thanked the girl and drove down the side of the mountain toward Clarkdale, the autumn light gorgeous on the stacked-rock walls lining the road. At the storage facility, the attendant didn't even balk at giving such an official-looking person a map to a customer's unit. Lucy left her car parked in the lot in front of the office and walked to it. A pickup truck was parked outside it, and the roll-up door to the unit was half-raised, as if someone didn't want passersby to see inside. What was Oliver hiding in there?

She ducked quietly under the door, expecting to catch him bending over crates of black market weapons or drugs. It took her a moment to process the scene. Oliver was seated on the corner of a storage bin talking to a skinny kid eating a sandwich on a makeshift bed.

Before she could even say Oliver's name, the boy had leaped to his feet with a look of abject terror and scrambled toward the door, and as he ducked to scuttle under it, his appearance changed swiftly. A skinny boy in baggy hand-me-downs crawled under the door, but a half-starved juvenile white wolf with red-tipped ears loped away on the other side, leaving the clothing behind.

"Colt, wait!" Oliver threw the door upward and ran after it, but the wolf had already scaled the wall and taken off into the hills. "Goddammit!" Oliver slammed his fist into the metal wall of the nearest unit and hissed another expletive as he wrung out his hand. "Do you realize what you've done?"

"Looks to me like I scared off a werewolf you've been protecting. How long have you been hiding him here?"

"He's a child, goddammit! And I swear to God, if you do anything to hurt that boy, I will hunt you down myself. Our working truce will be over."

"What the hell makes you think I would hurt a child?"

"Because he's not a human child, and to you, apparently, that makes him prey."

Too furious to respond, Lucy walked away from him. Oliver pursued her. "Are you going to tell me you don't think he's a menace to decent human society? That he doesn't need to be put down?"

Lucy whirled on him. "How the hell would I know whether he's a menace? You've been keeping him here like a pet. How long has he been here? You think keeping a child, human or otherwise, in a five-by-ten metal box is some kind of magnanimous gesture?"

"Oh, so you're just concerned about his welfare? Seems a little out of character for you and your *vast experience*. According to you, rogue werewolves are never benign. They only cause chaos and destruction."

Lucy opened her mouth and closed it again, thoroughly irritated to have her own words quoted back at her—and a bit impressed that he'd apparently memorized them.

"Nothing to say to that, I see."

"This clearly isn't a werewolf, and I doubt he's gone rogue."

The angry heat in his eyes cooled for a moment. "What makes you think he isn't a werewolf?"

Lucy folded her arms. "Because he shifted at will, just like our killer wolf."

His outburst of laughter was genuine. "You think Colt is our killer wolf?"

"Of course I don't. He's a boy."

"I see. So you think he'll grow *up* to be the same thing. May as well just put him down now to save time, then, right?"

"No, I think he's a hellhound."

Something seemed to click behind his eyes. "And you'd know, I suppose."

"Just what is that supposed to mean?"

"Well, you're Lucien Smok's sister. And Lucien, as

I understand it, is the head demon currently reigning in hell."

Prickling cold raced over her skin. She'd been extremely careful to control the flow of information about Lucien. "Who told you that?"

"Are you going to deny it?"

"I'm not obligated to confirm or deny any such absurdity to you. I want to know who's spreading this rumor about my brother."

Oliver glared at her wordlessly and yanked down the door of the storage unit before turning to step up into his truck.

"So you're just not going to answer me."

Oliver slammed the truck door and started the engine. "I'm not obligated to confirm or deny where I heard it. Have a nice day."

Oliver spent the better part of the day driving through the hills around Jerome and down into the valleys on either side looking for any sign of Colt, but the boy had obviously had plenty of practice avoiding humans in the time he'd been on the run. He hadn't seen Colt shape-shift before today, but Lucy was right, he'd simply shifted from one form to the other as he ran, like a chameleon donning camouflage. Was Lucy also right about him being a hellhound? Goddamn, she was frustrating as hell.

He laughed at the inadvertent pun. She was frustrating and infuriating and self-righteous, and it was a beautiful thing to behold. From one moment to the next, he couldn't decide whether he wanted to challenge her to a throw down in hand-to-hand combat or blurt out how goddamn much he wanted her, regardless of whether she was in cahoots with Darkrock or not—or in league with hell, for that matter. She made him feel like an inexperienced adolescent and an over-the-hill loser at the same time.

He gave up and called it a day, heading back to the shop to relieve Kelly. She looked frazzled, and from the state of the tip jar, it had been a big tourist day in town. It always was around the holidays. Oliver emptied the jar and gave her the lot and told her he'd close up.

As he emptied the espresso machine, the bell tinkled on the front door. Oliver groaned. It was five minutes until closing, and he'd hoped to get things cleaned up and shut down so he could get back out and search for Colt. He had a feeling he might find him in one of the old shafts after dark.

He turned with a plastered-on welcoming smile and found Lucy staring back at him. "What are you doing here?"

"Did you find the kid?"

"No. No thanks to you."

"I talked to my brother, the Prince of Hell, and he says the kid's part of a missing pack. There are four of them altogether, all juveniles, and they're not equipped to be on their own in our world."

"Four of them?" Oliver set down his cleaning rag on the counter. "So you're admitting that Lucien is a demon."

"I'd like to keep that from becoming common knowledge, so if you wouldn't mind telling me where you heard it—"

"From a siren. She owns—"

"Oh, I know all about Polly." Lucy came toward the back of the shop, looking relieved. "I thought maybe Darkrock had figured it out."

"If they did, they didn't say anything to me."

"But Polly did." Lucy slid onto one of the stools at the counter and swiveled to face him, one leg crossed over the other, her elbows—in her expensive and very businesslike suit jacket—resting on the edge of the counter. "What brought you to Polly's? Checking up on me?"

"No, I went to see if I could find some kind of safe house for Colt."

"And did you?"

"No. She said she wasn't running an orphanage."

"So how did Lucien come up?"

Oliver put his hands in his pockets and shrugged. "She kind of guessed I was curious about you, I suppose."

"Oh, you're curious about me?"

"You are a bit of a puzzle."

"I'm not a puzzle. You're just threatened by me."

Oliver's jaw dropped. "I'm *threatened* by you?"

"Oh, please. I kicked your ass the first time we met. And then I showed you up in front of your council with my knowledge of shape-shifters."

"You did not show me up. And you just caught me off guard that first night. I'm more than a match for you."

"Oh, really?" Lucy hopped off the stool and took off her jacket, tossing it on the counter. "You wanna go?"

"Do I *wanna go*?" Oliver laughed in disbelief. "What the hell are you—" His breath cut off with a grunt as Lucy punched him lightly in the gut. "Goddammit, Lucy."

"Come on, let's see what you've got."

"I'm not going to fight you."

Now she was rolling up her sleeves.

"Lucy—"

She ducked in toward him, her fist in a sharp extended-knuckle position, with a jab aimed at his right clavicle. Oliver stepped back with his right foot to avoid it and swung upward in a block with his left arm, but Lucy's move had been a feint, and she hooked her foot around his front leg and yanked him off balance as she dropped low for a sweep. Oliver ducked and rolled instead, darting up to tackle her at the waist and take her down as she turned. He narrowly missed having his windpipe punched.

Lucy rolled with him, using his weight to her advantage, and came up with one knee against his sternum as he landed on his back, her right arm poised for a strike. Instead of grabbing for it or blocking the punch, Oliver lowered his arms to the floor.

Lucy paused. "What are you doing?"

"Refusing to fight you. If you feel like punching me in the face to prove your point, go ahead." It was like dealing with a weird school yard bully who insisted on picking a fight, and Oliver wasn't having any of it. He voiced the thought that accompanied the image. "You're like one of those kids in grade school who keeps punching girls in the arm because he likes them."

"It's pretty weird to compare yourself to a defenseless schoolgirl." Lucy scowled. "And I do not like you."

"Oh, you do so. You just can't admit it without a fight first. And I don't feel like fighting you." He stretched his arms wide. "So have at it."

"What did you give Polly?"

"What?" She'd thrown him again, only mentally this time. "I didn't give Polly anything. What are you talking about? What does she even have to do with anything?"

"She's a siren. She never gives away anything for free. I just want to know what you gave her for the information."

Oliver was dumbfounded. Did all of this actually have something to do with the fact that he'd gone to the siren? "I didn't give her anything. I mean, she asked for a kiss—"

"You gave her a kiss?" Lucy's pale eyes had darkened.

Was she actually jealous? His head was spinning. "Yes, I gave her a kiss. It seemed like the polite thing to do."

"You very politely handed over a piece of your soul."

"Oh, come on."

Lucy moved her knee off his chest. "I'm not kidding."

Oliver sat up. "What would she do with a piece of my soul?"

"I don't know. Maybe nothing. She likes to keep her little 'trinkets' in case she needs them later. But that's a pretty costly piece of information you bought."

"So that's why you've been trying to beat me up? To get information out of me about what transpired between Polly and me? I already told you what I learned from her."

"She guessed that you wanted to know more about me, so she told you more about Lucien."

Oliver shrugged. "Which really doesn't tell me anything about you—except she did mention that you guard the gates of hell. I guess that's why you've been hunting this thing. It escaped from hell, like Colt."

Lucy straightened and stood. "Yes."

Oliver stared up at her. "I feel like that's supposed to be significant, that you guard the gates of hell, but I really don't get it."

"My brother rules hell because he has infernal blood."

He studied her for a moment. "And you…"

"Have infernal blood."

Oliver got to his feet. "You're telling me you're a demon?"

"A demi-demon, if you want to get technical."

"Okay."

"Okay?"

"Am I supposed to run screaming or something?"

Lucy threw her hands in the air. "Well, a normal person would."

"Well, thank God I've never been accused of being normal."

Before Lucy could respond, the little bell on the door handle jingled. He'd forgotten to lock up.

Kelly peered around the door and smiled tentatively at them. "I left my purse. I'll just run in back and get it."

"No problem. I was just about to close up." Oliver discreetly wiped the dust off the seat of his pants while Kelly dashed into the back. Good thing she hadn't shown up a few minutes earlier. That would have been awkward.

She returned with the purse strapped over her shoulder. "You guys looked busy when I came by, so I went to Rags & Riches for a little bit. Have a good night."

Oliver groaned as she closed the door behind her. At least they hadn't been naked wrestling. As much as he'd have preferred that, to be honest.

Lucy was still staring at him warily, as if she expected him to throw her out. Oliver walked to the door and locked it and pulled the shades.

Lucy's eyes were suspicious as he walked back toward her. "What are you doing?"

"Making sure we aren't interrupted. I thought I might give you a little piece of my soul."

Chapter 15

Lucy didn't stop him as he stepped in for the kiss. *Dammit.* He was right. She'd been picking a fight like some stupid, awkward adolescent. She did like him, and she wasn't at all accustomed to the feeling. For that matter, she couldn't remember ever having sex with the same man twice. Sex was for releasing tension, getting an itch scratched, and that was it.

She melted into Oliver as he slid his arms around her, ignoring the part of her brain that was reciting a litany of why giving in to her attraction for Oliver was dangerous, could compromise her integrity in doing her job, why she didn't deserve to be desired because she was bitchy and cold and picked childish fights. And had infernal blood—but not, as her dream-id hell beast had pointed out, enough infernal blood to be worthy of hell's throne.

She told her brain to suck it and indulged in the taste and texture of Oliver's mouth and the feel of his skin as she slipped her arms over his shoulders and curled her fingers into the hair at the back of his neck.

His hands had moved from caressing her to studiously, methodically undoing the buttons on her shirt, which he tugged from her waistband to get to the last of them. She shivered as he reached the bottom button and laid open the shirt, his hands inside the shirttails lightly stroking her sides.

To Lucy's disappointment, Oliver paused and released her mouth. "What are these?" His thumbs brushed over the healing marks of Rhea's artwork peeking out over the top of her waistband.

"Oh." Lucy hadn't expected anyone to see them. "Inkless tattoos." She sucked in her breath as Oliver unzipped the pants for a better view. "They were…ceremonial. They're not permanent."

"They're beautiful." He dropped to his haunches and kissed the top of one hip bone, letting his mouth linger and intensifying the shiver still rippling through her.

"My sister-in-law's sister…"

Oliver paused and looked up. "What?"

"Nothing. Never mind."

He returned his attention to the tattoos, kissing his way down from them to the band of her underwear. His mouth hovered over the fabric, damp heat from his breath drawing damp heat from between her thighs, and she gasped as he closed his mouth over the crotch of the panties, pressing his tongue between the cleft and against her clit.

Lucy closed her eyes, falling under his spell again, ready to throw caution to the wind, ready to break all her rules. Her irritating, rational brain was like a trapped animal rattling its cage in futility. *Don't do it. (Shut up.) You can't trust him. (Who cares?) You're pathetic.* She continued to ignore the voice as Oliver slipped her underwear down. *You're on your period.* Her higher brain seized on that one.

Eyes snapping open, she took a stumbling step backward.

Oliver was on his knees, looking puzzled. "What's the matter?"

"I'm on my period."

He blinked up at her with a sly smile. "I'm not seeing the part where that's a problem." Lucy's eyes widened, and Oliver laughed. "Honestly. I don't mind."

But she was already pulling things up and zipping things and putting herself back into place, feeling awkward. "I do."

Oliver straightened. "Okay. No worries." He watched her button her shirt. "I'm sorry. I didn't mean to upset you."

"You didn't upset me."

"You seem upset."

"I am not upset!" Lucy sighed and combed her fingers through the swoop of hair in front of her eyes. "Sorry. I am upset. I'm upset with myself."

Oliver studied her quizzically, as if she were a new species he'd encountered unexpectedly in the wild. "What for? You haven't done anything wrong."

"For wanting you." The words came out too loud and harshly, as if it were a condemnation of him instead of herself, and Lucy was horrified to feel tears burning behind her eyes. Worse, she could tell from his expression that he could see it. She turned away from him, blinking rapidly, and grabbed her coat from the counter.

When she turned back, he had his hands in his pockets, watching her with a frown. "I don't really understand what's going on here."

"Nothing's going on. I just made a mistake."

"By wanting me."

She shoved back her bangs in frustration. "No—it's not about you. It's about me. I have responsibilities—to Smok International, to your council. To the people of this town and this state."

"To yourself?"

She ignored that. "It's partly my fault that this hell beast is even in our dimension. It's here because a necromancer held the gates open to absorb hell's energy and prevent my brother from descending until the necromancer had gotten as much power as he wanted. And that necromancer used a shade—an unanchored spirit of the recent dead—to control me and lure Lucien into his trap. So for those few minutes before the necromancer was defeated, the gates swung both ways. And I've been tracking down every demon that escaped ever since. This is one of the last, and it's the worst. And while I'm indulging my sexual urges, someone else could be dying."

Oliver looked down at his feet, his forehead creased in thought. "I see. So I'm distracting you." He nodded thoughtfully and glanced up again. "Though I have to say that, from my end, at least, it's a little more than just sexual urges."

For some reason, the idea that it was more than sex made her cheeks warm with embarrassment in a way that sex itself did not.

"I think about you all the time. Half the time, it's because I'm furious with you." His mouth curved in a slight smile. "But you've gotten under my skin, Lucy Smok. And that doesn't happen to me very often. And if I've gotten under yours, even half that much, maybe you owe it to yourself to examine why you think you don't deserve that." He held up his hand before she could refute the statement. "Because that's what I see all over your face. That you think desire—whether it's for sexual pleasure or even just companionship—is selfish. And I wish I could confront whoever taught you that and give them a damn piece of my mind."

Lucy was speechless. She pulled on her jacket slowly, trying to formulate a response, any response.

"So that's it? You're leaving again?"

"I have a hell beast to kill. But I will. Examine it."

"It?"

"Why I don't deserve to desire or be desired."

Oliver frowned. "No...why you *think* you don't deserve to."

"Same thing."

His head shook definitively. "Nope. Not even close." He stepped in toward her once more before she could move past him, a question in his eyes as he brought his hand to the side of her neck and stroked his thumb along her jaw. "Am I wrong in thinking you feel what I feel? Just tell me if I am, and I'll keep my distance. I don't want to be that guy. Tell me you want me to back off, and I will. No hard feelings. I'll respect your boundaries."

Lucy closed her eyes for a moment, his scent and his touch making her heart beat faster and her breath quicken, everything inside her crying out for him—except for that holdout, that one corner of her brain saying she was stupid to let go and fall. She could regain her professional footing here, put up her wall. Feel safe. Feel nothing.

"You're not," she said.

His expression was puzzled when she opened her eyes. "I'm not?"

"That guy. And you're not wrong."

With both hands framing her face, he lowered his head and brought his lips to hers, and she was ready to lose herself in him, to tumble into the unknown territory of trust and emotional surrender and unfettered desire. But the kiss was brief and tender, almost chaste. No, definitely not *chaste*, but it was different from the frantic, overwhelming kisses they'd shared. It was a promise that there was more to come. He would be there. There was no rush.

But now he was all business, moving aside to let her pass. She'd almost forgotten she was leaving. She buttoned her coat, trying to adjust her internal compass as he walked her to the door.

"Have you considered my suggestion about teaming up?" he asked as they reached the front. "This thing has eluded capture twice—"

"Three times."

"Three?"

"It attacked me the morning I met you, right after I left Jerome. I stopped for gas in Clarkdale, and it was waiting for me."

"You never told me that."

"I wasn't working for you then."

"You're not working for me now. You're working for the council. And I think the cat's pretty much out of the bag that my experience makes me at least tactically qualified to help hunt."

She turned back at the door and studied him. Was it experience or current job skills?

He seemed amused by the way she was sizing him

up. "I *am* the one who recommended Smok Consulting to the council after all."

Lucy raised an eyebrow. "I thought you voted against it."

"I did. But since they were determined to bring in an outsider, I wanted to make sure it wasn't Darkrock." Maybe he was just trying to convince her that he wasn't on active duty, but he sounded sincere.

She tried to hide her surprise. "Do you promise to let me take the lead?"

Oliver smiled. "In every possible way. So, do you have a plan for where to hunt tonight?"

"Going back to the mine shaft."

"You think it's sticking close to it? Hiding out in there during the day?"

"I don't think it hides at all. I think it takes advantage of its human form to blend in. And I think it wants to fight with me, so it doesn't really matter where I go, it's going to be there."

"Then why the mine?"

"Because I can back it into a corner if I play my cards right."

She brought the crossbow again, despite Lucien's assertion that an arrow would be no more effective than a bullet. The creature had shown that it felt pain, so if nothing else, she could make it suffer, and hopefully slow it down long enough for Oliver to get off some shots of his own. He brought the tranquilizer gun loaded with darts containing a dose of ketamine designed for big game like ogres and trolls. And they took Oliver's truck just in case they needed to haul away a carcass—or an unconscious beast.

Lucy tried to ignore the little voice in her head that still didn't quite trust Oliver as they drove to the site. She was being ridiculous. No one could have two such distinctly different personalities. Still, on the remote chance that he really was the hell beast—or working with Darkrock—she held back a few details of her plan.

She left the sight off the crossbow this time in favor of thermal-imaging goggles—and Oliver, oddly enough for someone who was no longer a Darkrock operative, had a pair of his own. Her plan was to hit the beast from a distance with a single arrow followed by a barrage of rounds from her Nighthawk Browning to incapacitate it. She might get lucky this time, and it might go down. But if it didn't, Oliver would be standing guard at the entrance to the mine with the trank gun.

Oliver argued with her, wanting to head into the shaft with her, but Lucy "pulled rank" on him, reminding him that the council had hired her because of her expertise. She knew what she was doing. It would have been even better, of course, if she were half as confident as she sounded.

She chose the same entrance as before, going in as far as the tracks they'd left the last time—scuffed by their fight but still distinguishable. The cart rail tracks turned off here toward another section, while the path to the right was less defined. Lucy scanned the ground, her crossbow at the ready. There were tracks here, all right. Two sets. One large…and one small. The hellhound was here, and the beast was following it.

She paused and lowered the crossbow as she looked deeper into the tunnel. If she hit the hellhound, the Soul Reaper would shatter its corporeal form. The process was agonizing, but she'd hardened herself to it, knowing she was doing a necessary job. And the creatures she sent back to hell were fine, of course, once their matter reconstituted in their own plane. A little temporary agony was the price they paid for taking advantage of the breach to enter a realm they didn't belong in.

It was still her job to return the hellhound to where it was supposed to be. But she wasn't sure she could take aim at a juvenile wolf, much less a boy. She also wasn't sure she ought to. *Goddammit.* Oliver's sensitivity crap was rubbing off on her. And who knew how much harm his treating the hellhound like a human boy had done it? She'd checked out the storage unit after he left this afternoon. He'd brought the boy comic books and a little handheld video game system. He'd shown him caring and affection. How was a creature bred in hell for the purpose of hunting lost souls supposed to process that kind of information?

A piece of gravel bounced on the path behind her as though a boot had kicked it, and Lucy whirled, ready to let an arrow fly, only to see Oliver making his way down the tunnel.

"Jesus, Oliver. I could have killed you. I told you to wait at the entrance."

"I got to thinking that it would make more sense to hit the thing with the tranquilizer first. Isn't slowing it down the whole point?"

"Keeping it from escaping again is the whole point."

"But if we hit it with a trank dart, it won't be escaping."

"And if we don't hit it with anything and it gets past us, we've left a killer on the loose. Again. This damn thing has been toying with me. I can't afford to let it outsmart me anymore."

"If it comes at either one of us, we have each other's backs. Don't worry. We've got this. It's not going anywhere."

It felt like he was deliberately sabotaging her. Which would make sense only if he was working with Darkrock to take it in alive—or he *was* the hell beast. Lucy studied him through the night-vision goggles. She'd noticed a fading scar on his left shoulder earlier that her conscious mind had eagerly ignored. She'd hit the beast in its left shoulder the other night. But he didn't feel like a hell beast.

"Lucy." Oliver nodded toward the path ahead of them. Something was moving in the dark.

Lucy trained her crossbow on a flash of bright fur and a hulking shape, but Oliver knocked her arm aside with a shout as she fired, sending her arrow wide and high as her target headed deeper into the tunnel.

"Dammit, Oliver!"

"You were going to hit Colt."

"The hell I was. I had the beast in my sights, and you ruined the shot."

"It wasn't the wolf. It was the kid."

"Oliver, I know what I saw."

"I'm telling you, Colt was there."

"We can argue about what you think you saw later. We're losing it." Lucy took off in the direction the thing had gone. She spotted it around a corner and got off a shot this time. It hit the beast's flank but didn't go deep, and the creature shook it off and kept running.

"You hit him." Oliver grabbed her by the arm and spun her about. "You could have killed him!"

"I hit the damn hell beast!"

Oliver's face was a mask of fury. "You're so damn sure

that everything not fully human is evil that you're telling yourself stories about what you're hunting. At least have the decency to admit that you don't care what you hit."

Oliver was out of his mind. It was four times the size of the little wolf that had run from them this morning. She knew the beast when she saw it.

She shook him off. "Stay out of my way. If you mess with my shot one more time, I can't guarantee you won't take the next one."

"Now you're threatening me?"

"I'm telling you to stay the hell out of my way." At the end of the tunnel, the creature had turned to face them. Lucy raised her crossbow, and Oliver lifted the dart gun, but he was aiming it at her. "Jesus Christ, Oliver. Are you fucking crazy? Put that thing down or use it on the wolf!"

"I'm not going to stand here and watch you kill him."

"It's not a *him*, it's a thing."

"It's Colt. He's a goddamn kid."

"It is *not Colt*."

They'd lost their advantage by bickering, and it was coming for them, fast. Lucy tossed the crossbow aside and drew her gun, but Oliver had moved in front of her.

"Get the hell out of my way, or I'll shoot it right through you," she warned. But he'd cost her the shot, and the hell beast leaped on him, knocking him against the side wall of the shaft before turning to face Lucy with a grinning snarl. Lucy shot it. Twice. Three times. The bullets didn't faze it. It knocked the gun from her hand before she could shoot again, and Lucy felt the infernal blood surge in her veins as it struck her. The goggles were knocked off as they rolled in combat, the wolf snapping at her limbs and Lucy whipping it aside with a long-taloned wing.

At the periphery of her wyvern-enhanced vision, she was aware of something moving toward them, Oliver finally ready to use the gun, but something else moved from the other side, the juvenile wolf leaping at the larger creature in Lucy's defense. Oliver fired the dart gun at the same moment, hitting the smaller wolf in the flank, as the hell beast turned and threw the hellhound off with a slash of its razor-sharp claws and flung Oliver back.

The young wolf yelped and tumbled into the darkness, but the hell beast's attention was on it now, and it stalked toward it. While Lucy scrambled for her gun, Oliver fired once more from where he'd fallen, this time managing to hit the hell beast. It turned with a snarl and tore the weapon from Oliver's hand and backhanded him against the wall with a curled, clawed fist. The impact of Oliver's head against a metal railing was ominously loud in the enclosed space.

The beast's eyes locked on Lucy's as she got to her feet with the gun in her hand. It wasn't collapsing, wasn't slowing exactly, but something had given it pause. In an instant, it had taken on the form of a man—of Oliver. "I knew you had my toy," he snarled, recoiling with a roar as she fired. He stared down at the blood on his shirt where the bullet had struck and yanked the dart out of his chest beside it. "He's mine, and I *will* taste his blood. Mark my words." Just as swiftly as it had shifted into human form, it vanished.

Chapter 16

Her enhanced vision fading with the adrenaline surge, Lucy felt around in the dirt for her goggles. Oliver was slumped against the passage wall with his own goggles askew, looking dazed, and the young wolf lay motionless beside him.

Lucy crouched and felt for the wolf's pulse at its throat. It was weak, but it was there. She could see the movement of its narrow chest now, rising and falling shallowly.

"Oliver." Lucy shook him. "We need to get out of here. Colt needs help."

Oliver breathed in suddenly as if surfacing from underwater and opened his eyes wide. "What happened? Where's Colt?"

"He's right next to you."

He turned and checked the wolf as she had. "I think I hit him with a dart." He rubbed his chest absently and grimaced. "But I think the wolf got in a good blow, too, before he went down."

Lucy moved her hand over the softly panting body and felt something wet and sticky matting in the fur at the side of his rib cage.

She nodded. "It doesn't look like he's losing a lot of blood, but it definitely swiped him pretty deep."

Oliver got to his feet, straightening his goggles, and lifted the wolf in his arms. "We'll take him to my place. I've got supplies there."

"Yeah, I remember."

Lucy gathered up the rest of the weapons and followed Oliver back out through the mine shaft to the surface. Cold rain was drizzling over Cleopatra Hill when they emerged, and the dust on their clothes had turned to mud by the time they reached the truck.

"I'll drive," she insisted. "You took a pretty good blow to the head." She glanced at him as he laid the wolf on the seat and climbed in. "I'm honestly not sure how you're conscious right now."

"I have a very strong constitution." It was nonsense. He had something far more than a strong constitution. Only something inhuman could have gotten up and walked away from a blow like that. As something inhuman herself on occasion, she ought to know. For the time being, Lucy kept it to herself. She was still trying to figure out how the hell beast had looked like Oliver. And how it had disappeared.

"It's strange," said Oliver, echoing her thoughts as she drove toward his place. "I could have sworn you were going after Colt. I mean, I *saw* Colt. I didn't see anything else until the wolf jumped me."

"I didn't see Colt until he came to my rescue. And I

honestly don't believe he was there, except hiding in the side tunnel."

"You're saying I imagined I was seeing him the whole time."

"And maybe I imagined I was seeing a large wolf creature. Because we were both seeing what it wanted us to see." Lucy glanced at him. "I also saw you."

"What do you mean, you saw me? What did I do?" He grimaced. "Besides get in your way."

"I mean the hell beast, when it got mad, after we'd finally slowed it down. It looked like you when it spoke to me."

"How is that possible?"

"It's not a therianthrope—a human/animal shifter. It's something far worse. Like malevolent energy personified." Lucy's eyes went to Colt. "And it wants him."

Oliver stroked the wolf's fur. "Colt told me he was hiding from something that was after him, something dangerous. But why would that thing want him specifically?"

"Because Colt is something young and vulnerable. It probably followed the pack of juveniles out of hell. And it may have already gotten the other three."

"Well, it's not getting this one, goddammit."

By the time they reached Delectably Bookish, Oliver seemed to have fully recovered from the effects of the blow to his head, but Colt's condition hadn't changed. After cleaning and bandaging the wolf's wounds, Oliver put him in one of the guest beds to sleep off the drug.

Lucy watched him from the hallway as he closed the door. "You know he's not a human child. You can't keep him."

Oliver glared, arms folded as he stared her down.

"You're not going to put one of those bullets in him and send him back to hell."

"No, I'm not. But he has to go back. Somehow."

"He may not be a human child, but he's a scared—and now injured—kid. Let's just worry about protecting him from that thing for now. We can argue about where he belongs after we've figured out how to deal with the... malevolent energy."

"I'm worried about protecting *us* from that thing. I have no idea how to kill it."

Oliver headed into his room. "We'll figure something out. Right now I just want to get out of these muddy clothes and scrounge up something to eat. I'm absolutely starving." He stripped off his shirt and opened his dresser drawer to grab his pajamas, and Lucy admired his ass as he stepped out of the pants to pull on the blue-and-black flannel bottoms.

He caught her looking and threw a sly grin over his shoulder. "So you're staying, right?" He tossed the top of the pajamas to her, but Lucy's answering smile faltered as he turned to face her fully. Oliver tilted his head at her look. "What? What's the matter?"

Where his chest had been mostly scar-free just hours ago, it was now sporting four jagged craters of healing tissue.

Oliver followed her glance. "Oh. Yeah. Shit."

Chapter 17

He'd forgotten about the newest wounds.

Oliver rested his hands on his lower abs as he studied the marks. "I'm betting you want a good explanation for how I got these."

"Do you have a good explanation?"

He glanced up with an apologetic look. "No."

"Oliver."

"Where do *you* think I got them?"

"Are you serious?" Lucy's pale eyes had that dark, suspicious cast to them. "It looks like every bullet I've fired at that monster has somehow gone straight into you—and then immediately healed."

"That's because they have."

"I don't understand."

"I don't really understand it, either. All I know is that ever since I came to Jerome and started looking out for its

underground citizens, when one of them gets attacked…
it shows up on me."

"You're telling me that when I shoot or stab that hell
beast—I'm actually shooting and stabbing you?"

"Or when you or anyone else harms any other inhuman creature in the area, yes. Evidently, within at least a
five-mile radius, given the attack in Clarkdale. It doesn't
hurt, though, don't worry. I mean, it *does*, it hurts like
hell when it happens, but it doesn't cause me any harm.
And it heals up in just hours. As you can see."

Lucy was still clutching the pajama top like she was
trying to decide whether to run. "Why did you lie to me
about the scars I saw on you the other day?"

Oliver sighed. "Because I didn't know how to explain
it." He crossed the room and uncurled her fingers around
the shirt. "Your hands are freezing. Why don't you warm
up in the shower and join me in the kitchen when you're
dressed? I'll try to tell you what I know about it. But
fair warning, it really isn't much." He kissed her—and
at least she didn't recoil—and left her to give her time to
absorb what he'd told her while he whipped up a jumbo
omelet with chorizo and green chilies for them to share.

Lucy appeared at the doorway to the kitchen dressed
in his pajama top just as he was dishing up the omelet.
He left some in the pan for Colt in case he woke up later.

"Perfect timing." He smiled and set the plates on the
table. "Do you want anything to drink? It's a little late
for coffee, but I've got orange juice if you want the full
midnight breakfast experience."

"Juice is fine." Lucy sat and dug into her omelet, obviously having worked up as much of an appetite as he
had. And she wasn't even burning his peculiar metabolism. "So?" She wasted no time as he joined her. "Why

are you taking on other inhuman creatures' injuries? And what does that make you?"

"I honestly don't know what it makes me. I don't have any other extra-human abilities. That I know of," he added carefully, since that wasn't entirely true. "It never happened before I moved to Jerome, and I don't know why it's happening now. It's been going on for about three years. The first time it happened was right after I moved here and became aware of the underground community. I had a run-in with a pickpocket, a young were-coyote who lifted my wallet. He didn't realize I was onto him, so I followed him for a while to see where he'd go. It turned out he was stealing for his dealer, apparently wholly human, who was supplying him with meth. I confronted the dealer and told him he didn't have any business exploiting these kids and that if I caught him in Jerome again, I'd kick his ass."

Lucy concentrated on her omelet with a slight smirk. "Sounds familiar."

"Yeah, well, I'm nothing if not consistent." He smiled down at his food. "The pickpocket asked if I was their protector, and I said sure, I'd protect them if I could. I didn't have anything against shifters and sub-vamps and whatnot, and as long as they weren't hurting anybody, I'd defend them from anyone who wanted to hurt them. It seemed like they needed someone to look out for them. They weren't underage, but they were still really just kids, and they obviously didn't have a lot of human life skills. So the next night, I'm downstairs reading, and it feels like someone has knifed me in the gut. I look under my shirt and see the wound closing up. By morning it was almost undetectable. I found out later the dealer apparently came back and stabbed the pickpocket as a message to the rest of them. And the kid just got up and walked away."

"And you have no idea what gave you this power."

Oliver shrugged, eating his eggs. He had a suspicion, but it wasn't one he was prepared to voice, because it would only lead to more doubts he didn't want to bring up. She already suspected him of working with Darkrock, and in a way he *was* working with Darkrock, and the less said about it the better.

"What about your parents?"

"My parents?"

"Were they fully human? Did they have any abilities?"

Oliver sat back in his chair, pushing his food around the plate for a moment. "I didn't know my parents."

"Oh… I'm sorry, Oliver."

"Don't be sorry. I had terrific foster parents. I just never got to meet my birth mother. She was institutionalized—she died in a mental hospital when I was six. And she never identified the father—*my* father—on the birth certificate. All I know is that he was from the UK. From Wales. He'd gone back home before I was born, and her family wasn't able to take care of me. They're Navajo, but I don't know anything else about them." Oliver waved his hand to dismiss any misplaced sympathy she looked like she was about to express. "Anyway, it's never really affected me, since the only people I knew were the ones who raised me. But if my birth mom had any special abilities, certainly no one ever told me about them."

He hadn't talked this much about himself in years— since Vanessa—and having the focus on himself was making him uncomfortable. He glanced up to find Lucy smiling at him oddly.

"I guess we've all got our family skeletons. My father forced my mother to sign a nondisclosure agreement that said she would never tell us who she was when he granted her a divorce—then he hired her as the family doctor." Lucy took a sip of juice. "And he bargained my brother's soul to save his own while we were still in the womb. So, you know, knowing where you come from isn't always a bonus."

"Yikes. I guess not. But you had Lucien."

"True. We fought a lot trying to one-up each other for our father's approval growing up, but Lucien is the one person in the world I know I can be completely myself with, who really gets me, in all my ugliness. Even if he is a self-centered pain in the ass."

Oliver coughed on a bite of omelet that had gone down wrong. "Back up a sec. Ugliness? I can't imagine how anyone could find you anything other than stunningly beautiful."

Lucy looked down at her plate, her dark brows drawn together. "Thanks, but I wasn't talking about my looks."

"Neither was I." Oliver laughed at the expression of annoyed disbelief on her face as she glanced up. "I mean, obviously, *also* about your looks. But from everything I've seen, you're exceptional inside and out."

"You haven't seen everything."

"I'd like to."

Lucy put her napkin on the table and pushed back her chair. "Okay, this just got way too serious. I should probably get dressed and head home."

"You don't have to go. It's late, and you're all dressed for bed. Besides, I might need help with Colt when he wakes up."

"Oliver."

"Lucy." He smiled at her exasperated look. "We'll just sleep. That's it." He gave her a teasing grin. "You kind of owe me after disappearing last time."

"Oh, do I? I didn't know that was required."

He nodded, managing a mock serious expression. "It's in the rule book. If a man manages to give you two orgasms, you have to spend the night."

"I see." Her eyes were amused. That was a good sign. "Just so you understand, we *are* just going to sleep. I don't like messes."

"Or menses."

"Very funny."

Oliver grinned. "You're the boss." It was about time he finally won a round.

After cleaning up in the kitchen and checking on Colt once more, they climbed under Oliver's sheets as if it were the most natural thing in the world. He'd kind of expected Lucy to lie stiffly to one side, avoiding him. When he kissed her, she didn't pull away. And he'd come to the conclusion that, as Polly had said, if you did it right, kissing was everything. It certainly was when it came to kissing Lucy.

He drew back and studied her a moment, trying to figure out how he could be so comfortable with someone he'd only met a few days ago. And someone who wasn't Vanessa.

Lucy's brow wrinkled. "What?"

"I was just looking at your eyes. They're so…"

She rolled the pale blue eyes in question. "Yeah, I know. They're stunning. You've never seen any so pale, especially with the dark color of my hair. I've heard it a thousand times."

"No, I meant…they're just so serious. Melancholy, even."

"Melancholy?"

"I've never seen that kind of gravity in the eyes of anyone who hasn't been through war."

The pale blue eyes blinked in surprise, a bit of brightness in them, moisture, that hadn't been there a moment before. The question was, with whom was she at war? He had a feeling it was herself.

He'd gotten too serious again. Oliver smiled and propped his head in his hand, playing with the buttons on Lucy's pajama top.

She raised an eyebrow, crossing her arms behind her head. "I thought we were going to sleep."

"We are." He unbuttoned the top one. "Eventually." Oliver smoothed her hair behind her ear and kissed her temple. Her short cut was growing on him, even though he'd loved running his fingers through her hair while she was naked beneath him. "What made you cut your hair? It looks fantastic, by the way. Just took a little getting used to."

"Why does something have to have 'made' me cut my hair?"

"It doesn't. You just seem like a person who very carefully considers her appearance."

"And I carefully considered that I needed a haircut."

There was more to it than that, but he wasn't going to push it. Not when he could be doing other things.

He kissed her lightly on the lips. "I'm impressed by how long that lipstick stays on. Doesn't seem to come off on anything, either."

"It's Blood Moon lip stain, specially blended for me by an aesthetician at Smok Biotech. I can get you some if you're that into it."

Oliver laughed. "I'm only into kissing what's under it, but thanks for the generous offer."

"You seem really curious about my beauty routine tonight. Is there something else you wanted to ask me?"

"Not at all. Just appreciating having the time to…appreciate you."

"I thought maybe you were wondering about something you saw tonight."

He paused in kissing her neck. "What would I have seen?"

"If you didn't, then nothing."

"Okay, now you have me curious."

Lucy pushed him onto his back and climbed over him. "There's nothing to be curious about. I just…get a little ugly when I'm fighting mad."

So that was what she'd been talking about earlier. Something must happen to her appearance whenever she tapped into the infernal blood. But he'd been so out of it from the blow to his head that he hadn't noticed. And she thought he'd find her less attractive because of it.

He opened his mouth to tell her that nothing could make her unattractive to him, but a sudden pressure squeezed his chest, knocking the breath out of him. Before he could make a sound or signal in some way to let her know, Lucy's phone rang.

She glanced at it on the bedside table and bit her lip. "I'm sorry. I have to take this. It's Lucien. He's topside."

He managed to sit up as she climbed off him, still trying to figure out what was going on. The pressure was getting worse. God, was he having a heart attack?

Lucy frowned at her phone as she listened. "What do you mean you have to go to Polly's? Where are you?"

Oliver clutched his chest. He was having trouble breathing.

"You see? This is why I don't like owing people anything. All right, all right. I'm on my way." Lucy clicked off the call. "I have to help Lucien with something. I'm really sorry." She paused as she slid off the bed and stared at him. "Oliver? Are you okay?"

"I don't know. I don't think so. I feel very strange."

Lucy considered for a moment. "You gave her a kiss."

"You're bothered about that right now?"

"Polly's Grotto is under attack. Certain trinkets she's received—like the kiss you gave her—are designed to keep her protected. Those who've gifted her with them feel compelled to come to her aid. She calls them her gammon—part of her siren 'gam,' like a dolphin pod. Lucien and his wife belong to that group. And from the look of you right now, I'm guessing you do, too. That's what she's doing with that little piece of your soul." She grabbed his hand to pull him from the bed. "Come on. You'll feel better when you answer the call."

"Answer the call? I can't leave Colt here alone. He'll be scared when he wakes up in a strange place."

"With the dose of ketamine he got, he won't wake up for hours. But if you resist Polly's call, I think you're going to get very sick."

Oliver sat on the edge of the bed with his head in his hands. Just the mention of Polly's name was starting to feel like an imperative. God, how stupid had he been? Lucy was right. He had to go. The thought of doing so made him feel instantly better.

He went to the dresser to grab some clothes while Lucy put on the suit she'd been wearing earlier. "Did Lucien say anything else about what's happening? Who would attack Polly?"

"He called it a 'raid,' but he doesn't know anything else. He's still on his way there."

"A raid?" Oliver frowned as he buttoned his pants. "Darkrock." They'd followed him the other night, and he'd led them right to a treasure trove of inhuman creatures.

Chapter 18

Lucy had been thinking the same, and their suspicions turned out to be right on the money. A small fleet of black vans and Humvees was parked in front of Polly's when they arrived. The Grotto was normally protected by its own dimensional displacement, which meant Darkrock must have possessed some kind of magic to counter it. Only people with enhanced blood were able to find the place easily. It currently sat in a little corner of Sedona on the banks of Oak Creek—access to a living body of water was essential for the siren's well-being.

Lucy wondered why Darkrock hadn't already rounded up Polly's clientele and carted them off in the vans to Darkrock's headquarters. After all, it had taken Lucy and Oliver more than thirty minutes to get there. But it became obvious as soon as they entered the club. The doors to the outside disappeared.

Polly, in layers of red velvet and sporting a mane of

flaming ruby hair to match, was surrounded by a group of her loyal gammon—Lucien and Theia among them. Even Rhea, apparently, had given Polly a drop of blood at some point in the past. She was there beside her sister, while the Viking, Leo, stood off to the side looking ready to start ripping souls out of the assembled operatives. Like Lucy, he was only there to help someone he cared about. And Darkrock had brought a small army. Which of course was their specialty. But their weapons would do them no good within the dimensional displacement field of the Grotto.

Oliver's entrance caused a small stir among both groups.

"Hey, there he is. Chief Benally." One of the operatives, a short, stocky ginger built like a fireplug and sporting a flattop with shaved sides, came forward and slapped Oliver on the back.

Oliver nodded tersely. "Artie."

Polly's eyes glittered with menace in the candlelight being thrown by a sort of rippling disco ball at the center of the club. "Son of Gwyn. You know these assholes?"

Who was Son of Gwyn? Lucy glanced around, surprised when Oliver moved away from her toward Polly. The gammon parted for him, as if they shared one mind.

"I know them," said Oliver. "They're my former comrades. I didn't send them. But I believe I must have led them here the other morning." He turned to stand as a sentry in front of her, arms crossed to display his pecs and biceps to excellent effect in the white T-shirt he'd thrown on. "They won't come any closer."

"You keep interesting company these days, Chief," said the one Oliver had called Artie. "Quite a change from our Red Squad days."

Oliver ignored the implied insult. "What have these

people done to warrant the deployment of a full platoon of Darkrock troops?"

"That's not a question you used to ask."

"It's a question I should have asked." He addressed the other operatives. "One you should all be asking yourselves."

"They follow my orders here," Artie reminded him.

"And you follow Darkrock's. Blindly."

Artie rolled his eyes. "Oh, my God. When did you become such a cuck?"

Lucy couldn't contain the sharp outburst of laughter the word always evoked.

Artie turned in her direction and looked her up and down contemptuously. "Oh, right. That's when." He turned back to Oliver. "Vanessa would be ashamed to be seen with you right now, man."

Oliver's arms unfolded slowly, as if he was about to take a fighting stance, his eyes smoldering. "Don't talk about Vanessa."

"What really happened the night you got her and the rest of the team killed? Were you standing there with your thumbs up your ass trying to decide whether a bunch of murdering bloodsuckers deserved a little consideration while they drained her dry?"

The siren put a hand on Oliver's shoulder. "Never mind your concerns. You can settle whatever score you like with them on your own time."

Oliver nodded reluctantly and stepped back into formation. "Looks like we're at an impasse here, boys. Maybe you should move along. Hunt your prey elsewhere."

One of the other operatives made a sweeping gesture with his gun toward the group. "Looks to me like the predators are all in this room. What the hell is that freak?" He gestured toward the were-tiger beside Polly, the same one that had welcomed Lucy the last time she was here. The tiger growled low in his throat.

Polly stroked his fur. "Now, now, Giorgio."

"I'm in command here, Finch," Artie barked. "I'll handle it."

Polly sighed audibly and sat on the bench seat of the booth next to her, the velvet layers of her gown spreading out around her like a sea of flame. "I find this all very boring. And *male*." She said the word as if it represented the height of banality. "What would be a really lovely twist to this little drama would be to watch all of you boys do each other. All that sweating and grunting and groaning and clutching each other as you gave in to your primal desires." She emphasized the active words with approximations of their sounds, and pumped her fists with a lewd insinuation to punctuate the sentence. "Just really *giving* it to each other. A strutting, hyper-masculine man orgy for our entertainment."

"Pols." Lucien shook his head at her. "Let's not get carried away."

Lucy folded her arms and tilted her head with interest. If that was really something Polly could compel them to do, Lucy was here for it.

Artie spat on the floor, his fragile masculinity obviously threatened. "We're immune to your mind games, bitch. Darkrock wouldn't send us in here without adequate protection."

Polly laughed. "Well, feel free to use all the protection you want. Safer sex is always advisable."

"Very fucking funny."

"So is your Freudian little tongue, you adorably angry little bundle of roid rage."

Close enough for Lucy to hear, Finch leaned toward his team leader. "Stop provoking her, man. She's just trying to get a rise out of us."

Polly evidently heard it as well, judging by the ripple of delighted laughter that flowed out of her.

"Maybe you should quit while you're ahead," said Oliver, watching his former comrades with amusement.

"We'll quit when we have what we came for," Artie snapped.

"And what would that be?"

"These freaks." He indicated the obviously inhuman creatures with a wave of his AK-47. "I'd particularly like to see Darkrock cut open the brain of that one." For some reason, these guys were fixated on Giorgio, the tiger. Probably because he wore only fur and they were forced to acknowledge his furry, uncut junk.

Giorgio, however, had apparently had enough. He sprang forward with a snarl, and Artie opened fire—and discovered his weapon didn't work. Oh, the humanity. Giorgio knocked him to the floor.

Polly examined her nails, demonstrating her eternal ennui. "Your little toys don't work in here, boys. Did I forget to mention?"

Artie scrambled to his feet with as much dignity as he could muster, giving Giorgio a wide berth.

"You see, you may be immune to my influence—to a degree—but my Grotto is utterly immune to yours. You can certainly challenge my gammon to hand-to-hand combat if you like, but I wouldn't recommend it." She looked up and nodded at Lucien. "Lucien, sweetheart, would you take off that skin, please?"

Theia and Rhea stood back automatically.

Lucien, whose human appearance in the physical world was only an illusion facilitated by Theia's presence, rolled his shoulders and cracked his neck. With the sound of the joints cracking, his skin literally fell away, and he emerged from the shell he'd occupied as a full-size brilliant blue wyvern—reptilian eyes, horns, wings, tail and all—as far from human as one could get. With a roaring hiss, he took two steps forward on his lizard-like back legs, the shortened forearms ending in vicious claws, and his webbed wings raised above his head in a threatening posture, while his barbed tail switched in warning.

Lucy stole a glance at Oliver to see if he was making the connection between Lucien's appearance and her infernal blood. He seemed unconcerned, perhaps under Polly's thrall in some way that connected all of the gammon to each other with a collective consciousness.

The Darkrock troops wisely took a step back toward the front wall of the club, their AK-47s trained on Lucien despite the demonstration they'd just seen of the futility of the gesture.

Polly smiled at their alarmed expressions. "Who wants to challenge the Prince of Hell? Anyone? Or perhaps you'd feel more comfortable going up against the lovely twins? I believe the last time someone challenged them, he ended up being dragged straight to the bottomless pit, where he's spending eternity sulking. You boys look like sulkers. Maybe we should just skip the formalities."

"What the hell do you want?" Artie shot back, his voice shrill with frustration.

"Ah, now it's what *I* want. A moment ago, you were making demands. You see, the thing about my little Grotto is that I decide who enters and who leaves. And if I choose, I can open a back door straight into hell, where lovely Lucien here will be happy to escort you to your eternal rest."

Theia took an apologetic step forward. "It doesn't really work like that," she murmured.

"Nevertheless…" Polly glared at her. "I call the shots here. The Grotto is neutral territory, and any aggression toward my patrons will be met with the severest reprisals. So now that we understand each other, just let me know when you're ready for me to show you the door. Literally. It's still there, but I've kept you from seeing it." She rolled her eyes. "Immune to my influence, my ass." With a wave of her hand, the doors reappeared.

Without waiting for orders from their team leader, the rest of the Darkrock troops beat a hasty retreat.

Artie tried to save face. "This isn't over, Benally."

"Of course it's over," said Polly. "You won't remember where the Grotto is by morning. I wouldn't be surprised if you drive around all night trying to find your way back to the highway."

The atmosphere in the club shifted from tense to relaxed, with people going back to their drinks and conversations, and the electronic dance music that had been just barely at the level of hearing now pumping and thumping as if nothing had happened. Lucien appeared human once more, and Leo had joined him and the twins, the four of them joking about something like they were old friends. Maybe they were. Lucy had never been one for friendships, and she hadn't really kept track of what was happening with Lucien's social life during his brief stays in the mortal plane.

She supposed she should tell Lucien the latest about the hell beast—and find out if he had any corroborating information. Oliver was occupied with Polly for the moment.

Lucy approached the group. "Hey, baby brother. Nice display earlier."

Lucien grinned. "Yeah, sometimes being a monster comes in handy."

"Speaking of monsters, I had another run-in with the creature I've been tracking. I think you're right about it not being one of your fugitives."

"Well, of course I'm right. I think I know what kind of creatures I have in my domain."

"This time I was with Oliver, and we both saw something different, like it was manipulating our perception. I think it must be a coincidence after all that it showed up at the same time as the breach. Or maybe the breach drew it out of wherever it had been dormant."

"Why do you say that?"

"Because it wants those hellhounds in a bad way. And I think it may have already gotten some of them."

"Damn. I was afraid something might have happened to them."

She was about to tell him about Colt, but the idea of sending the boy—creature—back was too fraught with personal conflict, and she wasn't ready to have that conversation yet.

"So, this Oliver you mentioned." Lucien glanced toward Polly's infamous booth, where Oliver still stood as if he were on guard. "That's him with Polly? The ex-Marine?"

"Yeah, he's my client."

"Looks like he's a little more than a client."

Lucy realized how it must have appeared that they'd shown up together and had obviously been together when he called her and got her out of bed. For once, she didn't have a smart comeback. Which was even more damning.

"Lucien, leave her alone." Theia took Lucy's arm. "I wanted to tell her about a dream I had." She drew Lucy aside.

"A dream?" Lucy was skeptical of dream premonitions, but she couldn't entirely dismiss them after having Theia dream-walk into hers.

"You were in the middle of a burning building, but the flames didn't touch you. And there was a man made of flame holding your heart in his mouth."

"A man made of flame?"

"Interpretation is always tricky. I wasn't sure if it was a herald of something or a warning, you know? Good news or bad—it's hard to tell. And sometimes it's nothing. Anyway, I thought I'd pass it along. Often the meaning of the symbol is clearer to the subject of the dream. So…make of it what you will."

"Uh, thanks."

"I know what I'd make of it." Rhea bounced over to them, draping an arm on her sister's shoulder. "A man made of flame? As in a hot guy?" She gestured with an exaggerated roll of her eyes toward Oliver. "And I bet it's not your literal heart in his mouth. Heart can be a euphemism for lots of things, like heart as in your core, your center. As in your—"

"Okay, MoonPie," Theia interrupted and turned Rhea around, shoving her back toward Leo. "Go find a Valkyrie to play with or something."

"Hey." Rhea put her hands on her hips as Leo hooked his arms around her shoulders and rested his chin on her head. "I told you that in confidence."

"That was your first mistake."

Lucy raised an eyebrow, not sure what that was about, but she was beginning to feel like the odd man out. After a nod to Lucien in a nonverbal goodbye, she made her way to Polly's booth, where the siren was monopolizing Oliver's attention with a stern lecture.

"I'm not at all impressed with your friends, Son of Gwyn."

"I assure you, they're not my friends."

"The short one who kept barking orders and insulting people—he came here by himself earlier today, pretending to be a patron. I see now that he was taking inventory. I'll have to beef up my wards that keep out nosy parkers like him. Thankfully, I can always count on my gammon to deal with any riffraff."

"About that," Lucy interrupted.

Polly glanced up at her with a sly smile. "Lucy, dear. Did you find what you were looking for Sunday afternoon?" She gave Oliver an appreciative look. "Oh... I guess you did. Well done."

Oliver's brow wrinkled. "You were here Sunday afternoon?"

Lucy ignored the question, addressing Polly. "You had no business tricking Oliver into joining your little gam. He'd never been here before. He hadn't been warned about you."

Polly picked up her drink and held it out for someone to fill, and in seconds, a waiter appeared at her side to do it. "You needn't worry about Oliver, dear. He's special. I haven't conscripted him, merely linked with him." She fingered the solitary pearl in a silver filigree cage that hung from a delicate chain at her throat. Lucy had the distinct impression she was looking at the physical manifestation of Oliver's kiss.

"Linked?" Oliver and Lucy repeated the word together.

"Oliver's magic is unique." She smiled at him. "You're a natural protector. I'm rarely in danger of physical harm because my gammon are so loyal. But a little extra protection never hurts." She sipped her drink. "I mean, it might hurt *you*, and for that I apologize, but it *is* your nature. What's one more little undergrounder under your protection?" Polly winked.

"You're telling me that those chest pains I was having, that pressure and shortness of breath that I thought was a heart attack…that was your pain?"

"Oh, no, sweetie. I think I've misled you again. A link to me isn't simply a link to *me*. It's a link to all that I am. You're linked with the entire Grotto."

Lucy took Oliver's arm as his face clouded with anger. "We should probably get back to Colt, don't you think?"

After a deep breath that seemed like he was swallowing his rage, Oliver nodded. "My apologies for leading those idiots here. Let's hope there are no similar incidents in the future."

Lucy steered him out before Polly could toy with him anymore—or with her. She'd narrowly missed Oliver finding out about Finn and her out-of-control hormones.

As they drove back to Jerome, it turned out the miss was narrower than she'd hoped.

"What were you doing at the Grotto Sunday afternoon? Was that where you were when I called you about the Henderson interview?"

"I was just getting some information from Polly."

"I thought you were all about not giving anything to the siren."

"Well, it wasn't information, exactly." Lucy felt her cheeks growing hot. "I was just looking for someone, and

she pointed me in the right direction. No token required."
She hoped he wouldn't ask for whom. She felt his gaze
on her for a few moments longer, but he didn't press her.

Delectably Bookish was dark and quiet, the way they'd
left it. Oliver went into the guest room to check in on Colt
but came back out into the hallway abruptly.

"What's the matter?" Lucy glanced at the door. "Is
he awake?"

"He's gone. And Darkrock took him."

Chapter 19

"How do you know it was Darkrock?" Even knowing Colt wouldn't be there, Lucy looked around Oliver into the room. "Maybe he just woke up and ran off."

"Because they left this." Oliver held out his hand, a small black pebble resting in his palm. "It's their calling card. They staged that entire goddamn thing at Polly's Grotto just to get to him."

"Are you sure? How would they even know about him?"

"They must have been keeping a closer eye on me than I thought. Jesus. I've been such a colossal idiot."

Lucy rubbed the back of her neck. "If you're right about how they found you, this is my fault. I think I must have a mole at Smok Biotech." Thanks to Lucy's suspicious nature, Darkrock now had knowledge of an entire paranormal underground it could seek to exploit—and had taken a young boy to be tortured. She noticed Oliver wasn't exactly rushing to absolve her. "I'm sorry. I know that's inadequate. I had no idea my research department was vulnerable to Darkrock operatives." And she intended to do something about it the minute she had a free moment.

Oliver was watching her speak, but she had a feeling he wasn't listening to her. "Maybe we can use Smok's influence to get Colt back."

"Smok's influence?"

"You said Darkrock had tried to arrange a partnership in the past."

Lucy drew her hand away from the back of her neck, curling her fingers into a fist at her side. Maybe it was the other way around. Maybe Darkrock was using Lucy's vulnerability to Oliver and his to Colt to force a partnership.

"No way am I joining forces with those assholes."

"You don't have to join forces with them, just make it seem like you're willing to. Make them an offer, anything to get them to hold off on whatever plans they have for Colt. Maybe tell them *you* had plans for him. Or, hell, tell them the truth, that you want to send him back to hell. It'll probably be more effective if you can keep me out of it, anyway. Let them think we've had a falling-out because you disapprove of my sympathy for inhuman creatures."

Something was off between them, and it wasn't just that Colt was gone. It was as if something had wedged its way between them since they left Polly's. Or maybe at Polly's. Maybe his connection to Polly had done something to sever theirs. He was bound to the Grotto through a piece of his soul. Or maybe it was Lucy. She'd screwed up with Colt at the storage facility, and now she'd screwed up by leaving him here. And as open and vulnerable as Oliver had been with her, she'd insisted on playing things close to her vest. Were they actually having a falling-out? And, dammit, when had she fallen so far *in*?

Oliver voiced her worry. "And it wouldn't exactly be untrue, would it? You don't approve."

"It's not that simple, Oliver."

"At least they haven't hurt him yet." He still wasn't listening to her. "I'd feel it if they had. Please do what you can. What you think is right. In the meantime, I'm going to see if I can find out where they're holding him."

"What are you going to do, try to bust him out by yourself? They'll probably have him in an armed facility."

Oliver's gaze focused fully on her at last. "You know where it is, don't you? You know where they're holding him."

"What? Why would I know?"

"You've dealt with them before. Smok must have information on their sites in the area."

"That doesn't mean I automatically know where they took Colt. I have no idea where their holding facilities are. I'm not just walking around with all of my company's resources in my brain like I'm hooked up to some kind of neural net."

"But you can find out. In minutes, I'm guessing."

"Oliver—"

"Is there some reason you don't want to give me that information?"

"*Oliver.* I'm on your side here. It just isn't that simple."

"It is simple. You could make one phone call right now and get a map of every site they own in the Southwest."

Lucy swore and took her phone from her pocket. "All *right*. I'll see what I can find out. But you're acting like this is some kind of conspiracy against you—like I can just magically find Colt for you and I'm refusing—and I have no idea why."

After walking away from him for a few minutes to talk to her assistant and give her Oliver's email to send him everything on Darkrock's properties, Lucy put the phone away and turned back to him. "My assistant is on it. She'll send you anything she can find. But this isn't like swinging a magic pendulum over an enchanted map. They have dozens of operations, and I'm sure there are plenty of black sites Smok has no way of knowing about."

"It's a start. Thank you."

Whatever had come between them was still there, like an invisible field of mistrust. Maybe seeing what Lucien was and extrapolating it to Lucy had hit him on the drive home.

And maybe Lucy had lost her damn mind and let her hormones convince her there was something between them in the first place. She'd never bothered with more than the occasional hookup, and there was a reason for that. Sex was a release valve, something that was useful every so often so she could go back to concentrating on what was really important. Relationships were unnecessary complications that distracted her from her work. But Oliver had been right. It was more than just sexual between them. And that had been her big mistake.

Lucy slipped her phone back into her pocket. "I'd better get going. My assistant reminded me of several clients I've been neglecting."

Oliver's expression was inscrutable. "It's three in the morning. I thought you were going to sleep here."

"I told you, I don't sleep."

Lucy was keeping something from him. Over the past twelve hours, he'd forgotten who she was, letting desire—

and the fact that he'd felt it again for the first time since he'd lost Vanessa—cloud his mind.

Oliver fiddled with his ring as he sat in the kitchen drinking coffee in an attempt to get a little clarity. What Artie had said at the Grotto had gotten under his skin. Vanessa would be ashamed of him. Not because he had compassion for people who weren't fully human but because he'd lost sight of his personal integrity. Lucy Smok and Smok International were inseparable, and he'd allowed himself to forget that.

He still couldn't even be sure that Darkrock finding him hadn't been part of her plan. They could all be playing him. Except he didn't really think that of her. What the hell was his problem?

The ring gleamed at him again as he turned it. *Semper Fi*, the motto of the Marines, was engraved on the inside. It had been Vanessa's and his promise to each other: they would always be faithful, always stand by each other, always have each other's backs. And the knowledge that he hadn't had her back on that last mission ate away at him like a slow-acting corrosive agent. They had argued about the mission beforehand. Argued a lot beforehand, in fact.

Vanessa had talked about getting out, and Oliver was dead set against it. Despite his misgivings about Darkrock's overall mission, he'd thought they were providing a useful service. They were getting lowlifes off the streets—both human and otherwise. And fewer predators on the street was a good thing, even if Darkrock wasn't entirely ethical in how they went about it. Vanessa had talked about going into business together, a private enterprise where they offered their services on a consulting basis, setting their own terms. Darkrock was too much like the military, too much unquestioning loyalty, with someone else always calling the shots.

The night they'd gone to the meth-and-blood lab, Vanessa had given him an ultimatum: Darkrock or her. He would have chosen her. He had to believe that deep down, she'd known it. But he was too stubborn to let her "win" the argument. Even though he'd already been privately questioning his loyalty to Darkrock, he wasn't going to let her push him into making a decision. They'd argued on the way there. She'd announced that she was pregnant, and Oliver had accused her of doing it on purpose.

And ten minutes later, a vampire lord had smiled at him with Vanessa's blood on his lips and told him how delicious it was to get two for the price of one. That was when Oliver had burned the place to the ground. Vanessa was lost, and he couldn't let the bastard drink from his child who would never be born. And the possibility that the bloodsuckers might keep Vanessa's body alive to incubate not only her own fresh blood but also their child as a blood slave was horrifying.

Even then, it hadn't been a conscious decision. He'd told Artie he'd used incendiary tear gas to ignite the fire. But it had been Oliver himself. His rage had shot out of him like chaotic energy, sparks of uncontrollable grief and fury catching on everything in sight. Without an accelerant or an incendiary device, Oliver had called the fire through some primal, unconscious power he hadn't known he possessed. And tonight, the siren had told him what it was.

The same thing that gave him the power to absorb the injuries of the underground folks in his "territory"— something he'd unwittingly laid claim to that night three years ago with his promise of protection to the young pickpocket—had given him the ability to manifest his rage through external control over the element of fire. Polly had told him who his father was, showing him with a touch of her hand on his. Images had come to him in a flash, a vision of a dark green place by the sea. He'd always known his father had been Welsh. It was the only information he'd gotten from his grandparents—the reason they'd refused to take him in was his "Anglo" paternity. He just hadn't expected his father to be the ruler of the Welsh Otherworld—or a son of the ruler of the Welsh Otherworld, at any rate.

Son of Gwyn, Polly had called him when they first met. Gwyn ap Nudd was the king of the Ellyllon, the Welsh elven race, and Oliver's father was apparently one of Gwyn's numerous offspring. And his father, Oliver had seen in Polly's vision, had been there at his birth and had kissed Oliver's head "with fire," as Polly put it. It was the reason for the reddish highlights in his otherwise dark brown hair from his mother's side. His mother, consequently, had gone mad. Or maybe they'd just believed she was mad if she'd made any claim to have been impregnated by an elven prince. The vision hadn't told him that, but it seemed like a reasonable assumption.

Oliver set down his cold coffee and pushed back his chair. This was too much to deal with right now. Not unsurprisingly, his head felt like it was on fire with all this knowledge. He'd spent the past five years cultivating a practice of daily meditation to keep from burning anything else down, not knowing how he'd done it in the first place, and if he didn't stop thinking about it, he'd end up setting his own house ablaze.

He could kill two birds with one stone. Sitting on the floor of the room where Colt had last been, he cleared his mind and let go of his anger and his guilt and tried to let his mind fill with unconscious knowledge. Lucy's assistant had sent him the list of Darkrock's properties, and he meditated on those, letting the locations float by in his mind—Bagdad, Skull Valley, Bullhead City, Quartzite—not assigning any significance or judgment to them, as if they were meaningless.

But they weren't meaningless. He opened his eyes. Blackstone Ranch in the desert south of Golden Valley near Bullhead City on the Nevada border was the site of the compound where Darkrock had trained Oliver's unit. The compound, three hours west of Jerome off I-40, had supposedly been decommissioned afterward.

He took the pebble out of his pocket. Darkrock had left him a small black stone. They'd wanted Oliver to know. Colt's abduction served more than one purpose. They wanted Oliver back, and Colt was their leverage.

Lucy had changed clothes in her car once more before leaving Oliver's place. Her go bag had never gotten more use. It was time to get this job done. Something Theia had said had gotten her thinking. Not about the flaming man eating her heart—because what the hell?—but in the dream they'd shared. She'd mentioned that Leo Ström had a wolf aspect. And while Rhea had worked on Lucy's dream tattoos, Leo himself had brought up Fenrir, the giant wolf destined to swallow the sun—or the world; she could never remember which—during Ragnarök. She doubted this thing was Fenrir, but it was definitely something otherworldly.

She just hoped she wasn't the only one who wasn't sleeping tonight. She'd solicited Leo's help before to track the beast. As the chieftain of the Wild Hunt, he had a direct line to a well of knowledge about the murderers, sexual predators and "oath breakers" in the region. Who better to help her catch a malevolent, murderous energy that presented itself as a wolf than the wolf aspect of the chieftain of the Wild Hunt?

Lucy texted Leo's number, hoping she wouldn't be waking him up. A minute later, he replied. He was, in fact, on the Hunt tonight. It was the usual season. Lucy had forgotten. Odin's Hunt normally rode during the period between the late harvest and Yuletide, though Leo, as a mortal chieftain, had the power to call up the Hunt at will.

In moments, she heard the blast of the hunting horn and found herself sitting in the midst of a freak winter storm at the base of Cleopatra Hill. Roiling clouds and thunder and lightning ushered in a hailstorm that pelted the soft top of her little Alfa Romeo Spider, and the thundering of hooves soon distinguished from the atmospheric thunder as Leo and his entourage emerged from the clouds.

She stepped out of her car when Leo slowed, while the rest of the Hunt thundered past them into the hills.

"How do you manage to ride a phantom horse if you're not a phantom?" she asked as he dismounted and tipped his cowboy hat at her. In keeping with the setting, his Hunt had taken its inspiration from the Western "Ghost Riders in the Sky."

"Everyone contains a phantom self. Most people just keep theirs locked up at night in their dreams. My *hugr*, my thought-self, is awake when others sleep, even though it no longer leaves my body as it did when I was immortal."

"So...your thought-self inside your mortal frame is what's keeping you on the phantom horse?"

Leo grinned. "If that makes sense to you, then, yes. I don't even understand it." He patted the horse-that-wasn't-a-horse and rubbed its nose. "Your message said you'd thought of something I had that might help you track the beast."

Lucy nodded. "I'm not sure if this is an indelicate request, so please don't be offended if I'm way off base here, but Theia mentioned that you had a wolf aspect, as well."

Leo removed his hat and ran his fingers through his permanently tousled light ginger hair. "You think my wolf has something to do with this monster you're hunting?"

"No, sorry. I didn't make myself clear. I was hoping I could...borrow your wolf."

"You want to borrow my *fylgja*?"

"If your *fylgja* is your wolf-self, and if you're not using it—and if this isn't totally rude of me to ask—yes."

"It's not rude. I've just never been asked to lend out part of myself." Leo shrugged. "I don't see why not. But how is it going to help you?"

"It's your harbinger, if I understand correctly. A representation of your essential spirit that's intimately connected to you and your fate that presents itself to others."

"That's a rough approximation, sure."

"So since you can sense malevolent energy, your wolf can sense it."

Leo nodded slowly. "I think I see what you're getting at. As the wolf, it will be a more primal tracker, and it can home in on the wolf aspect of this evil, a sort of sympathetic magic."

"Exactly. I'm not sure it will work, but I'm willing to try anything at this point."

"But Lucien tells me you still don't know how to kill the beast."

"No," Lucy admitted. "But now that I'm convinced that it isn't a strictly physical being and more of a projection of malevolent intent, I'm hoping that projecting my own intent when I fire on it will do the trick."

"I suppose it's worth a try." Leo closed his eyes and gave his broad shoulders a little shimmy, and the wolf appeared beside him. It looked more like a scruffy hunting dog with wolf ancestry, but hopefully it would do. "Just don't get it killed," said Leo. "If my *fylgja* dies, I die. And Rhea would haunt you to the depths of Náströnd if you were responsible for my death." He grinned, but it was a warning that sobered Lucy a bit. She was asking a lot of him.

"Thanks, Leo. I promise to take care of it as if it were my own."

As the dog trotted over to her, Lucy opened the door of her car, and it promptly hopped in. "Do I need to do anything special to communicate with it?"

"He'll understand you. Just talk to him like he's me." Leo hopped back into the saddle and galloped into the air before she could thank him again.

Sliding into the car beside the dog, which had obligingly settled into the passenger seat, Lucy studied it for a moment. "I assume you got all that. But in case you didn't, I need your help to find the wolf I've been hunting. I don't think it's really a wolf, but I'm hoping the wolf energy it's putting out is something you can tap into."

The dog panted at her. What the hell was she doing? Was this dog even listening to her? She was starting to feel a little nuts. But she'd suggested this, and Leo had been extremely generous in lending her his *fylgja*. The least she could do was commit to her own idea.

"Okay, let's hit the road, I guess. I'm heading back up to the mine shaft where I've fought this thing before. Hopefully, you'll let me know if I'm off track." It didn't seem to object, so she went ahead with the plan.

At the end of the dirt road, she parked and got out and opened the door for the dog. It hopped out while she grabbed the crossbow and quiver and put on her thermal-imaging goggles. When she turned around, it was trotting toward the path to the open mine shafts. So far, so good.

The dog's hackles rose as they neared the opening she'd used before, and it growled low in its throat. Lucy took out her Nighthawk Browning. She'd loaded it with specially modified bullets this time, containing ketamine instead of Soul Reaper serum, with twice the dosage as the darts Oliver had used. If she could get enough bullets in the thing, maybe she could finally knock it out and shoot some Soul Reaper arrows straight into its heart.

Leo's *fylgja* ran ahead of her into the shaft, and Lucy called out after it. She'd promised Leo she wouldn't get him killed, and now he was already charging ahead to face the monster.

She switched on the goggles and hurried inside. The dog was halfway down the tracks. "Leo—Leo's *fylgja*—whatever—wait!"

Thankfully, it slowed and waited for her to catch up. She stepped up beside it, petting its scruff. Maybe she should have asked Leo for a collar and leash. Yikes, no. *That* would have been rude. If she was going to trust Leo to help her, she had to trust the dog's instincts, as well.

"So you've brought your own little hound."

Lucy whirled at the sound of the rough voice behind her. Oliver stood between her and the exit. Beside her, the *fylgja*'s growl kept her grounded. This wasn't Oliver.

She managed to maintain a cool demeanor. "I thought maybe you two could relate."

"Do you think I'm afraid of the master of the Wild Hunt? I *am* the Wild Hunt."

This thing seemed to have an ego bigger than Lucien's. Maybe if she got it talking about itself, she'd get some more information about it and distract it from the shot she was simultaneously getting ready to take.

"How exactly are you the Wild Hunt and Death and the Pit and a ravenous devouring maw all at the same time?"

The Oliver-beast grinned lasciviously. "You forgot Sex. I'm also Sex."

But that part had been in her dream, not something the actual beast had said.

"Did you think I didn't join you in your sleep, lovely Lucy? I'm everywhere you are."

The dog moved closer to her with another throaty growl.

"What do you mean?"

"You breathed life into me."

A chill crawled over her skin. "When the hell did I breathe life into you?"

"Don't you remember my birth? You and my father were there on the hill before the great cross."

"The hill before the… The Chapel of the Holy Cross?" She was having trouble not breaking down into a full body shake as it began to dawn on her.

"Now she starts to remember. You could feel me there, couldn't you? My father held open hell's mouth and let the seed of his hatred spill over the ground through Lucien's infernal blood. Through you." He'd been stepping slowly closer to her, and Lucy was locked in a paralysis of bone-chilling fear.

Carter Hamilton had been absorbing hell's energy while the gates were open—and Lucy had been possessed by a shade under Carter's control.

"You remember now, don't you? Mommy." The Oliver-beast was right in front of her, and he slipped his arm around her waist and thrust his pelvis against her with a rude gesture.

"I am *not* your mother. And ew." She tried to take a step back, but her legs weren't working.

"You were the vessel. My father let the energy of hell flow into the dirt and up into you, open and willing for him."

"No."

"That's why I take this form. The form of your desire."

"No."

His other arm went around her, pinning her gun arm to her side. "How else could Father have used you to lure your own twin brother to him on that hill? Your own blood, once half of yourself. How else could he have used your hand to take the charm that was keeping your own father alive from around his neck and let him slip into oblivion? You were born to break Madeleine Marchant's curse, and Father was ready to help you do it. Just let me in and we can devour everything together."

"I don't want to devour anything." She could barely get the words out. Her jaw felt frozen. Her brain felt frozen. She couldn't think. What had she come here for? She'd had a plan. "Leo," she murmured. "What do I do?"

The beast laughed, his breath warm against her cheek,

and he ran his tongue over her skin from her temple down to the hollow of her throat. "You think a dog is going to help you? Look down. He ran away like a coward."

Lucy glanced down, turning her head. *Goddammit.* The *fylgja* had abandoned her. If she lived through this, she and Leo Ström were going to have some fucking words.

The Oliver-beast kissed her throat. "Let me in, dear heart. I'll give you more pleasure than you've ever known. More than you ever dreamed. I was made for you. I am the embodiment of your desires."

"Get. Off. Of. Me." With a monumental effort, she managed to squeeze her finger against the trigger of the gun and fire a tranquilizer bullet into Oliver's leg. The beast's leg. Well, damn. Oliver's leg. Because he was going to feel it.

Oliver-beast shuddered with the impact, and his eyes went dark. "That wasn't very nice. I'm offering to give you supernatural orgasms, and you shoot me in the thigh?" He grabbed the gun from her hand and tossed it aside. "Maybe I shouldn't have wasted my time with you. I could be sucking the marrow out of tasty little hell-hound pup bones." He licked his lips. "You have no idea how delicious that is. If you're good, I'll save you some."

"You're not getting anywhere near Colt." Whatever else Darkrock's minions had done, they'd gotten the hell-hound safely out of the hell beast's grasp for the time being.

The Oliver-beast laughed. "I have news for you, Mommy dearest. I know precisely where your little puppy dog is, and he is far from safe. Your fool of a fireman is retrieving him for me right now."

Fireman? Jesus. Fire *man*. Man of flame. She was an

idiot. And so was Oliver, apparently. They'd both played right into this thing's hands. If it actually had hands.

The Oliver-beast stroked her arms, nipping at her neck. "I'm saving him for later, though. Because you taste like warm p—" He made an odd grunting noise against her at the same moment that a shot rang out, and his knees buckled, forcing Lucy to grab hold of him to keep them both from hitting the ground. Behind the Oliver-beast, Leo stood holding Lucy's gun. He'd shot the beast in the ass.

"Fucking…dog," the beast murmured, and shoved Lucy away, turning on Leo. He grabbed for the gun, and Leo fired again, this time into his neck. Oliver-beast's hand went to the blood streaming from the wound. Leo had hit a major artery, and the drug was going rapidly to the beast's brain. He slumped onto his knees with a gurgling roar and shifted into wolf form before vanishing with a strangled little snarl.

Chapter 20

"Leo, thank God. I thought your *fylgja* bailed on me."

"It's Gunnar."

"I'm sorry… Gunnar?"

"I'm Leo's *hamr*, a projection of his physical self. The *fylgja* warned us there was trouble, and Leo sent me, imbued with his luck-self, the *hamingja*. We thought you could use some backup."

"Ah. Thanks, Gunnar. You saved my ass."

The dog trotted up behind him, eyeing Lucy with reproach as if to chastise her for having doubted him.

"And you, too," she acknowledged. Unfortunately, they hadn't killed the thing. But she knew more about it now. More than she'd ever wanted to know. Now she just needed to figure out where Oliver had gone and make sure the beast hadn't managed to rematerialize there to take Colt.

"I hate to ask for another favor, but can either of you

help me find someone who isn't a murderer or an oath breaker?"

Gunnar smiled. "With our extra luck from the *hamingja*? I can help you find anyone."

"Fantastic." She was really going to owe Leo one after this. And Rhea, for that matter—if she didn't kill Lucy first.

Oliver's instincts hadn't been wrong. The Blackstone Ranch compound lit up the night like a sparkling power plant in the flat expanse of the farming valley southeast of Bullhead City. And like a power plant, it was well guarded. And they were expecting him.

Finch and another agent approached him as he walked up to the gate. "Benally." Finch eyed him with apparent newfound uneasiness after what had gone down at the Grotto.

Oliver handed him the pebble. "You have something of mine. I want it back."

"Artie didn't think you'd show up here without that Smok bitch."

"Watch your mouth."

"Sorry. Don't mean anything by it." He was definitely rattled by Oliver's connection to the siren. "I'm supposed to escort you to him. To Artie, I mean, not the kid." Finch nodded to the guard at the gate, and the gate buzzed loudly, sliding open on heavy wheels. "I gotta say, I don't know what's so special about that kid. He hasn't done anything but sleep."

So at least he wasn't awake and terrified or being physically or psychologically tortured. That was something. "There isn't anything special about him. He's just a kid. Darkrock's intel is fucked up."

"Tell it to Artie. This is his mission."

They led him inside the compound to a brightly lit corridor, industrial bulbs buzzing within metal cages in keeping with the power plant theme, to where Artie and his security retinue were waiting outside a locked door.

"Here comes the chief." Artie sneered.

Oliver stepped in front of him. "One of these days, Artie, you're going to call me that, and I'm going to split your skull before you finish saying the word. So if you like to gamble, just keep saying it."

"Relax, man. It's a nickname. It's meant with affection."

"It's racist, and I've asked you a dozen times to knock it the hell off with that. I'm also having a hard time seeing how there should be any affection between us at this point."

"All right. Jesus Fucking Christ. Goddamn snowflake." Artie's hand rested on the butt of his gun in his holster as if he expected Oliver to attack him at any moment. "I take it you get why we brought you here."

"For a trade."

"Hey, he's a bright boy. Give him a medal."

"I want to see Colt first."

Artie nodded to the guard at the door, who unlocked it and pushed the door open. Inside, a bright bulb hung from the ceiling, illuminating Colt's sleeping form on a foldout cot. They'd put him in an oversize uniform—he'd been unclothed under the covers at home, since he'd still been in wolf form. The fact that he was in human form now meant he must be closer to consciousness. And according to Finch, they hadn't seen him as a wolf when they abducted him. With any luck, they didn't know what they had.

"See?" Artie stood between Oliver and the open doorway. "No harm done."

Oliver folded his arms. "You didn't have to bring him into this. He's an innocent kid."

"Is he your kid?"

Oliver's jaw tightened. "No, he's not my kid. He's a street kid. I'm trying to find him a safe place to stay."

"Kinda looks like he could be your kid. Plus, there's the fact that he ain't human. And you…" Artie shook his head. "We're not too sure what you are."

A few hours ago, Oliver would have scoffed at that. Despite his odd ability to take wounds that weren't his and heal them in record time and his inexplicable control over fire, he hadn't doubted his own humanity. Now… what did being half Welsh elven royalty make him?

"Finch said you were willing to trade. I'm here. What are you going to do with him?"

"We don't need him, so as soon as he wakes up, he can go."

"How's he going to go anywhere? We're out in the middle of nowhere."

"That's his problem."

Oliver didn't doubt that Colt could travel back to Jerome—or wherever he wanted to—on his own. But they weren't just in the middle of nowhere; the hell beast was still looking for Colt.

"Let me take him back to Jerome. You can follow me, and I promise to turn myself over to you as soon as he's safe."

"No deal. You're not going anywhere." Artie nodded to the guard, who pulled the door shut and locked it once more. "Take him to the interrogation room, Finch. Blake wants to talk to him."

Oliver stood his ground as Finch took hold of his arm. "I'm warning you. If I don't have proof that Colt has been allowed to leave, there's going to be blood spilled."

Artie rolled his eyes. "All right, Chie—tough guy. We'll get you the footage from the camera on the gate when he leaves. Now move."

Gunnar turned out to be better than metaphysical GPS. It was nice having luck on her side for once. Lucy had shown him the list her assistant had sent of the Darkrock sites, and he'd perused them for a moment, before pointing to the Bullhead City site.

"This looks like a good bet," he said. "It's out near Golden Valley and there's nothing else around for miles, so they have good visibility for keeping it secure. Which of course doesn't exactly work in our favor, since they'll see us coming."

"I don't care if they see us coming. I just want to get there before the hell beast thing wakes up and rematerializes."

"Gus will alert us if it does."

"Gus?" Lucy glanced at Gunnar as they got into her car.

He nodded to the dog lying down patiently on the back seat. "That's what I call him. Easier than saying 'the *fylgja*' or 'the harbinger' all the time."

"Makes sense. Okay, Gus, we're counting on you."

The drive west from Jerome was a roller-coaster ride through dozens of switchbacks. If the road up the mountain from Clarkdale was slow, this was a virtual crawl. Golden Valley was a three-hour drive once they'd gotten to flat ground.

As they neared the lights of the compound, eerily illuminated against the predawn sky, Gus began to growl quietly from the back seat.

Lucy steeled herself. "The hell beast?"

Gunnar glanced back at Gus. "I think it's the hell-hound. We must be on the right track. Gus isn't sure what to make of him. Smells funny."

"How do you know what Gus thinks?"

Gunnar laughed. "Lucy, he's me. We're all Leo."

"This is just weird."

"That's what Rhea always says."

Armed security guards lined the gate in front of the compound, and Oliver's truck was parked just outside. Lucy parked next to it. So she'd been right about what he'd do. And so had the Oliver-beast. And Darkrock. Everybody was batting a thousand tonight.

She approached the guards at the gate. "I want to see Oliver Benally. Now."

The pair closest to her glanced at each other, and one of them addressed her. "Who the hell are you?"

"Lucy Smok."

The other guard called it in on his two-way radio. "Lucy Smok is out here demanding to see Ollie Benally."

The gate buzzed and started rolling open. Apparently, that was her answer. She started inside with Gunnar and Gus at her side, but the guards stopped them.

"Not them. Just you."

Great. So she was leaving her extra luck outside as well as her hell beast alarm. Her own luck and intuition would have to do.

"Thanks, guys. I can take it from here. And thank Leo for me."

Gunnar smiled. "Already done. Good luck."

Lucy grinned. "Nice one."

A guard on the inside of the compound stopped Lucy as she reached the entrance. "No weapons."

"It's only loaded with trank bullets."

"No weapons," he repeated, holding out his hand.

With a sigh, she turned over the Nighthawk Browning. "I want this back." He continued to hold out his hand.

Lucy rolled her eyes and slipped the knife from her boot and the larger tactical knife from inside her belt holster at the small of her back. "That's it. I swear. I left my crossbow in the car."

He didn't crack a smile, but he let her in. "This way."

Lucy followed him down the overly bright corridor to what looked like an interrogation waiting room. "What is this?"

"You're supposed to wait here."

"I want to see Oliver Benally."

He shrugged and took his place to stand guard at the door. After several minutes, a dazed-looking, half-awake Colt was escorted into the room. His eyes widened when he saw Lucy, and he pulled away from his escort and ran to stand behind her.

Lucy drew him close to let him know she would protect him. "Where's Oliver?"

Colt's escort held the door open. "You and the boy are free to go. Agent Benally is remaining voluntarily as an employee of Darkrock."

"I want to talk to him."

"Send him a letter."

Getting Colt away from them—and getting him somewhere safe from the beast—had been Oliver's singular goal. Short of taking on the entire compound single-handedly and unarmed, there was nothing she could do here. Lucy let the escort lead them out to her car, making sure he returned all her weapons.

Still out of it, Colt fell asleep on the way back to Jerome, and despite the fact that it was morning by the time they returned to Oliver's place, after drinking enough water to operate a fire hose, Colt climbed into the guest bed and went back to sleep. Lucy had figured Oliver's place would be more comfortable for Colt than her own, but she was going to need a better solution. They were sitting ducks here. What she needed were some magical wards. There were witches on retainer at Smok Consulting, but it was better to keep something like this off the books, and if the Carlisle sisters were Lucy's family now, as Rhea had said, Lucy had one of the most powerful witches in Sedona in her family.

She didn't really know Ione Carlisle at all, but there was no more talented witch in Arizona than the high priestess of the Sedona branch of the Covent, the world's largest organized coven.

After calling Leo to thank him for his help last night, Lucy dialed Ione's number. Halfway through explaining the nature of her request, she realized what a tricky subject this was going to be for Ione. The beast Lucy needed to ward against was a creation of none other than Carter Hamilton, the last person Ione ever wanted to hear about. His campaign to steal whatever power he could get his hands on had begun with Ione, who had unwittingly dated him while he was stalking her sister Phoebe in order to steal Rafe Diamante's "quetzal" power—Rafe was an avatar of Quetzalcoatl, who could command the dead. At the same time, Carter had been murdering local sex workers to use the shades of his victims as "step-ins" to control other women during sexual transactions his clients paid for.

"There's something I should tell you about the thing I've been hunting," she said to Ione. "But I think it would be better to talk about it in person. I'm kind of babysitting the subject in need of protection here in Jerome. Could I possibly impose on you to drive all the way out here?"

Ione was gracious. "I don't have anything on my calendar this morning. Anyway, it's stronger magic if the work is performed on-site by the witch providing the wards, so it only makes sense for me to come to you."

When Ione arrived, she wasn't alone. Phoebe had come along for the ride. As the lawyer who'd put Carter in prison, she'd also been a victim of his ongoing campaign for revenge when he cultivated the Carlisles' long-lost half sister Laurel as an apprentice to try to steal Phoebe's soul. This was going to be awkward.

Phoebe and Ione were as much a contrast in style as the twins. Where Ione's style was button-up conservative—even more so than Lucy, who was going for professional but chic—and her dark chestnut hair, highlighted in gradually lighter tones of auburn to dark gold from top to bottom, was professionally straightened, Phoebe looked like something out of a vintage pinup calendar— Bettie Page bangs, bouncy curled ponytail, tight sweater, cigarette pants and all.

Phoebe glanced around the café after Lucy let them in—double-checking to make sure the Closed sign was still up and the door was locked. "This is fantastic. What are you doing in Jerome? You don't own this place, do you?"

Ione frowned at her. "I'm sure that's none of our business, Phoebe."

"It is," said Lucy. "But it's fine. There's no reason for secrecy. I'm kind of watching the place for the owner, Oliver Connery. He's my client."

Phoebe turned back from perusing a stack of arcane books. "A client, huh? That's not how Rhea described him. I think the term she used was 'that insanely hot silver fox that Lucy bagged.'"

"Phoebe." Ione was still playing the disapproving mom. A role she'd apparently taken on after the Carlisle sisters' parents were killed when she was only nineteen. Lucy found Ione more relatable, even if—or maybe because—her manner was a little cool. Early responsibility was something Lucy knew well, even if she hadn't had to raise any siblings. Unless you counted Lucien's years of playing the irresponsible screw off. "You'll have to forgive Phoebe," said Ione. "She's just giving you the Carlisle treatment. Take it from me, it never ends, and it's maddening."

"The Carlisle treatment?" Lucy raised an eyebrow.

Phoebe laughed. "Affectionate ribbing about our marvelous taste in men. And it's not really the Carlisle treatment. The twin terrors started it. It just rubbed off on me. Love the hair, by the way."

"Thanks." Lucy fingered the back of it reflexively. "But Oliver really is a client. And I wouldn't call him a silver fox, exactly." The words were accompanied by a burgeoning heat in her cheeks, which ruined the whole protest. "I mean, he's not even forty. He's just…" She was digging herself in deeper. "Oh, crap."

Ione smiled politely. "Welcome to the family, Lucy. It only gets worse from here. Now, what kind of wards were you looking to put up? Is it a general protection spell you're looking for, or is there a specific threat you want to address?"

She hated to ruin Ione's day when she was being so generous. "I think you're both going to want to sit down."

Phoebe and Ione exchanged looks as they sat on one of the plush couches.

"The creature Oliver's group hired me to hunt is something I've never encountered before."

"Right," said Phoebe. "Some hell beast Lucien let out."

Ione was more diplomatic. "Theia mentioned to me that there had been a brief period during Lucien's transformation that allowed some unorthodox creatures to enter our world from the underworld."

"That's true. But it turns out this isn't one of them. At least, Lucien has no record of it in hell."

"Thank goodness." Phoebe breathed a sigh of relief. "I was afraid this was going to be another Carter Hanson Hamilton nightmare where he was using power from hell somehow, still letting things out."

When Lucy cleared her throat, Ione groaned. "Oh, no. Don't say it."

"Sorry. But if the beast itself is to be believed, Carter created it."

Phoebe jumped up and paced in frustration. "Goddammit. Why the hell can't he just die already?"

"Well, technically, he did," said Lucy. "Being dragged to hell will do that to you. But, sadly, there's no way to wipe out someone's soul from the universe itself, or I'd be happy to help do it."

Phoebe clenched her fists. "We should have had Leo take him to Náströnd and throw him into that corpse lake to let the dead feast on his bones along with that damn

Nazi's. You know how Carter met that guy, right? In prison. They met through Carter's Aryan Nations pals. That bag of Nazi dicks. I'm surprised he didn't end up as a special adviser to the White House."

"The thing is," said Lucy, wanting to get to the point, "I apparently...helped."

Phoebe stopped pacing. "Helped what?"

"Create this thing. It claims to have been...sort of... birthed...by me as Carter channeled the energy he was stealing from hell through the earth and into me—something he was able to do because of the step-in that was possessing me." Lucy sighed. "Because I'm weak and empty, apparently."

Phoebe sat carefully on the couch. "Being accessible to step-ins does not mean a person is weak and empty."

Lucy blanched. She'd forgotten that hosting step-ins was what Phoebe did. "I didn't mean to suggest—"

"No, of course you didn't." Phoebe smiled thinly. "Most people don't appreciate the strength it actually takes to host someone else's essence for an extended period of time without going completely insane. You simply weren't prepared for it, and Carter took advantage of that. But he wouldn't have been able to use you if you were weak. It's quite the opposite."

"I see."

"I don't think you do, really. Theia told me you were able to regain control long enough to do your dragon shift thing and save her from falling off a cliff that night. The fact that you were able to do that without any training while a seasoned, powerful necromancer was actively directing a shade to control you is nothing short of amazing."

"I don't think it's amazing that I stood there like a zombie while Carter filled me up with hell energy and hatred to bring this nasty thing into being."

"No, sweetie, that's not amazing, it's horrifying. And I'm so sorry he did that to you."

Lucy ran her fingers through the hair hanging over one eye. "I thought you guys would be furious with me." Maybe Ione was, though. She hadn't said anything yet. Lucy glanced at her nervously.

Ione's hands were clasped in her lap. She was the kind of person who tried to keep everything in. "We are most certainly not furious with you, Lucy. We're furious *for* you. So I take it that's the reason for the wards you need, to keep this thing from coming for you."

"No, I'm still coming for it. I just haven't figured out how to destroy it yet. But I need to keep it from getting to Colt, the little boy who's asleep upstairs."

Phoebe glanced at her curiously. "Oliver has a son?"

"No, Colt…well, to be perfectly honest, Colt is one of those things Lucien let out. He's under Oliver's protection."

Ione frowned. "An escaped creature from hell hardly qualifies as a boy. I'm surprised you'd approve of harboring something like that."

"Not half as surprised as I am." Lucy shrugged. "But he hasn't done anything to harm anyone, and he even risked his life to save me when the beast was attacking me, and it was four times his size. I know we can't keep him here. He has to go back where he belongs. But I'll be damned if I'm going to kill a little boy to right the dimensional balance—or stand by while a malevolent energy I helped into the world kills him for sport. Until Oliver gets back, Colt is staying right here."

"And where is Oliver?" Ione asked.

"In the belly of the beast. So to speak."

Chapter 21

Artie and Finch had been sent to "debrief" him. Oliver refused to engage until he had proof that Colt had been freed unharmed. After several unsuccessful attempts to coerce him physically, Artie gave in and brought in a laptop, pulling up the footage from the surveillance camera showing Colt walking out the front gate—hand in hand with Lucy.

What had Lucy been doing here? He had no way of knowing whether she'd taken his advice and proposed a cooperative effort as a ruse—or was actually in league with them. But for all appearances, Darkrock had fulfilled its end of the bargain with Oliver.

"Satisfied?" Artie closed the laptop and set it on the steel desk behind him.

Oliver licked blood from the corner of his split lip. "For now. Are you going to keep these cuffs on me and keep punching me like a coward?"

Artie ignored the dig. "If I have your word that you'll cooperate, I think we can take the cuffs off, sure." He nodded to Finch, who stepped forward with the key.

"You already had my word. I was just waiting for you to stand by yours."

"Fair enough. Finch." While Finch unlocked the cuffs, Artie waited with arms folded to accentuate his overdeveloped pecs and his legs planted in a wide, imposing stance, clearly not intimidated by Oliver at all. "So let's hear it."

Oliver rolled his shoulders and wiped his mouth with the back of his fist. "Hear what?"

Artie's broad arms unfolded. "Don't fuck with me, man."

"I'm not fucking with you. You asked me about forty questions before honoring the deal. Which one do you want me to answer?"

"All right. If you insist on being belligerent, let's start with the firebombing of the blood lab. There was no explosion, despite the official story given to the press. No incendiary devices or accelerants were found. Was it or was it not accomplished through telekinetic means?"

"I don't know about 'telekinetic,' but I don't have a natural explanation for what happened."

"You admit that you were the cause of whatever unnatural phenomenon occurred there."

Oliver sighed. "As far as I know, yes."

"And how long have you had this ability?"

"I don't know. It had never manifested before that night."

Artie looked doubtful. "There's another question that's been on my mind, personally. Did you start the blaze before or after your team was compromised?"

Oliver steadied his breathing. "I'm not sure I'm hearing you correctly. It sounds like you're accusing me of betraying my own people. Of *murdering* my own people."

"Nobody said the word *murder*." Artie's face was stone hard. "I'm asking when this mysterious blaze started. You said yourself you didn't know how it happened. I'd just like to know if it happened after your teammates were killed…or before."

"My *wife* was on that team."

"Yeah. Oh, I get that, man. So maybe you wanna answer the question carefully. Because a lot of us cared about the guys on that team. A lot of us cared about Vanessa."

He had to swallow this rage before he let Artie provoke him into doing something he'd regret. Which was probably what Artie was hoping for. Not that it made what he was insinuating any less despicable.

"You want all the ugly little details, Artie? Fine. When Vanessa and I broke down the back door, Baker's and Keene's bodies were being held upright while a couple of vampire lords drank from where their heads used to be like they were their own personal fountains. Another one grabbed Vanessa and cut her throat before either of us could even process what we were seeing. So if you want to get technical, yeah, Vanessa was still 'alive' when I started burning things. I doubt her spine was fully severed by the human bone blade the vamp was holding and licking, because her limbs were convulsing when he started drinking the blood straight out of her mouth."

"Jesus Christ."

"Fuck, man." Finch looked green.

Artie actually took a moment to compose himself before he went on. "So you just…went nuclear." He nodded as he processed the idea. "Guess I can't blame you for that. But Darkrock's going to want to get to the bottom of how this ability of yours manifests."

Oliver shrugged. "Guess you've gotta do what you've gotta do."

"As for the other thing…"

Oliver wasn't giving them anything. Whatever they knew, they were going to have to tip their hand first. He sure as hell wasn't going to tip his. "What other thing?"

"Come on. Are we really going to do this again?"

"Why don't you just be clear? I'm not a mind reader."

Finch laughed. "Well, that's one thing he can't do."

Artie glared at him. "Shut up, Finch." A little something, almost imperceptible, flashed in Finch's eyes. He'd been with Darkrock longer than Artie had. Oliver imagined he didn't appreciate having a pompous jarhead promoted over him. "There's a rumor that you've been protecting subhumans in Jerome. That you're some kind of sin eater."

"Sin eater?" Oliver laughed. "How does that work, exactly?"

"We've interviewed a few of these subhuman locals. They say any violence done against them is somehow countered by you. They get punched, but the bruise disappears. Somebody stabs them or shoots them, the wound closes up without leaving a scar."

"That's very imaginative, but I have a feeling they're exaggerating my pledge to protect them. It's just magical thinking. Using the idea that they can't be harmed as a sort of ward against anyone who threatens them."

"Well, we'll see about that."

Oliver frowned. "What do you mean?"

Artie switched on a screen behind him, showing another room like the one they were in. Watched over by a pair of Darkrock troops, a young were-badger was seated in a metal chair like Oliver's. Oliver recognized him—Pete, he thought his name was. He hung around the Mine Café sometimes, looking for scraps.

"Is this one under your protection?" Artie asked.

Oliver kept his mouth shut.

Artie spoke into the intercom on the wall. "Let's try one."

One of the agents punched Pete in the face. Nothing happened. Oliver could have told them it wouldn't. Only drawing blood seemed to trigger the protective magic.

"Why don't you try a sustained effort?" Artie said into the intercom. "Let's make it good this time."

Despite his outrage, Oliver tried not to react as the agent punched the were-badger, beating him relentlessly until Pete was semiconscious. Only when Pete's face was dripping with blood did it start to affect Oliver. He sucked in his breath, partly in anger and partly because of the pain.

Finch peered closely at him. "Damn, Artie. I think it's actually working." He touched the left side of Oliver's face, where pain was starting to throb in his cheek and his jaw as if bones had been broken. "Those are new bruises."

Artie smiled. "Hard to tell with all the others."

Through the video feed, Pete's bruises were fading.

Artie hit the button again. "Let's have another demonstration."

This time, the agent unsheathed his knife and stabbed Pete in the gut. The initial pain was clearly felt by Pete, despite his disoriented state, but the agent lifted Pete's shirt to reveal that although the blood was still there, the wound had already closed.

Artie nodded to Oliver. "Lift up your shirt."

Oliver didn't move, not because he was trying to defy Artie, necessarily, but because the pain from the stab to the gut had taken his breath away.

"Finch, do the honors," said Artie.

Finch pulled up the hem of Oliver's shirt to reveal the stab wound. It would be a few minutes before it began to heal.

Artie, looking pleased with himself, directed the agent with Pete to perform one more test. The agent took out his gun.

Oliver jumped to his feet. "All right, dammit. You've made your point. You don't have to keep putting him through this."

"Putting him through it, Ollie? Or putting you through it?"

"Maybe just skip the middleman, then, and do it to me yourself, if you have the guts."

Glaring, Artie barked an order to shoot.

The agent fired into Pete's knee, and Oliver buckled with a shout, falling back into the chair, swearing profusely. With a nod from Artie, Finch took out his knife and cut the bottom half of the jeans away from the leg that should have been affected. There was no blood—Oliver rarely bled from these wounds—but it was clear the kneecap had been shattered.

"I gotta say…" Artie shook his head. "I'd love to find out what would happen if we blasted away half that thing's skull or hacked off its head, but I think this demonstration has been sufficient to prove the claims." He opened up a case next to the laptop to reveal a med kit with syringes and an array of filled pharmaceutical vials.

Oliver bit back the pain still throbbing in his knee. "What the hell is that for?"

"Per your own admission, you don't know what the basis of your fire-based telekinesis is. Do you want to change your story about that?"

"Since it's not a story, no. I'm telling you the God's honest truth."

"And despite your earlier lies, I'm willing to give you the benefit of the doubt about this. So what we're going to do is see if we can find the biological triggers." Artie uncapped a syringe and picked up one of the vials. "This is a little something we borrowed from Smok Biotech's labs." He unsealed the vial and filled the syringe. "I don't understand the science gobbledygook, but the idea is to provide an incentive for your body to do its thing. This stuff is kind of like a flu vaccine, as I understand it. Introduces a little something to your bloodstream that your body has to fight off. Darkrock's research team is hoping it will fight it off with a little pyrotechnic demonstration."

Artie held up the syringe. "Now. Are you going to be a good little freak or do we have to cuff you again?"

Oliver sighed and held out his arm for the injection. There wasn't much point in fighting it. And maybe this drug wouldn't do a thing. Though he'd technically been honest with them about not knowing how his ability had come about, he knew his uncontrolled rage had been the catalyst, and he wasn't about to let them know that.

So far he'd been able to control his anger. Depending on what this drug did to him, he hoped he'd be able to continue to maintain an even keel.

Artie tossed the used syringe and bottle in the trash. "Since we don't know exactly what you can do, we've made sure there's nothing combustible in this room ex-

cept some boxes of paper." He grinned. "And Finch and
I are going to take our combustible bodies outta here.
Have fun." They took their equipment with them and
left Oliver in the chair. No doubt they'd be watching over
their video feed.

While he steeled himself for the drug's effects, Oliver
closed his eyes and repeated his mantra in his head—
Semper Fi—because it was easy to remember, and it
worked on so many conscious and unconscious levels.

He cleared his mind, focusing on nothing but the
sound of the words in his head. Let any other thoughts
flow in and out without responding to them, without
being affected by them. Thoughts were mere impulses
in the brain, snatches of memory that floated about in his
head like wisps of smoke and dissipated. Meaningless.
He was empty. Unencumbered by physical needs or desires. There was nothing but the silence and the words.

Semper Fi. He wasn't feeling any effects from the
drug yet. Oliver opened his eyes. He ought to be feeling
something by now. Maybe it wasn't formulated for his
kind of trigger if it wasn't biological in nature. Or maybe
the drug was nonsense, a placebo designed to get Oliver
so worked up that he'd display his ability unwittingly.

Semper Fi. Always faithful. Oliver played with the
ring on his finger. Had he been faithful? Never during
their five years of marriage had he strayed in thought or
in deed. But was that the meaning of faithfulness? Checking off sins he'd resisted and winning brownie points?
Did it matter that he'd been faithful then if he wasn't
being faithful now?

And what would Vanessa think of him now? She'd
probably think he was a joke, imagining he had some
duty to protect things that weren't human. Just as Lucy

thought he was a joke deep down. And Lucy... Vanessa would think he was even more of a joke for imagining someone as sophisticated and wealthy—and young—as Lucy would be interested in him.

Semper Fi. He was having trouble concentrating on what he'd come here for. Some kind of Darkrock debriefing. Right. They'd called him in from the field to report on the progress he'd made in... What was his mission? Damn, that drug really must be messing with his head. How could he forget his mission? Maybe that was the test. The experimental drug was something that affected his short-term memory, and they were testing him to see if he could remain faithful to the mission despite the lack of immediate context.

Other than a little bit of brain fog, he was feeling pretty good.

Semper Fi. What was his ring doing on his right hand? Oliver chuckled at himself and switched it back to the proper finger. Vanessa would kick his ass if she thought he was playing around on her.

The door opened, and Oliver glanced up to see Artie Cooper and Tyler Finch.

Artie smiled. "How's it goin', Chief?"

"Hilarious, Artie. Very original." He slapped his palms against his legs and got to his feet, adjusting the weight on his right leg as his knee gave him a twinge. "So, did I pass?"

"With flying colors," said Artie. "Fit as a fiddle. You're cleared for active duty."

Oliver grinned. "Fantastic. What's our target?"

Chapter 22

Ione's wards were extremely effective against the hell beast. Lucy could tell by the escalating reports of sightings nearby. It was circling Jerome, unable to get within a half-mile radius of Delectably Bookish. What Lucy hadn't counted on was that something else might come for Colt. Or rather, someone else.

Just before dawn, she was instantly alerted by a sound on the stairs. In a light sleep in Oliver's room, she'd kept her conventionally loaded gun by her side. Lucy leaped from the bed, bare feet silent on the hardwood floor, and crept to the door, weapon in hand. Scanning the landing, she was relieved to see Oliver at the top of the stairs. Dark-rock had released him after all. But before he turned and saw her standing there, more noise came from below. Three armed men were mounting the stairs behind him. That didn't bode well.

"Oliver?" Lucy lowered her gun but kept it ready at her side. "What's going on?"

He whirled and aimed his Beretta at her, his eyes scanning her—with a brief pause on her bare legs below the flannel nightshirt—as if he didn't recognize her. "Lucy Smok." Evidently, he did. But there was something a little off about him. "They told me you'd be hiding out here, but I guess I had to see for myself."

"Hiding out? What are you talking about?"

One of the other operatives moved toward the closed door to the guest room where Colt was sleeping.

Lucy stepped in front of him and blocked the door. "Unh-uh. You'll have to go through me." With her gun trained on the operative, she glanced at Oliver. "Are you going to do something about this? What are these guys doing here?"

"Following my orders." Oliver hadn't lowered his pistol. "Step aside, or we *will* go through you."

The other two operatives raised a pair of AK-47s in her direction. Darkrock was nothing if not predictably overarmed.

"Give me one good reason."

"Because you're harboring a monster in there, and it's my job to collect it. I would have thought it was your job, too, as the acting head of Smok International."

There was more than a little something off about him. There was something off about this whole thing.

"He's not a monster, and you damn well know it. If you're working with Darkrock, you should be going after the hell beast, not a harmless kid. And why let him go just to come straight here after him? Is this a test for you or something?"

Oliver's finger moved closer to the trigger of his Beretta. "I'm not going to have a discussion with you about my mission, and I'm not going to tell you again. Drop the weapon and step aside."

Instead, she fired her weapon at the operative to her right. Not to hit him—well, maybe just graze him a little, give him something to think about. It would be the warning Colt needed. They were fast, the other operative striking her arm and going for her gun and the one she'd grazed firing off a round that just missed her as she ducked for a counterstrike against the first operative. The bullet whizzed over her head and hit the wall. After elbow punching the one in front of her in the sternum and knocking the other gunman off his feet with a roundhouse to his shins, Lucy looked up into the barrel of Oliver's gun.

He pressed the Beretta against her forehead while one of the others disarmed her. "Step. Aside."

With her enhanced hearing, she caught the snick of the latch on the window in the guest room. Colt had taken heed.

Lucy shrugged and moved out of Oliver's way. "You could have said please."

Oliver kicked the door in—his own door, which wasn't locked—and his eyes swept the room. Lucy leaned against the busted door frame with her arms folded, giving Oliver a smug smile when his gaze finally came back to her.

"Where is he?"

"Beats me."

Oliver checked the window. Finding it ajar, he opened it to look down into the alley but evidently saw nothing. A faint acrid scent drifted into the room through the window, like a brush fire burning in the distance, and something yipped, and another something answered, like coyotes calling to each other.

He turned back to Lucy, studying her with a closed

expression. If he was playing a role for Darkrock to save his own skin, he was hiding it well. He also looked painfully attractive in his Darkrock gear—black combat fatigues and heavy boots, black long-sleeved cotton T that hugged him perfectly. It made him look younger, tougher. He also had a few bruises on his face that appeared to be his own, as though someone had worked him over. And it wasn't the only thing that was different about him. The gray in his hair was significantly less—and his ring was on his left hand.

Oliver holstered his handgun. "This isn't over, Smok. We've got eyes on you."

Lucy followed him to the top of the landing. "What the hell is that supposed to mean?"

"Figure it out." He gestured to his men and headed back down the stairs.

Lucy watched them clomp through the artfully arranged stacks of books, Oliver treating the decor with the same disinterested contempt as his men, and stared after them as the door to the street swung shut behind them with a sharp rattle of the little bell.

The air outside was icy. Lucy shivered and rubbed her arms after locking the door. What had happened at that compound?

"Figure it out." Was that a message of some kind that he was trying to give her without alerting the Darkrock team, or was he just being a dick? Whatever he'd meant, she damn well *was* going to figure it out. All of it—what he was up to, what Darkrock was up to. But she was also going to have to figure out where Colt had gone.

Dammit. After all the trouble Ione had gone to in setting the wards to keep the hell beast out, Colt was out there on his own, defenseless, with both Darkrock and the hell beast hunting him, and Lucy felt responsible for both. As she went back to the bedroom to get dressed, that little echoing yip from the hills haunted her. She had no doubt the first had been Colt's cry. But who had answered?

Before she could head out the door to go in search of Colt, someone rang the bell. As Oliver had made a point of that first day, the shop didn't open until noon. It was probably a delivery. Lucy pulled aside the shade to look and was surprised to see Phoebe Carlisle-Diamante standing outside.

"Phoebe?" She unlocked the door and opened it. "What's wrong? Has something happened?" The Carlisle sisters weren't known for being early risers.

"You might say that. Can I come in?"

Lucy shrugged and held the door open. "Would you like some coffee?"

Phoebe glanced around at the place as if she hadn't seen it before. Or as if she had, actually, and was a little choked up, like someone coming home after a long absence. "No, thanks." She met Lucy's eyes, and Lucy had the distinct impression that her eye color had changed. Didn't Phoebe have the sort of blue eyes that were described as violet? Right now they looked more hazel, almost brown. "I want to tell you, first of all, that this is all on the up-and-up. I have the evocator's consent."

"The evocator?" Lucy's eyes narrowed. It was the term for what Phoebe did, letting shades speak through her. "You're not Phoebe."

Phoebe shook her head and pulled awkwardly at the habitual ponytail, as though its height on the back of her head bothered her. "My name is Vanessa Benally. I'm Oliver's wife."

Chapter 23

Lucy sank onto the nearest chair. "I see. How can I help you, Vanessa?"

"I know you have a physical relationship with Oliver. You don't need to feel awkward about it. It's only natural that he'd find somebody eventually."

"I wouldn't call it a relationship—"

"But you care about him."

Lucy bristled. She didn't do emotional attachments. She hardly knew Oliver. "I'm not sure what difference it makes whether I do or I don't. Whatever you have to say to me, just say it."

Phoebe smiled—a little thin, slightly sad smile that was nothing like Phoebe's. "I am saying it. I've been here for years trying to get Oliver's attention. He talks to Jerome's regular haunts all the time, even though he can't see them. But as much as he's attuned to their vibrations and to the folks he likes to call undergrounders, he's never noticed me. Or maybe he doesn't want to notice me. The point is, when I saw Phoebe here yesterday, I followed her home because I knew she could sense me. I had to find a way to speak to you." She tugged down the edges of her faux jaguar winter coat as if adjusting a military uniform. "Darkrock is up to their old tricks. They used to treat us all like guinea pigs, telling us they were giving us vitamin shots or inoculations against vampirism. They've used something on Oliver, some kind of mind control drug to make him compliant."

It certainly explained his odd behavior this morning. "So he thinks he's still working for them."

"Yes. And I know it goes against everything he is now. He doesn't want this." She chewed her lip. "There's more, but I need to tell Oliver directly."

"This drug." Lucy rubbed the buzzed hair at the back of her neck. "You don't happen to know what it was called, do you?"

Phoebe's eyes clouded for a moment, literally changing from the muddy hazel to violet right in front of Lucy. "She sees something, a symbol on the bottles, but she can't articulate it."

"Phoebe?"

"Yeah, sorry. Didn't mean to interrupt."

"The symbol...was it a wyvern? A small dragon in silhouette?"

Phoebe thought for a moment, her demeanor changing once more, along with her eye color. "A dragon. Yes. The labels had a dragon on them."

It was Smok's trademark. A sneaking suspicion had begun to nag at Lucy as Vanessa spoke about the mind control drug. Smok Biotech had one in development, one that enabled the person administering it to literally inject a suggestion into the subject's mind. A suggestion like "you're on a mission for Darkrock." The subject wouldn't question it, because it would come with its own little story line to assuage any cognitive dissonance. And it could even include enhancements to make the story work—like getting rid of his prominent gray so he would believe he was younger.

Another detail she'd noticed about Oliver this morning took on greater significance. "He was wearing his ring on his left hand."

Phoebe's expression was puzzled. "His ring?"

"Vanessa's ring. Your ring. His wedding ring. He wears it on his right hand. But he was here with some Darkrock operatives this morning, and the ring was on his left hand." Lucy's gaze fixed on Phoebe's color-changed eyes. "I think Darkrock has convinced him that you're still alive. And still married."

Phoebe's expression shifted into a dark frown. "Then he thinks he's the person he was then. They can make him do anything." She rose and headed for the door. "I have to go. I have to keep an eye on him."

Lucy stood, ready to run after her, but Phoebe stopped at the door and hunched over, gripping the door handle, as if someone had punched her or she was going to be sick.

"Balls. I hate it when they do that. They get all excited and drag my body along for the ride as they're leaping out." She turned to look at Lucy, her face a little green. "Sorry. She's gone." Phoebe glanced hopefully toward the back of the shop. "Did you say you had coffee?"

"I did." Lucy put the coffee on and sat back on one of the stools at the counter as Phoebe hopped onto the other. "Do you remember everything we talked about?"

"Yep. Every word. When I let someone step in, I insist on having full conscious control, even if I let them take over my voluntary movements."

"That must be strange."

Phoebe shrugged. "I've gotten used to it. They've been coming to see me since I was little, so it's pretty much second nature. When they're polite and cooperative, it's mostly a breeze."

"Daisy sure wasn't a breeze." The shade that had possessed Lucy at Carter's command had made her feel dizzy and sick, and her departure had given Lucy a migraine.

"Yeah, it's not pleasant being entered without your consent. Ever. So, how are the wards holding up? Any visits from that thing?"

"No, no sign of it. But unfortunately, I had a visit from Oliver and his new Darkrock teammates. I'm not sure he even knew me. He called me by my name, but he was behaving as if I were someone he'd read about and never actually met."

"Maybe he did. Read about you, I mean. As part of his indoctrination with that mind control drug."

Lucy nodded. "Yeah. And the great thing about that? I think it's my company's drug. That dragon symbol Vanessa saw is Smok's. It's the wyvern."

"How would they have gotten it?"

"It's not on the market. It's one of our private label experimental pharmaceuticals. So the only way they could have gotten any was if someone at Smok Biotech was working for them on the inside." Lucy got up to pour the coffee. "So it looks like I've got a mole."

"That sucks."

Lucy set a cup in front of Phoebe and sipped her own. "Yeah, it does."

"So, where's the kid? The...what is he?"

"Colt is a hellhound."

"An actual, honest-to-God *hellhound*?"

"Looks that way. And thanks to Oliver and Dark-rock—Colt is gone."

"You mean they took him?"

"No, but they intended to. He ran away." Lucy sipped her coffee and shook her head. "So now I've got to some-how find the kid and try to keep him safe while simul-taneously hunting the hell beast and figuring out how to get to the bottom of who's working against me in my own company. Not to mention trying to figure out what to do about Oliver."

"Can I make a suggestion?" Phoebe offered her a gen-tle smile. "Maybe don't try to do everything yourself."

"Sure. I'll just fucking outsource some of that." Lucy's patience was starting to wear thin. She didn't "people" well. She'd gotten into a bad habit of thinking out loud to try to problem solve, and she hadn't been looking for advice from Phoebe.

"Why not?" Phoebe was eternally upbeat. "You know, I have my P.I. license now. Maybe I could do some sleuth-ing at Smok Biotech for you."

Lucy laughed. "I think you underestimate your local infamy, Phoebe. Everyone there knows exactly who you are."

"Well, I wasn't talking about going undercover, but now that you mention it, I do have one sister who's very good at flying under the radar, and she's right there in Flagstaff near the lab."

"Is Theia still topside? I don't see how she'd get any-thing out of anyone, even with her access. They know her, too."

"Not Theia. Laurel."

"Laurel…"

"She's one of our half sisters."

"No, I know. I'd just forgotten about her." Lucy considered it. "You know, that's not actually the worst idea I've ever heard."

Phoebe laughed. "Thanks."

"She has past ties to Carter, and if anyone at the lab is sympathetic to him—which I have a strong suspicion is how someone from Darkrock managed to get embedded there—that might be her in."

"Do you want me to have her call you?"

Lucy shook her head, the wheels already turning as she plotted the best course of action. "No. Have her call HR at Smok Biotech. I'll set up an interview with someone I trust and have them hire her as part-time holiday clerical help somewhere in the company where she could do some unobtrusive snooping. Do you think she'd be willing to do it?"

"I have a feeling she'll be eager to do anything that vitiates Carter's influence. She still feels terrible about her part in everything he did to us. And rightly so." If Lucy recalled correctly, Laurel had even once tried to kill Phoebe. Lucy wouldn't have been so forgiving. "But she's a good kid. And I know she can probably use the extra holiday cash, too. I think it'll be perfect. Meanwhile, I'll see if I can get Vanessa to talk to me again. She might be able to tell us more about what's going on with Oliver."

"Thanks, that would be… I'd appreciate that." Lucy smiled awkwardly. She wasn't used to having people offer their help without wanting something in return, and she wasn't really sure how normal people responded to such a thing. "You don't really have to do any of this."

"Nonsense." Phoebe reached across the counter and squeezed her arm, making Lucy twitch in her effort not to physically recoil. She was *so* not a touchy-feely person. "That's what sisters are for." Phoebe grinned. "Or sisters-in-law-once-removed, anyway."

With the mole situation being handled, Lucy could focus on what she did best: hunting things. She needed every bit of information she could get on the hell beast's habits, so she spent the day methodically conducting the eyewitness interviews she hadn't gotten to yet, including a drive around the little community—or a walk, which was easier for much of it—to visit each of the locations of the sightings. Like the previous eyewitnesses, these either backtracked, claiming they must have seen a coyote or a mountain lion, or were unwilling to speak to her at all. She'd written off the significance of the Hogback Cemetery, but it was time to leave no stone unturned. And the cemetery happened to be full of stones.

The cemetery trail, with its rusted wrought iron enclosures around the crumbling headstones among the brush, provided little opportunity for anything to hide in, but Lucy thought she caught a glimpse of a kid who looked a great deal like Colt panhandling in the parking lot. When she tried to get close to him, he bolted, and there was no recognition in his eyes. Lucy had the feeling she'd just seen another of the missing hellhounds. And maybe Colt had found his friends, but there was no way to know for sure. The only way to guarantee his safety was to get rid of the hell beast once and for all.

The sun was low in the sky as she drove back up

Cleopatra Hill, and as dusk fell, a sort of prickling sensation at the back of her neck made her look in the rearview mirror repeatedly. There was no one behind her, but she couldn't shake the feeling that the hell beast was near. She was beginning to suspect the hell beast was always near, as if it used Lucy herself as a focal point. Which meant Lucy could end up leading the thing straight to the hellhound if she found it.

Even so, she drove to the storage unit just to check to see if Colt had returned to someplace familiar, but there was no sign of him. Darkness was falling by the time she got back to the top of the hill. If the hell beast was focused on her, then she needed to draw it out on her terms. No more ambling about in caves letting it box her in where it limited her ability to use her own assets. She needed to be out in the open to take advantage of her strengths.

Lucy drove to the first site Oliver had shown her and walked down to the tailings pond. A half-moon lent a cool glow to the night, and the field of stars overhead was phenomenal.

She drew her gun and turned slowly to take in a panorama of the hillside. She'd left the crossbow in the car. If neither the arrowheads nor the bullets were going to kill it, she might as well stick with what she was best at to slow it down.

"All right, you goddamn piece of shit," she yelled at the sky. "Show yourself. Or are you afraid to fight me?"

"You're the one who's afraid."

Lucy whirled at the sound of Oliver's voice behind her. He was wearing his Darkrock commando gear, armed as he'd been earlier when they stormed the place. Was it Oliver, or was it the beast?

"What am I afraid of?"

"Of power." He moved toward her, slowly, steadily closer. "Of what we could do together." He was standing in front of her.

"And what would that be?"

Oliver reached out and touched her cheek. "Devouring the world." The last word was delivered on a sexy little growl, and he lowered his mouth to hers. Lucy, her gun still ready at her side, let their lips touch, let his tongue slide between her teeth. And fired a round directly into his gut.

The Oliver-beast roared and reared back, blood swiftly soaking the dark shirt. She'd hurt him this time. Lucy aimed again, and the beast transformed with the swiftness of thought and charged her, knocking her to the ground. She managed to hang on to the gun, but her arm was pinned, and there was no way to hit him with another round even if she fired.

His wolfish eyes glared down into hers, inches from her face, foul breath nearly choking her. "The only thing stopping me from devouring you myself is the tasty treat you keep from me. But I'm growing tired of this game. I can find it on my own."

"Why do you want it so bad?"

This seemed to give it pause. "Because the things of earth are protected here. But *they* are not of earth. They are of hell, and I long to taste its sweet infernal essence."

The things of earth—inhuman creatures that weren't hell fugitives—were protected here because of Oliver. But the claw marks from the swipe Colt had taken from the beast hadn't shown up on Oliver. Was it because Colt wasn't of this earth? But the "hell beast," as she'd grown so used to calling it, was. And Oliver, inadvertently, was protecting it from every bullet Lucy fired into it, every arrow she struck it with.

"If the things of earth are protected... I'm protected. Isn't that how it should work?"

The creature's laugh sent chills up her spine, like the screeching cackle of a reanimated corpse, and it morphed back into Oliver's form. "You, Mommy? You're not of this earth. You're a demon whore."

His transformation back into human form had given her just the moment's advantage she needed. Lucy fired several times in succession into his side and scrambled out from under him when he recoiled from the impact. As he returned to wolf form and leaped at her once more, she released her wings and grabbed it by the throat, digging her talons into the thick, furred flesh as she launched herself into the air, hanging on with all her might.

She spun with it, jamming the talons on her thumbs into the fleshy underside of the creature's chin, preventing it from using its powerful jaws on her, but it had recovered its brute strength, and it sank its claws into her shoulders and scored her arms, digging furrows into them.

Lucy screamed, her own voice unnaturally enhanced into a bloodcurdling wyvern shriek, but there was no way she was letting this fucker go. Not now. Let it shred her arms to the bone if it wanted to. It wasn't getting away.

And then something slammed into the back of her leg, like a bolt of fire. A second later, something struck the hell beast. The red fletching of a tranquilizer dart was sticking out of the beast's thigh. Which meant Lucy was sporting one, too. And it meant Oliver and his commandos were below them, waiting for the drug to take effect so she and the beast would fall to the ground and they could take them both in.

Things were already getting a little fuzzy. Lucy hissed in anger and let go of the hell beast, flapping her wings to knock it away from her, and took off toward the wooded hills.

Chapter 24

Finch scanned the horizon with his binoculars. "Damn, I think we lost it." He headed back down from the top of the ridge to where Oliver and Artie stood over the body.

"We'll get it later." Artie kicked at the massive werewolf lying unconscious at their feet. "We got this thing. Whatever the hell it is."

Oliver took another look through the binoculars while Finch and Artie loaded the dead weight of the beast into the cage in the back of the van. There was something oddly familiar about that bat-winged thing the beast had been fighting with. He'd thought…but it couldn't be. The thing had definitely been female, though.

As Finch came around to the front of the van, he glanced at Oliver. "You sure you're okay?"

Oliver had felt like he was being strangled, something stabbing into the underside of his jaw as the creatures had struggled in the air, and his gut and side were still aching. Must be the transference magic they'd warned him about. The creature could project its injuries outside itself to make someone else take the brunt of them. Though why it only affected him, he wasn't sure. At least the tranquilizer hadn't had much effect on him.

Oliver untucked his shirt and lifted it up to examine the mottled bruises and rapidly scarring flesh. Darkrock had given them all inoculations to prevent any such magic from doing them permanent harm, and it encouraged rapid healing. Thank God. Otherwise, he'd be a shredded mess. He'd taken four "transference" bullets, evidently, in addition to the injuries to his throat.

"Yeah." He tucked his shirt back in. "Yeah, I'm good."

Something wet was touching the side of her face. Lucy jolted awake, going for her gun, only to find a white wolf curled by her side.

"Colt?" She sat up, her head thick and groggy, and glanced around in the early morning light. How the hell had she ended up asleep outside in the snow? She raised her palm into the air. The snow was still falling. The hellhound whimpered softly beside her, its tail wagging and thumping the ground. She remembered now—flying off as the tranquilizer kicked in, going as far as she could until unconsciousness took her and she plummeted to the ground among the firs and brush of Mingus Mountain north of Jerome.

Lucy scratched the wolf's ears, and it panted happily. "Thanks, kid. I think you may have kept me from freezing to death." Her wyvern blood made her core temperature higher than normal, but it wouldn't have prevented hypothermia. Colt had saved her life.

The snow was coming down harder now. The white patches around them would soon be a respectable winter covering.

"We'd better get somewhere warmer than this, though, huh?" Lucy got to her feet, ignoring her throbbing head, and headed for the nearby forest road. Colt jumped up and trotted along beside her as if he'd always been at her side. She supposed it wasn't that odd, really, now that she thought about it. Why shouldn't the sister of the Prince of Hell have a hellhound?

They were both solidly wet by the time they hiked the three miles down the mountainside to where her car was parked. She'd never appreciated the heated seats more. Colt seemed content to stay in wolf form, curling up on the seat beside her as she drove back to Delectably Bookish. She'd noticed a fireplace upstairs in Oliver's sitting room. It seemed like a good day for a fire. Colt lay on the rug while she piled up the logs from the firewood holder by the hearth and threw on some kindling. Before she could light it, however, the distant tinkle of the bell on the door downstairs alerted both her and Colt to the entrance of an intruder.

Colt bolted upright, growling, as she straightened, his hackles raised. Had she remembered to lock the door? Maybe it was a customer. She really ought to put up a sign saying the place was closed for the holidays until she figured out what to do about Oliver.

Lucy unsnapped her holster and moved to the doorway in front of Colt. Whoever it was had started up the stairs. Before she could stop him, Colt had darted past her to the landing, but instead of attacking, she found him greeting Oliver on the top step.

Oliver patted the wolf, looking friendly, but there was no reason to believe he'd suddenly remembered himself.

With her gun drawn, she waited for Oliver to acknowledge her.

"I thought you might come back here." There was no smile in his eyes. "Though I didn't expect to find you both. Makes things easier." He slipped a collar around Colt's neck and held on to it with his left hand, keeping the wolf at his side.

"You're not taking him anywhere."

"I have my orders."

As Lucy opened her mouth to tell him where to stick his orders, her phone rang. She took it out of her pocket, intending to silence it, but the caller ID displayed Phoebe's number. With her gun still pointed at Oliver, she answered the phone. "Find out anything?"

"I did, but there's something more pressing."

"What's that?"

"Vanessa wants to talk to Oliver."

"Okay." Not even questioning how Vanessa could know Oliver was here, Lucy started to hold the phone out to him, but an odd sensation rushed through her as if a little static jolt had zapped her from the phone.

And then she "heard" Vanessa inside her head. *Let me speak to him.*

It wasn't exactly what she'd meant by "okay," but it seemed she'd agreed to let Vanessa step in to her.

Lucy shrugged. *Have at it.*

It was an odd sensation feeling herself move toward Oliver without actively willing it. It reminded her of the possession by Daisy, but this was more conscious. She felt she could stop Vanessa at any moment if she chose to.

"Hey, Ollie," she heard herself say. Oliver's eyes narrowed, but he didn't respond. Vanessa continued. "This will be hard for you to understand, baby. I know they told you we were still on the mission, that we'd meet up after I got back from doing recon. But I'm not coming back."

Oliver bristled. "What the hell are you talking about?"

"It's me, baby. It's Vee. I'm so sorry."

Oliver's right hand had gone to his sidearm. "Stop it."

"Do you remember our last mission? The blood lab?"

"I've never been on a mission with you. You're not Vanessa. You're some kind of demon. I saw your wings and your claws. So you goddamn leave my wife out of this."

"Okay, baby. Calm down. Let me put it this way. Just hear me out. Do you remember your last mission with Vanessa?"

"I don't know what you're trying to prove here."

"Just tell me what you remember. Did you go to that house with Vanessa?"

Oliver frowned, his fingers curled around the butt of his sidearm. "The blood lab? You mean the meth head vamps? Yeah, we…we took the back while Baker and Keene took the front. So what?"

"What happened when you went in?"

"Same thing that always happens. We busted down the door, Vanessa went first, and…" The blood drained from Oliver's face. "No. This is some bullshit demon-craft head game."

"It's not, baby. It happened. It's real."

A wave of horror washed over Lucy at the images in Vanessa's mind. She wanted to grab her throat to stop the blood, even though she knew her own throat hadn't been slit, but Vanessa was dominant, and her arms stayed at her sides. The image of a younger, darker-haired Oliver was superimposed in front of her, his eyes reflecting the pain and horror Lucy was experiencing through Vanessa's memories.

"It wasn't your fault," said Vanessa. "You did what you had to do. I ain't mad, baby. You spared me from what that thing was going to do to me. And our child. You're a goddamn hero, and I love you so fucking much."

Tears poured down Oliver's face as his hand moved away from his sidearm. "No. No. Fuck, no. Please. This can't be true."

Lucy found herself crossing the landing to him swiftly, her arms wrapping around his neck at Vanessa's willing, the gun dangling in her hand. She could feel Vanessa's love and heartache at the loss of Oliver—the loss of the baby she would never know—and it was impossible to bear.

Her own feelings for Oliver were tangled up in Vanessa's, with all the pain and love and all that history between them, and when he kissed her, there were three of them in the kiss. She wanted to stop him hurting, and she couldn't tell whether the thought was Vanessa's or her own. Oliver's love and passion for Vanessa was also apparent in the kiss, and a kind of desolation settled over Lucy as she moved back into her own mind, leaving Vanessa to him.

She had never been loved like that. Would never be loved like that.

"Well, isn't this sweet?"

Lucy and Vanessa released Oliver as one, stepping back to see Artie on the stairs, with Finch and Ramirez behind him. The names came to Lucy instantly with Vanessa's recognition. Along with something else. The knowledge of their part in how Vanessa's last mission had gone wrong.

Artie nodded to Finch as they came up onto the landing. "Get the hound."

Before Lucy could thrust her own will to the fore to take action, Finch had hooked a leash onto Colt's collar and was steering the panicked, yelping wolf down the stairs. Something about the collar seemed to keep him from shifting. Darkrock had planned for everything.

Artie aimed his sidearm at Lucy. "Drop your weapon." As Lucy glared at him and refused the order, he called over his shoulder, "Shoot that fucking thing if she doesn't comply."

Finch had a gun pointed at Colt. With a sigh of resignation, Lucy tossed the gun onto the carpet runner.

Artie looked her over, shaking his head. "Just what the hell are you, sweetie? I'm sure the world will be very interested in knowing that the CFO of Smok International is some kind of demon freak." He jerked the gun toward the stairs. "Come on. Let's go."

Lucy glanced at Oliver, but he looked lost. Darkrock still had a hold on him.

Firecracker, Vanessa whispered in her head. *When you find the right moment, when you think he's broken their hold, use it. Firecracker.* And just like that, Lucy could no longer sense her. Vanessa had gone. She had no idea what the hell "firecracker" meant. Lucy sighed and went down the stairs.

"What are they going to do with him?" Lucy sat beside Oliver in the front seat of the Humvee that followed the van they'd loaded Colt into.

"That's on a need-to-know basis."

"Are you going to let them experiment on him?"

Oliver glanced at her and looked quickly away, eyes focused on the road. "I don't know exactly what you did to me back there, but don't think for a minute that I'm buying any of it."

Lucy sighed and leaned back against the seat. "Believe what you want to, Oliver. I didn't do anything back there, and I think you know that as well as I do."

"You talk to me like you think you know me. You don't know a damn thing about me."

Lucy shrugged. "I suppose that's true. I know what you look like when you come, but that's about it."

The Humvee lurched forward as Oliver's foot slammed the gas pedal to the floor inadvertently.

He eased up, deliberately not looking at her. "And how exactly would you know that?"

"You don't remember the last few years, let alone the last few days." Lucy shook her head. "I don't know what to tell you."

"You expect me to believe I have some kind of relationship with you."

A sharp little "Ha!" burst out of her. "No, Oliver. We don't have any kind of relationship. You can be assured of that."

"But you're saying we've had sex."

"A few times."

He was silent for the next several minutes, the Humvee following the twists and turns of the road through the mountain to Prescott Valley in the west in a rhythmic, almost-wavelike motion—forward, slow turn, back toward the mountain, slow turn, forward toward the next curve of red rock. It was calming. Almost hypnotic.

"Okay, let's say what you're claiming is true."

Lucy jumped slightly. Her eyes had been half-closed. "Sure."

"Did I know about your…aberration?"

"My aberration?" Lucy turned an icy gaze on him. "You mean the fact that I share infernal blood with my twin brother, the current ruler of hell? Yeah, you knew about that."

He made a scoffing sound. "Why would I willingly have a sexual relationship with something inhuman?"

"I'm not inhuman. Darkrock has you convinced that there's some kind of purity test that can be applied to people, and anyone who's a little different is impure, not worth the dignity of being treated like a human being." It struck her that Oliver might have said the same to her when they first met. And she'd willingly perpetuated the belief she was now accusing Darkrock of harboring. That shifters and sirens—and demi-demons—weren't people.

"Look, I'm just doing a job."

God, she'd said that, too. Lucy studied his profile, little worry lines creasing his forehead. Vanessa had almost snapped him out of it. He wanted to know the truth, but Smok's pharmacogenetics were the best in the world. It wasn't going to be easy to undo a biologically induced false reality.

"You know that bookstore café Darkrock keeps having you raid? That's yours."

Oliver darted an incredulous glance at her. "Delectably Bookish? You're out of your mind."

A subconscious impression she'd retained from Vanessa's step-in came to her. The bookstore café B and B had been Vanessa's dream. She'd hoped they could retire and raise a family in a place like that.

"You bought it for Vanessa. To honor her memory."

He glanced at her again, this time not so incredulous. "How do you know that?"

"Vanessa's shade told me. She was touched when she saw it. That's where you've been living for the past three years. You changed your name to Oliver Connery—"

A hearty laugh interrupted her. "Now, that I can almost believe. That's kind of a private joke of mine. I used to do a Sean Connery impression for Vee—Vanessa."

"In your spare time, you're a volunteer firefighter." Despite the circumstances, she gave him a little sidelong smile. "The uniform looks very nice on you, by the way. I may have a little bit of a fireman fetish."

"Oh, really?" An answering smile flickered at the corner of his mouth.

"And you sit on an unofficial town council that monitors the paranormal activity in the town of Jerome."

Oliver's eyebrow lifted, but he didn't offer a comment.

"That's how we met. Your council called me in to deal with that thing you guys took down last night."

That interested him. "The werewolf?"

"I call it the hell beast. I thought it had escaped hell. That turns out not to have been the case."

"What do you know about it?" His voice had taken on a sort of falsely disinterested tone, something he'd been trained to affect. He was in full commando mode.

If she told him what she really knew, it would be like telling Darkrock. He wasn't ready to believe what she was telling him about himself. He would report on everything she said to him.

"I asked Lucien—my brother. He has no record of it in hell's inventory."

"You brother is *actually* the ruler of hell."

She probably shouldn't have mentioned that. But she

figured whoever was leaking information and biotech from the firm had probably leaked that already, as well.

"It's kind of a family tradition."

"So you already knew about this thing before this 'council' called you in. The council I supposedly sit on."

"No. I mean, I was tracking something that was killing people up north of here, so when I got the call, I figured it was probably the same thing. But I didn't know what it was at the time." She watched him, wondering how much more he was able to hear right now. "Are you aware that when the hell beast is wounded—you share the wound?"

"Darkrock thought that might happen. It has the ability to project transference magic to keep itself from being fatally injured." It was an interesting theory on Darkrock's part.

"That isn't why."

"Oh? I suppose you're going to tell me why."

"If you want me to."

"It's been a really entertaining story so far. Makes the drive seem shorter."

"The morning I met you—the morning before your council called me in on the job—I was tracking the thing, like I said. I ended up in Jerome, unaware of the paranormal population, and I went after a reptilian shifter—a single mom working as a waitress in a Jerome coffeehouse. You jumped me when I tried to take her out. Said you were Jerome's self-appointed protector of all things 'extra-human.'"

Oliver laughed. "This story just keeps getting better."

"You told me later that you'd promised a young shifter that you'd watch out for his kind after some drug dealer tried to take advantage of him. Somehow you've inadvertently managed to take on any injuries to paranormal creatures in the vicinity ever since. And you have no idea how or why."

"That sounds like a load of crap."

"Yeah, that's what I thought when you told me, to be perfectly honest. I figure you know exactly how. You just didn't feel like telling me. Maybe you don't really trust me."

"Should I trust you?"

There was something about the way he said it that seemed like more of a sincere plea, as if he needed to be able to trust her, to trust someone.

"Yes. You should. I may not know everything about what you're involved in or what's going on, but I would never lie to you." And that, she realized, was a pretty rare thing for her. She considered lying to be a business necessity much of the time. Though she preferred to call it "creative omission."

They'd reached the valley, and they picked up speed on the highway, heading for Bullhead City.

"One of the creatures you protect is that wolf they've got in the back of the van."

Oliver's jaw tightened. "I'm protecting society, as a matter of fact, by getting things like that off the street."

"And things like me."

Oliver met her eyes for the moment, obviously conflicted. "Yeah. And things like you."

Chapter 25

The sense of familiarity he'd had the night before as he watched the winged creature—Lucy—fly away was even stronger now. It was uncanny how her scent seemed as familiar to him—and as essential—as Vanessa's.

Oliver tossed his gear aside as he undressed for decon. It was some bullshit she was projecting, some hell thing—infernal blood, she'd called it. She'd managed to make him believe for a few minutes that he'd really seen Vanessa die. And what kind of sick imagination would have put that method of death in his head? Trying to play to his emotions, she'd made him see Vanessa pleading with her eyes for him to put her out of her misery after her vocal cords had been severed by a vampire lord's knife. And that extra little detail about Vanessa being pregnant—that was the giveaway that this whole thing was bullshit. Vanessa would have told him if she'd been pregnant. He'd never have let her go on the mission if that were true.

Except that he could remember a conversation with Vanessa now in vivid detail where she had. He'd accused her of lying and tried to pull rank on her to keep her from doing the job. She'd read him the riot act for that dumb stunt.

No.

Oliver hit the button on the decontamination shower and stepped under the scalding spray. That wasn't real. It was all a lie. And as soon as he met up with Vee later this morning, he could stop letting that demon mess with his head.

As the water streamed over his abs, he noticed the bruises from the transference injuries had already faded, the scars looking like they were from weeks or months ago. Quite a trick that thing was able to pull off. They'd have to neutralize that somehow if they were going to do any exploratory surgery on the beast, because those bullet wounds had felt all too real. He didn't relish having to experience every cut of the scalpel. It probably wouldn't have the ability to project its injuries on to him if it were unconscious, but Oliver knew better than to hope Darkrock would want it sedated. They were big fans of the vivisection.

"Stop stroking your dick and get moving." Artie tossed a towel at him as he came around the wall from the dressing room, and Oliver managed to step out from under the spray and grab it before it got soaked. Artie grinned. "I'm sure we're all very impressed, but they're waiting for you in Block D for testing."

Oliver wrapped the towel around his waist as Artie stepped under the shower. "Your mom was very impressed last night."

"I think you're confusing my mom with that four-hundred-pound werewolf you shagged in the back of the van while it was out cold, but it's a common mistake."

"Jesus, dude."

Artie shrugged. "What can I say?" He indicated the thick hair on his chest as he rubbed the soap over it. "The whole family's hairy."

Oliver rolled his eyes as he went around the partition to get a clean uniform out of his locker. "Hey, any word from Vanessa? Shouldn't she be reporting back from her recon mission today?"

"You know that's classified. Relax. If I'd heard anything negative, I'd have let you know, rules or no rules. I'm sure she's fine."

He couldn't shake the images Lucy Smok had infected him with as he got dressed and headed down to Block D. He wasn't going to be able to get them out of his head until he saw Vanessa in front of him.

They'd put Lucy and the wolf—the small one—in two adjacent cells with the same magic-dampening technology as the cell they'd put the bigger wolf in. He couldn't see what damage these two could possibly do even with their abilities intact, but it wasn't his area of expertise. Oliver kept his eyes straight ahead as he passed the bulletproof glass front walls of the cells and reported to the technician on duty.

"Hey." He nodded to the tech. "Artie says you need me to take some tests."

"Actually, we need you to oversee some tests."

"Oversee?"

"They want you to observe the intake procedures for the new acquisitions."

"Why would they need me to observe them?"

The tech shrugged. "Beats me. Just passing along the

orders." He switched on the screen in front of him to reveal side-by-side feeds of the cells where Lucy and the hellhound were being kept. The wolf was now in human form, huddled naked in the corner, and the glass between the cells allowed the two to see each other, as well. Security guards were stationed inside each cell. The tech spoke into the mic on his laptop. "Ready when you are. Let's start with Subject A."

One of the guards in Lucy's cell stepped forward without warning and punched Lucy in the jaw. He got his ass handed to him as a reward, with Lucy moving so swiftly to immobilize him and drop him to the floor with a knee to his throat that it took his partner a moment to recover and pull his sidearm on her, ordering her to back off. She did so, her stance ready to take them both on if she had to. He had a feeling she might be evenly matched despite being unarmed.

The tech glanced at Oliver and marked something down on his notepad. "Nothing so far. Let's try option two."

While the second guard had his weapon still trained on Lucy, the first took out his knife. "Give me your arm," he ordered.

Lucy looked him up and down. "How badly do you want me to break yours?"

He looked a little nervous. "I'm just going to make a small superficial cut."

"Or I can just shoot you," the other offered.

She studied him with a withering look. "What exactly are you hoping to achieve here?"

"That's on a need-to-know basis."

"For fuck's sake." Lucy sighed, holding out her arm. The guard pushed her sleeve up and drew the blade across the top of her forearm, painting a thin line of blood.

"Nothing," the tech reported, making another note.

"We probably should have cuffed that one," Artie observed as he came up behind Oliver and the tech at the desk. "Can you imagine what she's like in the sack?" He grinned as Oliver looked up at him. "But I guess you don't have to imagine, eh, Chief?"

Oliver decided to let the slur go—for the millionth time—and focused on the insinuation. "What's that supposed to mean? If you're trying to suggest that I'd ever cheat on Vanessa—"

"Oh, right, sorry. Vanessa. Of course you wouldn't. I forgot. You're not only a chief, you're a Boy Scout."

"If by 'Boy Scout' you mean 'not an asshole,' then, sure. I'm a Boy Scout." Oliver studied the monitor. "What's the point of this exercise?"

"Just seeing if either of these two has the same magical transference capacity as the ugly one."

"Nothing so far," said the tech. "Shall we move on to Subject B?"

Artie nodded. "Go for it."

Oliver's brows drew together. "Why would either of them have the same skill?" He cringed, a little flare of anger sparking in him, as one of the guards in the boy's cell punched the kid in the gut hard enough to cause internal injuries.

Artie nodded at Oliver. "Lift up your shirt."

"I didn't feel anything. This is absurd. Why would they have it? And why would it affect me if they did?"

"Just humor me. Let's see."

With a tight-jawed sigh, Oliver lifted up his shirt to reveal an unbruised surface.

Artie raised an eyebrow. "Huh."

While the hellhound was doubled over, the guard stabbed him in the side, eliciting a doglike yelp of pain and fear.

Oliver held up the shirt on the same side. "Nothing, goddammit. Now leave the damn thing alone."

"Grow a pair, Benally. Or do you let Vanessa keep them for you in her purse these days?" Artie turned to the technician. "Looks like these two are duds. I think we can call this test done. Captain Blake wants to have a word with the Smok bitch. Have Ramirez and Daniels bring her up to his office. We'll meet them there."

Lucy shook off her escorts as they brought her into their CO's office. When they'd moved on to torturing Colt, she figured they were trying to gauge whether she and the hellhound were under Oliver's protection. They hadn't figured out what she'd only just learned herself from the hell beast—that she and Colt didn't count because they weren't "of the earth."

Oliver stood off to the side with his buddies, but the focus of this room was an older man seated behind the desk who projected an air of authority.

The older man rose and offered Lucy his hand. "Captain David Blake. So nice to meet you, Ms. Smok. I've heard a great deal about you."

Lucy didn't take the offered hand. "Yeah? Well, I've heard nothing about you. Who the hell are you supposed to be?"

He seemed unfazed by her rudeness. "I'm the commanding officer of this facility. Of the entire Southwest division of Darkrock, in fact. We've had our eye on Smok for a long time. I tried to broker a deal with your father a few years ago, but he turned me down."

"Let me save you some time. I'll be turning you down, too."

Blake laughed. "You're not here to be offered a deal, Ms. Smok. The time for that has passed. I've brought you here to meet with me because as interesting as the prospect might be, keeping you in a cage and experimenting on you would be too high risk. Unlike most of our guests, you would no doubt have people looking for you. Someone would be bound to leak the information, and it wouldn't look good for either of us. I think you can agree that having the world know about what you are would be bad for business. Not our business," he amended. "Yours."

"I see. So Darkrock intends to blackmail me into cooperating with its efforts. Is that it?"

"Not exactly. As I said, we're no longer interested in cooperation. We intend to launch our own biotech center, specializing in the same discerning clients who've previously depended on Smok Biotech's monopoly. We already have someone on the inside at Smok who's been gathering information and acquiring intellectual capital. What we want is to be assured that Darkrock's efforts won't face any legal challenges from Smok for trademark violations. And to that end, we intend to document your transformation into an inhuman monster as our assurance. We'll have your dirty little secret on file, and you'll let us operate unfettered."

Lucy laughed. "You're out of your damn mind."

"I figure all you need is the right incentive." Blake picked up a remote from his desk and clicked it to display a large video screen beside them showing Colt in his cell—and the hell beast in the cell beside him, a wall of glass between them. The beast was awake. It paced like a tiger in a cage, salivating, as it watched Colt huddling in the farthest corner. "As you may have noticed earlier, there's a dampening field in operation around these cells preventing its occupants from transformations and any other magical influences they might otherwise be able to project. I'm about to turn that off."

Oliver made a startled motion from where he stood. "Sir…do you think that's wise?"

"We've cleared the level." Blake clicked another button on the remote. "I've left the dampening barrier in place between the two cells for now. But let's see what they do."

The lack of a dampening field was clearly felt immediately by both. Colt rose onto all fours and transformed into his wolf form, hackles raised, while the beast broke into one of its inhuman grins. Lucy held her breath as it charged the glass, but the barrier held. The beast stood upright and drew its claws along the glass as if testing it.

"Now," said Blake, "with a click of a button, I can dissolve the magical barrier between them, and we can let the little wolf take his chances against the larger."

A rush of rage-fueled adrenaline surged through Lucy's veins as she started toward him, but the guards held her back. "You can't do this."

"I most certainly can." Blake smiled. "But I'm betting that right about now you're feeling much more compliant. If you give us what we want, I'll leave the barrier intact and restore the dampening field to the whole cell block."

Lucy shook off the guards. "And what exactly is it you want?"

"We just need you to make a little video stating your identity—and your aberration. Before you demonstrate it."

The beast had made another run at the glass, snarling in frustration when it refused to budge. But now it was looking at the glass to the front.

"All right, dammit. Restore the dampening field and I'll make your fucking video."

"Make the video, and then I'll restore the field. It will give the whole thing a nice artistic sense of urgency."

One of the operatives had taken out a camcorder and pointed it at Lucy. "Whenever you're ready."

The hell beast charged the front wall of its cell, and the glass cracked.

"All right." Lucy glanced around. "But you all need to step back." She faced the camera. "My name is Lucy Electra Smok. I'm the CFO of Smok International. And I have infernal blood." She felt like she was at an AA meeting. "It gives me enhanced senses and strength when I experience a partial transformation into a wyvern."

Blake's brow wrinkled. "Sorry, a what?"

Lucy sighed. "It's a kind of dragon. It's my demon form."

"Okay, let's see it."

She'd never done this on command before. Usually, fury combined with the fight-or-flight response triggered it. But she'd put off taking the suppressing meds. Watching the beast make a larger crack in the glass as it rammed it with its shoulder did the trick.

Lucy closed her eyes and shook her shoulders, feeling the heat of the bony chitin that formed the horns on her head, the talons on her fingers and the wings on her back. The fabric of her T-shirt tore as her wings erupted. She allowed them to expand, and the Darkrock operatives took a few steps farther from her as she stretched them as far as she could within the office.

She opened her eyes, avoiding Oliver's, and glared at Blake with the full fury of her wyvern mien. "Restore the barrier. Now."

She'd evidently startled them all a bit, and Blake had to shake himself. "Of course. Thank you for your cooperation." He clicked the button a split second too late, as the glass front of the beast's cell shattered on the monitor. It was out now, loose, but it sensed the change and knew that it couldn't get inside the other cell. It made a snarling howl of anger as it battered its shoulder against the glass before turning and looking straight into the camera.

"I will tear off all your heads," it hissed in a voice that sent a surge of discomfort through Lucy's bowels—and from the looks of it, through everyone else's. "And I will suck the marrow from your bones while I fuck your corpses."

"You're sure the area's secure," said Ramirez.

Blake glared. "Of course I'm sure. Cooper, Benally—get down there and put that thing under again."

"You're going to need my help," said Lucy as the two men moved to follow the order.

Blake hesitated, but another rage-filled howl from the beast made him swallow visibly. "Go ahead." He indicated the video camera. "We've got everything we need here."

Lucy folded her wings and followed Oliver and Artie Cooper to the elevator. They had already grabbed a few weapons from the locker beside it.

Oliver glanced at her curiously after checking his ammunition as they stepped inside the elevator. "Is that as far as the transformation goes?"

Artie snorted. "What, you think she's got dragon tits or something?"

Lucy turned her wyvern gaze on Artie. "How would you like to find out about my dragon teeth?" That seemed to shut him up, at least temporarily. "Yes," she answered Oliver finally. "This is the whole deal."

The elevator arrived at Block D. Oliver and Artie raised their weapons, Artie armed with the tranquilizer gun and Oliver holding an AK-47, and the doors slid open. There was no sign of the beast as they scanned the corridor, but Lucy could sense it. It was using its ability to visually confound them.

"It's here," she cautioned. "Don't trust your eyes."

"Maybe we should stay between it and the elevator," Oliver suggested. "If we can't see it, it could get past us and escape."

"Good thinking," said Artie. "Let it come to us."

Three cells down, Colt's wolf form was pacing and growling, watching something.

"It's close," said Lucy. She could feel the skin-crawling sensation of its breath, even though the stench of it was absent.

Artie took a step forward. "How the hell are we supposed to shoot it if we can't see the fucking thing?"

Lucy put out a cautioning hand. "I don't think you should—" Her words were cut short by a guttural sound of surprise and a shuddering recoil from Artie, as though something had punched him hard in the gut. His black T-shirt was growing darker black at the center as if it had gotten wet, and he began to cough up blood.

The beast materialized in front of them, grinning, its claws dripping with Artie Cooper's blood. Artie managed to get off a shot that went wildly off target before he buckled and fell to his knees.

Oliver fired—and shouted with pain as the bullet

ripped through the beast's shoulder. Any shots he took at the beast—and any damage Lucy managed to do— were going to be felt by Oliver.

Lucy leaped at the beast with a kick to the head and knocked it back several feet on the slick tile, giving them the briefest moment to strategize. "Oliver, you have to re-linquish your protection," she urged. "That's the only way we're going to be able to kill this thing without killing you."

"What are you talking about? What protection?" He seemed reluctant to use the gun again as the beast picked itself up and rushed toward them, but he fired once more and hit the beast in the chest. The impact knocked them both backward an equal distance.

"The hell beast isn't projecting its injuries. You made a vow to protect all unnatural creatures in the Jerome vicinity. That's why you feel the wounds. You're taking them for everything inhuman."

Oliver winced, trying to line up his aim once more as the beast got to its feet. "Ridiculous. How would I even be able to do that? Besides, it didn't happen with you or the kid."

"Because we're both infernal, not earth-based. This thing is as earth-based as it gets. It was born out of rage and hate." She met the beast's charge, but it demateri-alized as she swung at it, reappearing behind her.

Oliver fired again and fell to his knees as the shot hit the beast in the stomach at close range. He was doing some serious damage, even if it was temporary, and it was taking its toll on them both.

The beast backed off for a moment, snarling, but some-thing behind it caught its attention. The white wolf was standing in the corridor growling. Someone had unlocked the doors.

Lucy cried out as the beast bolted toward Colt. It slashed its claws across the smaller wolf's side, spraying blood across the white tile and whiter fur.

"Revoke your protection!" she yelled at Oliver as she barreled after the beast to try to get between it and Colt.

"How?"

"Just say it! 'I revoke my protection!'"

Oliver groaned, the AK-47 falling out of his arms. "I revoke my protection."

As she reached the beast, Colt suddenly leaped for its throat, his eyes glowing with red fire and his teeth unexpectedly razor sharp as he bared them, and the hell beast seemed to stop dead with surprise at its attack. The young wolf had torn out its throat. After the instant of shock, the beast flailed, claws swinging wildly, its eyes almost plaintively on Lucy's as Colt eviscerated it.

Its unwitting "mother" or not, Lucy had no sympathy for the creature. She turned to make sure Oliver wasn't also lying shredded on the tile, but he'd stood up, beginning to recover already.

Oliver stared aghast at Colt. "He was holding back to keep from hurting me. I didn't realize. All this time, Colt was suppressing his own power to kill the damn thing and putting himself in danger. Because of me."

"Colt?" Lucy scrutinized Oliver's face. "You said Colt."

"That's the name I gave him, because he—" Oliver wiped blood on his pants from the hand he'd been gripping his gut with. The left hand. Blood clogged the ring. He stared at it. "Oh... God, how did I forget that?" He raised his eyes to Lucy. "How could I have forgotten you?"

Self-conscious discomfort at her wyvern state gnawed at her as it hadn't while Oliver was under the influence of the drug. Sometimes it took a while for the transformation to subside when she hadn't taken her monthly dose of shift control. And now everyone would see her this way if she didn't acquiesce to Darkrock's scheme. Smok International would be ruined either way.

"We should probably get Colt out of here." She turned toward the blood-covered wolf. She was glad he hadn't returned yet to his human form. The blood and gore smeared across his face would have been even more unsettling.

As Colt trotted toward her, a crack of gunfire went off beside her. At first she thought it was Oliver's weapon, but she spun about to see Artie Cooper holding his handgun as he slumped against the elevator door. And Oliver... Oliver didn't look like himself. His face had filled with a white-hot rage, and his eyes were glowing orange, like flame was igniting inside them.

Lucy turned back to the corridor, trying to make sense of what was going on. Had the hell beast somehow managed to rally after all that? But Colt was lying on his side, blood pouring from his hip and his breathing rapid and shallow.

"No." She moved toward him in a daze and sank to her knees beside him. "Colt." She was vaguely aware as she laid her hand on Colt's rising and falling rib cage that Oliver had dragged the wounded Artie to his feet.

"What the fuck did you do?"

"Just following orders," Artie gritted out. "You've gone soft, Chief. I had to take care of it. Like I had to take care of you and Vanessa."

"What are you talking about? What about Vanessa?"

"Your last mission. It was *supposed* to be your last,

anyway. Made a deal with those vamp lords to have you taken out. Your team was collateral damage."

"You sold us out."

Artie was gasping for air. "Vanessa…submitted her resignation. Said she wanted out. We knew you'd follow."

"You son of a bitch."

Lucy lifted the wolf in her arms and watched as Artie choked out his last breath.

Oliver let him slip to the floor. "Darkrock did this." His voice was unrecognizable. "They did this to me. To Vanessa." Tears poured down his cheeks, steaming as they fell. "To Colt."

The word that Vanessa had said echoed in Lucy's head, and she voiced it aloud. "Firecracker."

Something seemed to snap inside Oliver. As the rage exploded across his face, the tile beneath their feet began to melt, and in an instant, flames were licking up the walls.

"Run," he said, his voice like crackling fire, and Lucy ran for the stairs, charging up to the surface with Colt in her arms. The building was burning, and explosions were sounding throughout the compound. Ignoring the shouts of the operatives running past her in the opposite direction and the sprinklers raining down on her, Lucy burst through the door into the yard and took flight under the cover of night, carrying Colt's body away and leaving Oliver to the inferno of his fury and grief.

Chapter 26

Lucy took Colt to the only person she could think of who might be able to save a hellhound: Fran.

"He doesn't deserve this." Lucy felt hollow as she watched Fran work. "He killed that thing—the monster Carter used me to make. He protected us."

"I've stopped the bleeding, but he lost a lot. And there's something else going on with him. His temperature is spiking. I don't know what to make of it. It's as though he's fundamentally unwell. My guess is it's something infernal. He might not be suited to living in this plane. I think the only thing we can do now is send him home."

Lucy exploded at her. "I am not going to use the Soul Reaper on him!"

"Sweetheart." Fran touched her arm gently. "I wasn't suggesting that you shoot the poor thing. Of course not. But you need to contact Lucien."

"Oh." For some reason, her eyes were stinging. She'd

transformed back while Fran was working on Colt. It was probably just a residual effect of the shift in her irises.

"You know it's okay to care about him. To care about anyone."

"Ha!" The sharp, dismissive laugh circumvented a less dignified emotional response. "You make me sound like some cold, inhuman bitch."

"That's not what I meant. I've watched you your whole life swallowing your emotions, believing they made you feminine and weak."

"That's not—"

"And I'm partly to blame for that. I gave in to Edgar. I relinquished my right to be your mother. I abandoned you."

"No, you didn't."

"I did. Don't do that."

Lucy scowled irritably. "Do what?"

"Bury your hurt and anger under the Smok stoicism. Let everybody else off the hook but yourself."

"Well, what do you want me to do? Scream at you? Fly into a rage because I didn't have a real mother because you protected yourself instead of protecting us? What goddamn good is that going to do either of us? Edgar made us both what we are."

"No. He doesn't have the power to make you—or me—anything. Don't give him that. He failed you, and I failed you, but that doesn't define you, sweetheart. You are who you are—brilliant, strong, compassionate—because you have the power to be whatever you want to be. To feel however you want to feel. And to express it." Fran touched her once more, despite knowing that Lucy didn't do touching, and let her hand linger on Lucy's forearm. "It's okay to cry. It doesn't make you weak."

"Dammit." Tears were pouring down Lucy's cheeks. "Maybe it doesn't make me weak, but it sucks. It feels like shit. I hate it. I hate crying." And now she was blubbering.

She let Fran hold her, crying a little harder when she realized it was the first time she could remember her mother hugging her—partly because of the NDA Fran had signed relinquishing her parental claim but also because Lucy had always refused any displays of affection. It was sentimental. And made her have feelings. And she fucking hated feelings. Because feelings hurt. Like the little piece of glass that seemed to be stuck in her heart whenever she thought about Oliver's bond with Vanessa—and that seemed to twist deeper when she wondered whether he'd made it out of the compound alive.

By the time she'd pulled herself together, Theia had answered the text she'd sent her while Fran was stitching Colt up. Yes, she was still topside, and she'd go get Lucien immediately. They could meet at Phoebe's place. The quaint, cozy ranch house seemed to be the hub for the Carlisle clan, despite the fact that Rafe Diamante owned several high-end properties around town.

Fran helped Lucy load the unconscious Colt—still in wolf form—into Fran's Range Rover, since Lucy had flown here. "Bring it back when you can." She gave Lucy a quick little hug, which was really pushing it, but Lucy allowed it.

Theia and Lucien hadn't returned yet when Lucy arrived at Phoebe's. Sometimes time passed at a slightly different rate when they were below. Lucy hoped this wasn't going to be one of those times when an hour below was a day above.

Phoebe helped her bring Colt inside and put him in the guest bed.

Lucy observed him as Phoebe tucked a blanket around the little wolf. "He might shift when he wakes up." *If he wakes up.* "I should go get him something to wear."

"I'll text Laurel and have her pick up something. She's on her way here to report back on her undercover assignment."

Lucy had forgotten all about the mole at Smok Biotech. "I'm not sure it matters what Laurel found out, to tell you the truth. Darkrock command bragged that they had someone inside, and they've blackmailed me into outing myself if I don't let them basically destroy everything the company has worked for and let them take what they want."

"Well, just wait to see what Laurel has to say. You may be surprised."

Lucy raised an eyebrow but didn't ask what that meant. Right now she was too tired and worried to care.

"Around what size is Colt's human form, would you say?"

Lucy shrugged. "He's about four and a half feet tall, maybe seventy-five, eighty pounds?"

Phoebe texted the details to Laurel. "She's on it."

Lucy doubted it would matter. From the way Colt was breathing, it wouldn't be long before it became a moot point.

"Do you want something to drink? I have hot mulled cider brewing for Yule—Leo wanted glögg, which I thought was mulled wine, but when I told him that, he said to leave it alone. He'd do it himself." Phoebe laughed. "Apparently, real glögg is more like eating soggy chunks of drunk fruit and nuts out of a glass."

Lucy followed Phoebe down the hall while she chattered on. "Cider's fine." She hadn't thought to drink or eat anything. Phoebe opened up a steaming slow cooker in the delicious-smelling kitchen to ladle out the drink. "Yule…isn't that closer to Christmas?"

Phoebe made a little obvious glance at the huge Christmas tree in the corner. Come to think of it, there were lights all over the outside of the house that Lucy hadn't been paying attention to when she arrived. "What day do you think this is?"

"Um…" God, what the hell day was it? Sometime in early December, Lucy thought.

"Today's the solstice. We're celebrating Christmas early because Ione has to give a big convocation thing or something at Covent Temple, and Leo prefers to celebrate Yule, so it all works out."

"I'm sorry. I didn't realize I'd be interrupting a family gathering."

Phoebe handed her a mug of cider with a little half slice of orange on the rim and a cinnamon stick in it. "Lucy. You're family. And I really should have invited you. I didn't even think of it. I'm sorry. We didn't think Theia would be able to get here for it, so it was just going to be small. But it's all good." She smiled and clinked her mug against Lucy's. "I've got a huge rib roast in the oven."

So that's what that fantastic smell was. She was actually feeling a little faint with hunger now that she thought about it.

Phoebe watched her for a moment. "There's a tray full of *saffransbullar* and meat pies on the coffee table. Have a seat and dig in. That's what they're there for."

Lucy sank onto the couch and loaded a little plate with savory and sweet saffron buns. Her wyvern metabolism needed some serious replenishing.

Laurel arrived shortly after, quickly followed by Rhea

and Leo, while Phoebe made the introductions. Phoebe dragged them to the kitchen to help with chopping things, and the kitchen seemed to bubble over with laughter and joy. Lucy had always wondered what it would be like to have a sister. Or a joyous family celebration, for that matter. The Smoks' had always been grand, solemn, corporate affairs designed to show off Edgar's money and might.

With her hunger slightly mollified, she set her plate down as Laurel sat in the chair adjacent to the table with a cup of cider. "So Phoebe says you have some news for me."

Laurel nodded, cupping her mug in both hands and breathing in the mulling spices. "First, I wanted to thank you for the job. Things were pretty tight this year, and I wasn't sure how I was going to make my rent next month."

Lucy wasn't sure what to say to that. She'd never even considered the idea of rent—or missing a meal, or having any material need met, really.

"I'm glad it worked out for you," she said awkwardly. She felt like an asshole.

"Oh, I know it wasn't about hiring me, exactly, so I'm just pleased that our needs coincided." Laurel smiled warmly and took an experimental sip of cider. "Ow. Too hot. So here's the thing." She set the cup down on the table. "I don't know if Phoebe mentioned to you that I have one of Madeleine's gifts." The Lilith blood passed down from Madeleine Marchant was the source of the Carlisle sisters' abilities.

"She didn't, but I assumed you must. What's your gift?"

"I see certain near-future events when they intersect

with events in front of me. It's kind of hard to explain. It's like a probability projection of the butterfly effect. If A happens, B will happen, causing C to happen and on down to the most likely outcome."

"And you saw something at Smok?"

"I did. I mean, first, literally, I saw your assistant putting an entire terabyte drive in her purse. She wasn't very subtle about it."

Lucy gaped. "Allison? She's the mole? But I vetted and hired her myself."

"No, I don't think she's the mole."

"I don't understand."

"I don't think you have a mole. I think you have a magical virus. Something a certain necromancer put in place before he got dragged to hell." Laurel wrinkled her nose with distaste. "It had his nasty smell all over it."

"A virus." A vein throbbed at Lucy's temple. She really wished she'd had the opportunity to punch Carter in the throat. "He infected my staff?"

Laurel nodded. "All of them. They don't even know they're doing it, and no one notices it when anyone steals something right in front of them. I wear an amulet that prevents necromancy from affecting me. Otherwise, I think it would have just drifted onto me from close contact."

"Why don't I have it?"

"Because of your infernal blood, maybe?" Laurel shrugged. "I disinfected the place with some help from Ione, so I don't think you'll be having any more problems."

"Wow. Well, thank you, Laurel. I never imagined it would be something this widespread. Of course, it doesn't actually matter now. Carter played every hand just perfectly to continue screwing Smok after his departure."

"What do you mean?"

"Stolen data and research were being sent directly to Darkrock, and they used Colt as leverage to get me to let them record my transformation. They've threatened to release the video if I try to sue them for anything they've done. They can just take it all now with impunity. Or I can let them release the video, and I can kiss everything goodbye."

"Colt is the little boy?" Laurel looked over at the bag she'd set at her side and passed it to Lucy. "Oh, here's the clothing, by the way."

"Thanks." Lucy rose. "I'd probably better check on him." She started toward the guest room but remembered what Laurel had said about things being tight. Damn. She really needed to start paying more attention to her privilege. "How much do I owe you?"

Laurel waved her away. "Oh, it was nothing. Don't worry about it. I'm happy to help."

"Laurel." Lucy walked back to the couch. "To me it's nothing, because people have been giving me things all my life without me giving any of it a second thought. To you, it matters. Tell me how much it was."

Laurel blushed. "It really wasn't much. I stopped at the dollar store." Lucy took out her wallet and handed Laurel a one-hundred-dollar bill, but Laurel balked. "No, no. I mean it. It was like twenty-three bucks."

"I don't have anything smaller. Just consider it a thank-you for everything you've done." Lucy set the bill on the table and took the bag into the guest room.

Colt's condition hadn't changed, except that he seemed even warmer now. She took out the clothes and removed the tags and laid them out on a chair just in case.

As she adjusted the blanket around him, however, the

rapid breathing sped up like an engine revving, and the wolf opened its eyes. Three things happened in rapid succession, almost too swiftly for Lucy to register: the wolf recognized her, Colt resumed his human form and a ball of fire seemed to roll off Colt's skin and onto the bed, setting the bedding aflame.

Colt bolted out of bed as if he meant to crash through the window, but Lucy grabbed him around the waist and swung him back toward her. He looked up at her with anxious eyes, shaking his head vehemently. Another little ball of fire dripped off him onto the floor, and Lucy stamped it out, but the fire on the bed was spreading rapidly. She could either keep him here or keep Phoebe's house from burning down.

As yet another ball of fire rolled across the carpet, Lucy shoved Colt through the door toward the bathroom across the hall. "In there! Water!" He'd drunk gallons of water at Oliver's place, and perhaps this was why. She prayed she wasn't sending him to set the whole house ablaze as she threw another blanket on top of the bed to smother the fire and yelled for help.

The smoke alarm had been triggered, and Phoebe came running with a fire extinguisher and put out the bedding and a streak of smoldering carpet.

She turned to Lucy when it was under control. "What the hell happened?"

"Colt," said Lucy. "I think he was dehydrated." She grabbed the clothes from the chair and pushed through the crowd in the doorway that now included Rhea, Leo, Ione and Ione's husband, Dev Gideon, to reach the bathroom and make sure she'd been right.

Colt had climbed into the porcelain bathtub—smart

kid; he'd minimized his flammability—and was drinking from his cupped hands under the running water.

Lucy closed the door. "I'm so sorry, Colt. I didn't realize." She should have had Fran hook up an IV drip to keep him hydrated, but it had never occurred to her what the consequences would be of his not getting sufficient water. And she'd honestly thought he wouldn't make it through the night. "I brought you some clothes." She set them on the toilet seat lid. "Once you've cooled down a bit, you can put these on, and we'll get you some proper water from the kitchen. And something to eat."

Colt nodded and continued drinking. Whatever it was that kept him from speaking—whether it was a choice or a physiological impossibility—he seemed to fully understand human speech.

She stepped out to find the hallway had cleared—except for Leo, who stood waiting in the guest room doorway, arms folded as he leaned one broad shoulder against the door frame. "The little wolf," he said, pushing himself away from the wall. "He's a hellhound."

"Yes."

"You know they're meant to hunt."

Lucy shrugged. "I guess, yeah."

"But he's not one of mine."

"I'm not sure what you mean. One of yours?"

"One of my hounds. They accompany the Wild Hunt. They're spectral, but Colt is flesh and blood. I think he may be part of a hunting pack meant to join another Wild Hunt."

"Another?" Lucy pushed back her hair. "I didn't know there was more than one."

"Oh, yes. They come from many regions of the world, many traditions."

"Lucien said he'd escaped hell with a small pack of juveniles. Maybe you're right. But why is that significant?"

"Because I think these hellhounds would have escaped with a purpose. To hunt—or to seek the hunter." Leo started walking back to the living room as if he was done with the conversation.

"Leo." Lucy walked after him. "Do you know something about this hunter?"

Before he could answer, the front door opened at the end of the hall. Theia and Lucien had arrived. Behind Lucy, a soft growl sounded. She turned to see Colt, dressed in his new clothes, standing with legs planted wide, arms out at his sides, ready to run. His eyes had gone red, and they were fixed on Lucien.

Lucy returned to him and took his hand. "It's okay, Colt. He's not here to hurt you. You're not in trouble."

Lucien seemed to recognize Colt as well, whether simply because of his description or because of some infernal sense, Lucy wasn't sure. "So there you are. You and your brother and sisters have caused quite a bit of chaos, my little friend. I don't suppose you know where they are?"

A narrowing of the red eyes was Colt's only response.

Lucy drew Colt a little closer to her side. "He doesn't have to go right away, does he? I know he can't stay, but he seems to be doing much better than he was."

Phoebe came out of the kitchen with oven mitts on her hands. "He could at least stay and eat something, couldn't he? I mean, you guys just got here."

Rhea stepped past her and grabbed Theia's hand, dragging her toward the breakfast counter that separated the living room from the kitchen. "Of course they're staying. It's Yule. And Leo's making honest-to-God glögg. I bet you don't have that in hell."

Lucien put his hands in his pockets, gazing after his stolen wife. "Well, actually, hell isn't really that different. It's just on another..." He stopped and rolled his eyes. "Oh, for fuck's sake. I'm devilsplaining. Never mind. Let's eat, drink and be merry!"

Chapter 27

The food and drink were as amazing as they smelled, and the company, despite the crowded little house, was far more enjoyable than Lucy had expected. After dinner, the Carlisle sisters shared a tradition of "passing fire"—one person lighting the next person's candle and continuing around the circle as they welcomed the return of the light—and even Colt participated, blowing a little bauble of flame onto the candle in Lucy's hand with a shy smile.

Colt never did warm up to Lucien, but Lucy took the boy aside before the evening wound down and explained to him that he had to go home and that Lucien was her brother and she trusted him. She wasn't sure if Colt finally agreed or simply gave up, but it broke her heart a little to see his head hanging as he walked out between Lucien and Theia.

As she headed home, she remembered her car was in Jerome, and she had to get the Range Rover back to

Fran. She parked the SUV in the lot at her place and called Allison in the morning to have a car sent to drop her off in Jerome and have the Range Rover picked up and returned. She hesitated a moment when Allison answered, remembering that she—and everyone else at Smok Biotech—had been sabotaging Lucy for months. But it wasn't Allison's fault, and if Laurel was right, it was all sorted now. Whether it mattered or not. If Darkrock had uploaded that footage to the cloud, she was screwed—even if everyone in the compound was dead.

Lucy stared at the tiles while she stood under the shower. Was Oliver dead? How could he not be? He'd been in the midst of the flames fifty feet below the ground, and unlike Lucy, he couldn't transform into a dragon and fly away.

She felt empty again, the way she'd always felt before Oliver. The difference now was that she knew she was empty. All she'd lived for was her work. And now she might not even have that. Oh, some semblance of Smok International would survive, but the usual consulting jobs—exorcising demons and chasing down wayward therianthropic millionaires who'd forgotten to take their meds—didn't hold the same appeal they once had. Biogenetics was the real excitement. That was where the future was. And Smok Biotech was finished.

The water had run cold. Lucy shut it off and stepped out to get dressed. She wasn't really feeling the Prada suits today. A pair of khakis and a black cotton turtleneck would do. She slicked back her hair with a little glosser and applied her signature stain to her lips. She was going to have to report back to the council today that the creature was dead…and that Oliver was, too. Might as well grab a suit jacket and wear the boots that gave her a little height. People seemed to respect her expertise more when she was taller.

Even in the daytime, colored lights and strings of white seemed to drape everything as her driver took her through Sedona, the red rock formations above them sprinkled with snow making it look like a holiday postcard. How had she not even noticed it was almost Christmas? What, even, was the point of Christmas? She might as well be spending it in hell. Goddamn Lucien. He always got the better end of the deal.

She'd emailed Nora that she had news to deliver, and they'd agreed to meet at the Civic Center building at noon. Nora and Wes rose to greet her as she entered the meeting room.

"I've tried calling Oliver to let him know about the meeting, but his phone seems to be out of service, so it's just the two of us today." Nora smiled tentatively as they sat. "I hope it's good news you have to share with us? No new sightings have been reported recently, so that's a good sign."

"It is," said Lucy. "I'm happy to report that the problem has been handled. You shouldn't have any more trouble."

"Oh, that's marvelous! And just in time for Christmas."

Wes was a little more reserved. "Was it a werewolf, like we thought?"

"It was a…" Lucy paused. "I'd call it a malevolent shape-shifting entity. That's really the closest I can come to describing it."

Nora shuddered. "Well, thank goodness it's gone. Oliver's nose is bound to be out of joint when he finds out he was wrong."

"About Oliver—"

"What about Oliver?" The words were delivered in an amused baritone from behind her.

Lucy turned to see Oliver standing in the doorway looking remarkably none the worse for wear—not even a singed eyebrow to show he'd been in a fire. She started to her feet, relief so complete rushing through her that her knees went weak, and she dropped back onto the chair.

"Oliver…" She'd lost the capacity for professionalism. Or human speech.

"I had a little trouble with my phone. Sorry I'm late." He came into the room and sat across from her. "So, did I hear right? You were talking about our shape-shifting menace in the past tense?"

"I…"

"Yes." Nora beamed. "Ms. Smok explained that she's taken care of it."

"Oh, *she's* taken care of it."

"I didn't say…"

"Well, that *is* terrific news. I have to admit that I wasn't sold on the idea of bringing in an outsider to handle town business, but I think we were totally out of our league here. Bringing in Ms. Smok was the right call." Oliver's smile had a devious twinkle to it. "So, Nora, I trust you've handled the payment details?"

Nora pulled a check from her purse and held it out to Lucy. "Absolutely. The fee we agreed on, plus a little extra as a thank-you."

Lucy took the check, still feeling like she was several seconds behind everyone, and the others rose.

Oliver offered his hand to help her up, evidently aware that she was feeling shaky on her feet. "Can I treat you to a coffee and a muffin over at Delectably Bookish, or are you off to your next appointment?"

"I'm…no, I'm good."

Oliver raised an eyebrow. "No, I can't treat you?"

"I mean, yes to the coffee and muffin. No appointments."

Nora and Wes had left the room.

Oliver closed the door. "Sorry to surprise you like that."

"I thought you were dead."

"I gathered. You look like you might even have been a little upset at the idea." He'd stepped closer to her, so close, but not touching. Lucy was having trouble forming words. Oliver leaned down so that his mouth was next to hers. "Were you? A little?"

"Oh, shut up." Lucy grabbed him by the collar and breached the distance between their mouths. Slipping his arms around her, Oliver pressed her close, deepening the kiss until Lucy pulled away breathlessly, realizing how horribly unprofessional this was. And that Oliver was still in love with his dead wife, who might even show up at any moment and want to take over.

"We should probably get going. You mentioned coffee and muffins."

Oliver put his hands in his pockets and studied her for a moment. "You are a damn hard nut to crack."

Lucy turned and pushed open the door. "I'm not any kind of a nut."

Oliver snorted. "I beg to differ."

At the shop, he paused as he unlocked the door. "Before we go in, I should warn you that we're not alone."

She'd managed to regain her composure on the walk over, and she glanced at him curiously. "Oh, is Kelly working?"

"No, she has the week off for the holidays, but I have a couple of houseguests."

Lucy's skin prickled with apprehension. Had some of his Darkrock compatriots managed to survive along with him?

Oliver opened the door and stepped back to let her go first, and Lucy glanced around. "I don't see anyone."

"They're upstairs." Before the words were out of his mouth, three juvenile white wolves with red-tipped ears came racing down the stairs with wagging tails, bouncing around Oliver in greeting.

Lucy watched with amazement. "You found the other hellhounds."

"Actually, they found me. When I used my power to call fire, it apparently called them, as well."

"Why would the hellhounds come to you?"

"It turns out, at least according to a certain siren, that the father I never met was a son of the king of Annwn."

Lucy blinked. "Of where?"

"The fairy realm of Welsh mythology. Which is apparently not so mythical."

"So you're…"

"Half Fae. And it seems these little wolves belong to the Cŵn Annwn, the Hounds of the Otherworld. And they consider me their pack leader."

"You're the hunter."

"The hunter?"

"Leo Ström told me Colt was looking for the leader of the Wild Hunt. Or *a* Wild Hunt. Leo is my sister-in-law's sister's…" Lucy paused. "Oh, hell. There's too many layers. Suffice it to say, he happens to be the leader of Odin's Hunt—you can thank him for the extra-snowy winters we've been having—and he said there were many Wild Hunts, and that Colt must belong to one."

Oliver's expression grew sober. "Where *is* Colt? Is he okay?"

"He's fine, but I…"

"Lucy?" His brows drew together with displeasure. "What did you do?"

"They can't live in this world, Oliver. I had to send him back."

For an instant, the flames returned to his eyes. "You what?"

"I didn't hurt him. I told you, he's fine. But Lucien and Theia came to collect him. He's gone home." Lucy folded her arms, tucking one hand tightly at her side, uncomfortable under his continued glare, though the flames had receded. "My mother's a doctor—she's the one who took the bullet out of his hip and stitched him up. She said he seemed 'fundamentally unwell,' as though something essential to his continued survival was lacking in our world. I imagine the same is true for these three." She shrugged helplessly. "I'm sorry."

The wolves had settled around him, sitting on their haunches and watching Lucy intently.

"You don't know anything about them," Oliver said at last.

"No, I don't. You're right."

"I'm right about something?" Oliver threw his arms in the air. "Let me mark this day on my calendar." Light glinted off the ring on his left hand.

Lucy uncrossed her arms. "I think I'd better take a pass on the coffee and muffins."

"Lucy—"

"See you, Oliver." She turned and walked out to her

car without glancing back, and he didn't follow her. Whatever had happened between them, whatever she'd thought might happen in the future, he was already taken. Better to make a clean break. She had enough experience with broken bones to know that it was the best chance at healing. This was why she didn't do relationships. Because all you had to do was disappoint someone once and they would disappear from your life.

And maybe she wasn't thinking about her almost-relationship with Oliver at all. Maybe she was thinking about how she'd spent the first twenty-five years of her life walking on eggshells around her father, always being so careful never to disappoint him the way her mother had. But the fact remained that not getting involved meant not having to feel like she felt right now. Because somehow, she *had* fallen for Oliver.

When she got back to the villa, Lucy left instructions with Allison to clear her calendar for the next few days and not to put any calls through to her or bother her unless it was an emergency. It was Christmastime, she realized, so she gave Allison the rest of the week off, as well.

She was tired. Tired of being on alert all the time, tired of trying to suppress her wyvern nature, tired of trying to navigate a world where people kept insisting on dragging her into their emotional nonsense. She stripped out of her clothes and turned off her phone and took the remaining dose of the dreaming compound she'd gotten from the lab—along with her shift control meds—before climbing into bed. Time to sleep. Finally. Maybe hibernate. Fuck the world.

Chapter 28

A persistent rapping dragged her out of a deep and—despite the drug—blissfully dreamless sleep. Who the hell could be at her door? Lucy pulled on her robe and slipped her gun into the pocket. She couldn't even remember what her last job was. Were there still any hell fugitives left to collect? Not that they would knock.

The pounding was growing louder.

"Goddammit. What the fuck do you want?" Lucy yanked the door open to find Oliver standing on her doorstep. She said it more quietly. "What the fuck do you want?"

"Can I come in for a moment?"

"Why?"

Oliver sighed and looked up at the falling snow—there were already several inches of it on the ground, unusual for Sedona—before meeting her eyes once more. "Does everything have to be a contest of wills?"

"Yes." Lucy moved away from the door without closing it. That was all the invitation he was going to get.

Oliver stepped inside and closed the door. "I talked to your brother's sister-in-law's—I talked to your friend Leo. Polly hooked me up with him. And don't worry, I didn't give her any more tokens of my gratitude. You were right about the hounds. They aren't meant to stay in this realm long-term. Leo put me in touch with the rest of the Carlisle clan." He smiled and shook his head. "They're an interesting bunch. Rafe Diamante and Dev Gideon arranged for me to communicate with the other side, as it were. Dev apparently shares his physical form with a Sumerian dragon demon that simultaneously exists within the underworld. Were you aware of that?"

Lucy shrugged. "Yes."

Oliver tilted his head like one of his hounds. "Your family and extended family are chock-full of extra-humans, and yet you spend your time hunting them down."

"I hunt the ones that don't belong here. Can you just get to the point?"

"The point is, I spoke with someone in Annwn and got the boys back to where they belong, including Colt. They weren't supposed to be in Lucien's domain. Some necromancer temporarily thinned the walls between some of the underworlds in an attempt to escape hell."

"Oh, for God's sake." Carter Hamilton was like some kind of killer maniac from an '80s slasher movie that just kept coming. Someone should buy him a goalie mask. And then punch him in the junk.

Oliver smiled. "The Carlisle women all had the same reaction. At any rate, the thinning has been repaired and the Cŵn Annwn are safe and sound. Including Colt. He's been reunited with them."

"I'm glad." And she was. Those little downcast eyes had been haunting her. Lucy rubbed her arms. She hadn't bothered to turn on the heat, and her wyvern hormones had finally tapered off now that she'd taken her meds.

"You look cold."

"Yeah. I had the heat off while I was sleeping."

"I could help warm you up."

"Oliver."

"Can you just tell me why you're so mad at me? I know I overreacted about Colt—"

"I'm not mad at you. I just… There's a certain time of the month when my infernal blood is more active, and it makes me lose perspective around…certain things. And I think I allowed myself to get a little carried away. So I'm the one who should apologize."

"I see. So you're not attracted to me now."

"I didn't say that." *Shut up, Lucy.*

"Okay, so you just don't like me now."

Lucy let a little half smile slip out. "I never liked you. I told you that."

"Oh, right. I forgot. Well, would you like to punch me again? We could start with that."

She wanted to laugh, but the sound that came out was more like a whimper. "Oliver, I…" She closed her eyes so she wouldn't have to see his expression. "You still love Vanessa. She's never left your side. I don't want to come between that. I can't compete with a ghost."

"Lucy." He'd crossed the distance between them, and she opened her eyes to find him just inches away. "I will always love Vanessa. But she's gone. She's been gone for half a decade. Phoebe let me say goodbye to her."

"She told me she had more she needed to tell you."

Oliver's eyes flickered with emotion. "She did. She

wanted me to know what happened that day—the day she died."

"I saw it." Lucy shuddered. She didn't need to hear that story again.

"Not that part, but before. She was part of a secret task force. So secret, I didn't even know about it. Because it was about me. Darkrock had dug up my father's identity, and they knew about my magical blood. They hadn't seen me demonstrate it, and they wanted to find out what it was I might be able to do so they could find a way to use it for their own ends. Vanessa was chosen to administer the catalyst and to give me a trigger word while I was under a hypnosis spell."

"You mean—"

"Probably don't say it just now." He smiled wryly. "Just in case. But yes. The word she told you to say to me. She wasn't supposed to try it that night. But when we went into that nest and she saw what had happened to the rest of our team—and knew what was about to happen to her—she breathed that word to me in the instant before her throat was slit. Darkrock had no idea that she'd triggered my magical ability. And neither did I. I just acted on instinct, out of pain, and I…"

He paused for a moment, lost in his thoughts. "At any rate, it was the reason she wanted out of Darkrock so badly. She couldn't live with the knowledge that she was being used to manipulate me. That's what she wanted to tell me. To tell me she was sorry. Which, it turns out, was all *I* still needed to say to her. But Vanessa's business is finished here. She's crossed over. And getting the chance to say goodbye to her freed me from the oppressive cloud of her specter that I'd allowed to hang over me." He touched Lucy's fingers, and she didn't pull away immediately. "There's nothing to compete with. And I know you have some issues with relationships…"

Lucy let out a sharp little laugh, but her fingers curled around his involuntarily. He wasn't wearing his ring. She glanced down at the other hand, but all his fingers were bare.

"I have some issues with a lot of things," she admitted. "I'm kind of a mess. You have no idea what you're getting yourself into."

Oliver's brow lifted hopefully. "Am I? Getting in?"

Lucy's heart gave a little involuntary leap. "I think you already have."

He kissed her, and this time Lucy didn't feel that sense of panic, the urge to flee, that usually accompanied emotional intimacy. There was just the heat of his lips and his tongue, and that sexy just-rained scent on his skin— even though it was snowing—and the rightness of his body as it fit around hers when his arms enveloped her.

The tie had slipped loose on her robe, and Oliver stepped back slightly, his hands on the lapels. "Close it? Or open it?"

"Open," she said. He took that invitation as far as he could.

As they spooned together under her blankets later, Oliver kissed her neck sleepily. "I brought you a Christmas present. I don't know if you do Christmas."

"It's a little early for Christmas presents, isn't it?"

"It's Christmas Eve."

"It's what?" Lucy turned toward him, incredulous.

Oliver laughed. "Lost track, did you?"

"I… But I came home after talking to you and went straight to bed. That was the twenty-third."

"You've been asleep for more than a day? I thought you were just ignoring my calls."

"My phone was off."

"I thought you didn't sleep."

"I guess I was saving it up. I took a sleeping pill—it was kind of a heavy dose. One of Smok Biotech's special formulae." Lucy lay back against the pillow and closed her eyes. "I guess that's Darkrock's special formulae now."

"Oh, that's the other present. I forgot to tell you." Oliver turned and propped his elbow on the bed. "All records of your statement, your demonstration of the wyvern shift, have been destroyed."

Lucy's eyes opened in surprise. "It's what? How do you know they hadn't backed it up to the cloud somewhere?"

"Darkrock protocol. Nothing is stored remotely via internet connection, not even over a VPN. They would have taken the SD card off-site and made a backup at one of their hubs, but they never had the chance. I burned the card myself."

Lucy breathed a sigh of relief. "Thank you. I was sure my career was over and Smok stock was going to be in the toilet." She kissed him gratefully. "So, what's this other present? I didn't get you anything."

Oliver threw off the covers, letting the shock of cold roll over them. "Come on. Get dressed. Wear something warm."

With an ivory cashmere coat over her jeans and long-sleeved thermal T—along with boots, gloves, hat and a scarf at Oliver's suggestion—Lucy followed him outside.

"They should be arriving…" Oliver looked at his smart watch. "Right about now."

"Who?"

Oliver put his index finger and his thumb between his teeth and whistled sharply. A Christmas sleigh appeared promptly from around the corner…driven by four young white wolves with red-tipped ears.

Lucy threw him an amused glance. "I thought you said they'd gone home."

"They did. But apparently I can call them for the Hunt whenever I need to. They love pulling this thing. Trust me."

Oliver helped her into the sleigh and climbed in beside her, laying a blanket over their laps before he took the reins. "Let's go, boys. Mush!" He grinned and put his arm around Lucy as the hellhounds took off.

Despite their size and the weight of the conveyance, the hounds seemed to have no trouble navigating the still-falling powder as the sleigh skimmed through the parking lot toward the private hiking trail behind the villas. On the trail, the hounds drew them at a brisk pace between sparkling snow-covered acacia bushes and desert broom, the powder-dusted domes of Thunder Mountain and Coffee Pot Rock rising in the distance.

"So, what are we hunting?" Lucy murmured against Oliver's side.

"Nothing," said Oliver. "I've already found you."

* * * * *

We hope you enjoyed this story from

H HARLEQUIN®

NOCTURNE™

Unleash your otherworldly desires.

Discover more stories from
Harlequin® series and continue
to venture where the normal and
paranormal collide.

Visit **Harlequin.com** for more Harlequin® series reads
and **www.Harlequin.com/ParanormalRomance**
for more paranormal reads!

From passionate, suspenseful
and dramatic love stories
to inspirational or historical...

With different lines to choose from
and new books in each one every month,
Harlequin satisfies the most voracious
romance readers.

"I think I might be pretty good at motivating myself," Lila confessed.

"Everybody should know how to motivate themselves," Travis agreed with a wicked smile. "Aren't you going to ask about my stress levels?"

"Are you stressed?" she asked, taking one step backward.

"That depends."

"Depends on what?"

"On if you're interested in doing something about it." His smile sexy enough to make her light-headed, he moved forward one step.

Since his legs were longer than hers, his step brought him close enough to touch. To feel. To taste.

She held her breath when he reached out. He shifted his gaze to his fingers as they combed through her hair, swirling one long strand around and around. His gaze met hers again and he gave a tug.

"So?" he asked quietly. "Interested?"

"I shouldn't be. This would probably be a mistake," she murmured, her eyes locked on his mouth. His lips looked so soft, a contrast against those dark whiskers. Were they soft, too? How would they feel against her skin?

Desire wrapped around her like a silk ribbon, pretty and tight.

"Let's see what it feels like making a mistake together."

With that, his mouth took hers.

The kiss was whisper soft. The lightest teasing touch of his lips to hers. Pressing, sliding, enticing. Then his tongue slid along her bottom lip in a way that made Lila want to purr. She straight up melted, the trembling in her knees spreading through her entire body.

Don't miss
Navy SEAL to the Rescue *by Tawny Weber,*
available February 2019 wherever
Harlequin® *Romantic Suspense books*
and ebooks are sold.

www.Harlequin.com

HRSEXP0119

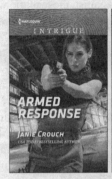 

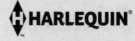

Love Harlequin romance?

DISCOVER.

Be the first to find out about promotions,
news and exclusive content!

Facebook.com/HarlequinBooks

Twitter.com/HarlequinBooks

Instagram.com/HarlequinBooks

Pinterest.com/HarlequinBooks

ReaderService.com

EXPLORE.

Sign up for the Harlequin e-newsletter and
download a free book from any series at
TryHarlequin.com.

CONNECT.

Join our Harlequin community to share
your thoughts and connect with other
romance readers!
Facebook.com/groups/HarlequinConnection

HARLEQUIN®

**ROMANCE WHEN
YOU NEED IT**

HSOCIAL2018

Reward the book lover in you!

Earn points on your purchase of new Harlequin books from participating retailers.

Turn your points into **FREE BOOKS** of your choice!

Join for FREE today at
www.HarlequinMyRewards.com.

Harlequin My Rewards is a free program (no fees) without any commitments or obligations.

MYR18